"Enough!" Lucais cried, settling the matter by simply rolling over and pinning Elspeth beneath him.

"I'd heard the court was a wicked place, my lady, but I had no idea 'twas the custom there for women to ravish men in their beds."

Elspeth trembled with the force of her emotions. "You think I want to couple with you?" At Raebert's death she had sworn she'd never again be vulnerable to a man. And here she was, spread-eagled beneath one who had good cause to hurt her. Yet the feel of Lucais's muscular body trapping hers did not unleash a rush of primitive female panic. It made her skin heat and heart pound with the overwhelming urge to press closer, to wrap herself around him....

Dear Reader,

This month, award-winning Harlequin Historical author Miranda Jarrett continues her dramatic saga of the Sparhawk family in *Sparhawk's Lady*, a sweeping tale of danger and romance with a dashing hero who is torn between duty and desire. Don't miss this stirring adventure that was given a 5★ rating by *Affaire de Coeur* and a 4+ rating from *Romantic Times*.

And from author Suzanne Barclay comes *Lion of the North*, the second in her new medieval series featuring two clans of Scottish Highlanders, the Sutherlands and the Carmichaels, who have been fighting for generations.

Our other titles for June include our warmhearted WOMEN OF THE WEST title, *Saddle the Wind*, by author Pat Tracy, and the first Western from author Kit Gardner, *Twilight*, a story of love and redemption.

We hope you'll keep an eye out for all four selections, wherever Harlequin Historicals are sold.

Sincerely,

Tracy Farrell
Senior Editor

Please address questions and book requests to:
Harlequin Reader Service
U.S.: 3010 Walden Ave., P.O. Box 1325, Buffalo, NY 14269
Canadian: P.O. Box 609, Fort Erie, Ont. L2A 5X3

SUZANNE BARCLAY

Lion of the North

Harlequin Books

TORONTO • NEW YORK • LONDON
AMSTERDAM • PARIS • SYDNEY • HAMBURG
STOCKHOLM • ATHENS • TOKYO • MILAN
MADRID • WARSAW • BUDAPEST • AUCKLAND

ISBN 0-373-28872-7

LION OF THE NORTH

Copyright © 1995 by Carol Suzanne Backus.

Books by Suzanne Barclay

Harlequin Historicals

Knight Dreams #141
Knight's Lady #162
Knight's Honor #184
†*Lion's Heart* #252
†*Lion of the North* #272

*The Sommerville Brothers
†The Lion Trilogy

SUZANNE BARCLAY

has been an avid reader since she was very young;
her mother claims Suzanne could read and recite
"The Night Before Christmas" on her first birthday!
Not surprisingly, history was her favorite subject in
school, and historical novels are her number one
reading choice. The house she shares with her husband and their two dogs is set on fifty-five acres of
New York State's wine-growing region. When she's
not writing, the author makes fine furniture and car-
pets in miniature.

With much love to Amy, Jon and Melissa, the youngest member of our "clan"

Prologue

Scottish Highlands
June—1367

Pale moonlight filtered through the mist that clung to the treetops, liming the hard faces of the Sutherlands who drove their mounts up the steep, rocky gorge. Beneath their iron helmets, red-rimmed eyes narrowed in concentration, lips pulled back in grimaces of rage and determination. Only their harsh breathing and the clatter of shod hooves broke the eerie silence. Behind them lay the smoldering ruins of one Sutherland croft. Ahead, the trail taken by the bastards who'd left their kinsmen to die. It pointed straight toward Bran Sutherland's farm.

The scent of wood smoke reached them as they topped the ridge. Sharp and ominous, it hung in the damp spring air, taunting the men who'd raced to the rescue.

"Too late," Lucais Sutherland snarled between clenched teeth. Still, he did not slacken his pace as he led the way down the tricky slope to the bleak moor and the fire that lit up the darkened landscape. The alarm had sounded well past midnight, dragging the Sutherlands of Kinduin Castle from their beds for the second time this week. As he pulled his stallion to a halt beside the body of young Bran, Lucais cursed the fact that his lands were so far-flung. He simply could not be everywhere.

"Is he dead?" Lucais demanded as Cathal Sutherland knelt to the bloodied form on the ground.

"Nay, but sore hurt, I fear." Cathal gathered his eldest son in his arms and looked up at Lucais, tears glinting in the seams of his leathery face. "Who could ha' done this?"

"I dinna know," Lucais said, low and tight. "But I'll—"

Niall drew rein beside him, his young face a mask of fury. "The tracks lead nor' by nor'west," his cousin growled.

"Munros," Cathal hissed, the hatred in his voice echoed in the curses of their kinsmen. Harness jangled, horses pranced, sensing their riders' eagerness to be off after the enemy.

Lucais checked them with an upraised hand. "'Tis sheer stupidity to lay a trail straight to Scourie Castle."

"Are ye sayin' we willna pursue them?" Cathal demanded over the grumblings of the other Sutherlands.

"Nay." Lucais glanced at the burning hut, the wounded crofter. "But whatever else he may be, Seamus Munro isna a stupid man. This doesna make sense. I canna ride off without knowin'—"

"I want blood," Cathal cried, surging up to glare at Lucais.

"Guilty blood? Or just any blood?" Lucais asked with the canniness that had earned him the leadership of his fiercely independent clansmen though he'd not been raised among them.

Cathal's grizzled brows lowered. "The Munros *are* guilty."

"Mayhap." The worn leather of the saddle that had carried his grandsire into battle against the Munros creaked as Lucais shifted his big body to study the scene. Backlit by the leaping orange flames, two sheep lay bleeding on the ground, but a trio of Highland cattle huddled untouched in the far corner of the nearby pen. "'Tis a foul piece of business," Lucais said. "And greedy as he is, I wouldna put it past Seamus to break the peace between us for profit, but he left his plunder behind."

"We came too quick upon them," Cathal spat. "But we lose the advantage standin' about like timid nuns. It makes nae difference what they took or didna. I say we hunt them down and make them pay for this night's work," he added, and more than one man raised his voice to agree with the old man.

Jesu, could they not learn to think with something besides their swords? Lucais pried off his helmet, ran a weary, frustrated hand through his sweat-drenched hair. The fire picked out the red in its deep chestnut, glinted on the gold flecks in his hazel eyes so they glowed as fiercely as the live coals he studied. If this was the Munros' doing, they must be made to pay. Still, he couldn't shake the sense of foreboding, the gut instinct that there was more here than a simple raid. "We'll follow," he allowed at last. "But slowly . . . with an eye to—"

"Nay! I want them dead." Cathal grabbed Lucais's stallion by the bridle, making Black Jock dance back a pace before Lucais regained control of his mount.

"Cathal! Ye forget yerself," Niall exclaimed. " 'Tis Lucais who's laird here, and from the time our grandsire named him heir, Lucais has been worthy of the title. Are ye forgettin' how much better off we are now? How prosperous we've become? Are ye forgettin' that we havena suffered a Munro raid these three years because Lucais forced old Seamus to cry peace wi' us?"

Which made this all the more puzzling, Lucais thought as he shot his cousin a quick smile of gratitude. Though six years younger than Lucais's five and twenty, Niall had been born and raised at Kinduin Castle, and many had expected he'd be the next laird. Winning Niall over had been the first of many battles Lucais had waged with fists, swords and words since being unexpectedly named his grandsire's heir.

Despite his warrior's skills, Lucais still found his quick mind and facile tongue his greatest weapons. "Cathal, you and one other carry Bran back to Kinduin so his wounds can be tended." When the man made to object, Lucais added, "Your son is a good friend. I'd see he gets the best care so he doesna lose the use of that injured arm. None will be more assiduous in that than his own father." Having reminded Cathal of his duty, Lucais turned his attention to hunting down the bastards responsible for a total of four burned crofts, two men dead, six wounded and the loss of several valuable sheep and cattle.

The moon had reached its zenith and cast no shadow to confuse the tracker who trotted ahead of the Sutherlands across the grassy moor and into the woods. Here all was dark and silent, the ominous stillness broken only by the rustle of tree branches, the suck of mud on hooves as they pushed deeper into the forest. The smell of wet leaves and rich earth was a welcome antidote to the smoke that still clung in Lucais's nostrils.

Damn. These attacks had all the earmarks of a Munro raid. Greedy, brutal and lazy, for generations the Munros had made their living by preying on weaker clans. Thanks to his training and the English-style armor and weapons Lucais had purchased shortly after becoming chief, the Sutherlands had convinced the Munros to hunt elsewhere or risk being killed off. Why had that suddenly changed? Could this be Raebert's doing?

Hatred coiled deep in Lucais's gut. Though they'd met only once face-to-face, he loathed Seamus's only son and heir. Raebert had robbed him of the only woman he'd ever loved. *Elspeth.* Jesu, even after four years, it hurt to recall how she'd dismissed his suit and wed Raebert instead. And then there was the matter with Jean. If losing Elspeth had dealt Lucais's heart a bitter blow, what had happened to Jean was a blot on his immortal soul, even though it had been Raebert who'd done the foul deed.

"Lucais! Look here," the scout cried, kneeling in the mud.

Pushing both women from his mind, Lucais dismounted to examine the signs. Two horses had continued on up the trail. Only a broken branch betrayed the spot where the rest of the men had turned into the woods. Had the Sutherlands been riding hard after the reivers, they'd have missed this.

"That'll shut the lads up," Niall murmured.

Lucais shrugged off the compliment. The grumbling behind him stopped after that, but he was not one to gloat. He focused his attention ahead, increasingly troubled but not surprised when the raiding party doubled back toward Kinduin.

"Do ye think 'twas a ruse to get us away, then attack the castle?" Niall said over the clatter of hooves.

Lucais shook his head. "'Twould take six times the men Seamus can raise and a score of siege engines to pry us from that old black tower." Still, he increased the pace till they were galloping along the steep, uneven trail, so intent on reaching home they nearly missed the next twist their quarry took.

"Halt!" Lucais cried, and behind him horses screamed and men cursed as they skidded to a stop. "Look there. Unless I miss my guess, they've taken that fork to the left."

"There's naught that way but the old broch," Niall said.

"Unless they're thinkin' of comin' around the loch and attackin' the fishin' village," Lucais replied, wheeling his horse to follow the fresh hoofprints. At the first raid two days ago, he'd shifted men from patrolling the loch to watching the hills. Had the village been the Munros' real target all along?

If so, they'd strike the Sutherlands a crippling blow. The trade in smoked and salted salmon Lucais had arranged made the Sutherlands prosperous. The income had not only provided the weaponry to help quell the Munros but allowed the Sutherlands to barter for luxuries, as well. Without the boats and the fishermen, his clan would be ruined.

His heart in his mouth, Lucais rode flat out. The old, seldom-used track ran through a pine forest dripping with dew, then curved upward to scale a rocky hill before dipping down to the stony shores of Loch Shin. Here he called a halt.

A chill breeze ruffled the dark surface of the loch, icing the sweat that clung to Lucais's skin beneath his woolen tunic and chain mail. All was silent save for the harsh breathing of the winded horses and worried men. Dreading what he'd find, he rose in his stirrups and looked toward the village. "No smoke..."

"They went north, again," the tracker softly called. "And nae too long since."

"Ah. We'll catch them, then." Lucais's grin was a white slash in his tanned face. But the smile faded when they'd ridden the half league to the broch and found the ancient stone tower deserted. Fresh horse droppings and a hastily discarded rope ladder were the only signs that anyone had been here.

"They've fled into the hills," the scout came back to report. "Scattered in a dozen directions."

"Do we follow?" Niall wanted to know.

"Too risky. We'd have to split up to follow them, leavin' ourselves open to ambush." Lucais looked up at the deserted broch. Tall as a four-story tower and made entirely of rough stone cut from the cliffs behind it, the fort had no windows and only one entrance, a small doorway set into the face two stories above the ground. Thus the ladders. Clearly the attack on Bran's croft had been merely a diversion, but why had the Munros wanted to get inside an empty, long-abandoned fort?

True, this place was sacred to the Sutherlands, who claimed the builders of the broch as ancestors, but it commanded no vital crossroads or fertile valley. Lucais knew Seamus well enough to know the old bastard would not risk rekindling the feud between their clans unless he saw a way to profit by it...or strike the Sutherlands a crippling blow. Which was it, greed or vengeance?

"What do we do, then?" Niall asked, finding it natural to look to Lucais for leadership. He was as able a warrior as their grandsire had been, big, strong and so fierce in battle the Sutherlands called him Da Lyoun...The Lion. Yet it was Lucais's canny mind that had led the Sutherlands from the brink of extinction at the hands of the Munros to peace and prosperity. Aye, though Lucais's inbred caution occasionally chafed at a few of the older men like Cathal, Niall and most of the others would have followed Lucais to the gates of hell itself.

"Mayhap Seamus plans to use the broch as a base from which to capture the village and wrest the salmon trade from us," Lucais said slowly. 'Twas the only thing that made sense. "We'll double the watch around the loch and see what happens next." Though 'twould spread his men thin if they were to guard the outlying crofts, as well. "Ever been inside the broch?"

Niall blinked. " 'Tis forbidden."

"So 'tis." Lucais gave orders for a patrol around the broch. Still, as he rode away, he couldn't resist one last glance at the old tower. There was something about the forbidden that drew a man. Mayhap that was why he hadn't been able to forget Elspeth Carmichael.

Chapter One

Carmichael Castle
June—1367

Even at midmorn on this warm, sunny day, it was cool and dark inside the chapel. But it was apprehension, not the damp seeping out of centuries-old stone, that made Lady Elspeth Carmichael Munro shiver as she reluctantly slipped inside.

"Steady," she breathed, eyes narrowing as they probed the dimness for her quarry. Her pulse beat too quickly and her hands were damp with a nervousness that belied the stiffness of her spine and her resolve. She would do this. She must, for the pain and the guilt had become unbearable.

A flicker of movement at the front of the nave distracted her. Father Patrick, bent with age but still guardian of the Carmichaels' souls, rose from his knees and crossed himself. The rasp of coarse black wool whispered through the chapel as he backed from the altar and started down the main aisle.

Elspeth stepped from the shadows. "Father. A moment of your time." She gazed at him through a protective veil of thick black lashes. He'd always read her like an open book.

"Eh?" Father Patrick stopped midstride. His squint reminded Elspeth of her mother's comment that the old priest was losing his eyesight. No need to worry about keeping in place the mask she wore for her family, she thought, and relaxed fractionally.

"'Tis Elspeth. Elspeth Carmichael . . . Munro," she tacked on.

"Indeed?" Father Patrick withdrew his gnarled hands from the sleeves of his robe and reached unerringly for hers, knotted deep in the folds of the bright woolen surcoat she'd put on to raise her spirits. "What troubles ye, daughter?" he asked, voicing the one question she'd avoided answering since returning to her family a fortnight ago. "Come, let us pray together." Giving her fist a gentle squeeze, he urged her toward a nearby bench.

Elspeth sank down beside him, grateful for the support of the solid oak. *Oh, Father. Prayers willna help. Nothing will.* Elspeth felt the sting of moisture in eyes that had already shed too many tears. Bitter tears, frightened tears, guilty tears.

Father Patrick sniffed, his own eyes looking suspiciously wet. "I wondered why ye hadna been to see me since ye returned home. Thought mayhap livin' at court all these years, ye'd become too grand for the likes of us." The seams around his thin mouth deepening, he thumbed an errant tear from Elspeth's cheek. "Hush, child. It canna be that bad."

Aye, it can. Grief made her throat too full for words.

"What happened to the feisty lass who used to sneak down to the tiltyard and match swords wi' her brothers?" he teased.

Elspeth smiled as she recalled those happy days. "'Tis been a long time since I did something that impetuous." Four years ago she'd wed Raebert and that last hasty act had cost her dearly.

"I sense ye've changed." He cocked his head, bald but for a fringe of snow white hair. "And it isna all to the good."

"Nay. 'Twasna all good." A gross understatement.

"Yer mother says ye're grief-struck by yer husband's death."

Elspeth nearly choked on that, assaulted by memories from the four terrible years of their marriage. Raebert, drunk and foul. Raebert, sober and cruel. Raebert, foul and cruel. He'd stripped her of her dreams, her property and, nearly, her sanity.

"Could be true," Father Patrick mused. "As I recall, ye were so keen to wed him ye even quarreled over it wi' yer father."

"Aye, I did." Miserable, Elspeth looked down at their joined hands. Headstrong, thoroughly spoiled and possessing a temper to rival her doting da's, she'd flown into a rage when Lio-

nel Carmichael had refused to let her wed Raebert Munro. *Stupid fool.* If only she'd listened to her family's objections.

"Was life at court, being feted as wife of the king's champion, as grand as ye'd expected?" the priest said quietly.

"Nay." They'd lived well...on her money. Which was all that Raebert had wanted from the bargain. All his fine words and loving looks had been a lie. He hadn't wanted her. He'd wanted what she could bring him . . . a rich dowry.

"I'm sorry ye grieve for Raebert."

Elspeth sighed. 'Twas not grief she felt when she thought of him, but anger at herself for not being strong enough to somehow escape the trap her marriage had become. And guilt. Guilt over the part she'd played in Raebert's greatest cruelty. "Father, I need to..." *Confess.* She'd never been overly pious, yet she was smothered by the terrible weight she'd borne since learning her father had been ambushed and crippled... mayhap for life. Her fault. All her fault. The pain was unbearable.

"Father, I want to..." The words stuck in her throat.

Father Patrick sat stock-still. Eyes calm, patient and endlessly forgiving, he waited for her to open her heart to him. She longed to; she ached to. On the day Raebert died, she'd fled Edinburgh. Run home like the wounded animal she'd become, seeking the healing bosom of her family. They'd made her welcome, yet their gentle smiles had increased her guilt.

I'm not worthy of your love, she'd wanted to shout, and hated herself anew for lacking the courage to speak. As penance, she'd forced herself to tend her father, though every moment spent in his company tore at her troubled heart. If he knew what she'd done, he'd hate her forever. So she'd come to beg Father Patrick's intercession with a God she'd stopped believing in on her wedding night when Raebert had...

"Is it somethin' to do wi' yer marriage?" he gently asked.

"Aye," Elspeth whispered. Then her will faltered. *Sweet Mary, she could not do it.* She could not bear to see the love in that dear, lined face turn to revulsion when she revealed her weakness. No more than she'd been able to tell her puzzled family the real reason she had not once been back to visit after her marriage. *Pride.* She'd had too much damned pride to

confess that in wedding Raebert she'd made a serious mistake. Now she was afraid the truth would cost her her family's love.

"Give it time," the old priest said. "'Tis glad we all are to have ye home." Gripping her hands in his, he offered to pray with her. She accepted the escape he provided. The stone chapel echoed with his earnest promises of God's love and forgiveness, but the familiar words rang hollow in her aching heart. "We've been that worried about ye," he added after the amen.

Elspeth nodded, by no means at peace, yet oddly comforted by the hope that in time she might be able to forget Raebert and forgive herself for being so weak. "Mama's intent on fattening me up, and Da . . ." Her voice caught.

"Laird Lionel's on the mend. Wi' God's help, he'll soon be up, orderin' all about to suit him," Father Patrick said quickly. The way he avoided her gaze put a lie to his smooth assurances. Her father had taken an arrow in the thigh two months ago while defending a Carmichael croft from a band of brigands. She alone knew who'd sent those outlaws and why. Her fault. All her fault.

"He's the worst patient in all of Scotland," Elspeth said hoarsely. How could she live with herself if he never walked again? "I—I'd best go relieve Mama at his beside."

Father Patrick stood with her, gave her cold hands a final pat before releasing them. "Have ye tried readin' to him?"

She snorted. "Just yestereve. He threw the book at me. 'Damned romances are stuff and nonsense,'" she growled in fair imitation of the sire she so resembled, even to her black hair and the temper that had been her bane till Raebert beat it out of her. Nay, she'd not think of that. "Mayhap a rousing tale of some bloody battle," she said over her shoulder as she fled.

"I pray ye find the happiness ye deserve."

"I dinna deserve happiness," she whispered as the door thumped closed behind her. The sunlight blinded her momentarily, but the sight without had been etched into her mind since infancy. A wide, cobbled courtyard bounded on four sides by the imposing gray towers her ancestors had built. Even the dependency buildings, the kitchens, buttery, brewhouse and so on, were neat and orderly. Her parents had worked hard to make it so.

While her father had seen to the fortifications and trained the large garrison needed to defend the castle, her mother had directed the weaving, the cleaning, the cooking and such. Elspeth had chafed at being instructed in these duties when she was a lass. Now she was sorry the place was so well run because there was naught to occupy her time . . . save regret and recrimination.

"Aunt Elspeth!" A compact body careered into hers, driving her back a step. She'd have fallen if it hadn't been for the strong arms strangling her waist.

"Nephew Kieran." Elspeth returned his hug, smiling down into a face so like his father's it took her back. Back to her youth when her oldest brother had been the center of her world. Poor Lion, dead these nine years without even knowing he'd sired a son. Siusan Sutherland, the woman he'd loved but not wed, had lived just long enough to give her newborn son into the tender care of her sister, Megan, to raise.

"We've a visitor, and Papa sent me to fetch you."

"Papa" was Ross, her second brother, heir in Lion's stead, and husband to Megan. She wondered if Kieran knew he was not their own child. More to the point, what would happen to Kieran now that—miracle of miracles after nine barren years—Megan was expecting a child? "Someone to see me?" she asked warily.

"'Tis just a wee woman wi' lots of rings," Kieran said with the disdain of a lad who at nine was only an inch shorter than her own five feet and three inches. Aye, he had the Carmichael height and solid build . . . along with the fiery temperament her father had bequeathed to Lion and herself. Poor lad. She hoped his rashness did not lead him into the trouble hers had. "We could sneak down to the tiltyard and watch the men practice," her nephew offered, clearly sensing her hesitation.

Elspeth smiled. "Whatever gave you the idea I'd do that?"

"Papa...he and Grandpapa were talkin' about how wild you used to be before you wed." Kieran's eyes, a violet several shades darker than her own, widened as he released her. "Did Sir Andrew really teach you to fight with a dirk and a sword?"

"Aye." A shudder coursed through her as she recalled to what use she'd put another of the old knight's lessons. That

Raebert had richly deserved so foul an end didn't ease her conscience.

Kieran's face shone with youthful male fervor. "When I'm laird of the Carmichaels, I'll be as great a warrior as Papa is."

Was, Elspeth thought with a twinge. Lion had been a superb fighter. A big, bold knight, expert in arms, fearless in battle, honorable to the core. That Raebert had physically resembled Lion, except for his brown hair and eyes, was what had drawn her to him. She'd always dreamed of wedding a warrior. But beneath his knightly trappings, Raebert had been rotten and evil.

"Ah, there you are," a deep voice called, and Elspeth turned to find Ross bearing down on them. Tall and solid, with only a hint of gray in his black hair for all he was two and thirty. "I should ha' known I'd find you two huddled together. Like to like," he said fondly as he ruffled Kieran's hair. "Sir Andrew awaits you in the exercise yard, lad."

Kieran looked at his boots. "Sword's broke."

"Mmm. And how did that happen?" Ross winked at Elspeth.

"Well . . ." Kieran toed a line in the fresh grass.

"There's a dent in that old suit of armor in the barracks." Ross gently prodded, where Lion or their sire would have blustered. Once she'd seen such loud displays as a sign of strength and scorned Ross's quieter ways. Being wed to Raebert had taught her to fear the masculine brawn she used to admire.

Kieran sighed, but the eyes he raised to her brother were unwavering. "I did it. I didna mean to, but . . ."

"Mmm." Ross squeezed Kieran's shoulder in much the same way Father Patrick had Elspeth's, and she felt the love flow between the two. She'd sorely missed such closeness during her marriage, hurt as much by Raebert's coldness as his physical cruelty. "If you'll wait a moment, Elspeth, I'd speak wi' this unruly pup." Ross drew Kieran aside and spoke earnestly to him. Whatever he said made Kieran grimace, then nod grudgingly. The lad's boot heels dragged as he crossed the courtyard and disappeared out the gate that led to the lower bailey and the tiltyard.

"Whatever did you say to hurt him so?" Elspeth asked Ross.

Ross sighed. "I'd planned to give him a metal sword . . . wi' a dull edge," he added in response to her gasp. "Now he'll have to wait until he's proved his worth to me and to his worried mama."

"Kieran doesna know he isna your son, does he?"

If she'd slapped him, her brother could not have looked more stricken. "Kieran *is* our son," he said fiercely.

"In all ways save one," Elspeth replied. "What will happen if the bairn Megan carries is a lad? As your legal get, he should be the next laird, not Kieran. But Kieran thinks—"

"Kieran will remain my heir, no matter if Megan should bear me a score of sons. That I swore on Lion's grave."

"And Megan?"

"She supports me in this. Siusan was her sister, after all, so the lad is doubly dear to us."

"I wonder if my wise brother isna making a serious mistake."

"You'd be the one to recognize a mistake," Ross mocked.

"Oh! That was low," Elspeth snapped at the brother who had always known how to make her blood boil. Jesu, but she hated men who used their clever tongues to twist her words. Just like Lucais Sutherland, she thought, and the mere fact that . . . that nobody still haunted her made her tremble with impotent rage.

"Aye, get angry wi' me." Ross grabbed her arms. "Kick me as you used to when we were young. Even a bruise is preferable to that pasty-faced, stricken look you've worn since you came home. Faith, you've got Megan and Mama tiptoein' about and worryin' themselves into a state. Even Da's noticed you're nae yourself."

"I *am* a widow," Elspeth replied, shuddering as wave after wave of emotion tore her apart. Anger. Fear. Remorse. Even the mention of her sire's name made her belly knot with all three.

Ross, her calm, controlled brother, snarled a word that would have gotten him switched when they were young and gave her a little shake. "If you've grown pale and skinny mournin' Raebert Munro, I'll . . . I'll eat my sword."

"With or without salt," Elspeth replied, but the raw edge of her rage faltered under the intensity of his gaze. She felt the coil of grief in her chest rise to choke her. "Damn you. Damn you for seeing too much...." Her words were muffled against the rough wool of his surcoat as he hauled her against his chest.

"Let it out, Lizzie," he crooned, taking her weight when her knees failed her. "Cry it out, lass."

She wanted to. Sweet Mary, her chest ached with four years of pent-up misery, but she dared not let loose for fear the awful truth would pour out with her tears. Trembling with the force of her emotions, she was dimly aware of Ross leading her to the stone bench in the chapel garden. He held her till the shuddering had eased and she was back in control. "Ross...I...thank you."

"No thanks needed, bratlin'. I've become expert in dealin' wi' weepy women since Meggie became pregnant." Ross grinned and tugged on one of her braids, but his eyes glinted with tears.

It amazed her that Ross could cry yet be bold and forceful enough to lead their clan. Such a dichotomy unnerved her, for she'd only encountered it in one other...Lucais. Damn, why did he keep popping into her head? "I'm nae a weepy woman." She snatched her black braid from his grasp and tossed it over her shoulder.

His face turned grave. "What's wrong, Lizzie? Whatever 'tis, I'll understand."

Nay. He would not. Ross Carmichael, the perfect, always-in-control-knight, would never know what it was like to be alone, frightened and vulnerable. As a lass, she'd rued being born female, had trailed after her brothers determined to become a knight, too. She'd put the notion aside at eleven, when Megan had come and shown her a woman could be strong, useful and powerful. It had taken Raebert Munro exactly fifteen minutes to destroy all that, to reduce her to a quivering lump of weak female flesh.

Baring her soul now would not change what had happened, and the telling would only upset Ross. "I dinna know what to do, where I belong now that I'm...I'm widowed." 'Twas partly true.

"Do? Why, you'll stay here with us...until you wed again."

Elspeth shook her head so hard her braids flew. "I'll never marry again...never."

Ross blinked in astonishment at her vehemence, his heart aching for his fiery little sister. Prickly as she was on the out-side, she had a tender core. Never had it been more evident than these past two weeks when he'd watched her play with the bairns he and Megan had adopted or read to their irascible sire. But pain had shadowed the brave front she'd put on for her family. Raebert Munro's doing, he thought darkly, and wished the man alive so he could kill him for hurting Elspeth so.

"What man will want me?" she asked, cheeks flushed with emotion. "I dinna have any property and am likely barren."

"What happened to your dower lands? The farms?"

"Raebert mortgaged them to the moneylenders months ago."

"Bloody hell!" Ross exploded off the bench.

"I'm sorry. I tried to stop him, but..." He'd beaten her, then locked her up for days with naught but bread and water.

Ross wheeled on her. "You..." *Stupid fool for not coming to me with this.* He sighed, recognizing the Carmichael pride in her stiff spine and aggressively angled chin. "As your hus-band, the property was Raebert's to dispose of, but the farms were solid ones wi' a good yield. I'll see to buyin' them back."

"Thank you, Ross." Elspeth rose and laid her hand on his arm, soaking up the warmth, the strength. Megan was a lucky woman to have him to husband. "I'm sorry to be a charge on you. If—"

"Hush. There's room aplenty here, and Mama and Megan claim you dinna eat enough to keep a fly alive."

"Still..." Elspeth lifted her gaze to the sturdy walls that guarded the castle and beyond to the rolling green hills she'd explored as a lass. "I canna just stay here."

"Why? Now that your temper's turned up sweet, 'tis a pleasure to have you about," Ross teased, expecting an explo-sion. What he got was a shrug that worried him greatly.

"I enjoy playing aunt to the bairns and being with you all again, but 'tisna enough. I'd have a place of my own."

Ross frowned. "A lass, alone? How would you manage to feed and protect yourself without a husband?"

"I'll hire men." Just where she'd get the money to pay them was neither here nor there. Elspeth lifted her chin. "Many la-dies manage their own households. Frances Gordon, for one."

"Ah, Jesu." Ross smote himself on the head. "I clean forgot why I'd sought you out in the first place. Lady Frances Gordon's waitin' upstairs in Mama's solar."

"Oh, how wonderful." Her heart lighter than it had been in days, Elspeth headed across the courtyard with Ross beside her. They were met at the front door by Megan and Ross's *brood*, five lads and lasses the couple had taken under their wing over the years because the fall from a horse that had lamed Meg's leg had also made it unlikely she'd ever have any of her own. Unlikely, but not impossible, as time had finally proved. Would that time could work a miracle for her, Elspeth thought.

"Mama says we canna have any of the cakes till you and Aunt Elspeth come, Papa," announced nine-year-old Flora. Her fragile blond beauty was marred by a puckery burn that ran across her right cheek, down her neck and over much of her back. Yet here was no shrinking violet. Indeed, she was the leader of the pack.

More of Megan's magic, Elspeth thought as she allowed herself to be led upstairs by Thomas and Timothy, lively five-year-old twins whose whole family had died of the plague. Kara, six and likewise an orphan, pushed her from behind. Ross brought up the rear with three-year-old Anne in his arms.

Much as Elspeth had come to love them, the bairns brought a pang of sorrow. The idea of bearing Raebert's babe had repulsed her, yet the thought of never having one saddened her. Her dismal mood lifted when she entered the airy second-story chamber that was her mother's solar and saw her friend standing at the window.

"Frances!" Elspeth dashed across the room and threw herself in the older woman's arms.

"I wasna certain you'd be anxious for company." Lady Frances gave her a quick hug, then held her at arm's length. As usual, she was dressed in the height of fashion, her dark hair concealed by a rolled headdress of red silk that matched her surcoat. Despite her five and thirty years, her face was unlined, her figure slim, her energy inexhaustible. She claimed it was because she didn't have a husband to sap her strength.

" 'Tis always a pleasure to see you," Elspeth replied honestly. In Frances she'd found a kindred spirit, a woman whose keen wit and sharp tongue matched her own. If not for this lady's friendship at court, she'd probably have gone mad. But even Frances had been powerless to save her from Raebert.

Lady Frances's dark eyes turned troubled. "Elspeth, I . . ."

"Come partake of the refreshments before the bairns gobble them up," Lady Carina called, turning them from the window.

"A moment, Mama," Elspeth replied. "What is it, Frances?"

"Later," her friend mouthed, and moved toward the hearth. Apprehension sizzling down her spine, Elspeth pasted on the bland mask she'd worn since coming home and crossed to take the wine cup from her mother. "How is Da today?" she asked.

A smile smoothed the lines bracketing her mother's mouth, but failed to lift the shadows from her blue eyes. There was a bit of silver mingling with her red gold hair, yet she'd retained her slim figure. "Better. Sittin' in the garden tired him . . ."

"It did nae such thing," grumbled a deep voice, and Elspeth spun to find her father in the doorway, dressed in a long bed robe and leaning heavily on his two squires.

"Lionel! Ye shouldna be up," her mother exclaimed.

"I'm fine," he growled. But he yet carried too little weight on his large body, and his face, framed by a mane of hair more white now than black, was far too pale for Elspeth's liking.

Oh, Da! her heart cried, and the strands of fear in her chest twined tighter. Much as she longed to throw herself in his arms and weep to see him so, she knew that, like her, he hated pity. "Well, I see you've decided to stop moping in bed."

He raised one bushy brow, then chuckled and cast his hovering wife a smug glance. "Aye. 'Tis sick I am of bein' fussed over. Thought I'd best come down and see what sort of hash Ross has made of managin' things in my stead." The words were lightly spoken, but a fine sweat had broken out on his brow, and Elspeth wondered how best to trick him into sitting down.

"You've come in the nick of time, Da," Ross interjected. Displacing one of the squires, he threw an arm across his father's shoulders and supported Lionel to the high-backed chair that had sat empty while the laird mended. "There's trouble brewin'," he began, then lowered his voice.

Lady Carina drew in a ragged breath and turned away from the two heads bent together in earnest conversation.

"Mama?" Elspeth took her mother's icy hand.

"I'm all right." She smiled through her tears. "It has just taken so long. I love him so, and I've felt so...so helpless."

"I know." Elspeth looked over at her father and brother, felt love mingle with her pain. "When did Ross become so wise?"

Lady Carina chuckled. "He was born so, I think. Ye were just too busy worshipin' Lion to appreciate his quieter ways."

"Aye." And that had led her to make a terrible mistake. But never again. "Mama. Do you think Da will force me to remarry?"

"Ye dinna wish to?" Her mother's expression turned soft. "I ken ye loved Raebert very much, dearling, but ye're young. Ye have yer whole life ahead of ye. Surely in time, ye'll want—"

"Nay." Elspeth shook her head, sick at the thought of being vulnerable to another man. "I...I never want to remarry...ever."

"I hope 'tisna our brood that's given you such a distaste of marriage," Megan said, strolling over with Lady Frances.

"Nay," Elspeth quickly replied. She glanced over at the table by the window where the bairns gobbled their treats under the watchful eyes of the trio of maids charged with keeping them from mischief. "Especially now, when they're quiet."

"'Tis a temporary thing," Megan said, laughing. Her honey-colored hair was plaited in two fat braids, and her face positively glowed with health and joy. "And lively as this lad is—" one slim hand caressed the silk-covered bulge that was her babe "—things'll be twice as wild when he gets here."

Elspeth felt envy slice deep and sharp. Reminding herself that she'd have been hard-pressed to love anything Raebert sired did not quell it. "I'm content to play aunt to your brood," she said, though the words sounded hollow even to her own ears.

"What do ye mean, Raebert sold Elspeth's farms?" her sire bellowed. Turning in his chair to confront her across the thick Turkish carpet, he demanded, "Is this true, lass?"

Elspeth shot Ross a reproachful look. "Aye, but—"

"Nay buts about it," the laird raged. He surged from his chair, then groaned and sagged back down again.

Elspeth and her mother were beside him ere he settled.

"Lionel, ye should be in bed," his wife cried.

"Da, I'm sorry, I—"

"Leave me be, the pair of ye," he rasped, color high. "There isna any harm done. I but moved too quick. 'Tisna right that he sold off yer property. The farms should ha' served to dower yer next marriage," he told Elspeth.

"I dinna intend to wed again." Quiet, yet firm.

"Nonsense," he boomed, hinting he was indeed on the mend. "I ken ye were daft for young Munro, but that ache'll heal in time."

Fine. Let them think she pined for Raebert. "Nay. I will never get over him." That, at least, was true.

"Oh, dearling." Tears welled in her mother's eyes.

"I dinna want your pity, Mama, just your understanding." Elspeth glanced around the circle of her loved ones.

Lady Frances was not fooled, Elspeth saw. Small wonder, for the woman had helped her over more than one rough spot, knew most of what had gone on behind closed doors at the Munro residence. 'Twas to her Elspeth had first run when she'd been rescued from the fire that had claimed Raebert's worthless life. "I'm sure we all want what's best for ye," her friend said at length.

The others were quick to agree. Then an uneasy silence fell over the room, as though Elspeth's grief had cast a pall they knew not how to throw off. A shriek from one of the bairns broke the tension. Megan and her mother by marriage went to solve the problem while the two men returned to their talk.

"I've news for ye," Lady Frances whispered, and drew Elspeth back to the window overlooking the gardens. "Alain Munro left for the Highlands to tell his brother, Seamus, of Raebert's death."

Elspeth shivered. Seamus was twice the monster Raebert had been. If he ever found out how his only son had come to die...

"I owe Alain much." For befriending her over the years. For coming to her aid the night of the fire. 'Twas he who had pulled her from the raging inferno of her bedchamber and gone back inside to look for his nephew. It had been too late. Raebert was already dead. Another terrible secret that must be guarded or...

"He wants to wed ye."

"Alain? But . . . but he's old."

Frances smiled ruefully. "Four and thirty isna such a great age. I'm a year older myself."

"You scarce look older than I am, and you know it," Elspeth said, frowning. "Alain's never wed. Why now? Why me?"

"He's always been fond of ye. Ye were sunk too deep in your troubles with Raebert to see it. Now ye're free."

"Nay." She was still hostage to Raebert's memory. "You never remarried . . . and neither shall I," Elspeth declared.

"My case was different," Frances said gently. "My castle and lands were mine when I wed. Because my lord loved me well, our marriage contract insured they'd remain so even did he die before me. Thus I have a home and income. Over the years, my men have had to fend off an attack or two from greedy men anxious to kidnap me and force me into marriage to gain my property."

"Men!" Elspeth snarled.

"Ah, malignin' us again?" Ross asked at her elbow.

"Aye. Men use their strength to wound and imprison."

"Some do," he said levelly, and she feared his piercing gaze saw too much. "But I didna come to defend my sex. I came to ask about the Highland property. Surely Raebert didna sell that."

"If you mean Scourie Castle, that, and the lairdship of the Munros, will fall to Alain when Seamus dies."

Ross frowned. "You were obviously too taken wi' Raebert to read the marriage contract. There is a piece of land on Loch Shin, and a tower, too, I think, that are yours. Because Da and I wanted you to have something that was yours, we insisted the property remain yours should Raebert die before you."

"I have land and a tower?" Elspeth blinked, trying to take it all in. Why had Raebert not mentioned this? Because he'd wanted to keep her weak and totally at his mercy. "Oh, Ross. Thank you." She hugged him, then danced back. "I'm going there."

A chorus of denials rang round the solar as their mother, father and Megan protested the plan. Only Ross failed to join in. Expression bland, he hushed them and told Elspeth that if she'd agree to a few stipulations, mayhap she could visit her lands.

"Anything, so long as I may go," Elspeth breathlessly promised. "Frances, come with me while I set the maids to packing. Ever since I was a lass, I've craved adventure," she confided as they left. Her cheeks were flushed, eyes bright and lively as they hadn't been in four long years.

"Have ye taken leave of yer senses?" Lionel roared when the door shut behind the capering Elspeth.

"Not entirely." Ross strolled across the room and propped one shoulder against the mantelpiece as he regarded his worried kin. "She's had a rough time of it, and I'd see her happy."

"She'll be killed," his mother moaned, and even Megan looked as though she doubted his judgment.

"Loch Shin is only a day's march north of your parents' castle, Meggie," he reminded her. "We'll send a goodly escort and a letter to your papa requestin' he send someone to look over the property while your mama entertains Elspeth at Curthill."

"Why could she nae wait here?" his mother demanded.

Ross sighed. "You've seen how she is since she came home."

His parents nodded in unison, and Carina said, "She's so quiet and...and forlorn. Though she was a trial growin' up, I'd give anything to find her sneakin' away to prowl the woods."

"She hasna lost her temper once," Lionel added unhappily.

"Exactly," Ross said, turning to leave before they came up with more objections. "I'd best be about gettin' the men ready to accompany her." He did not get clean away, though, for Megan followed him from the solar.

"Ross Carmichael, what are you up to?" Megan demanded.

"Helpin' my sister."

"Ha. And you thought I wouldna remember that Lucais Sutherland holds Kinduin Castle . . . *on Loch Shin*."

"Why, so he does."

"Ross. She already turned him down once, and for all we know, he's wed and the father of four by now."

"He isna and she was a fool to refuse him."

"She didna just refuse. She called him a scrawny, unco' Highlander . . . and laughed in his face."

"He's grown some since then. Should they meet, I dinna think she'll find him the sort of man to laugh at."

"Aye, more like they'll claw each other to death. He's arrogant as the devil and his pride more than equals hers."

"Too true." He kissed her and turned away, smiling.

"Where are you goin'?"

"To tell Giles to pick thirty men and escort Elspeth. I think I'll send Wee Wat along, too. He's the only one I can trust to keep my sister from doin' somethin' foolish."

"I didna think there was a man born who could manage her."

"Nay, Wat canna do that." But Lucais had, once. Knowing Elspeth as he did, Ross had often wondered if that wasn't why she'd refused him. Mayhap all they needed was a second chance.

As adventures went, this was undoubtedly the most boring, Elspeth thought as she descended the steps of Curthill Castle ten days later. The sail north to Dornoch Firth had been tedious and uneventful. When they'd landed, Megan's elderly parents, Eammon and Mary Sutherland, had greeted her like a long-lost daughter, fussing and hovering worse than her own family.

Inside Elspeth, a storm was brewing to rival the one ruffling the sea below the cliffs that supported the old castle. She was done with waiting, done with following orders. Primed for a fight, she stopped at the foot of the stairs and glared at the men preparing to travel into the Highlands ... without her.

Dawn had not yet broken, and over the castle walls the mountains stood out like fretwork against the pale sky, dark, sullen, mysterious. A chill wind moaned around the castle, whipping the torches that rimmed the courtyard, casting eerie light and shadow over the seasoned fighters Ross had picked for this journey. Beneath their thick woolen cloaks, she caught the glint of armor and the gleaming lengths of wide broadswords, bathed red in the firelight so they already looked bloodied.

"M-m'lady," stammered the maid her mother had chosen to accompany her, a plump older woman whose constant complaints grated on Elspeth's frayed nerves. "I dinna like this."

Despite her resolve to be away, a shiver worked its way down Elspeth's spine. If she had any sense, she'd stay safely behind at Curthill while Sir Giles and his troop inspected her property. But she did not feel sensible; she felt reckless, her dormant spirit stirred by the rising wind. She was not staying here.

"See my bundles are tied on a pack animal, Ann," Elspeth ordered, then marched across the courtyard to confront Sir Giles.

"But...but m'lord expressly said ye were to stay here whilst we inspected the tower," the unhappy knight sputtered.

Elspeth crossed her arms and tapped her foot, a gesture her family had long ago learned to dread. "I can ride as well as any of your men. If you dinna take me with you, I'll only follow."

Sir Giles's mustache twitched in alarm. "Ye wouldna—"

"Aye, she would." Wee Wat stepped from the shadows into a circle of torchlight. Leathery and brown as a dried plum and scarcely taller than herself, the wiry man scanned Elspeth from her coronet of tightly pinned braids to the hem of the split woolen riding skirt that had been Lady Frances's parting gift.

Elspeth resisted the urge to squirm beneath his piercing black eyes. Lifting her chin, she stood her ground. "I need answer to neither of you. I'm going, and that's final."

Wee Wat hawked and spat. "Ross said ye were to stay."

"*Lord* Ross isna my keeper." Whatever did her brother see in this rude, disrespectful little man?

"Well, ye need one, that's sure," Wee Wat snapped. Ignoring her outraged gasp, he turned to Sir Giles. "Best ha' another beast saddled. I can keep a better eye on yon spoiled bairn if she's beside me, not bumblin' about on the trail behind us."

Spoiled bairn! Elspeth's eyes narrowed. She longed to wrap her hands around his skinny neck, but she had what she wanted. And if she caused a row in the courtyard, 'twas certain to rouse the castle. Better Wee Wat's sarcasm than Lady Mary's weeping and hand-wringing when she discovered her guest was departing.

"See ye've learned to control yer temper," Wee Wat muttered moments later as he boosted her up into the saddle. "But I'm thinkin' this trip'll take some of the steel out of yer spine."

"You willna hear me complain," Elspeth said boldly, but not naively. Ross's tales of his own long-ago journey through the rugged Highlands left her few illusions this would be an easy ride. Yet once they left the level plain of the coast and started to climb, her resolve faltered. The world narrowed to a single track abutted by sheer walls of rough-hewn stone. As far as the eye could see marched the stark mountains, shoulder to shoulder like a band of giants that nearly blocked out the brooding sky.

Fog lay close in the glens, turning the damp air so moist 'twas some time before she realized 'twas, in fact, drizzling. She looked ahead to Sir Giles, a dark blur in the mist. "I expect he'll call a halt and erect tents to shelter us."

Wee Wat grunted. "Stoppin' in the Highlands is dangerous."

Elspeth's heart leapt at his ominous words, then beat thickly in her throat as she recalled Ross's warnings about the perils of venturing away from Curthill Castle.

"The Highlands may be part of Scotland," Ross had said. "But they are as wild and lawless a place as ever God created."

Elspeth had brushed aside his dire predictions of what she would encounter. Now, with home far behind and only this cold, inhospitable land all around, she felt less certain she'd made the right decision. What if they were set upon by outlaws? Worse, what if they ran into Lucais Sutherland? She knew not what place he called home, only that it lay somewhere north of Curthill, a disastrous coincidence she'd avoided thinking about till now.

Her mood as somber as her surroundings, Elspeth allowed her mind to stray into forbidden territory. Aye, Lucais was that. A thorn in her side from the moment they'd first met, a threat to all she held dear. A danger she'd escaped the only way she could . . . by wedding someone else. Still . . . regret burned deep in her soul. She shouldn't have rejected his suit so cruelly.

Four years had not dimmed the horrible memory of his lean features twisted in agony as her words flayed him. If they did meet again, she'd explain . . . Explain what? That his marriage proposal had shocked her and terrified her. Nay, she could never lay bare the secret fear that had driven her to hurt him so in order to save herself. She'd seen hatred in his eyes as he'd spun away and walked out of her life. Better he should continue to hate her than learn the awful truth. If their paths did cross, he'd be far more likely to spit on her than talk to her.

Besides, the Highlands were vast, and she vaguely recalled Lucais describing the property he'd inherited as remote and run-down. Doubtless he was too busy running it and siring a horde of red-haired bairns even to remember her. This time her regret was more personal, but it changed naught. Marrying Lucais would have been an even bigger mistake than wedding Raebert had been.

"Elspeth?"

She jerked around, startled to see it had grown nearly dark and they were stopped on the trail. "What is it?"

"Giles thinks we're at the turnoff." Wee Wat nodded to where the knight and the scout Eammon Sutherland had loaned them sat hunched over a white square. The map her da had insisted the Munros supply when the marriage contract was signed. Elspeth had another copy in her pouch, and secreted in the false heel of her boot lay the precious deed to Broch Tower.

"It willna be long, then?" she asked hopefully.

"Wi' any luck. I've no likin' to pass the night here." Her leathery protector frowned and looked over his shoulder, making Elspeth's skin crawl as she did the same.

"We turn here." Sir Giles wheeled his horse to the left. "Swords at the ready. Stay close." The rasp of steel clearing two dozen scabbards was swallowed up by the forest.

Elspeth crouched low, striving to keep clear of the wet branches that slapped at her face. 'Twas dark as pitch, and the earth steamed with fog, stank of soggy peat. According to the map, this trail led to the banks of Loch Shin and thence to the tower a half league to the north. She hoped these choking woods soon thinned, for she could not shake the feeling that unseen, unfriendly eyes marked their progress.

The woods ended as abruptly as they had started, and they found themselves on the stony shores of the loch. Black water lapped at the ferns that crowded its edge and reflected a string of lights in the distance to their right.

"Is that my tower?" she asked, nudging her mount forward.

"Stay back." Wee Wat took the horse's bridle and drew her into the shelter of the trees. "Let Giles look things over."

"I willna sit here with the rain pouring down my neck when my tower lies yonder," Elspeth said through chattering teeth.

"Yer tower's to the left," Wee Wat said tersely. "That must be the village of Kinduin."

Kinduin. The name sounded vaguely familiar. Before she could comment, mounted men erupted into the clearing. Elspeth gasped; Wee Wat cursed and started them both back up the trail, but retreat was cut off by a wall of horses. Behind them, she heard the rattle of steel-shod hooves on wet rock, the clang of swords as Sir Giles and the others engaged the enemy.

"Hold!" The sharp command rose above the shouts of her escort, cutting off all sound save the thudding of her heart. The bulky shapes of their attackers pressed closer, ringing them with iron-banded shields, yet making no attempt to use their swords.

"Yield and we'll spare your lives," the same voice called.

Elspeth glanced at Wee Wat, gauged the frustration in the grim gaze he spared her. If not for the need to protect her, the men would likely try to fight their way clear. Once again, she was a liability to people she cared about.

"What are yer terms?" Sir Giles demanded.

The crowd parted to reveal a huge black stallion. At some signal from its rider, the beast stepped from beneath the shadow of overhanging branches into the misty gloom. Though his face was hidden by his helmet, Elspeth fancied this powerful man stared directly at her. "Terms? An interestin' phrase," he said, voice deep and dark as the night, yet laced with a mockery that set her teeth on edge. "Considerin' we've snared you right and proper."

"What do ye brigands want?" Wee Wat growled.

"What every outlaw wants," the leader mocked. "A swift horse, a trusty blade and a willin' wench to warm our beds when the night's work's done." He leaned forward to rest his arms on his saddle horn. "Niall, see to collectin' our guests' weapons...so there's no chance of an accident...and bring them along. Since my night's work is done, I'll see to the wench."

Elspeth swayed where she sat, shivering as every lurid story she'd ever heard about such lawless reivers flashed through her mind. Her adventure had just taken a decidedly nasty turn.

Chapter Two

Elspeth Carmichael, here?

Nay, 'twas Elspeth Munro now.

Lucais's hands tightened on the reins, mirroring the tension roiling in his gut as he led the way through the wet woods.

Thank God he'd recognized the Carmichael banner and called off the attack, he thought, mind still reeling from shock. Twin shocks. Hard on the realization that the band his men had attacked were Carmichaels, not Munros, had come the stunning discovery that Elspeth was with them. Elspeth was here!

Even a quarter hour later, the pain of seeing her again was still a grinding, gnawing ache in his chest. Part denial, part... part yearning. The sight of her pale, hauntingly beautiful face had pierced him like a lance, stealing his breath, scattering his reason. He hurt. God, how he hurt. He'd thought he was over Elspeth, but seeing her again had frozen him in place at the edge of the clearing, then burned him to the quick.

Anger. It had to be anger at the way she'd dismissed him. He couldn't let it be anything else because losing her had nearly killed him. Losing her to Raebert had made the blow doubly cruel. Aye, she was Raebert Munro's wife. He couldn't forget that, nor the damning fact that she had suddenly appeared a league from the broch. Coincidence? Lucais couldn't afford to believe in them.

So he'd pulled his shattered wits together and retreated behind the mask of mockery that had been his most effective weapon against her potent appeal. Shored up by the reminder that she was wed to his enemy, Lucais had coldly ordered the Carmichaels disarmed and bound... all save Elspeth. Though she was more dangerous to him than her escort of thirty battle-trained men, he couldn't bring himself to hurt her.

Fool! he thought, and cursed his weakness where she was concerned. Black Jock noted his tension and sidestepped, bumping them against Elspeth's mount. The palfrey tried to balk, but was held in close check by the reins twined in Lucais's fist.

Elspeth gasped and turned on the man who rode knee to knee beside her, his features obscured by his helmet, all save the eyes that glittered from inside the shadowed metal sockets. Big. Powerful. He must be, for he'd quelled a battle with just one word. Aye, he exuded the kind of raw vitality that made others jump to obey his terse commands without his even raising his voice. Sweet Mary, but he frightened her, she thought, instinctively glancing around with an eye toward escape.

"Dinna even think about it," the reiver growled. "I know these woods. I'd find you...if the beasts didna get you first."

Elspeth lifted her chin, teeth clenched to still their chattering. "Better ripped apart by a wolf than raped by you."

"I've never forced a lass in my life," the wretch drawled. "There's more profit in ransom."

Ransom. The word kindled a tiny flame of hope in Elspeth's frozen body. Still she was too terrified to relax. Nor did she trust him. Nerves taut, she rode beside him through the dark forest and into a small village.

"Niall, take these men to the dryin' hut and see what you can learn," their captor said as he reined in before the largest of the neat dwellings. That brought a chorus of protests from her Carmichaels. He silenced them quickly. "Your lady is safe with me...providin' you cooperate. All I want is ransom."

Elspeth's fears grew as she watched Giles and the others ride away. The reiver, who had removed his helmet, watched them, too. She chose the moment of inattention to spring into action. Leaping from the saddle, she darted into the night, intent on reaching the woods and hiding there until—

"Nay!" Hard hands grabbed her from behind, lifting and turning her so she was mashed against a body encased in steel.

Lucais had expected her to fight. She did, kicking and bucking like a wild thing and calling him every foul name she'd learned from her sire's soldiers. The words were interspersed with grunts of pain as her soft flesh met his armor. "Cease. You're only hurtin' yourself," he growled, but she thrashed on till he trapped her milling arms with one of his and wrapped his other hand around her throat.

Self-preservation stilled her instantly, though he applied little pressure. Beneath his palm, her pulse beat a frantic tattoo. 'Twas strangely heady to feel her life's blood rushing against his flesh, to smell the lavender in her wet hair, to warm her chill skin with his hand. He'd wanted so much for them, once. A joining of the flesh, surely, but more...respect, happiness, love. Sweet dreams that had died hard.

Her eyes were wide now, reflecting back his own grim image in the flickering torchlight—rough-hewn features, slashing brows, strong jaw and a beak of a nose. No wonder she'd turned him down. He looked more like a nightmare than a lass's dream.

"A-are you going to kill me?"

"Nay. 'Tis ransom I'm after," he murmured, his voice made huskier than usual by the things warring inside his head. "But if you try to escape me again, 'twill go hard with your men."

"You are despicable." Though she did not fight him again, her whole body trembled, mirroring the impotent rage in her face. "I hope you choke on your *blood money,* you bastard."

'Twas her low opinion of him that stuck in his throat. Still, Lucais was grateful that she docilely accompanied him into the hut...the one he'd asked the village headman to vacate for this interview . . . and took a stool by the simple hearth.

Under cover of rebuilding the fire in it, Lucais cast a sidelong glance at the lass who had haunted him day and night since their first meeting nine years ago. The oval face with its high cheekbones and full, mobile mouth was as deceptively sweet and delicate as he remembered. She'd thrown back her wet cloak to reveal a woolen tunic, damply molded to the curve of full breasts. Lass no more, then, but a woman grown, bonny and self-assured, even under these trying circumstances.

Aye, she was as achingly beautiful as ever . . . and as proud, he mused. Even wet, muddy and bedraggled, she sat on the simple fireside stool as regally as royalty on a throne. Only her pallor and the grimness in her eyes betrayed her fear. Such control was new, coming from a lass whose flaming temper and towering rages he well recalled. No doubt a skill she'd picked up at court, where everyone hid behind a mask, posturing till it fair made a body sick. Had she learned deceit and treachery, too? He didn't want to think so, any more than he wanted to recall she was Raebert's wife, but what honest reason could have brought a fine court lady, a Munro, to his corner of the Highlands?

"Are you going to crouch there all night?" she demanded, jaw set, tone indignant. "I'm tired, wet and chilled to the bone, and I want to know what you plan to do with us, Sir Brigand."

So, her temper was not completely tamed. Perversely pleased, Lucais smothered a grin and stood slowly. He'd brought the Carmichaels to the village instead of to Kinduin, not wanting them inside his stronghold until he'd determined their purpose.

"Well?" she snapped, but the flames gilded the fear in her eyes. *Damn.* He did not want her fear; he wanted, had always wanted, only one thing from her. Something he'd never get.

His hands tightened around the stick of wood he held, knuckles white with the force it took to keep from reaching for her and soothing that fear. 'Twas better this way, for her fear kept between them a distance he needed to maintain . . . for his own sake. Disgusted at his lack of control, he threw the wood into the fire and stood. "They're safe enough. You have my word."

"Your word." She leapt up, toppling the stool behind her. "The word of some nameless, lawless outlaw."

Lucais blinked. Though he'd removed his armor and helm, she didn't know him. It hurt to see no hint of recognition in the magnificent violet eyes that had first drawn him to her. Worse were the pain and vulnerability that ghosted their depths.

Who hurt you? he longed to ask, but he dared not get that close. Instead, he concentrated on her cutting comment. Damn, he was leader of his clan, a man who'd worked long and hard to make something of himself and fulfill his grandsire's trust in him, yet she made him feel like the raw, lowly page he'd once been.

"What do you intend to do with us?" she demanded. He gave her high marks for bravery and shored up his own defenses.

"That depends on who you are and why you've come here."

She glanced at the fire. "I—I am Lady Elspeth Carmichael. I was visiting relatives and fancied a ride in the Highlands. We . . . we became lost . . . it got dark, and—"

She lied! "What kin?" he snapped. If she mentioned the Munros, flaunted her marriage to Raebert, he just might be sick. Come to think of it, where was her husband?

"I was visiting Curthill. Lord Eammon is father to my sister by marriage, Meg Sutherland. To what clan do you belong?" Her curled lip said she doubted any would claim such as he.

The bitter anger that rose inside Lucais steadied him, drove out the pain and confusion that had tormented him from the moment he'd recognized her in the clearing. *Ugly, unco' Highlander,* she'd called him when she'd scoffed at his marriage proposal. Aye, she'd preferred Raebert's pretty face and lofty title to his own craggy features and meager holdings. 'Twas still the worst cut of all. The sooner Elspeth was gone from his life again, the better. But he'd not release her till he knew why she'd been sniffing about the broch. The survival of his clan was more important than any hurt he might suffer at her hands.

"I belong to the clan that's captured you." Spinning away from her dangerous beauty, Lucais drew a flask from his saddle pack, uncorked and proffered it. "Here, this'll put some steel in your spine whilst I decide what to do with you."

"My spine is just fine." She snatched the flask and upended it in her mouth before he could warn her that— "Oh!" She wheezed and coughed as the strong liquid burned its way down her throat. Her face turned red and tears filled her eyes.

"*Osquebae* isna for the fainthearted." He reached to take the flask from her trembling fingers.

She snatched it back, raised her chin and downed another, albeit more careful, swallow before thrusting the flask at him. *So there,* she silently challenged, and he applauded her in kind. There was a strength behind her bravado that had been missing before, a new piece of the puzzle he dared not explore.

"Have you eaten?" he inquired.

"'Tisna your concern." Her belly rumbled its disagreement.

Lucais smothered a grin and fetched the food he'd asked the headman's wife to prepare. Dark bread, sharp cheese, the village's own smoked salmon and ale. He set the plate on the packed, earth floor before the fire and sat down. "Hardly the sort of thing a fine court lady's used to."

"How do you know that's what I am?"

Damn. He'd forgotten how quick she was. Lucais glanced up at his damp adversary and grinned. "You've the airs of one."

"'Tisna airs to refuse to break bread with my...my..."

"Captor?" he supplied, though by her suddenly stricken look, *rapist* was the word hovering on the tongue that nervously wet her lips. He'd dreamed about her mouth, about feeling it beneath his own. Some of the desire that sizzled through his body must have shown in his face, for she retreated a step. He frightened her. Good, because she terrified him. When she did not speak, merely watched him as a mouse would a hungry cat, he relented and patted the nearby stool. "Come, I willna tell the Guild for Females Who've Been Abducted that you slipped and ate with me."

"Dinna tease me," she snapped, but after eyeing the food, she kicked the stool a foot farther from him and sat.

Perverse little baggage. Fondly. Yet he did not want to like her, not at this point, and he could ill afford to have her learn she tied him in knots. Studiously avoiding her fulminating gaze, he divided the food, laid a portion on his thigh and handed her the plate. From beneath lowered lashes, he studied her while she tucked in with nary a complaint about the simple fare.

He liked her new lack of airs, too, damn her. His own appetite faded. How often had he daydreamed about sharing something as ordinary as a meal with her? Her refusal had killed those dreams, yet here they were, sitting alone together in the enforced intimacy of the dimly lit hut.

"What's this?" she asked at length.

Lucais blinked, refocused his attention on her plate. "Smoked salmon. The fish comes from the loch. The villagers smoke it or pack it in salt, then we ship it to market."

Her delicate black brows rose. "We?"

He cursed silently. "I've hauled a net or two in my time." 'Twas the truth. Though his father had been a tailor, Lucais had grown up by the sea at Curthill and fished with the other lads. When he'd first come to Kinduin and been desperate to win the respect of the kinsmen his grandsire wanted him to lead, he'd lived in the village and worked alongside the fishermen.

"Mmm." Skeptically, but he was not certain if she was wary of the fish or of his words. She sniffed the salmon, took a tentative bite. "'Tis delicious." Her smile stopped his breath.

Mercifully for the state of his rioting body, someone knocked on the door. "Aye," he called.

Niall stuck his head in. His eyes widened at the sight of his proud chief sitting cross-legged on the floor at a lass's feet. "I need to speak wi' ye a moment."

Lucais nodded. Setting his untouched food on Elspeth's plate, he climbed to his feet. The stiffness in his limbs was caused by tension, not the long day he'd spent in the saddle patrolling his lands against Munro encroachment.

"What of me?" Elspeth demanded, guilelessly beautiful in the flickering firelight, her face framed by tendrils of raven hair come loose from the braid that now hung over one shoulder. Her bedraggled state was an ugly reminder of how she'd come back into his life. Even uglier was the notion that mayhap Seamus and Raebert had sent her in to spy on him or gain entry to the broch.

"Finish your meal," he said with a curtness that made her blink. Struggling to ignore her fear, he glanced around the windowless hut, saw nothing that could be used as a weapon and strode out to join Niall.

"Jesu, ye looked right cozy with yon lady," his cousin said before he'd gotten a step from the hut. "Never say ye've found a replacement for Jean?"

"You know better than that," Lucais snapped.

"I'm sorry, Luc, but I think 'tis about time ye put what happened to Jean behind ye and found a lass who—"

"Niall," Lucais warned. Jesu, he didn't want to think about the price poor Jean had paid for loving him. And as for Elspeth . . . Close as they were, he hadn't told Niall about his impossible yearning for Elspeth, or his disastrous marriage proposal.

Niall frowned. "Back to *this* lady, then. What's to be done wi' her and the men?"

Damned if he knew. "We need to find out what they were doin' on Sutherland land. She claims they were out for a ride..."

"And they lost their way. The men tell the same story, only they claim they were makin' for Larig."

Lucais snorted. The mountain village was two leagues and a dozen hills farther east. "Clearly they *are* up to something." He speared one hand through his damp hair and paced before the hut. Most of the fisherfolk had retired, for they'd be back in their boats before dawn. The few people who walked by stared at their chief but none intruded on his privacy. *Loneliness, isolation are the price of being a leader,* his grandsire had warned. Niall was the closest thing Lucais had to a friend and confidant. Once he'd hoped to have a wife to share his toils and triumphs. But Elspeth had not wanted to be stuck in the Highlands with an impoverished bard playing at being a knight. Which made her sudden appearance here all the more curious.

"These Carmichaels are led by a Sir Giles," Niall said. "He alternates between promisin' a grand ransom if we free them and threatenin' to kill the lot of us if we harm Lady Elspeth. Mayhap I should bring him by to see how famously ye two are gettin' on."

"Niall."

"Ye're so damned perfect, ye canna blame me for gloatin' when I find a chink in yer armor."

Elspeth was that. 'Twould be too damned easy to ignore the evidence and let her ride away before she recognized him and things went from bad to worse. That he was even tempted to let her go scared him. "Sir Giles isna well-known to me, but there is a small, dark man ... Wee Wat, by name."

"Aye. The little old man who asks a lot of questions and looks fierce enough to chew nails. How do ye know them?"

Lucais stopped pacing, dragged in a lungful of damp air to steady him as he looked back. "Nine years ago I was page to Megan and Siusan Sutherland. A blood feud had sprung up between the Sutherlands and the Carmichaels over the death of Lord Lion, who was Siusan's betrothed. Ross Carmichael, the same man who sells our salmon and is brother to the lady we've captured, was ordered to Curthill to wed Megan. He came, married the lady and untangled the web of lies and betrayal to prove 'twasna a Sutherland murdered Lion, but Comyn MacDonnel.'' Lucais had been along on that desperate ride into the Highlands to rescue Siusan and baby Kieran from the mad MacDonnel. "Wee Wat was Ross's most trusted man, so if he's come with Lady Elspeth . . .''

"Her brother knows she's here and was expectin' trouble,'' Niall put in, frown deepening. "Ye meet Lady Elspeth then, too?''

"Aye, but that's of no import,'' Lucais hedged. "Ross has been a good friend.'' 'Twas Ross who had found markets for the Kinduin salmon and Carmichael ships that took them from Curthill's docks to be sold in Edinburgh. "And Lady Megan is dear to me. For their sakes, I wouldna harm these men.''

"Or the Lady Elspeth?'' Niall prompted, grinning.

Though there had been a time four years ago when he'd cheerfully have choked her for refusing him, murder was the last thing on Lucais's mind when he thought of Elspeth. Damn her. "Or the lady,'' he grumbled. Some of what he felt must have shown in his expression, for Niall cursed and grabbed his arm.

"Jesu, she's the one. Four years ago ye went to Edinburgh to fetch a bride, wi' black hair, ye said. Ye came back wi' black-haired Jean, but ye never wed her.''

Aye, desire for Elspeth drove me to that piece of madness. Lucais clenched his teeth over the howl that rose in his throat. "Elspeth's naught to me.'' Not anymore. "Now if you've finished pickin' at my past, I've decided to keep the Carmichaels here as our guests for a few days . . . see what we can learn. The men can stay in the village, but I'll take the lady to Kinduin.'' The knowing grin that split Niall's wide face made him add, "Wee Wat and Sir Giles may be quicker to speak if their lady's nowhere in sight and they're a wee bit worried over her . . . fate.''

Elspeth finished off the last of the fish, set the plate down on the floor and leaned back on her stool. Hands clasped loosely around her knees, she stared into the crackling fire, dimly aware that she should be up looking for a way out, but too warm and tired to stir. The combination of a full belly and the *osquebae* had doubtless dulled her thinking. Her mouth still hummed with the smoky taste of the salmon, an unexpectedly pleasant mix of sea and land. As surprising as her host.

When she'd first seen him in the clearing, big and unyielding as the granite cliffs soaring over the loch, she'd expected to be thrown to the ground, raped, robbed and murdered along with the Carmichaels who'd accompanied her. Instead, she'd been brought to his village and treated as courteously as an invited guest...except that she'd been separated from her men. Oddly, their captor seemed more concerned about why they were here than how he could profit by it.

Or was he?

This village lay close to her tower. Suppose this mysterious brigand coveted her land. Worse, suppose he already lived in it. That notion drove Elspeth to her feet, reminded her that she knew next to naught about this place she'd come to claim. Pressing her fingers to her lips to still their trembling, she frantically ransacked her brain for every scrap of information.

Raebert had never mentioned the Highlands except to curse the bleak land, drear weather and dour people. To her knowledge, he'd visited Scourie Castle only once in the past years, and that shortly after their wedding. On the occasions when Alain and old Seamus had visited Edinburgh, they had grumbled about the difficulties of wresting a living from their mountain holdings. There had been talk of raids and retaliations, of lifting cattle and burning crofts. The names of their enemies had been roundly damned...Gunns, MacKays, MacLeods and Sutherlands.

References to the last had always made her worry about the Sutherlands she knew. Laird Eammon and Lady Mary lived on the seacoast, nowhere near the Munros. And she'd supposed Lucais didn't have anything worth stealing. 'Twas some other branch of the far-flung Sutherland clan that harassed the Munros, she'd told herself, and closed her ears to the talk. Now she wished she'd paid more careful attention. Wished she knew whose lands bordered hers, who was warlike, who could be trusted.

Her outlaw knew, but she did not trust him.

Her outlaw.

Elspeth lowered her hands and shook her head in disgust. 'Twasn't like her to be fanciful. He was a brigand, an ambusher of hapless travelers . . . mayhap even a murderer, for all she knew.

He didn't act like a murderer.

Awareness tingled along her jaw and down her neck as she recalled the way he'd thwarted her escape attempt. Painlessly, but effectively. Caught as much by the intensity that darkened his eyes as by the callused palm warming her skin, she'd felt . . .

Cherished?

"Bah!" Elspeth whirled away from the fire, annoyed with herself. Men were not what they seemed, were not to be trusted. Hadn't living with Raebert taught her that?

Aye, it had, but as she surveyed the hut looking for a way out, the image that lingered in her mind was of a rugged Highlander dressed in damp wool and leather, thick dark hair falling forward to conceal features as rough-hewn as the mountains that had spawned him.

Elspeth closed her eyes, swaying where she stood. In the dim room, she'd caught only impressions of his face, but the feelings he'd roused in her were anything but vague. His height, the width of his shoulders, the way he moved, graceful and quick as a cat despite his size, made her pulse quicken and her skin feel a size too small. Mayhap she was sickening from the wetting she'd taken. 'Twas the only explanation for her feverish fascination with the man who'd taken her prisoner. Sweet Mary, she even fancied the rogue seemed familiar somehow. 'Twas impossible. If she'd met a man as big and vital as this one, she'd have remembered him.

Still, there was something about his eyes. Something . . .

Elspeth snorted, opened her own eyes and marched toward the door, driven by equal parts fear and anger. It must be some sort of spell. The clan legends she'd helped Megan copy down were filled with them. She had the uneasy feeling she'd fallen in with a tortured hero from some ancient tale. The sooner she left this place, the better. But as she touched the latch she heard voices.

"I've decided to keep the Carmichaels here. . . . The men can stay in the village, but I'll take the lady to Kinduin." 'Twas her reiver, but the rest of his words were garbled. Then, "Wee Wat and Sir Giles may be quicker to speak if their lady's nowhere in sight and they're a wee bit worried over her . . . fate.''

Oh, sweet Mary. Her heart in her mouth, she turned and began a frantic search for a weapon, a way out, anything. A scant few minutes later, the rattle of the latch alerted her to trouble. Rounding from a basket of fishing tackle, she snagged a length of rope in one hand and sprinted for the door. In the time it took him to bid his cohort good sleep, she tied one end of the rope to a table leg, stretched it across the threshold and crouched on the other side of the door, praying the gloom would hide her.

It did. He walked into her trap, unsuspecting until the second she tightened the rope, catching him about the ankles and sending him crashing to the floor like a felled timber. With the hut still shaking and his curses ringing in her ears, she jumped up, leapt over her victim and headed out the door.

'Twas full night and dark as pitch, except for the weak light seeping from the shuttered huts and a few wind-whipped torches sprinkled through the village. Where were her men? Which way to the horses? Panicked, confused, Elspeth headed away from the light toward the forest. She had only a few seconds to choose her course and savor her freedom before *he* thudded up beside her.

'' 'Twas a nasty trick,'' her nemesis said as calmly and effortlessly as though they'd been strolling through the palace gardens, not running flat out over rocky soil. He reached for her; she instinctively shied away, lost her footing and fell.

Strong hands closed on her, snatched her up a scant inch from the ground. Holding her tight against the hard wall of his chest, he skidded to a halt. The feel of those muscular arms wrapped around her sent her pulse careering faster than the fear that had driven her to flight. *Better he'd let her fall.*

Elspeth twisted in his grasp, though oddly she wanted to go limp, to absorb his warmth and strength to bolster her sudden weakness. Nay. Men were not safe. 'Twas an illusion born of her fear and desperation. She struggled harder.

''Easy, bratlin', or you'll hurt yourself,'' he said, rough mockery overlaying his concern.

That tone; those words. She'd heard them before. Elspeth stilled, mind racing back, straining to dredge up a splinter of memory that lay just beyond. "Who are you?" she whispered.

A tremor raced from his body into hers. He cursed softly, then slowly turned her to face him, yet did not release his iron grip on her. "I'm a nobody from your past, Beth."

The pet name, used only by one person, brought her head up. She frowned at the man towering over her, dark hair wildly ruffled by the night wind, face gilded in the torchlight. Stoic. Proud. Arrogant. Beneath the hands she'd splayed across his chest, she felt not a youth's bony ribs but the hard muscles of a body honed to fighting trim. It couldn't be Lucais. It could not.

"You often claimed I was a lowly bard...called me worse the day we parted." His bitterness pulled the scales from her mind.

"L-Lucais?" Her voice stuttered with her faltering heart as she tried to fit her memory of a lanky, intense lad over the reality of this...this warrior. Nay. It could not be. 'Twas too cruel a twist of fate even to contemplate. That she should endure so much at Raebert's hands only to end up in the arms of the very man she'd wed Raebert to avoid. "Y-you've changed."

"Aye." His eyes probed for answers she couldn't give him, for he must never know how she truly felt. "You havena," he said.

Hysterical laughter burned in Elspeth's throat. Mayhap he couldn't read her as well as she'd always feared. "Time changes us all," she murmured. But some scars were too deeply rooted to be seen except by a loving heart. Her family had seen her pain, yet not guessed its cause. 'Twas partly why she'd fled...never realizing she'd face an even more discerning heart. Lucais's. "Is that why you've captured us? Because I was cruel to you?"

It did *her* heart good to see his gaze falter, but her triumph was short-lived. "Nay, *I* wouldna be so petty." Meaning she had been. True. Sadly, achingly true, but at the time, she'd thought she'd taken the wisest course for both of them.

Elspeth lifted her chin, determined to play the role she'd been forced to accept years ago. "Then you'll let us go?"

"When I know what really brought you to my lands."

Oh God. He lived here! "This is your village?"

"It may have slipped your mind that I am chief of the Sutherlands hereabouts."

It had. She'd closed her ears to his words that day, blinded herself to his announcement that he'd inherited his grandsire's estates and could offer her both his name and a home. Desperate to end the interview as quickly as possible and make certain he never tried to contact her again, she'd ruthlessly cut his proposal to ribbons. She'd had no choice, but she doubted he'd have agreed with her...then or now. 'Twas too late...for both of them. "I mean you nae harm." How could she live so close to him?

"So you say." Lucais's tone was as cold as the ice wedged in his chest where his heart had been. "Knowin' firsthand how capricious is your nature, I'll reserve judgment for tonight."

She shivered and sagged in his grip. "What will you do?"

"Take you back to Kinduin with me."

"Then God have mercy on us both," Elspeth whispered.

Chapter Three

Weary, wet and chilled to the marrow, Alain Munro climbed the circular stairway in Scourie's lone tower. 'Twas well past midnight and he'd just rode in, would have loved to tumble into bed and sleep till noon, but he had news that wouldn't keep.

Despite the thickness of the stone walls, he could still hear the men drinking and grousing in the hall below. They didn't understand why Seamus ordered them to strike at the Sutherlands, then leave half the plunder behind and head for that decrepit old broch. But they followed orders because no one defied Seamus.

Even his own brother. Half brother, Alain amended as he stopped before the door to Seamus's chamber. He hated every drop of blood he shared with his evil brother, yet lacked the strength to oppose Seamus. Alain sighed and knocked.

"Who is it?" came the prompt, gruff reply.

"Alain. I've news that willna wait till morn."

"Go let my brother in," he heard Seamus grumble.

There was a grating noise as the bar was lifted, then the door opened to reveal Mari Gunn. Clad only in her long, tangled hair, eyes averted, she stood aside to let Alain in, then hurried to fetch the ale Seamus demanded. What a difference from the defiant lass Seamus had kidnapped two months ago.

Alain's heart ached as he spied the lash marks on her back, the bruises on her pale flesh. *Do something about it,* his conscience chided. But he knew he wouldn't. Any more than he'd confronted Raebert over his treatment of Elspeth . . . until the end.

"Well, speak up." Seamus sat in a tangle of blankets, the ale cup resting on his hairy barrel chest. Mari had crawled under the covers beside him. Her eyes were wary and haunted . . . as Elspeth's had often been . . . especially toward the end.

Alain sighed. He didn't want to do this. 'Twas like betraying Elspeth all over again, but he knew if he didn't tell Seamus what he'd seen, one of the men who'd been with him would. "We were watchin' the broch, as ye ordered, tryin' to find a flaw in the Sutherlands' defenses, when the Carmichaels arrived."

"Carmichaels!" Seamus sat up straighter. "Why . . . ?" His beady eyes narrowed. "They've come for the broch. Damn, I thought the deed burned up in the fire that claimed my puir lad's life."

Alain nearly gagged on the description. Raebert had been ten times worse than his brutish sire. "Nay, we managed to rescue some of Elspeth's belongings. I saw the deed myself."

"And didna think to take it from her?"

"Why? The deed's useless wi'out her," Alain observed.

"Aye, her cursed brother saw the land was tied to her. Damn, I never should ha' agreed to Carmichael's demands for property."

Alain didn't bother to point out that Seamus had used a forged document to give Elspeth something that wasn't his in the first place. "We thought it worthless and we needed her money."

"They cheated us. She wasna as rich as they claimed."

Untrue. Raebert had squandered her fortune on his mistress and abused Elspeth when the well ran dry.

Seamus scowled. "That fire was suspicious, happenin' just when Raebert was fixin' to set her aside. And, too, why'd she leave before ye'd even recovered Raebert's body from the ruins?"

Alain knew why she'd run, had the moment he'd found his nephew's body. But Elspeth's secret was safe with him. Raebert had deserved to die. Alain was only sorry he'd lacked the courage to kill him himself. "We've more immediate problems. Elspeth was wi' the Carmichaels, and Lucais has captured them."

"Bloody hell!" Seamus leapt from the bed. "Lucais has been a thorn in my side since he came here. We ha' to get the wench and that damned deed back from him."

Alain agreed heartily, but for a very different reason.

"What if she persuades Lucais to let her inside and they find the treasure?" Seamus demanded, pacing restlessly.

'Twas possible. Duncan Munro had done so. Returning from a raid a month ago, he'd been chased by a Sutherland patrol. Desperate to elude them, Duncan had found a way into the broch and stumbled upon the secret hidden there all these years.

"Damned pup," Seamus snapped. "I should just kill Lucais."

Alain snorted. "The Sutherlands'd send the Fiery Cross through the Highlands and summon their clan to war. We wouldna get inside the broch if the glens were crawlin' with vengeful Sutherlands. 'Tis proved impossible so far, what wi' Lucais's patrols and the way the old fortress is constructed."

"We dinna ha' enough men," Seamus muttered. "Pity Raebert died. I'd counted on him to bring his mercenaries here and keep Lucais busy whilst I looted the broch." He slammed down his empty cup and returned to the bed. "We'll just ha' to find a way to get Elspeth from Lucais before they discover what's inside the fort."

Amen to that, Alain thought. He wanted Elspeth for himself. Had always wanted her. Mayhap with her beside him, he'd find the courage to overthrow Seamus.

Elspeth woke to gray gloom and the nagging feeling that something was dreadfully wrong. Straw rustled in the mattress as she shifted to survey her surroundings, her first clue that she was not at home in her own feather bed or even in the borrowed one at Curthill. One glance around the tiny, stark chamber confirmed her worst fears. This was not another nightmare. She was a prisoner in Lucais Sutherland's Highland tower.

Lucais. His image rose up to haunt her. The changes time had wrought in him were startling . . . fascinating. His features were too chiseled to be classically handsome, but the strength in them drew her. His nose no longer dominated his face, it gave his profile a hawkishness that appealed to her. And his body...

Elspeth sucked in air, her skin prickling as her mind's eye roved over his image. She'd never stared at men as some women at court had, especially after Raebert had shown her to what cruel use a man could put his superior size. But she couldn't stop marveling at the way Lucais's tall, lanky frame had filled out in the intervening years. He was bigger even than Lion had been, yet he moved with the sleek grace of a hunting cat on the prowl, all rippling muscles and carefully leashed violence.

Dangerous. Aye, Lucais was even more of a danger to her than ever. Because his new guise made her feel things she'd thought herself immune to...deep, dark, forbidden things. Her pulse quickened; her skin warmed. Low in her belly a yearning coiled....

Nay! Elspeth sat up, trembling as she cast off the strange longing. 'Twas...'twas the shock of seeing him so changed. She couldn't forget she'd sworn off all men. With good reason. Speaking of reasons, Lucais had ample ones for hating her. He might look different, but he was still the man she'd rejected. Likely he was only biding his time before he extracted his revenge. Aye, Lucais had always been patient and proud. Surely that hadn't changed. He'd make certain she paid.

She'd make certain she was gone before he could.

Last night she'd been too numb with shock and exhaustion to examine her prison. Now she did so with an eye toward escape. 'Twas early yet, and long shadows crept from the corners to meet at the end of the narrow bed. A pair of iron-banded chests stood in one corner; a small table and high stool occupied the other. For light, there was only a thin arrow slit covered with hide.

If this was the chief's chamber, Lucais's clan was a poor one indeed. Her heart ached for him, knowing how such poverty must have grated on his pride. Tossing back the thick pile of blankets, she leapt out of bed and nearly stumbled over a brazier, still warm though the fire had burned to ash. 'Twas then she noticed there was no hearth. Someone had fetched coals to make sure she stayed warm during the night.

Lucais.

That her nemesis, the lad who had tormented her, the man who surely despised her, had gone to such lengths to ensure her comfort confused her. But then, Lucais had always been good at that. 'Twas partly why she'd refused to wed him. Partly.

Confusion became anger when she looked down and saw she wore naught but the linen shift that covered her to midthigh. *He'd undressed her.* Her cheeks heated, and she spat an oath that had been Lion's favorite. Dimly she recalled being brought to this room and waiting till Lucais had left to climb between the sheets—with her clothes on—and falling into an exhausted stupor.

Likely Lucais had returned with the brazier, stripped her and looked at her lying there bare and vulnerable. "Bloody hell." Her stomach knotted on painful memories of her marriage. When she'd defied him, Raebert had punished her by taking her clothes and emptying her room of anything she might use to cover herself.

Nay. Do not remember how it felt to be naked and humiliated. Elspeth drew herself back from the edge of madness, wrapped both arms around her waist to steady her shivering and felt . . .

The leather pouch that contained the map. Her fingers shook as she lifted her shift and opened the pouch attached to her belt. The map was there. Relieved, she sank onto the bed. Tense as things were between them, if Lucais found the map and realized she'd be taking up residence a few miles from his own tower, he might refuse to let her go. Provided *this* was not her tower.

Alarmed, Elspeth quickly scanned the map. Kinduin village lay at the southern end of Loch Shin, her tower at the northern end. Vague as her memories were of last night, she knew Lucais had brought them here through the hills, not along the loch. And the journey had been a short one. So this was not her tower.

Still . . . still she did not trust Lucais. A man who'd stoop to removing a sleeping woman's clothes wouldn't think twice about stealing her property. Sweet Mary, what if he learned she was a widow? Frances's tales of kidnapped brides set her heart racing. Fear sent her scrambling to find her boots. Thankfully they'd been set to dry beside the brazier. More important, the heel containing the deed was still sealed shut. She hugged the dirty things, then set them down while she looked for her clothes, but they were nowhere in sight.

Swathing herself in a woolen blanket, Elspeth crept to the room's only door. 'Twas not locked. Ha! If Lucais had been *her* prisoner, she'd not have been so stupid as to leave the door unbarred. Chuckling in spite of the seriousness of her predicament, she carefully lifted the latch, eased the door open a crack and slipped through...

Right into another chamber.

Elspeth paused, blinking in the spill of bright sunlight from a pair of open windows. 'Twas a bedchamber twice the size of her own at Carmichael and dominated by an enormous bed. Draped in dark blue velvet and raised upon a dais to her left, it faced a large hearth bracketed by floor-to-ceiling shelves filled with books. Even Ross did not own so many costly books.

Drawn by her love of reading, she reverently touched the titles gilded on the leather spines. Because he'd been trained as a bard, Lucais could read, but how had a simple Highlander come by so many books? she wondered, awed and envious. A slight sound from outside the door at the far end of the room alerted her to the fact that time was moving and she wasn't. Casting a wary eye at the curtains drawn tight around the bed, she tiptoed...

"You're up early," taunted a familiar voice.

Elspeth spun around and found the face that had haunted her by night grinning at her from between the drapery folds.

"And scarce dressed for traipsin' about," he added, his gaze scorching a path from her head to her bare toes and back, leaving a trail of tingling flesh in its wake.

Terrified by the sensations he roused in her, Elspeth fought back as she always had. With anger. Eyes blazing, she advanced on the smirking gargoyle. "'Tis you I have to thank for that." She planted her fist square in his grin. Or would have if he hadn't dodged at the last instant. Off-balance, carried forward by her furious momentum, Elspeth careered into Lucais, tumbling them both back through the curtains and onto the bed.

Lucais's grunt of surprise turned to pain as her fist struck his cheek. "Elspeth, stop." His plea made her fight harder. With his legs trapped in the bedclothes and one arm caught between them, Lucais was at her mercy. And well she knew it. She pummeled him with both hands, but his flesh was used to fiercer blows than she could land. He suspected from the "ouches" sprinkled in with her curses that she'd be the one bruised by this.

"Enough!" Lucais cried, and settled the matter by simply rolling over and pinning her beneath his greater weight. "Yield."

"Never." In the dimness of their curtained cocoon, her eyes glowed like live coals. Aye, Elspeth was more alive than any woman he'd ever known. 'Twas part of what had continued to draw him back to her despite her temper and her rudeness.

He resorted to the mockery he'd hid behind in the past. "I'd heard the court was a wicked place, but I had no idea 'twas the custom there for women to . . . ravish the men in their beds."

"You . . . you think I want to couple with you?" Elspeth trembled with the force of her emotions. Indignation and something deeper, something that should have been fear, given her terrible history. When Raebert had died, she'd sworn she would never again be vulnerable to a man. And here she was, spread-eagled beneath one who had good cause to hurt her. But the feel of Lucais's muscular body, trapping her though he held the full weight of his body in check, didn't unleash a rush of primitive female panic. It made her skin heat and her heart pound with the overwhelming urge to press closer, to wrap herself around him . . .

Nay! Fight. Do not let him know how he affects you. "Get off me, you loathsome beast," she snapped, trying to twist free.

Damn. For a moment he'd thought she wanted . . . Lucais sighed. "Wrigglin' about isna the way to convince me you're serious," he said truthfully. Despite his good intentions, his lower body stirred, aching to fulfill a dream long held at bay. He shuddered as a white-hot wash of desire roared through him, threatening to make a mockery of the honor pounded into him from birth.

As though feeling the tide of his rising passion, she stilled. Her violet eyes locked on his. The repugnance that flickered in them before fear took over brought him back to his senses quicker than a dip in the icy loch. She was not for him. Never had been, never would be. It took all his skills in self-control to keep the bleakness from his face as he levered himself off her. He dared not let her see how truly vulnerable he was.

Glad that he'd slept in his breeks in case she needed him in the night, Lucais settled his back against the pillows and watched her furtive efforts to wrap the blanket around her.

"Fiend," she snapped, covered to the chin and sitting as far away from him as she could without falling off the bed. That hurt, though he knew 'twas better this way.

" 'Twas you who sought me out."

" 'Twas you who took off my clothes and—"

"I've seen naked lasses before," he goaded, needing her anger to keep the distance between them. To help him forget.

"Well, you willna see *me* naked again."

She looked so much like an enraged kitten, silky hair standing on end, eyes spitting. Lucais couldn't help smiling or appreciating. Small wonder all women had seemed too tame compared to her...even Jean. Poor Jean. A sobering reminder he had ill luck with women. "One of the maids removed your clothes."

"Summon her here that I may ask her—"

"You doubt my word?" Lucais's eyes narrowed. His voice was low and deadly. "Whatever else I may be, I dinna lie."

"Oh, you're just an abductor of innocent travelers?"

Check. He'd forgotten she played a lethal, if somewhat erratic game of chess. 'Twas a game Lucais played to win. And the stakes in this game were high indeed. "Somehow I dinna think you're as innocent or as honest as you'd have me believe."

She had the grace to flush. He saw that even in the faint light filtering in through the part in the curtains. Still she did not back down. "My presence here has naught to do with you. Now, I must ask that you return my men so we can head back to Curthill. You wouldna want to worry Lady Mary and Laird Eammon."

True. But his first duty was to his own people. "You can leave when you've told me what you were doin' here," Lucais said quietly but firmly. He watched her face closely, but his mind was on the map concealed at her waist. Ena had found it when she'd undressed Elspeth and brought it to him at once.

A map showing Loch Shin, Kinduin village and the path that led to the broch. Only on Elspeth's map, the lands thereabouts were marked with a bold *Munro,* not Sutherland. Clearly the mapmaker had been a Munro. What troubled Lucais was the presence of the king's seal on the bottom. It lent credence to the lie . . . made it seem the lands did belong to the Munros. How had it been done?

Lucais itched to leap from the bed, ride posthaste to Edinburgh and set the matter to rights. But he had more pressing matters here . . . the raiding Munros and Elspeth. Beautiful, obdurate Elspeth. Much as he longed to confront her with what he knew and demand an explanation, one look at the determined set of her chin assured him the direct approach would yield naught. Past experience had taught him that she'd close up tight as a clam if prodded, and when you tried to pry open a clam, you too often cracked its shell.

The ache in his gut intensified. 'Twas one thing to *persuade* information from an enemy raider, quite another to contemplate harming one hair on Elspeth's proud head. Seamus and Raebert had known what they were about if they'd sent Elspeth here to spy for them, he thought grimly. But his own determination ran just as deep. And force was not his weapon of choice, at any rate.

"Enough of this lyin' about," Lucais announced.

Elspeth squeaked as he leapt from the bed and jerked open the drapes, giving her a heart-stopping view of more bronzed flesh than she wanted to see. His chest was broad, heavily muscled and lightly furred. Sunlight picked out the red in the dark swirling pelt, gilded the undulating ridges of well-honed flesh as he stretched his arms over his head . . . casual as you please. She was not pleased, but she couldn't look away.

Her traitorous pulse raced as her eyes traveled from the chestnut hair hanging wild about his wide shoulders, down his chest to the woolen breeks that rode low on his narrow hips. Sweet Mary, he looked as perfect as one of the statues in the castle gardens. *Nay, he was a dangerous beast.* Frightened now, Elspeth wrenched her gaze back to his face, found him watching her with an intensity that stole what remained of her breath. *An intelligent beast.* That hadn't changed. In order to succeed with her plans, she'd have to be very careful around him.

Lucais set his hands on his hips, head cocked, hazel eyes more green than brown and alight with mischief. "Will you dress and come down to break your fast? Or shall I bring a tray—"

"Nay," Elspeth exclaimed. Her tumultuous thoughts could not stand another moment cooped up in here with him. And well he knew that she was not as immune to him as she'd like. The wretch. She dredged up the haughty anger she had used so effectively on him in the past. "Though your hall is doubtless dark, dank and unfit for gentlefolk, I'll come down." Heiress to lowly page.

His teasing smile vanished, his eyes narrowed. "At least the rabble below will be wearin' clothes, not a blanket."

Elspeth gasped. "You'd deny me my clothes?"

"They're caked with mud, m'lady...scarce fit to touch your soft, pampered skin. We Highland louts dinna clean our clothes but once a year, and I fear you've missed wash day."

"Where is my baggage?"

"Spoils of war, I fear."

"Thief!"

"How else is a stupid lout like me to earn my bread?"

That he mocked her was as clear as the brogue that suddenly thickened his speech. "Surely there is something I could wear."

"Naught fine enough for you." He waved his right hand in her direction, and she saw that scars crisscrossed the long fingers that years ago had plucked a lute so sweetly she'd nearly cried. Could he still play? Or was he so thoroughly the warrior she'd thought she'd wanted that he no longer had the soul for music?

Bah! Now was not the time to turn fanciful. "I'll wear anything." Elspeth meant it. She had to get away from him.

He grinned and bowed low. "As Lady Elspeth commands. I'll send Ena with the garments and return to escort you below." Stopping only long enough to scoop sword and dirk from the floor beneath the bed, he strode from the room. And if the chamber suddenly seemed a little dimmer, she tried not to notice. She tried to concentrate instead on how she might escape Kinduin.

* * *

" 'Tis a fine fit, m'lady," Ena said, twitching at the skirts of the blue gown, one of several she'd brought along with wash water and a comb. "But it could stand a press."

"Nay. 'Tis fine. I'm anxious to be gone." Elspeth smoothed her hand over her hip, surprised at the softness of the wool, fine as any she'd worn at home. Though the style had not been worn in Edinburgh for years, the close cut flattered her slender figure. Falling in fluid lines from her shoulders to her feet, it was nipped in at the waist by a leather belt tooled in blue. The costume seemed made for a lady just her size and coloring. What lady? Belatedly she wondered if Lucais had a wife stashed away in the tower or a string of mistresses.

Not a wife, Elspeth decided, glancing at the big bed. This new Lucais seemed too virile a man to sleep apart from his wife as Raebert had ... thank God. "Who do I thank for the loan of this gown?" she asked of the maid crouched at her feet.

Ena's brown eyes clouded as she hefted her pudgy body up. "'Twas puir Jeanie's. She were about yer size. The things have been in a trunk since ... well, for a few years now."

Puir Jean? Spoken of in the past, yet a chest of her belongings remained at Kinduin. What, then, had happened to Jean? Before Elspeth could voice this new question, Lucais opened the door and strolled in.

"You might wait for permission to enter," Elspeth snapped.

"My own chamber?" He quirked his brow in a manner that grated on Elspeth's fragile temper. And if he'd noticed how well the borrowed gown fit, it wasn't evident in his blank expression. "Well, are you ready?" he asked a trifle curtly.

"Aye." Elspeth fought the urge to kick something ... him. "Thank you for your assistance, Ena," she said politely. Lifting the hem of the skirt to display the toe of her hastily cleaned boots, she walked to the door with the dignity that had gotten her through the terrible days at court.

"Allow me to assist you." Lucais took her icy hand in his warm, callused one. When she tried to tug free, he tightened his grip, holding her firmly but painlessly. "The gown becomes you, but 'tis an inch too long. I wouldna like you to trip."

Though Elspeth had never cared for compliments, his warmed her. And that troubled her anew. He was making a hash of her insides. "I am too surefooted to fall," she said curtly.

"Hmm." He studied her in the dim corridor. The rhythmic stroking of his thumb across her wrist played havoc with her senses. Or was it the warm glint in his eyes that made standing beside him seem...intimate? Made her recall how it had felt to lie in his big bed, pressed against the intoxicating strength of his body. "I seem to recall you nearly topplin' off a cliff."

Elspeth blinked, only too glad to drag her thoughts from a quarter hour past to nine years ago. "You were chasing me."

"You'd stolen my dirk, if memory serves. And if I hadna caught you when you stumbled, you'd have gone over the side."

"I've since learned to look out for myself," Elspeth said, hoping he couldn't read the bitterness in her words.

His features tightened. "Is that why you rode out from Curthill yesterday? Were you lookin' out for your interests?"

That he'd cut so close to the mark made her gasp. She covered it with a cough, but surely he felt her pulse leap. She sidestepped. "I wanted to see the Highlands."

"Hmm." This time the eyes that measured her were harder, less indulgent. "A word of caution, Lady Elspeth. I wouldna put it about here that you're wed to a Munro."

This time there was no covering the gasp that seared her throat. "I...I didna think you knew," she managed.

"I made it my business to find out who you'd chosen." *Over me.* The unspoken words heightened the tension between them so the air seemed to crackle. His face was as forbidding as carved granite; his eyes burned with the same raw fury she'd seen there when she'd turned him down.

"It mattered to you that I wed Raebert?"

He blinked, and when he lifted his lashes, his expression was shuttered once more. Would that she had as much control over herself, Elspeth thought, face hot, hands cold. "'Tis a moot point now. Suffice to say, we Sutherlands hate the Munros."

"I see." So 'twas a clan feud, nothing personal. Why did that hurt? "Raebert is—"

"Nay!" His hand gripped hers convulsively. A muscle jumped in his cheek as he flexed his jaw. "Dinna speak of him."

"But I just wanted to tell you that he—"

"Silence!" Lucais roared.

Before Elspeth could recover from the shock of the vehemence in one who was usually so controlled, a head appeared in the opening at the bottom of the stairs. "Ah, there ye are," the man called up. "We're waitin' the meal on ye."

Lucais groaned. "There isna any help for it now," he said cryptically. "Just keep your rotten opinion of me and my tower to yourself. We're that proud of what we've got, though I ken Kinduin's a rough, poor place compared with what you're used to. And for God's sake, dinna tell a soul you're wed to Raebert Munro." With that, he all but dragged her down the stairs.

"Faith, there's nae need to risk life and limb," mocked the man who met them as they emerged from the stairwell into the hall. "We met briefly last night, but I doubt you'll remember. I'm Lucais's cousin... Niall Sutherland." He bowed low over Elspeth's hand. "The one with all the charm." He had a shock of orange hair, lively brown eyes and an infectious grin.

"Elspeth Carmichael," she replied, conscious of Lucais glowering down at her. Was it her refusal to tell him why she was here or mention of Raebert that had infuriated him?

"Come and eat, then, m'lady." Niall took Elspeth's hand and led her toward a trestle table packed with men and women.

Never had she been the object of such intense curiosity, Elspeth thought as Niall helped her step over the bench and take her seat midtable. "Have I mud on my face?" she leaned over to whisper as he sat down beside her.

"Nay, 'tis just that Lucais hasna had a woman at Kinduin since... for a very long time," Niall smoothly finished.

Did he mean Jean? Elspeth longed to ask, interest sharpened by curiosity. Or jealousy? Nay. It couldn't be.

"Did ye really live at court?" asked the woman to her left.

Elspeth looked into the plain, earnest face and nodded. The questions came fast and furious then. Had she seen the king? Were the clothes grand? What of the tourneys? She answered each query easily, their smiles of wonder a balm to her frayed nerves.

"Did ye see the king's champion, the cursed Raebert Munro?" asked a man named Cathal, and the others echoed his loathing.

Elspeth shuddered inwardly. 'Twas true. They hated Munros. Sweet Mary, what would happen if they found out who she was?

"Here, here, let the lady eat," Niall interjected. "Though I doubt there's anything here good enough for you."

"B-bread and cheese is fine," she stammered. "Is that some of your delicious smoked salmon?" She looked at a nearby platter and it took wings as the Sutherlands passed it to her. "Lucais gave me some of this last night," she said as she helped herself.

Around her, people shifted, women whispered, men cleared their throats. She looked up to see them staring at her again, a sea of wide faces, red brown hair and curious eyes.

"They think ye're...involved wi' Lucais," Niall murmured.

Elspeth choked on a mouthful of salmon. Niall thumped her on the back until she stopped coughing. The first thing she saw when she opened her watery eyes was Lucais. He stood before the massive hearth that dominated one wall of the hall, head bent to speak with an older man, but his gaze was full on her. What was he thinking? Why was he keeping her here?

"When Lucais told us this morn that ye'd come visitin', he warned ye mightna like us," said a young, freckled lass.

"Said ye'd be so very grand ye'd look down yer nose at us wild, unco' Highlanders," put in the man across the table.

The very words she'd given him four years ago came back to haunt Elspeth, and she wondered why he hadn't told his people to shun her, especially given the way she'd come back into his life. She looked toward the hearth, but Lucais had vanished.

"My cousin's a busy man, but dinna fret. He willna stray far from so lovely a lady as ye," Niall confided.

That's what she was afraid of. With every passing moment, her need to leave here grew. The knot in her belly was partly anxiety over her strange new feelings for Lucais, mostly desperation to escape and reach the sanctuary of her own tower. "I've an urge to stretch my legs and see Kinduin," Elspeth said, and ten people stood up to offer their services as guide.

"Lucais asked me to look out for his lady," Niall said.

"Everyone is so friendly," she said as they left the table. "I'd heard that Highlanders were fierce, standoffish."

"We dinna take quickly to strangers," Niall allowed. "But there isna a person here who doesna owe a debt to Lucais for bringin' us peace and makin' us prosperous. They've made ye welcome because he asked it...and because ye're a bonny lass."

Elspeth smiled absently at the compliment. Why had Lucais treated her so kindly when he clearly suspected she was in league with his enemies? "Th-the hall is quite impressive," she said to divert her mind. Then she really looked and found 'twas indeed cleaner, bigger and grander than the drear Highland towers Ross and Megan had warned her to expect, with rushes on the floor and colorful tapestries to brighten the smoke-stained walls.

"Fit for a powerful chieftain," Niall said proudly.

Elspeth blinked. "Lucais is powerful?"

"Strong enough so even Seamus Munro leaves us alone." Clearly unaware of the tremor that stopped Elspeth in her tracks, he added, "Wealthy enough to reinforce Kinduin's walls *and* buy luxuries such as they have at Curthill, where Lucais grew up."

Like books. "I see," Elspeth said faintly. As her gaze swept the silken banners that hung from the dark rafters and moved down to the Sutherlands going about their daily lives with a smile and a jaunty step, she wondered what her life would have been like if she'd accepted Lucais's proposal. No one bound to Raebert had laughed or relaxed . . . least of all his wife.

"Would ye like to see what he's made of the place?"

"Aye." Shaken by conflicting emotions, Elspeth took his arm. She'd survey the place and make plans to escape. As they rounded the screen that separated the hall from the entryway, she prayed her tower would be as fine as Lucais's. *'Twould serve you right if 'twas a hellhole,* her conscience chided. *If not for your pride, you'd be lady of Kinduin.* But pride hadn't stopped her from wedding Lucais. It had been fear, pure and not so simple.

"Ye shivered. Are ye cold?" Niall asked.

"Nay." Elspeth managed a wan smile for her gallant escort. *Just sorry . . . for so many things.*

"Next to the tower is the kitchen," Niall said as they descended the steps into the small courtyard.

Elspeth blinked against the sunlight and looked around as he identified each structure. The bailey was hard-packed earth and grass enclosed on all sides by a stout stone wall. Helmeted guards patrolled the walkways atop the wall. The teeth of the portcullis were buried in the dirt; the iron-banded drawbridge was up, sealing Kinduin tight as a moneylender's strongbox. *Curse the luck,* she thought, dully listening to Niall's chatter.

The whole of Kinduin would fit in a corner of Carmichael Castle, but the stables, barracks and lesser dependency buildings were well built and in good repair. Listening to Niall rattle on about the improvements *Saint* Lucais had wrought here, Elspeth was impressed ... and surprised. Who would have guessed that a man so humbly raised could accomplish so much? Obviously she hadn't. Clearly there was more to Lucais than she'd ever suspected.

Sturdy as Kinduin was, there was a roughness about the place that cried out for a woman's touch to turn it from a fortress into a home. There should be gardens behind the tower and whitewash on the walls and a dozen other things. Knowing she'd lost the right to be that woman intensified the ache in Elspeth's chest. But she was not one to cry over what couldn't be changed. Instead, she focused her attention on leaving Kinduin for her own tower. For that, she needed a horse.

"I'll escort ye back inside, then I've a bit of work I must see to," Niall said at the end of the tour.

Elspeth smiled in apparent agreement, returned with him to the hall, nearly empty at this time of day, and thanked him prettily. She watched Niall stride off, counted to fifty, then followed. At the top of the steps she paused to scan the courtyard. A few people hurried to and fro, but she saw no sign of Niall or Lucais. Breath bated, heart pounding, she forced herself to slowly descend the stairs and cross the bailey.

At any moment, she expected Lucais to materialize and thwart her escape, but she reached the stables without incident. Inside, 'twas warm and dark, the pungent animal smells oddly comforting. In a world turned upside down, 'twas good to find something familiar. But she didn't linger to appreciate it. Squinting against the gloom, she peered into the first stall. A fat old pony blew in her face. "Not fast enough."

She moved on, glancing into each shadowy box in turn until she came to one that held a big, powerful black. "Ah, you're a beauty." Elspeth reached for the bridle hanging on the wall. "Now, if you'll just hold still while I get this on, we'll be—"

"Thinkin' of stealin' my stallion?" asked a familiar voice.

Elspeth spun toward the sound, found Lucais stalking toward her, movements lithe and coordinated as a hunter's. The glint in his eyes was just as predatory. He stopped so close his boots nudged the hem of her borrowed gown, his body blocking off the light from the single lantern. She could feel the heat radiating from him, warming her chilled flesh even through the layers of clothing that separated them. But 'twas nothing compared to the fire blazing in his eyes as he studied her in the dimness.

Warning flares ignited deep inside her, but 'twasn't his size or his obvious anger that intimidated her. 'Twas her own response to his nearness. Eyes locked on his, Elspeth felt breathless, suddenly nervous, apprehensive and, God help her, excited. Mind sizzling with memories of lying beside him in his wide bed, she wanted to take the single step forward and ...

"What are you doin' here?" Lucais growled, fighting the nearly overpowering urge to crush her close and kiss her.

She blinked, clearing her eyes of the soft, naked yearning that had sent his desire soaring. "I'd like to take a ride."

Jesu, if she'd been sent here to seduce him, she was doing a fine job of it. At the moment, he'd have sold his soul for just one kiss. "I canna spare the men to provide a guard for your little outin'," he snapped, furious with her, with himself.

Her chin came up. "My men can accompany me."

Lucais threw back his head and laughed. 'Twas that or throw her down in the straw and take what she seemed to offer.

Infuriated, frustrated, Elspeth kicked him in the shin. "Dinna laugh at me, you wretch." Her shout ended in a gasp as he grabbed her upper arms and lifted her off her feet.

"Say what you will to me in private," he whispered, low and hard, face so close she could smell the soap on his skin, taste the rage on his breath. "But dinna yell at me before my clan. It belittles us both, and that I willna allow."

Belatedly aware they were ringed by curious Sutherlands, but too angry to care, Elspeth snarled, "Dinna think to intimidate me. 'Tis been tried and failed at by a master in that evil art."

"Then he didna try hard enough," Lucais growled. "Since you've proved yourself untrustworthy, we'll see if some time locked away in my countin' room cools your temper and curbs your penchant for lies."

Chapter Four

A few moments after shutting his prisoner away in his counting room, Lucais mounted Black Jock and left Kinduin, his ears ringing from Elspeth's curses. She still had a repertoire a soldier would envy, though it now took more to anger her. There were other changes, too, ones that confused him, when he'd always thought he knew Elspeth so well. He'd seen a new patience in the way she'd talked with his people. And when she looked at him, he'd read respect in a gaze that used to damn him. But there was more, something like . . . longing. Aye, that soft yearning in her eyes pierced him to the quick. Made him wish for so much. . . .

"Elspeth'll prove a handful for the man she weds," Niall said as they rode out under the portcullis.

"She's already wed," Lucais snapped, angered anew by the reminder Elspeth was Raebert's wife . . . and likely his spy.

"But—but Ena said ye and Elspeth were rollin' about in that great bed of yers this morn."

Lucais jerked so violently Black Jock shied. He used the time it took to quiet the stallion to control his own turbulent emotions. "So that's why everyone smiled when we came down."

"Aye. All of Kinduin had ye weddin' Elspeth Carmichael."

If only that were true. But Elspeth did not belong at Kinduin. Despite her friendliness with his kin, her comments about his keep made it plain she found the place contemptible. He should count himself fortunate she'd refused him and saved them both years of pain. He knew firsthand how a mismatch could chafe. Much as his parents had loved each other, the differences in their station had caused heartache. George

Sutherland had oft bemoaned his inability to give Janet the kind of life she'd been born to. And though she'd never complained, Lucais had seen the sorrow in his mother's face when Kinduin was mentioned.

Janet of Kinduin had married below her station and been disinherited by her sire for her folly. 'Twas only years later, after his other heirs had died, that old Angus Sutherland had relented and named Janet's son his heir.

When the title had passed to him, Lucais had rushed to Edinburgh and offered for Elspeth. Having his suit so cruelly rejected by the lady he'd loved for years had hurt, caused him to seek a poor substitute... Jean. The consequences of that mistake would haunt him for the rest of his life, he thought, but he was older now, and hopefully wiser. "Elspeth is already wed."

" 'Tisna like ye to poach on another man's property," Niall said over the thud of the horses' hooves.

"I took naught from her... her husband," Lucais snarled. But he'd wanted to. He'd wanted to kiss her until they were both breathless, love her until they were too exhausted to...

"Never say 'twas chess ye were playin' that made the bed ropes creak and the lady shriek so Ena thought—"

"She was tryin' to escape. I stopped her." Lucais turned his flushed face into the cool wind and nudged Jock's ribs. Sensing his turmoil, the horse charged recklessly down the narrow mountain trail. But Lucais found it impossible to outrun his memories of Elspeth. All too soon they reached the outskirts of the village and he slowed Jock to a trot.

"Faith, 'twas a wild ride ye led us on," Niall exclaimed breathlessly, reining in beside him. "If not the bonny Elspeth, what's lit a fire in my usually cautious cousin?"

Lucais glared at Niall, then at the grinning Sutherlands who'd raced down the path behind them and now sat cooling their steaming horses. "Duty," he growled. Swinging down, he threw the horse's reins to the lad who'd run out to greet them. "I'd see what we can learn from the Carmichaels," he added, and set out for the drying hut with his cousin dogging his steps.

"Do ye want to know what I think about her?" Niall asked.

"Nay. But you'll likely tell me anyway."

"I think she's runnin' away from something...this husband, mayhap," Niall mused. "There's such sadness in her eyes."

"Nonsense," Lucais said to calm his leaping pulse, but he'd seen it, too. Was there trouble between Raebert and Elspeth? He should have felt satisfaction. After all, she'd chosen Munro over him. But 'twas fear, raw fear for Elspeth that gripped him, and a wave of protectiveness so strong it left him weak. Raebert was cruel, as poor Jean had found out. Was he depraved enough to hurt his own wife? *Fool.* Elspeth had come here to spy for Raebert. She didn't deserve sympathy. "Keep your nose from my affairs."

"But ye have none," Niall chided. "Leastwise, none we know about. Elspeth's the first lass ye've brought home since—"

"Niall," Lucais warned, but his cousin was persistent.

"I ken the attack on Jean and the sorry mess that followed shook ye, but..." His voice trailed off under Lucais's threatening growl. "Ye've a duty to the clan to produce an heir."

"You are my heir."

"Jesu, ye're just as stubborn as Grandda."

"High praise indeed." Lucais walked into the village. It was smaller than the town of Curthill, where he'd grown up, but the stone-and-timber huts were stout, the dirt streets between them free of garbage, bustling with activity...most directed at him.

Women held their bairns aloft to be patted and praised by their chief. The lasses sidled up with ale, fresh baked bread and shy smiles. The men stopped to ask Lucais's advice on everything from fishnets to weapons. Winning their trust had not been easy, for he'd been an outsider, raised on the coast with different customs, but once gained, their trust was unwavering.

Lucais felt a deep kinship with these folk who fished the loch and trapped the pine marten in the dark woods. Honest, hardworking people, not greedy and deceitful like the Munros, who lived off others...even to stealing their women. Aye, he'd do whatever he had to to guard his clan's safety and property.

The pair of guards posted at either side of the large stone hut straightened as Lucais approached. Windowless, with a stout, barred door, the building used to store the dried fish ready for market had been chosen to house the prisoners.

"Have they given you any trouble?" Lucais asked.

"They raised a fair ruckus till we tied them up. Been right quiet since," the short man said with a grin.

Lucais nodded. "I dinna want them harmed if you can help it. Bring me Wee Wat. He's a small dark man with eyes black as peat." He turned toward Niall. "We may need to keep them here a few more days. Will you see to arrangin' for more guards and food?"

"I dinna like leavin' ye alone while ye question this Wee Wat," he grumbled, but one glance at the wiry little man who stalked out of the hut and Niall brightened. "Guess ye can handle that one by yerself." He went away smiling.

Do not be too certain. Lucais braced himself for the coming ordeal. Wee Wat Carmichael was a fierce fighter and no man's fool. "Wat," Lucais said gravely. "Will you walk apart with me?"

Wee Wat hawked and spat. "Takin' up reivin', have ye, lad?"

"Dinna talk so to the laird." The guard started for Wee Wat.

Lucais stopped him with a glance. "'Tis all right. He knew me as a lad and still thinks of me that way."

"Only when ye're actin' like a stupid fool," Wee Wat grumbled and turned away. "Are we walkin', or what?"

Lucais sighed and fell into step beside the angry man. "The boats are out. 'Twill be quiet down by the loch."

"My head's full of the stink of fish." Wee Wat stomped up to the hill overlooking the village and sat down on a rock. "So?"

Lucais propped one foot on the boulder, forearms resting on his knee. "You've scarce aged these past nine years."

"Ye're still a cheeky lad." Wee Wat glared at him. "Though ye've filled out a mite. Ross said ye'd done well for yerself."

The praise warmed Lucais, but not as much as the satisfaction he felt looking out over the thatched roofs of the peaceful village to the deep blue of the loch and the hulking mountains beyond. "Aye. 'Tis a rough land. We've worked hard to wrest a livin' from it, but we finally have enough to eat, enough to trade and a measure of security. Question is . . ." He glanced down at Wee Wat. "Will the Munros let us enjoy our hard-won peace?"

Wee Wat's gray brows knotted. "There's been trouble?"

Lucais nodded and gave him the grim tally of crofts burned, livestock lifted and Sutherlands killed. "The trail leads straight to Scourie, and the raids follow the pattern set in my grandsire's time." He ground his teeth together. "I thought I'd convinced them we were strong enough to thwart them."

"Ye're extendin' the feud to include Elspeth?"

"You tell me," Lucais replied. "Why did she come here?"

"What did the lass say?"

"She claimed you'd gotten lost in the Highlands." Lucais snorted. "Led by the best tracker in all Scotland."

The little man acknowledged the praise with a grin. "Mayhap I'm losin' my sight, too." He lifted the woolen cap and scratched his bald head. "What harm in lettin' us cross yer land?"

"On your way to...?" Lucais prompted.

Wee Wat shrugged. "No place in particular."

"Only fools would ride into the Highlands for pleasure in the summer, when a storm could wash them down the glens. You recall how 'twas when I led you and Ross to Kilphedir to rescue Lady Siusan and wee Kieran."

"'Twas a hellish journey," Wee Wat allowed. "Are ye doin' this 'cause ye're still fashed she didna wed ye?"

Lucais shut his eyes, battling pain and weariness. "I wouldna be so petty, even though she did choose a Munro instead."

"But Raebert—"

"I didna bring you out here to discuss her husband," Lucais snapped. There was a wealth of bitterness behind the words.

The lass hadna told Lucais that Raebert was dead? Wat thought. Close on its heels came another notion. No matter that she'd hurt him gravely, Lucais still cared for Elspeth. Interesting. Wat suspected Ross had known exactly how the lad felt about Elspeth, mayhap had even had matchmaking on his mind when he'd agreed to let his sister travel to the Highlands. "If Lucais and Elspeth should meet," Ross had said with a wink, "'Twill be up to you to see they dinna kill each other."

No light task, Wat thought, considering they'd been at each other's throats from the time they'd first met. But then, he amended, glancing at the young Highlander's proud profile, if the man existed who could tame Elspeth Carmichael, *his* money was on Lucais. Even as a lad, he'd been braw, canny and loyal. A sight better man than that jumped-up court knight she'd wed.

"How long will ye hold us?" Wat's first loyalty was to the Carmichaels. Still, there was no harm in seeing what the lad intended. "I'm gettin' fair sick of the stink of fish."

Lucais smiled faintly. "Sorry. I'd bring you to Kinduin, but I fear *she'd* incite you all to escape. She's already tried once and 'tis scarce even noon."

"Really." The creases in Wat's face deepened as he smiled. "Ross'll be pleased to hear she's regainin' her spirit. She's been a mite peaked since she returned to Carmichael Castle."

Elspeth was home? Had she and Raebert fought? "She's as feisty as ever, and I've the scars to prove it."

"She's a temperamental lass, but likable all the same."

Like was so far from what Lucais felt when he thought of her that he nearly laughed. "Thus far today she has tried to flatten my nose, bruised my shin and attacked me in my bed."

"Ye did naught, of course," Wee Wat said dryly.

"Well . . ." Lucais grinned. "We seem to set sparks off one another. I canna resist teasin' a lass who rises so swiftly to the bait, and she's still determined to look down on me."

"Devilish difficult to do these days," Wee Wat replied, and Lucais knew he didn't only mean his added height.

The compliment, coming from a man who offered few, made Lucais's chest swell, but his brain was more pragmatic. "To her, I'll always be Lady Megan's page, the village lad who aspired to be bard of Clan Sutherland until fate intervened and made him laird of a ragtag Highland tower."

"Looks prosperous to me. Ross thinks highly of ye," Wee Wat added, slanting Lucais a measuring glance. "But I dinna think he'll take kindly to yer holdin' his sister hostage."

A muscle twitched in Lucais's cheek as he tightened his jaw. "No more than I do to being lied to . . . especially by friends. I want to know why you came here. What does Elspeth want?"

"Naught that's yers."

"Everything hereabouts is mine. Rumor has it the Munros have fallen on hard times. Their raidin' seems to bear that out. I think they sent Elspeth to spy on me and get hold of Kinduin."

Wee Wat rubbed his stubbled cheek. "She wouldna do that."

"Elspeth is used to luxury. Faced with financial ruin, she may decide stealin' from me is preferable to starvin'." He straightened, crossed his arms over his mailed chest. "Tell me you werena headed for a tower at the north end of the loch."

His adversary blinked. "She told ye that?"

"I found the map and I'd know what she wants with my broch."

His? Wee Wat frowned. So, the Sutherlands and Munros both claimed it. Mayhap 'twas why Elspeth hadn't told Lucais she was widowed. Many a lady had been kidnapped and forced into marriage for her estate. If Broch Tower was disputed land, even so fine a man as Lucais might be tempted to wed her to get his hands on it. After all, he'd wanted her before. "She'd a mind to visit there."

Lucais's arms fell to his sides, fists clenched. "She's come to steal it. Well, she'll be goin' home empty-handed."

Wee Wat stood. "Does that mean ye'll let us go?"

"Gladly. I'll provide you with an escort to the coast . . . once I have your word, and hers, that you'll stay there."

It took Elspeth nearly an hour, working with the tip of her eating knife and the skills she'd acquired escaping the rooms Raebert had shut her in, to pick the lock on the larger of the two chests that sat against the wall in Lucais's counting room.

She lifted the lid, looked inside and sagged back on her heels with a groan of disappointment. She'd been hoping for a weapon, but found his tally sticks and ledgers instead. Damn, not even a ceremonial sword . . . not that she'd expected a man like Lucais to wear such a useless thing, but he might have had one lying about. Raebert had had dozens, richly crafted and set with precious stones. He'd made a fine showing at court. The king's champion, posing and preening for his enraptured audience. But that's all it had been, a show, a facade.

Sighing heavily, Elspeth went to work on the smaller chest, but the lock proved more stubborn than she was. Angry, frustrated and more than a little worried that Lucais would return before she could escape, she snatched the tally sticks and ledgers out of the chest and stomped on them.

"Take that, you wretch," she cried, imagining that the crack beneath her heel was his neck, not the wooden sticks marked to show the rents paid by the Sutherland crofters. It felt so good that when she'd finished, she tore in half the parchment sheets that detailed which clansmen worked which plots of land.

"There," she said when she'd run out of paper to shred. "Cheat me of *my* land and I'll make certain you've a devil of a time figuring out what property is yours." But when she looked around and saw the shattered wood buried beneath an avalanche of parchment bits, she flinched. Escape was no longer a goal; 'twas a necessity. Lucais would kill her when he saw what she'd done.

With trembling fingers, Elspeth hid the mess in the trunk, then set to work on the door lock. The mechanism was old, rusty from years in this damp clime, but fear was a powerful motivator and the lock soon yielded. Holding her breath, she eased the door open and peered into Lucais's bedchamber. Empty.

So far, so good. Pressing a hand to her thudding heart, Elspeth crept into the room. The heavy drapes surrounding the bed had been pulled back and the rumpled linens straightened, but she recalled only too clearly what had taken place there hours earlier. The anger in his eyes, the mockery on his lips, the feel of his body pressed against hers...hard to soft. Her hands went cold, but her blood heated. Rage. It had to be rage that sent her pulse racing to coil low in her belly, not the memory of lying in the arms of a man who inspired ... What? Not fear or revulsion. These thing she would have welcomed, for they were old friends made during her marriage. So what did Lucais make her feel?

Confused. Angry. Vulnerable in ways Raebert never had.

Bah! Elspeth shook the cobwebs from her brain and turned it to better use than daydreaming—finding a way atop a horse and out of Kinduin before her nemesis returned. Just as she reached for the latch on the door leading into the corridor, she heard something drop behind her.

Whirling, Elspeth pressed her back against the oaken portal, mouth dry with dread, expecting Lucais to pounce on her. The room was empty as before, she found as her eyes swept frantically from bed to windows to hearth, probing every corner, every shadow that lingered where the pale sunlight couldn't reach. Empty.

Wait. There . . . on the far side of the table set before the hearth . . . something huddled on the floor beside a high-backed chair. Too motionless to be Lucais. Unless he was hurt.

Reflexively she started forward, drawn by a need to help that transcended her distrust of men, her fear of this male in particular. "Lucais?" she whispered as she rounded the chair. But the scrap of humanity balled up at her feet was too impossibly small to be Lucais. 'Twas a bairn.

"Oh. Are you hurt?" Elspeth sank to her knees, hesitantly reached out to touch the thin, bare arm that stuck out of the tangle of clothes. Cold. So cold she feared the mite was dead, but the limb flinched away and a low sob issued from the heap. "Dinna be afraid," she crooned. "I only want to help."

"Nae supposed to be here," lisped a small voice.

"Neither am I." Elspeth chuckled. Even at Carmichael the servants' bairns sometimes ventured into the forbidden realm of the laird's chamber. Just to see the wonders there.

A small, grimy face popped into view, pale, framed by a mangled mop of hair as black as Elspeth's. Wet, spiky lashes lifted to reveal golden brown eyes. "Ye're new," the bairn said.

"Actually, I'm quite old," Elspeth replied. This would have earned a smile, at least, from Ross's brood.

The lass's frown deepened. At least Elspeth guessed she was a girl. "Are ye wed to the laird?"

"Nay, thank God."

"Ye're in his room."

"So are you. Are you his wife?" Elspeth teased.

The bairn averted her face, small fingers pleating her woolen gown. "Nay. I'm naught to nae one."

I know the feeling, Elspeth thought, and her heart tightened painfully. "Surely your mama—"

"She died." Flat. Emotionless.

Elspeth recalled the pain, the anguish she'd felt when she'd heard her da had been gravely wounded. If she lost him or her mother, she'd be beside herself with grief. "Your father?"

The girl looked up then, delicate features tight with some fierce emotion that made her eyes glow. "He was glad. He didna like her." The fire went out. "He doesna like me."

"Oh, I'm sure that isna true...um, what is your name?"

"Gillie."

"I am Lady Elspeth...Carmichael."

Gillie swallowed hard. "Are ye gunna tell I was here?"

"Nay," Elspeth said softly.

"I'm nae supposed to come in, but I...I like to see the pretties." From beneath her, she pulled a book that looked too heavy for her to lift and opened it.

'Twas a Book of Hours, Elspeth saw, and very costly, with elaborate color drawings. Their serene beauty was marred by small grimy fingerprints. She could well imagine Ross's anger if one of his precious books had been soiled. Lucais was every bit as fanatical about books and even less likely to overlook having his property ruined by a maid's lass. "Mayhap I can clean the book," Elspeth muttered. That she was leaving and wouldn't be here to witness Gillie's punishment, mattered not one whit.

Gillie looked from the offending marks to her fingers, then up at Elspeth. "He'll ken 'twas me and he'll be that angry."

"I willna let him hurt you."

Gillie's lower lip trembled and tears welled in her eyes. "But he's the laird. Ye willna be able to save me."

A rattle at the latch was all the warning they had before the door opened and the aforementioned laird stalked in. His hair was rumpled from the wind, and he brought with him the fresh scent of trees and sunshine. But the set of his unshaven jaw and the grimness in his gaze bespoke a man ready to do battle.

Gillie groaned softly and buried her face in her hands. Elspeth surged to her feet and placed her hands on her hips, ready to defend the poor child.

"I should have known you wouldna stay where I put you." Peeling off his gauntlets, Lucais tossed them in the general direction of the nearby clothes chest, flung his cloak after them and advanced on her. "I have a proposition I'd...what is this?"

he demanded, dark brows snapping together as he spied Gillie.

Elspeth moved between them. "I . . . I invited her . . ."

"You know you are nae allowed in here," Lucais growled.

"Dinna lay a hand on her," Elspeth cried.

He recoiled as though *she'd* struck *him*. "I'd never hit a bairn." But his high color and ready fists did not reassure.

"She harmed naught." Elspeth's conscience barely flinched over the lie. 'Twas his fault for leaving so valuable a book down where a child could reach it. At home such things were kept on the highest shelves or under lock and key.

"She knows she isna allowed in here," Lucais said again, still without looking at Gillie.

Behind her, Elspeth heard a sound halfway between a sigh and a sob and turned as the poor lass stood. Head bowed, bare feet dragging, Gillie started for the door. The sight pierced Elspeth to the quick. "You fiend." She caught Gillie and swung the lass up into her arms. "How could you hurt her so?"

"What have I done but remind her my room is forbidden—"

"You've crushed her," Elspeth hissed.

"Nay." Still he didn't look at the lass. "For she'll keep comin' back here. Why do you care? She's naught to you."

Elspeth bit back a moan as she felt Gillie tremble in her embrace. "I *feel* for her. Something you obviously canna do or you wouldna hurt her so."

Anguish glittered deep in his eyes. Or was it some trick of the light? "You dinna have any idea what I feel."

True enough, but she was too angry to care. "I think you've become a cold, uncarin' beast." Like Raebert. Mayhap being a warrior did that to all men, save those in her family. "You scarcely even look at the poor—"

"Stop." Lucais shoved both hands into his hair and turned away, body trembling, breathing harsh in the still room.

Drawn by his suffering, Elspeth started toward him with Gillie still clinging to her. "Lucais, I am sorry, but—"

He flung away from her with a ripe oath and stalked to the empty hearth. Leaning both hands on the mantel, he stared into the cold ashes, then abruptly back at her, eyes dark and haunted as her own nightmares. "I neither want nor deserve your pity."

Dear God, what ailed him? Nay, she could not afford to know, to care. He'd always had the ability to draw her against her will. Hadn't she wanted to wed him even knowing they were all wrong for each other? "Very well, then," she said slowly. "I understand Gillie's mother is dead, but I'd like to speak with her father about the deplorable state of her clothes and hair."

"I am Gillie's father." Blunt, brutal words.

"Merciful God," Elspeth whispered.

"God had very little to do with it," Lucais said gruffly, his face a grim mask.

Elspeth stared at him, aghast. "Leave us," she finally said, too shocked to work past the idea that the man she'd once thought soft could treat his own bairn so coldly and cruelly. Thank God she hadn't married him, for he'd likely have turned on her, too.

Chapter Five

Lucais sat brooding before the hearth in the hall, a cup of ale in his hand, one leg thrown over the arm of the high-backed chair that had been Angus Sutherland's pride and joy. Out of the corner of his eye he saw yet another pair of serving women head up the stairs toward the sleeping floor, bearing armloads of folded clothes. Gillie's, no doubt.

"Faith, Kinduin's buzzin' like a hive of aroused bees," Niall observed as he threw himself into the small chair that had been their grandmother's. "What's afoot?"

Lucais turned his head, took in his cousin's wind-reddened face and dancing eyes and growled, "As if you didna know."

"Well." Niall paused long enough to accept a cup of ale from a smirking maid, then said, "I did hear a rumor in the stables when I rode in, but... 'Twas too farfetched to credit."

"What are they sayin'?" Lucais demanded, angered anew at Elspeth's high-handedness, but uncertain how to curb it.

"'Twas a bit garbled, something about ye being, er, barred from yer chamber by—"

"That black-haired witch threw me out of my own rooms." Lucais leapt from the chair, ale slopping from his cup.

"Easy, Luc." Niall took the dripping cup, set it with his on the rush-covered floor and stood. "Why did she...?"

"What does it matter why?" Lucais paced before the crackling fire, beyond reason for the first time in memory. Three hours had passed since he'd been forced to tell Elspeth that Gillie was his. Three hours of reliving the old guilt, the pain, the lies. Now he felt like a kettle set to boil over. "She's my prisoner, dammit. She canna just take over my rooms, order the servants about and . . ." And remind him of his duty to Gillie. Jesu, he could barely stand to look at the bairn, whose presence was a constant reminder of the grievous end Jean had come to because of him.

"Ah well, 'tis easy enough to resolve. She's a good deal smaller than ye are. A sound beating'll teach her her place."

Lucais whirled on Niall, scowling. "Beat Elspeth? Has all that drinkin' and wenchin' addled your wits?"

"Nay, but livin' like a monk seems to have warped yers . . . along with yer sense of humor, I might add."

"This amuses you?" Lucais fairly roared. Heads turned the length of the hall. Servants paused in setting up the trestle tables for dinner; men looked up from their dice and drinks.

"Easy, Luc, ye're givin' everyone a fright. They've never seen ye take on so. Even the day Jean died, ye—"

"Dinna remind me." Lucais turned toward the fireplace. He considered banging his head against the stone mantel. 'Twould be very like dealing with Elspeth. "That's the problem, you see. Elspeth's met Gillie."

"Ah." The word carried a wealth of sadness. Yet close as they were, not even Niall knew the truth about Gillie. "Did the grand lady look down her nose at yer wee bastard?"

Lucais turned slowly, lowered his hands to ball them at his sides. "Regrettably, she didna. After she'd finished dressin' me down like a murderer for my daughter's 'deplorable state,' she ordered me from my chamber, commandeered half my servants and has been up to God only knows what since."

Right on cue, Ena emerged from the stairwell and advanced on them like a woman with a holy mission. "The Lady Elspeth says ye're wanted above, m'lord," she said loftily.

"M'lord?" Lucais exclaimed, sending the old woman back a step. "Since when am I 'm'lord,' instead of Lucais?"

"Since when ha' ye taken to rantin' and stompin' around like a bull with a sore—"

"Thank ye, Ena," Niall interjected. "He'll be right up."

"Besides, Lady Elspeth says 'tis proper respect." Ena threw the comment over one fleshy shoulder as she beat a hasty retreat.

"Damn. Bad enough she's turned me out of my rooms, now she's got me shoutin' at people," Lucais grumbled.

" 'Tis proper respect, I suppose. You *are* the laird here."

Lucais scowled. "Proper for a Lowland fop, but I'm a Highlander. Grandda was always 'Angus.' He said the chief was like a father to his people and should never set himself above them. Besides, Elspeth's my prisoner. She has no right takin' over."

"Elspeth doesna impress me as a meek, biddable sort of female, content to stay where she's put."

Truer words were never spoken, Lucais thought ruefully, recalling other times, other rebellions. He'd laughed when Elspeth had defied her mother or wheedled something from her father. Now her defiance didn't seem so amusing. "Damned if I can figure why she cares what happens to Gillie." Unless she somehow knew the truth about the bairn's parentage. Impossible. Only he and Jean had shared that terrible secret, and Jean was dead. "The sooner Elspeth's gone from here, the safer we'll all be."

"Safer?" Niall's smile faded. "Ye found out somethin'?"

"Aye." Deciding it was time to share part of his burden, Lucais briefly told his cousin about the map Elspeth had been carrying. Niall was suitably concerned, but when he asked why a Carmichael would be interested in the broch, Lucais hesitated. Though he was a good lad, Niall was as inclined to drink as any young man, and Lucais knew only too well that disaster could befall a man when he was in his cups. Had he not drowned his sorrows in ale the day Elspeth had refused him, he'd never have taken up with Jean and Gillie would never have been conceived. If it got out that Elspeth was wed to a Munro, Cathal and those who'd lost family to the enemy might vent their hatred on her.

Distrustful as he was, Lucais couldn't bear the thought of Elspeth being hurt, proof he still cared for her. His brain warned him to keep his distance, but she drew him like iron to a magnet, the pull all the stronger for the changes he'd seen in her. The patience, the vulnerability, even the damned insistence on helping Gillie, bespoke a woman worth loving. Nay, he wouldn't . . . couldn't afford to love her. But then he recalled what had happened in the stables and his heart turned over. Despite the dimness of their surroundings, there'd been no mistaking the desire that had darkened her eyes as she looked up at him, lips parted breathlessly, expectantly awaiting his kiss.

A stir in the hall had Lucais spinning around. What he saw emerging from the shadows deepened the ache in his heart.

Elspeth, with Gillie in her arms.

Their two black heads were bent close together, Gillie's face and pinched, Elspeth's calm, determined, as she whispered something soothing to the lass. Like mother and daughter. The lump in Lucais's chest rose to fill his throat. *Gillie should have been theirs.*

The knowledge rocked him as nothing had since Elspeth had refused him, nearly drove him to his knees there in the hall, before all of Clan Sutherland. Pride alone kept him standing, head high, gaze carefully shuttered as they drew nearer. He would not crumble before the only woman he'd ever loved and the child he couldn't bear to look at because she reminded him of his worst failure. This pain, this grinding, ripping pain, was his penance.

"M'lord," Elspeth said, inclining her head.

"Lucais," he replied as stiffly. "We Highlanders dinna stand on formality."

"Is it a formality to ignore your bairn?" she whispered.

Lucais's glance flicked to Gillie, then away. Naught had changed. She still looked exactly like her mother…black hair, fair skin, cowed expression. How could he have thought Jean resembled Elspeth? Of course it had been dark and he'd been so gone with drink he scarce recalled meeting her, much less…

"Well. What have you to say?" Elspeth demanded. The hall was so quiet you could hear her toe tapping in the rushes.

Presumptuous little witch. Generations of Sutherland pride rushing to the fore, Lucais straightened to his full height and glared down at her. "Ena, 'tis well past the bairn's bedtime. Niall, see what is keepin' dinner," he snapped.

Elspeth watched the others flee to do Lucais's bidding, but 'twas the resignation in Gillie's expression as Ena bore her away that stiffened her own resolve. Though the maids had all assured her the child was well cared for, Elspeth had recognized the loneliness in Gillie's eyes, the yearning to fit in and be accepted. Mayhap because she had never fit into the woman's role that was her lot. Whatever, she wanted to make a difference for

Gillie the way Megan and Ross had for the orphans they'd taken in. "I'd have a word with you, *Lucais,*" she hissed.

"And I with you," he replied. "We dinna have gardens to walk in, but a turn about the battlements should cool your temper."

"'Tisna me shouting and stomping about the keep like a madman." Elspeth spun on her heel and marched from the hall.

Night had fallen and it was full dark with only a few torches lit to chase the gloom from the bailey. The air felt cold and damp. She should have taken time to fetch a cloak, but there was no going back now. In more ways than one, Elspeth realized as Lucais caught up with her at the bottom of the stairs.

"Here." He thrust a length of wool at her. "You're unused to our dank Highland weather. I wouldna want your family accusin' me of neglectin' your health."

"And what of Gillie's health?" she challenged, and wished she hadn't. Despite the lack of light, she saw the bleakness in his face as he flinched and turned away. What was going on here? Why did he ignore the child, yet look so...?

"Come, it grows late and dinner awaits."

Elspeth opened the cloak he'd handed her. 'Twas immense and she could not find the collar. "What manner of cape is this?"

"'Tis a plaid." He took the tumbled length of wool from her, folded it over, then wrapped it around her, securing it at the shoulder with a broach taken from his own tunic. She knew it for his clan badge, a heavy silver circle showing a wild Highland cat and the inscription *Sans Peur.* Without fear. Appropriate, for she'd always known he was a brave man. But now he was also a troubled one. 'Twas the vulnerability she'd seen in him that muted her anger as she followed him across the courtyard and up the stairs to the walkway that ran the length of the outer wall.

The Sutherland trooper on duty hailed Lucais by his first name, smiled as his chief asked after his family. She decided she liked this easy familiarity, so different from the deference paid her father and brother by their clansmen. Oh, there was respect aplenty in this Sutherland's tone when he answered Lucais's questions, but there was fondness, too, she thought as the guard bade them good-night and walked away.

Lucais's attitude added to her confusion. How could he take such care with his kinsmen and ignore his own bairn?

"I have a proposition I would put to you," Lucais said as soon as they were alone on the windswept wall.

"And I a favor to ask you."

"Ladies first," he replied gravely.

Instead of speaking, Elspeth turned to look out over the landscape spread before her like a shadowy tapestry, plowed fields giving way to dark forest and, beyond, darker mountains, their jagged peaks concealing the horizon. Glimpsed through the fringe of trees to her right, the black mirror of the loch reflected the stars just popping out overhead. 'Twas a forbidding land, raw and untamed, but breathtaking. She didn't know why, but it called to her, stirred a restless longing to be out and about, mounted on a swift horse, the wind in her hair.

The same powerful forces that had wrought this land had changed Lucais from a sensitive lad who would be a bard to a ruthless knight. Was there naught left in him of the gentleness she'd once, in her own youthful stupidity, decried? When she'd left the hall, she'd been so certain what she wanted to say, but now, alone with him in the night, she wasn't sure where to begin, what words to use to breach his hard shell. And even if she did, was there any softness, any understanding beneath? " 'T-'tis about Gillie."

"Aye." Voice colder than the wind that sent a shiver racing down her spine. Or was it despair?

"I was wrong to accuse you of mistreating her."

"The Elspeth I knew never apologized."

"I *was* a bit arrogant when I was young." The way his brows flew up made her smile faintly. "I still am, on occasion, but I've learned to admit my mistakes." Even if she couldn't atone for all of them, she thought. "Ena and the others say Gillie's well fed, clothed and such. If she's untidy and dirty, 'tis because she's quick as a darting minnow, into everything."

Ena's words had made Elspeth giggle. Lucais did not make a sound, just stood there looking out over the wall, eyes unreadable as the mountains he faced, jaw tense as a drawn bow.

"She needs more," Elspeth said softly. She went on to tell him about Ross's brood, the orphaned or unwanted babes he and Megan had taken in, raised with love. "Gillie needs love."

"I canna give her back her mother. Would that I could." So grim, so filled with pain.

Elspeth gasped. *He had loved Jean.* Likely loved her still. It shouldn't have hurt, but it did. Given Gillie's age—three years, three months, according to Ena—Lucais had wasted no time in finding someone else after Elspeth had refused him. That shouldn't have chafed, but it did. In the darkest days of her marriage, when Raebert flayed her pride and her self-esteem, she had consoled herself with the knowledge that Lucais had wanted her. But not for long, it seemed. Truly men were inconsistent beasts. "I'm sorry." *For so many things.*

"I dinna want your pity," Lucais snapped. More than pride made him turn away from her soft, bewildered eyes. He could barely stand to think about Jean's death, much less discuss it . . . and with Elspeth, of all people. "I have done my best to see Gillie cared for. She'll never be able to make her own way."

"What do you mean?"

"She's simple." That realization, on top of everything else, had nearly sent him over the edge.

Elspeth blinked. "She seemed normal to me. Very shy and she doesna speak much, but—"

"She doesna speak at all."

"Aye. She did. She told me . . ." *My mother is dead, and he doesna want me.* "She told me her name."

"You always did have a lively imagination."

Elspeth stiffened. "I didna imagine her speaking to me." But she couldn't recall if the lass had said anything to Ena or the other maids. "She was interested in your books." Belatedly, she remembered the smudges in the Book of Hours, now hidden beneath the bed in her counting room cum prison cell. Later tonight she intended to repair the damage and put it back.

"'Tis the colors she likes. She canna read, nor will—"

"Dammit, Lucais, she's only three. I couldna read at that age, either. But I know she could learn. I could teach her."

"You willna be here long enough." Jesu, it hurt to think he'd never see her again, but . . . "I'm lettin' you go. At dawn tomorrow my men will escort you back to Curthill Castle."

"But I canna leave. I havena even seen—" Oh, drat.

"Seen what?" he asked silkily. Too silkily. *He knew. Somehow he knew about her tower.* "What did you come here to see?" When she didn't answer, he growled, "Give it up. I found your map."

Elspeth gasped, hands reflexively going to the pouch concealed beneath her clothes. "Bastard," she hissed. "You did take off my clothes and . . . and look at me. How like a man to sneak about in the dead of night when a woman canna defend herself."

What an odd thing to say, Lucais thought, puzzled by her bitterness. "'Twas Ena who found the map and brought it to me."

Some of her outrage faded. "Still, that was my map."

"Confiscated when you were caught trespassin'."

"I was only crossing your land to get to Broch Tower," Elspeth blurted out, then once again cursed her hasty tongue.

"So. They did send you." If anything, his expression grew more grim, eyes glinting with anger. "Well, the Munros willna use what I once felt for you as a way to sneak under my guard."

What I once felt. That hurt, but she buried the pain deep, locked it away with her other scars. "I wasna sent by anyone."

"Ha! Deny you came here seekin' the ancient broch at the north end of Loch Shin." When she could not, he cursed, slamming his open palm on the top of the wall. The crack reverberated through the stillness, making her flinch. "Over my dead body will you or any other Munro lay claim to my clan's property."

"Yours?" Elspeth gasped, driven back by the fury radiating from him. He followed, stalking her till she reached the turning of the walkway and could go no farther. Trapped between cold, hard stone and Lucais's smoldering rage, she took a stand. "But . . ." *But the land is mine* The words burned on the tip of her tongue; the fire blazing in his eyes sealed her lips shut. What would he do if he knew she had a deed to the land and Broch Tower? Kill her? At the moment, he looked capable of that. Thank God the deed was still safe in the heel of her boot.

"Tomorrow you return to Curthill. If you, or any of the Carmichaels you persuaded Ross to send with you, venture this way again, I'll kill the lot of you."

Sweet Mary. "You've become a hard, cruel man."

"I do what I must to protect my clan. Besides," he added, eyes dark and tormented, "'twas you who said I was too soft. A weak bard. Not the seasoned knight you wanted for a mate."

Elspeth swallowed. "I was young then. I made a mistake."

"Did you?" he asked, low and tight. "I'm thinkin' 'twas I who made the mistake in offerin' for you, but I willna be taken in by you again. I want you gone . . . the sooner the better."

His rejection pierced Elspeth like a lance, so sharp and painful it stole her breath. Was this how he'd felt when she'd refused him? Dazed, wounded, she shivered and looked away from his scathing gaze, but her mind was already searching for a way out. Raebert had cheated her of pride and property; she wouldn't let Lucais do the same. Somehow she was going to Broch Tower.

Someone was in the room with her. Watching, waiting.

Elspeth's skin crawled with the knowledge. Fear welled inside her, dark, insidious, overpowering. She wanted to open her eyes but didn't dare. "Who's there," she whispered.

"Where have ye hidden the money?" Raebert. And behind him, framed in the open door of her bedchamber stood a woman. Raebert's plump, blond mistress, her face alight with greed. "Come, I havena got all night," he growled, stalking closer, hands outstretched like the talons of some great predatory bird.

Apt, for he used them to wound, reveling in her pain. Panicked, Elspeth tried to scramble away, kicking at the twisted bed linens that clung to her legs. But he was too quick for her. Grabbing her up like a rag doll, he slammed her into the mattress, cruel hands pressed to her shoulders to keep her there.

"Give me the money." His words were slurred, stinking of sour ale and evil intentions.

"Please, I—I dinna have any." She hated that pleading voice, but she was afraid. So afraid.

"The servants say ye had a message from yer da. He never fails to tuck a coin in for his darlin' lass. Do ye think he'd still have a care for ye if he knew 'twas yer fault he canna draw an easy breath or sit a horse?"

Elspeth shivered. "I didna do it."

"But ye did." A slow smile crept over Raebert's face, twisting aristocratic features into something demonic. "If ye hadna denied me what was mine, he'd never have been hurt at all."

"Nay," she whispered through numb lips, but she knew 'twas true. If not for her pride, her father wouldn't have been hurt.

"Give me the money, or yer brother'll be next. Think ye the Carmichaels will want him as chief if he has only one arm?" His laughter echoed through the room, chilling her blood.

"Nay, Raebert!" Elspeth screamed, jerking upright in bed, fighting the sheets and residual panic. "Not Ross! Dinna hurt Ross. Take the money. Take whatever you want, but spare him."

A door opened, slanting a wedge of pale light into the room. "Elspeth?" a deep voice called. "What is it?" A dark shape blocked out the light, advancing on her. The bed dipped; wide hands grabbed hold of her shoulders.

"Raebert," she whispered. *Oh God. It hadn't been a nightmare after all. He was not dead but here...* She lashed out with all her strength, striking flesh that felt like rock.

"Damn. Stop that. 'Tis Lucais."

"Lucais?" Elspeth stilled, tilted her head to see the man whose arms wrapped around her like a vise. The night concealed his features, but she knew his scent and the feel of his muscular body from this morn. It seemed a lifetime ago. A lifetime in which her greatest mistakes had come back to haunt her.

"What ails you?" His voice was calm, but his heart thudded in concert with her own, making her aware that unlike this morn, when the layers of her blanket had separated them, tonight only her linen shift stood between her chilled flesh and the hard, warm wall of his chest.

"N-nightmare." Elspeth's pulse raced with the awareness that here was no lad but a man, strong, vital, virile. With a man's needs. Raebert had shown her how cruelly men satisfied those needs. And yet the coil that tightened her insides as Lucais kneaded her back was not fear. She only wished it were.

"Are you all right now?"

Nay. She swallowed. "Aye." Shaky.

"I'll leave you, then." His voice was no more steady than her own. What was he thinking? Did he still hate her? Despite their argument and her resolve to stay clear of men, she didn't want him to leave, needed to understand the changes in him and the ones his nearness wrought in her.

When he loosened his grip and made to stand, she caught his arm. "Wait. I . . ." How to explain her sudden, overwhelming need to keep him here? It had been so long since someone held her, comforted her in the night. Mayhap that was it. The nights had been the worst, for 'twas then Raebert had prowled. 'Twas night now, and she was alone in a strange place. "I—I'm cold."

"I'll bring more coals for the brazier."

There weren't enough coals in all the Highlands to drive the chill from her bones. "A-all right." She bit her lip to still its trembling, but somehow he heard her unspoken plea.

"Your nightmare was about Raebert?" he asked gruffly, yet the concern behind his words brought a lump to her throat. At her nod, he asked another, softer question. "Did he hurt you?"

In more ways than she had known existed. Pride kept the terrible details locked inside, but she couldn't control the shudder that swept through her, even knowing he'd feel it. His curse rent the silence, and his hands tightened on her arms.

"Tell me what happened." His breath fanned the hair at her temples, hands sliding up to caress her shoulders, voice so tender she longed to bury her face in his chest and open her troubled heart. But could she tell part without revealing all? Once started, would she blurt out the terrible truth about the attack on her sire and her real reasons for coming here?

Nay, she could not trust him with her secrets. Not the ones she'd tried to leave behind or the truth about the land he somehow thought was his. "'Twas naught but a dream," she said, then added, "Could you stay with me a little longer?"

"And do what?" There was an edge to his voice she didn't understand, and he released his hold on her shoulders when she wanted him to wrap his arms around her, wanted . . .

Nay. Elspeth clamped down on her fanciful thoughts. He'd made it plain he wanted naught to do with her, and pride wouldn't allow her to beg. "Talk," she said.

"If you're tryin' to seduce me into lettin' you stay—"

"Me?" she squeaked, wishing she could see his face. Was he teasing her? Mocking her? "I wouldna know how." Truly.

He snorted. "I dinna believe that."

"But 'tis the truth." Raebert had made it plain enough that her slender body was unwomanly and unappealing. "Ena said you think all court ladies are wicked, but I am nothing like them."

"This has naught to do with the court," Lucais said honestly, his muscles so tight he could barely force out the words. 'Twas heaven and hell to sit hip to hip with her in the dark, feeling the warmth of her flesh through the bed linens, breathing in the unique scent of lavender and Elspeth. 'Twould only be a moment's work to lay her back in the tumbled bed, strip away her shift and bury himself in the secret haven of her body. Impossible. She was another man's wife. Wed to the man he hated most in this world...for stealing Elspeth and for another, even worse crime. "I have no business being here with you like this."

"But I need you to stay. I need . . . you."

The sensual promise hanging on her last, whispered word tightened every muscle below his waist. "'Tis the broch you want," he managed, struggling for control of his rampant desire.

Elspeth sighed. "I do want to know about Broch Tower."

Lucais blinked, then his gaze narrowed. Damn, she was bold. He wished he could see her face, gauge her intentions. "'Tisna Broch Tower. 'Tis a broch. An ancient fortress built by my Sutherland ancestors."

Seamus had told Ross the same tale when he'd proposed signing Broch Tower over to Elspeth. Only he'd claimed 'twas the Munros who had built it. "Who lives there now?"

"It hasna been lived in for hundreds upon hundreds of years. There is no roof, and 'tis . . . 'tis uninhabitable."

Oh, and what of the people who, according to the ledgers Seamus had shown to Ross, had been paying rent for the land they worked? "Are you trying to scare me off from visiting it?"

"Aye," Lucais growled. "To my people, the broch is a sacred place. 'Tis forbidden for anyone to go inside."

Elspeth snorted. "Next you'll be telling me 'tis haunted."

"In a way. There's a curse attached to the place."

How convenient. "Let me guess," Elspeth said quickly, at least as well versed as he in ancient legends. "Whosoever trespasses on this holy ground will . . ."

"Die a horrible death," he finished for her. "And 'tisna a matter for jestin'. In my grandsire's time, two curious men ventured inside and were never seen or heard from again."

"More likely they went hunting and fell into one of your deep Highland glens," she replied. "I'd still like to see it."

"You're leavin' tomorrow."

It must be rich indeed if Lucais was so determined to hang on to it. *Sweet Mary, all men were greedy sots.* "'Tis a waste of time." Broch Tower was hers. "I'd only come right back."

"Would you risk your life and those of your men?"

"If you didna kill me for ordering you out of your chamber, you willna kill me over this piece of land," she gamely replied.

"You dinna know what I'm capable of." Grimly.

True. She weighed the things she'd seen thus far, the well-kept tower, the clansmen who returned his respect, his treatment of her...kinder than she deserved, considering how she'd hurt him in the past. He'd changed physically, and there was now a hard edge to him, but the only person he cut with it was Gillie. Because he'd loved her mother. Elspeth understood that, too, for she suffered the same pain when she looked at her father.

"You wouldna hurt me," she said with renewed conviction.

"Damn your stubbornness. You dinna have any idea what I want to do with you." Without warning, his mouth swooped down on hers from out of the dark.

Anger. Frustration. Desire. She tasted them all in the instant his firm lips clamped down on her startled ones, kissing her with all the heat and pent-up fury of a summer storm. She tried to twist away, knowing all too well this would lead to pain and degradation. His mouth gentled instantly, one wide hand cupping her head as he apologized with a soft, fleeting kiss. And then another and another, each one light and tender. A slow, dizzying heat spilled through her, melting her bones.

"Oh, Beth. You taste even sweeter than I'd dreamed," he whispered, low and husky. His fingers tunneled into her hair, tilted her face up. "You are right. I couldna hurt you. No matter how badly you've hurt me." His mouth settled over hers.

Moist, warm and incredibly stirring, his gentle kiss shook Elspeth more profoundly than his earlier greed. Of their own volition, her arms stole around his neck; her lips parted to the questing tip of his tongue. The seductive tangling of their tastes and textures stirred something wild and primitive deep inside her, made her moan for the sheer wonder of it. The soft sound was lost in the growl that rippled from his body into hers as he deepened the kiss. Hot, needful things she'd never felt before shattered, splintered and grew apace with the rhythm he set. Closer, she had to get closer or die of the ache building in her sensitive breasts and low in her belly.

Elspeth's small whimpers, the feel of her mouth opening beneath his, the soft weight of her breasts pressed against his chest as she responded to his kisses ripped at Lucais's control. Perfect. She fit his arms as perfectly as he'd known she would, tasted as sweet as his dreams. Groaning, he ran his hands up and down her slender back, loving the way she shivered and moaned as she caught fire in his embrace. His. She had been made for him and no one else. She might have wed Raebert, but...

Raebert.

That single name cut across Lucais's passion-clogged senses, dousing the flames with icy reality. She was Raebert's wife.

"Damn." Lucais thrust her from him and leapt up. His pulse thundered in his ears so he barely heard her ask what was wrong. *Everything,* his battered heart replied, cut and bleeding from her latest wounding. "God," he rasped, dragging a shaky hand through his hair. "I dinna believe you let me...and you a married woman. You're even worse than your husband." He turned and left before he could say more, glad the darkness covered his shame and her betrayal. His only consolation lay in the fact that she'd not seduced him or gained access to the broch.

Chapter Six

Elspeth lay motionless in the narrow bed, eyes gritty from lack of sleep. Beneath the blankets, her body was so tense with apprehension her muscles hurt. The pale light filtering in through the hide-covered window warned her it was morn and her wait would soon be over. Any moment now, someone would walk through the door and order her down the stairs for the trip to Curthill. She prayed that someone wouldn't be Lucais.

How could she face him after what had happened last night?

Shame heated her skin, momentarily driving out the icy dread that had plagued her since he'd slammed from the room hours ago. She'd behaved like the veriest wanton. One kiss and she'd turned from her calm, controlled self into someone she didn't recognize. A wild, hungry thing. Just thinking about the feel of his mouth melding with hers, his hands stroking and caressing, made her pulse soar, her flesh tingle. She'd never dreamed a man's touch could turn her inside out. Especially not a man like Lucais.

Liar, mocked a tiny voice. *You knew he'd be your downfall.* Shivering, Elspeth tried to push the thought aside, but it clung like a pesky Highland thistle, a burr as persistent as the man himself. Aye, though they'd met only a few times, those meetings had been memorable, a contest of wills that had left her shaking with anger. She'd hated Lucais for so easily rousing her temper, hated herself more because beneath her rage there should have been contempt for the lad Megan had trained to take her place as bard of the Curthill Sutherlands. Instead, she'd felt respect for his bravery in leading Ross through the mountains to rescue Kieran and an even more grudging admiration for his clever wit. There had been something else, too, something soft and insidious.

Something she could not . . . would not put a name to.

The creak of the door made Elspeth jump. But 'twas Ena's broad face that peered into the room. "I knocked but ye didna answer," the maid said as she entered carrying a tray.

"I . . . I was asleep." Hastily gathering her scattered wits, Elspeth put into action the plan hatched during the long, sleepless night. She found she didn't have to fake illness. One whiff of the salmon Ena had brought and her stomach rolled.

"Is aught amiss?" the maid asked, setting the tray on the foot of the bed. "Ye look that pale." The crease in Ena's brow deepened as Elspeth admitted she wasn't well. "Small wonder after that wetting ye took two nights past." The maid bustled out and returned immediately with another blanket and the assurance that someone would be up directly with more coals for the brazier.

"I'm sure 'tis naught," Elspeth mumbled, her conscience pricked by the obvious concern with which Ena hurried away to fetch her chest of medicinal herbs.

"Still abed?" growled a horribly familiar voice.

Lucais. Elspeth squeaked and pulled the covers up under her chin like a shield. "Wh-what are you doing here?"

"Bringin' more coals." He strode into the room, emptied the shovel into the brazier beside the bed, then straightened to stare down at her. He looked every inch the Highland laird this morn in a woolen tunic and hose the color of dark leaves. They fit his tall frame like a second skin and brought out the green in his hazel eyes. Handsome. Unbearably handsome, she silently added. It still surprised her to see him so changed.

The glance he slanted her made her acutely aware that she lay on the bed, defenseless and vulnerable to him. A frisson of fear shivered through her. Before it could take root, his eyes moved down to her mouth and lingered there, glinting with the memory of the kiss they'd shared. Her cheeks heated with something she wished was anger or shame, but knew was not. Why were her feelings for him never the appropriate ones?

An answering heat flared in his gaze, then was carefully banked. "I've sent someone to fetch your men." Cool. Controlled.

Elspeth fumbled for a delay. "I . . . I'm nae well."

"Mornin' sickness?" he sneered.

She flinched, startled as much by his bitterness as by the question. "Nay. 'Tisna a polite question to ask a lady,"

"We both know you're nae a lady." His contempt reminded her of his parting comment last night.

Elspeth sat up. "How like a man to blame a woman for his own actions," she exclaimed, eyes shooting violet sparks.

Jesu, she was magnificent, Lucais thought, body tightening as his mind tumbled back to last night and the heady feel of her filling his arms. He could have sworn she'd been as caught up in the passion that exploded between them, but the ache in his heart reminded him that if she had, she'd had an ulterior motive. "'Tis neither here nor there. Get dressed. You'll be leavin' soon."

"You canna order me about like one of your clansmen."

"You are my prisoner," he reminded her, but he was her captive. More so this morn with the memory of her taste lingering bittersweet on his tongue. From her too pale skin and the mauve circles beneath her eyes, he guessed she'd slept little better than he had once he'd left her. But she was still gut-wrenchingly beautiful, he thought, gaze moving from the cloud of tumbled black hair to her breasts pushing against the blanket she held before her. Her fragility roused his protective instincts, made him long to lie down beside her and hold her...just hold her...while she slept. Dangerous. Sleeping with the enemy was dangerous. "You are my prisoner," he repeated to remind himself.

"I've done naught." Insides churning with fear and determination, Elspeth raised her chin another notch to meet the challenge glinting in his eyes. "You dinna have the right to—"

"I must protect what is my clan's from the Munros."

"I assure you I am *nae* in league with the Munros to steal anything from you." She only wanted what was hers for herself. "They would be the last people I'd ally myself with."

"You married one," Lucais growled, then he belatedly recalled her nightmare. "Or do you regret that now?"

Elspeth gasped. The terror that widened her eyes made him even more curious, but she recovered quickly. "Why should I?"

"Last night, when the nightmare had you in its grip, I heard you call out. You begged Raebert nae to hurt you."

"Ridiculous," Elspeth retorted, panic of a different sort knotting her insides. The fact that she was a married woman was the only thing that had stopped Lucais last night. If he knew she was a widow, he'd kiss her again. And this time, he wouldn't stop until he'd hurt her as Raebert had. Revulsion made her stomach heave. Kisses were one thing; submitting to the other was…unthinkable. She'd let Lucais think she was still wed. "You must have misunderstood. I am happy with Raebert." Bile rose in her throat, or was it lying to Lucais that burned?

Lucais cocked his head, studying the ghosts flickering in the depths of the violet eyes that met his so levelly. Was it only wishful thinking that made him sense she was afraid of her husband? Words dimly heard last night filled his mind, cries of horror that had driven him from his bed to hers in an instant. "Nay, Raebert," she'd screamed. "Take the money. Take whatever you want, but spare him." Whoever this *him* was.

Hardly a scene from a loving marriage, but just because she deplored her husband's greed did not mean she feared him. The image of another black-haired woman surfaced. Jean's face swollen from Raebert's blows. If he'd caught Raebert then, Lucais would have killed him. But that memory was nigh four years old, Jean was dead, and this was no business of his. Even Holy Church did not berate a husband's treatment of his wife. But in his heart of hearts, Lucais knew that if he found Elspeth had been mistreated, an army of Munros could not prevent him from making certain Raebert paid dear. And therein lay another danger. If he rekindled the feud with the Munros over this, all the Sutherlands would suffer. Nay, he could not put his clan in jeopardy for a headstrong woman who, after all, had chosen her own path.

Lucais cleared his throat and steeled himself for the ordeal of bidding her farewell…for good, this time. "'Tis well you are content," he said gruffly. "Come, I'd see you on your way."

"You'd send a sick woman into the harsh Highland weather?"

If she was ill, he'd eat his sword. His innards couldn't feel worse for the experience than they already did. Still... He eyed her too pale face, so at odds with her fierce temper, and wondered which to believe. Was there ever a more confusing lass? "I suppose one day willna matter," he muttered, though he didn't trust her. "I'll stay close by and work on my accounts."

"Thank you, I . . ." *Sweet Mary, the broken tally stick and shredded ledgers.* Elspeth went hot, then cold. She'd stuck them back in the chest, but if he saw them before she left . . . He'd doubtless take it as fresh proof of some Munro plot and take his anger out on her. Despite her brave words that Lucais would not hurt her, she knew no man's charity was unending. Especially one who could shun his own bairn.

She had to get away before he discovered the damage she'd wrought to his accounts. Forgetting all about her feigned illness, Elspeth tossed back the covers and leapt from the bed.

"Ah, feelin' better, I see," Lucais drawled.

Damn her impulsiveness! Elspeth shivered, acutely aware of her bare legs and her nakedness beneath the shift. She expected him to eye her lewdly from head to toe and was oddly disappointed when his gaze remained locked on hers. "I . . . I know you want me gone, and I wouldna want to strain your hospitality."

"Fine," he snapped, but she knew it wasn't. "Your men will arrive in a half hour. See you're dressed and downstairs."

Now what ailed him? Elspeth wondered as Lucais stomped from the room. He'd gotten what he wanted . . . her gone from his castle . . . yet he looked fit to chew nails. She felt a little offish herself. She had what she wanted, too. Lucais was letting her go, and once free she'd find a way to slip his guard and make for Broch Tower. So why did she feel disappointed and frustrated, as though she'd bought something from a merchant and been cheated?

Lucais went down to the hall, unable to sit in his chamber and listen to the sounds of Elspeth getting ready to leave him. The tower's main room with its two-story vaulted ceiling was nearly deserted at this time of day, his clansmen having broken their fast on bread and ale hours ago and set about their tasks.

Grateful for the solitude, Lucais threw himself into the chair he still thought of as his grandsire's and stared broodily into the fire that leapt in the hearth.

"Lucais!" Cathal skidded to a halt beside him. "A scout just rode in wi' news the Munros have been seen near the broch."

In the time it took Lucais to leap up, the scout joined them and added, "'Tis a small party . . . no more'n twenty."

"What are they doin'?"

"Sittin' in the woods. Watchin' the broch."

"They havena made an attempt to go inside?"

"Nay," said the scout. "They seem to be waitin' for someone.

Elspeth. Apprehension skittered down Lucais's spine, tied his gut in knots. They were waiting for Elspeth.

"Reinforcements, mayhap," Cathal put in. "'Twould be devilish tricky to protect yerself while climbin' up a ladder into the broch, and I wouldna want to get trapped inside."

Lucais nodded. According to the stories handed down through the generations, the old fortress had never been intended as a dwelling place. It was a defensive structure, erected to shelter the ancient hill people from attacks by marauding Vikings. The Picts lived in separate crofts scattered around the loch but kept their broch stocked with food and water. When danger threatened, they repaired to it with their animals and goods. The broch was impregnable to attack from without, but the only exit was through the second-story door. Those inside were effectively cornered until the enemy left.

"I spread the word in the barracks before I came in," Cathal said, shifting eagerly from one foot to the other. "The lads'll be ready to ride as quick as ye are."

Lucais nodded absently, his mind racing with possibilities. Was Elspeth supposed to lure him there alone on the pretext of seeing the broch? If he took with him the fifty clansmen presently at Kinduin, would they foil Seamus's plans? Or did the greedy old bastard have a superior force waiting in the hills for his signal to rush down and wipe out the Sutherlands once and for all? Given time, Lucais could summon two hundred clansmen from the outlying areas, but did he have time? And did he really want to embroil the Sutherlands in an all-out war?

Not if there was another way out of this damned mess.

And he thought there just might be. It was dangerous, but potentially less costly in terms of human lives. Cathal and the others might not understand, but they'd follow him.

From the shadowy stairwell, Elspeth watched Lucais confer with two of his clansmen. She recognized the stocky, gray-haired man as Cathal Sutherland of the loud voice and perpetually sullen expression. The younger man had the red hair and sleek, muscular body she'd found typical of most Sutherland males.

Lucais stood before the hearth, his back to her as he spoke quietly to the pair. Whatever he said made Cathal furious.

"Hang back! Why? We've got them right where we want them," the older man roared.

"Silence!" Lucais bellowed, looking over his shoulder so Elspeth was forced to retreat a few steps. When she ventured back down, it was to see the trio moving away from the fire, heads bent together in deep conversation. *Conspiring*.

The word raised gooseflesh on Elspeth's skin. She chafed her hands together and crept down another step, craning her neck to follow their progress through the nearly deserted hall. What need had Lucais to conspire in his own tower? Still, there was something furtive about the way he looked about before disappearing around the carved wooden screen that protected the hall from the drafty entryway.

Elspeth let go the breath she'd been holding and stepped down into the hall. Wonder of wonders, the place was entirely deserted. How curious. She'd at least expected to run into Ena and have a chance to thank her for the many kindnesses. Lucais must have told the maid about her miraculous recovery, for Ena hadn't even come up with the promised herbs. She was even sorrier not to have a chance to bid Gillie farewell. Likely the lass would wonder where her new friend had gone…at least Elspeth hoped they'd become friends, because they both needed one. Mayhap when she was settled in Broch Tower and Lucais had resigned himself to losing it, she could find a way to visit with Gillie, Ena and the others.

Ah well. Elspeth shrugged off the vague regret and concentrated on reaching the stables without arousing suspicion. She paused briefly in the entryway. Battered shields and huge, battle-scarred claymores decorated the walls. Much as she wished for a more formidable weapon than the puny eating knife in her belt, Elspeth knew she couldn't lift one of the heavy swords. Even as strong a man as Lucais would require two hands to wield the mighty claymore. Speaking of which . . .

Elspeth cracked the front door and peered out. The courtyard was likewise empty, the portcullis had been raised and the drawbridge lowered. Doubtless Lucais and his men had just ridden out . . . bound for the village to retrieve her men, mayhap. Which meant she'd best find a horse and leave while she still could. Mingled fear and excitement bubbled in her veins, but she forced herself to walk, not run. *Pretend you have naught more pressing in mind than visiting the jakes behind the tower*. So intent was she on her playacting, she didn't see Wee Wat until she rounded the corner of the tower and bumped into him.

"Easy, lass," the little man warned, steadying her.

Elspeth ignored his familiarity and threw her arms around him. "Oh, Wat. I was never so glad to see anyone in my life."

"What's happened?" He peeled her arms from his neck and demanded, "Did that young rogue have his way wi' ye?"

"Wat Carmichael! What a crude thing to ask a lady!"

"Well." He scratched his head. "He always was uncommon fond of ye," he muttered.

Now 'tis my land he wants. Elspeth stifled the pang that thought brought. "Come. We have to leave."

"Aye. Young Niall roused us two hours ago. We've been washed, fed and now we're waitin' on that escort—"

"Nay. We are leaving now . . . alone." When he still didn't budge, she grabbed his arm and tugged. "Hurry, Wat."

"Where are we going?" he asked, trailing in her wake as she made for the stables.

"To Broch Tower, of course."

Wee Wat dug in his heels. "Lucais said 'twas Sutherland property . . . some sacred old ruin."

"Lies." Elspeth prodded him into motion. "There's a feud between the Sutherlands and the Munros. I vaguely recall Alain saying there was bad blood between them, and Lucais confirmed it when he cautioned me against mentioning I was Raebert's wife."

"He's dead," Wee Wat pointed out.

"Widow, then," Elspeth said between clenched teeth.

"Still doesna change the fact that Lucais says this broch thing belongs to the Sutherlands, no' the Munros."

"Broch Tower belongs to me. I have a deed to the land... properly recorded and signed by the king himself."

"Dinna see how Seamus Munro could sign over somethin' that wasna his to begin wi'," Wee Wat mused.

"I hadna realized you'd studied the law," Elspeth snapped, thoroughly annoyed. Bad enough she had to fight Lucais for her property, now she had to convince her own man, as well. "You may stay here if you wish. Sir Giles and the others will—"

"Canna. Swore a solemn oath to Ross that I wouldna let ye out of my sight."

"Well. I've spent two nights and a day without you and gotten on just fine." *Mostly*. But even the presence of her sainted brother could not have kept her safe last night, because the demons that beset her were of her own making. Still, the threat of being left behind prodded Wee Wat into motion.

After that, all went smoothly. They found the Carmichaels and their horses waiting around outside the stables. The stable lad offered no objection when Elspeth requested a mount. *Too smoothly*, she thought as Wee Wat boosted her into the saddle.

"Damned odd, him lettin' us go," the little man grumbled.

Sir Giles shrugged and pulled on his helmet. "I gather there was some trouble in the hills. Most of the Sutherlands thundered out of here whilst ye were lookin' for Lady Elspeth. Likely Lord Lucais had better uses for his men than escortin' us. I hope we willna be drawn into the fightin'."

Trouble in the hills. A battle? Doubtless Lucais would be in the thick of the fight. Elspeth shuddered, suddenly flashing back to yesterday morn and the sight of his bare chest. Visible beneath the mat of red brown hair had been numerous scars, some old and white, others pinker, newer. She hadn't bid him goodbye, was her next thought. What if something happened . . . ?

"M'lady? Have ye changed yer mind?" Sir Giles asked, his brown mustache twitching over pursed lips.

"Nay." 'Twas too late to go back. Still, her heart lay heavy in her chest as she cantered out over the drawbridge. Even ringed by Wee Wat and the other Carmichaels, she felt oddly vulnerable. If Lucais had been with them, she'd have felt safe....

Elspeth killed the thought aborning. Sweet Mary, what ailed her? She needed no man in her life. Something in the chill Highland air must have stolen her good sense. Slinging her hastily rebraided hair over her shoulder, she concentrated on the trail ahead. With Sir Giles in the lead, they followed it through the hills to the level banks of Loch Shin.

Even by day, the water was black, bottomless, reflecting a dark sky crowded with scalloped clouds. Ferns grew thick along the edge, heads drooping over ledges of peat moss that muffled the sound of the horses' hooves and sprang back after them to leave no trace of their passing. As they left the loch the way grew steeper, the trees thinning to reveal a brown ridge backed by jagged mountains whose peaks disappeared in the mist.

The silence wrapped around them, broken only by the shriek of a circling hawk. They might have been the only people in the world, Elspeth thought, awed by the raw beauty of her surroundings. The air smelled damply of peat, but to her 'twas a whiff of freedom. No matter what challenges awaited her at Broch Tower, she could be happy here.

They'd been riding for more than an hour when the track abruptly began to descend again, dropping out of the boulders and into a heavily wooded glen. 'Twas a dark, mysterious place, massive tree trunks of stalwart oak standing out black against the green fringe of hardy Scots pine. "Are we lost, do you think?" she whispered to Wee Wat.

"I hope so. I dinna like the feel of this."

In a blink, they were free of the forest and into a clearing. At its center stood a structure like none she'd seen before. Elspeth tipped her head back, following the spiraled layers of stone as they rose to meet the tops of the trees.

Ancient.

The word whispered through the trees on a capricious breeze that sent a chill arrowing down Elspeth's spine. Around her, she was dimly conscious of the Carmichaels shifting and muttering.

"Haunted," someone murmured, and she fully understood why.

Broch Tower looked like something conjured up out of an ancient myth. Silent and sullen as a pagan god, it stared down at them from its single eye, a door-size opening two stories above ground. Fully as big around at the base as Kinduin's main tower, it tapered in at the top to resemble a large chimney.

"Lucais was right. 'Tisna a fit place to live. Might 's well head back to Kinduin." Wee Wat spat to punctuate his decision.

"Nay. I'd see inside," Elspeth murmured.

"But 'tis a barren, uninhabitable place," Sir Giles said.

"Godforsaken," another hissed.

"Wait," Elspeth cried, less afraid they'd leave her here alone than that they'd drag her away before she'd gotten inside.

"A wise idea," called a gravelly male voice, and suddenly the woods around them were alive with men and horses. Swords winked in the pale light as they pressed close around her escort, cutting off all hope of retreat. It was like reliving their capture two nights ago, but the man who approached was far too short and burly to be Lucais. When he tugged off his helmet, Elspeth saw a face she'd hoped never to see again.

"Seamus Munro," she breathed.

Chapter Seven

"**M**unros!" The word hissed through Cathal's clenched teeth and was softly echoed by the thirty Sutherlands hidden in the woods.

Munros. Reality pierced Lucais, quick and merciless as the thrust of a sword. Elspeth had lied to him about being allied with the Munros. Why else would she be meeting them here, in the shadow of the broch?

From atop a nearby ridge, Lucais looked down on the meeting through a canopy of leaves and wished himself anywhere but here. He was glad Elspeth's back was to him, so he couldn't see her face as she betrayed him. Bad enough he could read the smugness in Seamus's ugly smile as he approached Elspeth.

"What are we waitin' for?" Cathal demanded.

A miracle. Some proof that Elspeth had not come here to conspire with her family by marriage. "I'd see what they're about," Lucais said tightly, grimly.

"They're after the broch," Cathal shouted back. And again his accusation rippled through the assembled clansmen, had them turning to look at Lucais, eyes narrowed, faces lined with doubt.

Bloody hell. They'd not regarded him so suspiciously since the first day he'd arrived, a raw unknown, an outsider. Did all his hard work over the past four years count for naught? The knot in his gut tightened; his throat clogged with rage and frustration. "Why would they want it?" He spoke to Cathal but included the others in his hard glance.

Their own eyes were no less flinty as they stared back from the sockets of their helms. Seasoned veterans of many a reprisal raid against the marauding Munros. Hardy lads determined to keep what was theirs. In that, Lucais fully agreed. But . . .

His gaze flicked downward through the trees to the slender back, stiff and proud beneath a cape as black as her shiny hair. And her heart? Was it black, as well? Or was Elspeth a pawn, as much a victim in this as the Sutherlands? Jesu, he wanted to think so. 'Twas hell to sit here, not knowing if she was in danger or a danger to everything else he loved in the world. Awash with conflicting emotions, he still ached with the need to ride in and carry her to safety before the evil that was Seamus Munro could touch her, hurt her.

"Who kens why they want it?" Cathal snapped, jerking Lucais from his morbid thoughts and foolish dreams. "A Munro doesna need a reason to covet what belongs to a Sutherland."

Too true. Lucais drew in a ragged breath, exhaled slowly, his breath congealing to a fine mist on the chill air. His thoughts seemed just as clouded. "What say the scouts?"

"They havena seen any signs of a Munro army lurkin' nearby," Niall said from his other side.

Which meant Seamus hadn't expected to meet any Sutherlands. Lucais's mouth filled with the leaden taste of dread. "Our numbers are greater, then. If the Carmichaels side with us—"

"We dinna need them. A Sutherland's worth two of a Munro any day," Cathal growled, and pulled his sword clear of the scabbard.

"That may be," Lucais allowed. "But a feud profits neither clan. I'd see our truce with them stand if possible. We'll wait a bit longer, see if we can discover what they're abou—"

"Nay!" Elspeth's cry carried up the hill. Despite the distance separating the two groups, her fear rang clear, potent enough to send Lucais scrambling to free his own blade.

"Seize her!" This from Seamus as Elspeth attempted to wheel her horse away from him.

Lucais didn't wait to hear more. In the instant the Munros tightened their noose around the Carmichaels, he set his spurs to Black Jock's ribs and sent them racing down into the glen.

"Ride, lass!" Wee Wat shouted.

Elspeth flinched as the little man turned his horse between hers and Seamus's. Fear held her paralyzed, hands white where they clenched the reins, ears ringing with the cries of the men around her. Munros intent on capture, Carmichaels badly outnumbered but fighting back. The clash of steel on steel drowned out her own panicked gasp as the dark, mysterious glen suddenly became a battlefield.

From the time she was a wee lass, Elspeth had yearned to be a man... a knight. Learning domestic skills had seemed tame stuff indeed, measured against the thrill and excitement of knightly training. Now, with the grunts of embattled men, the screams of wounded horses and the smell of blood all around her, she heartily wished herself back at Carmichael Castle, clumsily plying a needle while her mother played the lute.

"Seize the wench," Seamus bellowed over the din.

"Ride! Get clear of here." Sir Giles's tone was as frantic as his attempts to keep the Munros from reaching her. At her other side, Wee Wat waged a desperate fight with Seamus.

Dimly it occurred to Elspeth that she was a liability. With her to protect, her men could not concentrate on fighting. But she saw no way through the hand-to-hand combat that raged all around her. Then she saw a tiny parting in the churning sea of men bent on murder. Just as she angled her nervous mount toward it, a gauntleted hand snagged the reins from her grasp.

"Hold! I've got yer lady," Seamus bellowed.

"Let me go." Elspeth glared defiantly at Seamus, but 'twas a useless gesture. Even if she managed to jump from the horse without breaking something, she'd never outrun his men. The sounds of battle fell away, leaving a silence broken only by harsh breathing and the agonized moans of the wounded.

"Laird Lionel'll kill ye when he hears of this infamy," Sir Giles growled, blood dripping from his left shoulder.

Wee Wat lay on the ground, a small, unmoving tumble of brown limbs. Reflexively, Elspeth leaned toward him, a broken cry rising from trembling lips.

Seamus jerked hard on the reins, drawing her closer. "'Tis a long way from Carmichael Castle to the Highlands," he sneered. "And yer laird isna a well man." That he knew how her beloved da had come to be maimed was clear in the glance he spared Elspeth.

"But 'tis hardly any distance at all from Kinduin, Munro," shouted a voice Elspeth had dreaded hearing again. Now it sounded like the sweetest music.

"Lucais!" She looked up to find the Munros surrounded by a ring of green-clad Sutherlands, whose swords rose and fell with deadly purpose as they cleared a path to her men.

Seamus's face flushed purple. "Seize them!" he screamed. But his Munros, outnumbered, caught between the advancing Sutherlands and Carmichaels eager for redress, lowered their weapons.

"Your kin have more brains than you do," Lucais said softly as he walked the black stallion closer. "What brings you here?" he asked, only the tautness of his lips betraying his tension.

Seamus cursed and hauled Elspeth's horse closer. She could see the sweat bead up on the old man's brow beneath his helmet. But he spoke as querulously as ever. "Mind yer own business."

"'Tis my business when someone tramples our sacred ground."

"I'm only reclaimin' what's mine," Seamus shot back.

"Meaning the lass?" Lucais responded without looking at her.

The hope that had blossomed in Elspeth's chest when Lucais first appeared faltered. She had expected he would be annoyed that she'd disobeyed him and visited the broch, but surely he was not so angry that he'd turn her over to the Munros. *Why not?* said a little voice. *He does not know the truth about them.*

"She *is* my daughter by marriage," Seamus replied.

"She's a Munro?" Cathal spit out.

The stunned gasp that followed Seamus's nod and the censorious glances from the Sutherlands, who had smiled at her yesterday, plunged Elspeth's spirits to her boots. Even Niall looked furious, lips compressed in a line of disapproval, and Lucais. Lucais looked cold, uncaring. 'Twas the worst cut of all.

"What has this to do with our broch?" Lucais asked.

"Not a thing," Seamus said quickly. "'Twas a place to meet."

"He lies," Elspeth interjected, seeing a way to escape her father by marriage. "Broch Tower is mine...deeded to me by Seamus when Raebert and I wed. Now he wants it back."

"This is Sutherland land. It wasna Seamus's to give away," Lucais growled, a sentiment echoed by his angry kinsmen.

Elspeth dismissed that with an impatient gesture. "'Tis no matter, I've a d—"

She got no further before a chorus of Sutherland protests cut her off. Led by Cathal, they cursed her and the Munros for presuming to covet their land.

"Enough!" Lucais roared, then turned his attention back to his enemy. "Why do you want the broch?" he asked Seamus.

"I dinna care a fig for yon pile of stones," Seamus blustered, and Lucais knew he lied. But why? "Still, 'tis Elspeth's, and since she's my son's widow—"

"Widow?" Lucais looked at Elspeth for the first time since riding down from the hills. The only color in her white, stricken face was her eyes, great wells of purple, frightened, beseeching. 'Twas true. She was a widow, yet she had not told him. The knot of fury in his chest tightened, turned to ice. He wanted to wheel about and ride away. To his everlasting shame, he could not.

"Aye," Seamus continued. "Raebert died three weeks ago. A matter I'm still examinin'." Ordinary words, yet the piercing glance he speared Elspeth with made her heart quail. *He knew. Somehow he knew what part she'd played in Raebert's death. And he'd make her pay.* "But I have a responsibility to look after his *dear* wife," Seamus said into the heavy silence.

Elspeth shivered, recalling Raebert's boast that he'd learned everything he knew from his father. She knew in her heart of hearts that she'd not last a day in Seamus's tender care. And what of Lucais? She peered at him through her lashes.

What she could see of his face beneath his helmet was not reassuring. Dark emotionless eyes, starkly chiseled lips, the mouth that had kissed her so hotly last night set in a cold, grim line. Her stomach rolled and a lump rose in her throat. Why were the choices never really choices? Still, she supposed Lucais's anger was preferable to Seamus's cruelty. "I would rather continue my visit at Kinduin," she said evenly.

Seamus snorted. ''Ye havena any say in the matter. Besides, 'tisna fittin'...ye, a lone woman, in a tower full of men.''

''What female companions will I have at Scourie?'' She hated the desperation edging her voice, but she was desperate.

''None needed. We're yer kin.''

''By marriage.'' Elspeth refused to be lumped in with such creatures as these. ''I am nae a Munro.'' This for the Sutherlands.

''Your concern for Raebert's *widow* is natural,'' Lucais said, his tone ripe with sarcasm. He edged his horse forward until it stood beside Elspeth's. ''But unnecessary. Elspeth will have my protection...as my wife.''

''Wife!'' Seamus's shout drowned out Elspeth's gasp.

''Wife,'' Lucais repeated. ''We agreed on it last night. What say you, Elspeth? Do you consider yourself my wife?'' His eyes bored into hers, fierce, intent, compelling.

Elspeth swayed where she sat, conscious of the precipice looming before her. If they declared themselves man and wife before witnesses, they'd be handfasted. Bound together for a year and a day by a knot just as binding as any tied in kirk. If at the end of their time, they decided they didn't suit, the union could be dissolved as speedily and tidily as it was made.

Lucais was offering her a way to escape Seamus, but at what price? That she'd scorned him once gave him every reason to hurt her in return. That she'd lied to him about Raebert and her reasons for coming to the Highlands was added fuel for the anger and contempt blazing in his eyes as he waited for her reply. And if those weren't enough to give her pause, there was the memory of what had happened between them last night. Once wed, she doubted anger and contempt would keep Lucais from exercising his husbandly rights over her. They hadn't stopped Raebert.

''Well?'' Seamus prompted, the promise of retribution gleaming in his tiny, piggy eyes.

Elspeth swallowed and stepped off the cliff. ''A-aye, Lucais is my husband,'' she said, her voice as strangled as her breathing. *And God help us both.*

God help us both, Lucais thought as they thundered over the drawbridge and into Kinduin some hours later. Slowed as they were by the wounded and the need for a rear guard, dark had overtaken them on the trail. The mist had turned to mizzling rain, adding to their misery yet not dampening the anger that radiated from his clansmen. If, in fact, they still considered him their chief.

"Angus is doubtless spinnin' in his grave to see a Munro bitch inside his walls," Cathal snarled as he leapt from the saddle and tossed the reins to a waiting stableboy.

Despite his own exhaustion, Lucais was on the ground, blocking the way to the keep as the old man turned. "Elspeth is my wife." He pitched his voice to carry over the creak of wet leather and the groans of weary men. The confidence in the words that echoed off the old stone walls surprised him. At any moment he feared Elspeth would shout a denial, claim she wanted no part of him. "Does any man seek to harm her, he'll answer to me."

Cathal raised his stubbled jaw. "Just 'cause ye're chief—"

"'Tis glad I am you've recalled that," Lucais replied as tightly. "Remember, too, that I've kept Kinduin from fallin' into Munro hands these past four years." He swept the torch-lit courtyard with an unwavering glance, forcibly reminding each man of the long struggle they'd endured...together. Lastly, he sought out Elspeth, though he was not certain why. To reassure her of her safety? Or remind her that she, too, owed him a debt?

He found her bent over Wee Wat as the Carmichaels lifted the makeshift sling that had borne the little man between two horses. Without looking back, she walked beside the litter, across the courtyard and up the stairs to the tower. The slump in her shoulders beneath the bloodied cloak made Lucais's heart ache for what she'd endured this day; the stiff determination in her step earned his grudging respect. She'd changed. Unfortunately she had not changed her opinion of him. The loathing on her face when she'd accepted his offer of a hand-fasting had made that clear.

Why had he done it? What mad impulse had made him...?

"Lucais." Niall laid a hand on his arm. "Come inside. We've hurts that want tendin', and this coil willna right itself whilst we stand about in the cold and the rain."

Truer words were never spoken. 'Twould take a miracle to right the mess he found himself in. Wed to the only woman he'd ever wanted, yet the recipient of her hatred and his clansmen's. That word of the handfasting and Elspeth's connections with the Munros had already spread was clear from the fuming sidelong glances that greeted him when he entered the hall.

"They'll get over it," Niall assured him.

Lucais sighed as he tugged off his helmet and raked the sweaty hair from his face. "In my lifetime?"

Niall grinned ruefully. "She isna really a Munro."

"But she was wed to one." God, that hurt.

"She's wed to you now."

"For a year and a day." If she stayed here that long. Looking past the servants rushing to set up the trestle tables, Lucais sought the opening that led to the sleeping rooms above. Would she share with him the wide bed that had been his grandparents? Or would she barricade herself in the counting room, preferring that narrow camp bed? The memory of the kiss they'd shared there last night rose up to haunt him. She'd been willing, nay, eager, for his touch. He'd been the one to stop things with the reminder that she was married. Why hadn't she told him Raebert was dead? Had it all been part of some elaborate scheme of Seamus's?

"Forever, if ye will it," Niall interjected.

Lucais shook his head. "I only wed her to save her from Seamus." *Liar.* Deep down, beneath the pain of her rejection and betrayal, he knew he still wanted her. But could he keep her? "She doesna want me. Likely she'll hie herself back to the bosom of her family first chance she gets."

"*If* she gets the chance," Niall said ominously. "Hatred of the Munros runs deep at Kinduin, as ye can see."

Foreboding crept down Lucais's spine as he followed his cousin's gaze to the men knotted about Cathal. *Plotting.* But was it Lucais's downfall or Elspeth's? He found he dreaded both equally. "My name will protect her."

"Then ye'd best make yer act convincin'."

"Act?" Lucais exclaimed.

"Ye looked shocked when Seamus said she was a widow, and she nearly toppled off her horse when ye claimed she was yer wife."

"I did it to keep the peace." The rest was just a dream.

"Shame on ye," Ena scolded. "Standin' about drippin' water and blood on me fresh rushes." Hands on hips, she regarded him as she always had at such times...with exasperation and fondness. "You've heard what happened?" Lucais asked warily.

"Aye. I've had the whole sorry tale." The old woman snatched the helmet from his grasp and shoved it at her youthful shadow. "Danny, see this is cleaned proper. There's water heatin' in the kitchens," she added as the lad, her grandson in training to become Lucais's squire, scooted away. "If ye'll go above..."

Lucais shook his head. "I willna take my ease till the men have been seen to. And Elspeth..."

"M'lady's seein' to that wizened excuse of a man. I've given her my wall chamber to lay him in."

Lucais started forward. "There's no call for her to do that. She's had a hellish day. She must be exhausted."

"Tried tellin' her that." Ena snorted. "Might's well talk to yon stone walls. Ye'll have yer work cut out tamin' her, that's sure," she added, chuckling. "'Tis short notice ye've given us, but tomorrow we'll put on a feast to celebrate yer marriage."

"There's many here who dinna welcome the union. And Elspeth had little choice in the matter. She willna feel like—"

"Nonsense. Every lass wants a fuss made when she weds."

Lucais thought of the contempt in Elspeth's face when she'd turned him down four years ago. Worse were the fear and resignation in her voice this afternoon when she'd fallen in with his desperate ruse. She'd tied herself to him out of necessity, naught more. He was the lesser of two evils. "Not this time." Her loathing did not lessen his determination to see the marriage stand, at least until he could discover what the Munros were up to...and what part Elspeth played in their schemes.

Some of his ruthlessness must have shown, for Ena sighed and shook her head. "Men. Insensitive, the lot of ye."

"I do what must be done." Still, Lucais's spirits were low as he turned away from her and got down to the business at hand.

He ignored his own aching muscles as he moved about the hall, checking on the wounded as usual. "A chief's first duty is to his clansmen," his grandsire had taught him. And Lucais had done just that. 'Twas to keep from plunging his people into another costly feud, as much as to save Elspeth, that he'd acted as he had and claimed her, Lucais thought glumly. Though at the moment, neither party appreciated his efforts.

Thanks to the element of surprise, the Sutherlands had taken few wounds. Scant comfort when some of the clansmen whose respect he'd fought so hard to win now shied away from his concern as though he'd contracted the plague. The men of Cathal's family refused even to look at Lucais. Faces sullen and remote, they huddled together at one table, plotting over their bread and ale.

"They'll come around," Niall murmured, making Lucais aware his cousin hadn't gone off drinking as was his want after a raid.

"I dinna need a nursemaid."

Niall quirked one red brow. "Nay, but just now ye can use all the *friends* ye can get."

Sighing, Lucais ran a hand over his stubbled face. Jesu, he was tired to the very depths of his soul. "You are right. I—"

"A word, m'lord," Sir Giles demanded, coming to stand in front of Lucais. Despite his pallor and the thick bandage on his left shoulder, the knight oozed belligerence.

Now what? Lucais wondered as he led the way to the relative privacy of a deeply recessed window. No sooner had he stopped and turned toward Sir Giles than Ena materialized with ale for them and a reminder that she had bathwater heated. He took the drink, shrugged off the bath and looked longingly at the wooden seat that ran beneath the window. Tempting as it was to sit, he doubted he'd have the strength to rise again.

"Come morn, I'd challenge ye for m'lady's honor."

Lucais frowned. "You think I've dishonored her?"

"I ken she didna come here to wed ye," the knight said, tanned cheeks flushing. "Since she agreed to, I can only assume 'twas because ye compromised her."

Bloody hell. This was all he needed. "I grant it seems the only reason she'd agree to wed the likes of me," Lucais snapped. "But I havena touched her." Well, only one kiss. One kiss that had made a mockery of the years he'd spent convincing himself that he'd gotten over Elspeth. "She agreed to the handfastin' for the same reason I proposed it—'twas the only way short of battle to get her safe away from the Munros." Practice made the lie flow easily from his tongue, but it rang false in his heart.

"Well." Sir Giles fingered the drooping ends of his mustache. "Ye'll let us go, then?"

"As soon as 'tis safe and your wounds have healed. And Elspeth has signed away her claim to the broch."

"'Tis Lady Elspeth's dower land at her marriage."

"The broch wasna Seamus Munro's to give away."

"But the king was witness to the transaction."

A troublesome point. Lucais dismissed it with a snort. "Seamus tricked the Carmichaels. He doubtless told Laird Lionel and the king the property was his, but the broch never belonged to the Munros. 'Tisna even fit to live in."

"Mmm. I grant it did look run-down."

Lucais pressed the advantage by describing the curse that went with the old stone fort. He hid a smile as the knight crossed himself. "She wouldna be safe there," he added for good measure, though he didn't believe in ghosts or curses himself.

Eventually Sir Giles sighed and nodded. "Well, 'tis best we rest here till the men are healed. Then we'll accept yer offer of an escort back to Curthill Castle."

Now if only Elspeth could be so easily persuaded. Lucais smiled and steered Sir Giles toward the table where the other Carmichaels sat. "You can bed down in the hall with my clansmen. You've only to tell Niall what you require and 'twill be provided." Just then Lucais caught sight of Cathal and his smile died. "Some of my people are angered that Elspeth was wed to a Munro," he murmured. "I dinna think they'll take it out on you, considerin' the way you Carmichaels fought the Munros, but..."

Sir Giles nodded. "We'll stay alert. Mayhap I'd best set someone to watch over Wee Wat." *If he lives.*

The unspoken fear in the knight's eyes matched Lucais's own concerns for the canny little man. "I was just on my way to check on him. Doubtless Ena will stay with him tonight."

"And Lady Elspeth, too, I'll wager. She was that broke up he was hurt tryin' to save her. Wee Wat's no swordsman, but he was closest to m'lady when old Seamus tried to seize her."

"You werena expectin' the Munros?"

Sir Giles snorted. "Had no idea there was a Munro within a hundred leagues of Broch Tower. We thought to find a keep such as Kinduin, under the control of a castellan. Lord Ross said if the man dinna open to us, we were to return to Curthill at once and send word we needed help claimin' m'lady's property."

Sutherland property, Lucais wanted to shout, but his quarrel was with Elspeth, not her sire's knight. "Well, eat and get some sleep if you can," he said evenly, and turned to pick his way through the crowded hall. At the doorway leading to the wall chambers, Lucais paused to locate Niall. His cousin had a cup of ale in one hand and his arm around the wench who tended the scrape a tree branch had left on his cheek.

The sight of Niall's cocky smile and the answering sparkle in the lass's eyes sent a pang of envy lancing through Lucais. For some reason this easy familiarity with the fairer sex had always eluded him. Oh, in his youth he had learned to play the pipes and lute, had memorized the heroic legends and romantic ballads the lasses were wild for. But there was no one he cared to impress, save Elspeth, and she'd always made him feel edgy, restless and angry. Aye, he'd raged against his feelings for her and the circumstances that made it impossible for him to act on them.

Now she was his wife. Tonight she'd lie in his bed. Heat blossomed deep inside him. More than desire. He knew what it was...refused to name it, even in his heart. For if he did, and she rejected him again, he wasn't certain he'd survive.

Niall lifted his cup in a silent toast and mouthed, "Good luck wi' Elspeth tonight."

Luck? Aye, he'd need the devil's own luck to survive this, Lucais thought as he turned away. After the noise and brilliance of the hall, the narrow corridor seemed quiet and dark as a tomb, illuminated only by a few torches set in wall brackets. Opening off from the passageway were the small chambers used for storage or as sleeping rooms by Niall and some of the others.

Lucais paused before the door to Ena's room, took a deep breath, then cautiously pushed it open. The light from four thick candles set in wrought-iron pike stands at each corner of the bed made it seem bright as day. The stench of herbs and burned flesh hung heavy in the smoky air. Elspeth and the herb woman from the village sat on stools flanking the narrow bed. Wee Wat, bandaged and tucked beneath a mountain of blankets, lay limp as a netted salmon, his leathery face gray, his breathing raspy.

"Elspeth?" Lucais whispered, creeping closer.

She bounded off the stool and threw her arms around Lucais's waist. "Oh, Lucais..." Though she weighed next to nothing, the feel of her burrowing into his chest nearly toppled him over. Reflexively, he folded her into his embrace, the air trapped inside his lungs, heart slamming against his ribs. She needed him. "I'm here, Beth," he managed past the lump in his throat.

"I'm so afraid." She tipped her head back, tears running down her cheeks. "We canna let him die."

"What can I do to help?" Lucais immediately asked.

"I've done all I can," the herb woman put in. "The rest is in God's hands. I'll sit wi' him. The lady should get some sleep."

The "lady" belatedly came to her senses. *Lucais was her husband now.* Suddenly the arms that had cradled and soothed seemed like vises intent on hurting her. Frightened, Elspeth tried to slip away. "I'd rather stay here with Wee Wat."

His grip tightened. "Be reasonable. You can do naught."

Elspeth was not feeling reasonable. She was terrified, sick with the memories of another time, another man. "Let go. I canna stand being touched." She pushed against Lucais's chest. 'Twas like trying to move a mountain. But even as she dug in her heels, he swung her up in his arms and headed for the door.

"Send word to me if there's any change," Lucais called to the herb woman on their way out of the room.

Oh God, he was taking her to bed. Elspeth began to struggle in earnest, bucking, twisting, sobbing as she tried to escape.

He subdued her with ridiculous ease. Pinning her arms to her sides with the steely muscles of one arm, he stilled her milling legs with the other. "Elspeth, what ails you?"

"I canna abide a man's touch," she snapped, panting with exertion, angered anew to find he was not even breathing hard.

"You didna mind it last night." His gaze locked on hers, eyes dark, probing for secrets she'd revealed to no one. "And I am your husband now, Elspeth."

As was the last man who hurt her. "Let me go."

Lucais sighed, his expression gentling. "I dinna know what you fear." Yet. "But you needna fear me."

"Men canna help inflicting pain on those who are weaker."

"You, weak?" He snorted. "Never."

But she had been weak. That weakness had cost her dear and nearly killed her da. Elspeth shook her head to clear it of the terrible memory and glared at her tormentor. "Fine. I am strong, then, strong enough to walk on my own. Now, *put me down.*"

"Presently." He loosed her hold long enough to reach for the latch. "I'm only doin' what's best for you," he growled.

"The way you did when you told Seamus we were hand-fasted?"

"Exactly." The door swung shut behind them, cutting out the light, reminding her she was alone in this keep, at the mercy of the man whose arms had tightened around her like a vise.

"I dinna want to be wed to you," she whispered.

"I'm aware of that." His voice was level, nearly devoid of emotion, but against her side she felt his heart leap . . . just as it had last night in the instant before he'd kissed her.

Her own pulse stuttered, and her mouth tingled. Fear. It had to be fear. Sweet Mary, she wished she could see his face, gauge his thoughts. "Wh-why did you do it?"

"To keep you free of Seamus Munro's clutches. Or did I misread the situation? Did you want to go with him?"

"Nay!" Too loudly. Too quickly.

"Why?" His words were hushed, yet echoed in her mind.

"Because . . ." Her eyes had grown used to the dim corridor, yet his expression was still inscrutable, stark planes, shadowy hollows. "I swore I wouldna put myself in a Munro's hands again."

"So . . ." His sigh was sharp and achy as the knot of fears and doubts in her own chest. "I am the lesser of two evils."

"Definitely that."

"Remember that if you are tempted to think ill of me." His voice gentled. "In all the years we've known one another, I have never harmed you, Elspeth. Nor will I. What I do now, what I did earlier today, were done for your protection."

He'd wed her to keep her safe from Seamus. It was not a real marriage; it was a . . . a convenience. As soon as the danger passed, he'd free her. She relaxed slightly. "What happens now?"

"Now?" Something flickered in his eyes . . . yearning, loneliness. She recognized them both before he blinked them away. "For tonight, we will sleep. In the morn . . ." He shrugged and started walking down the long hallway, taking her toward a future as dark and ominous as their surroundings.

Elspeth shivered, and he tucked her closer, making her aware that part of his steely strength was due to the chain mail he yet wore beneath his battle gambeson and woolen tunic. Concern pricked her. "Why has no one unarmed you?"

"I've been too busy."

Seeing to everyone else, Elspeth guessed, thinking of the time Raebert's squire had been badly injured fighting in a melee. Raebert had insisted his men remove *his* sweaty garments and bring fresh before seeing to the lad who lay bleeding on the ground. Selfish, where Lucais was selfless. The contrast touched her, made her want to help him. "I'll ask Ena for hot water."

"It waits above stairs, if you've the strength to bathe."

"'Tisna for me. I want the water for you. And food, too."

He stopped abruptly, head cocked. "For me?" Warily.

"Aye." Poor man. So many worries; no one to look after him. She'd see to his comfort. 'Twas the least she could do after all he'd done to save her. And mayhap if he was more in charity with her, he'd let her go. "You must be weary. Sir Giles said you must have ridden full-out to reach us in time."

"That we did," he allowed. "But why do you care?"

Because he was a good man. She was suddenly, inexplicably swept with the urge to reach up and soothe the tension from his lean jaw. "I am trying to show my gratitude, you great dolt," she snapped instead, appalled by her softness toward him.

"Ah. I thought it might be wifely concern."

"Nay. You know as well as I do this marriage is a sham. To-morrow I'll return to Curthill." With a detour to Broch Tower.

"I canna allow you to leave."

"What?" Shocked, she raised her head so fast she clipped his chin, used the momentary laxness of his embrace to leap free.

"Elspeth, get back here." Air eddied as he reached for her in the darkness. She dodged away, bumped up against smooth oak. A door. Shouldering it open, she found herself standing in the hall, the object of a dozen hostile male glances.

"'Tis the Munro bitch," a man shouted, jumping to his feet.

"My daughters were raped by a Munro," cried another. Face twisted with hate, he started toward her. "I'd see her pay."

"Nay!" Elspeth stumbled backward into Lucais, grateful for the swiftness with which his arms closed around her.

"'Tis Elspeth Sutherland now." Lucais's voice rang from the rafters, silenced the hall, stopped the advancing men in their tracks. "She's my wife and any who harms her will answer to me." With that, he swung her up and stalked from the hall.

As she peered over his shoulder, Elspeth's eyes swept the hate-filled faces of the people who'd laughed with her only this morn. She shivered, haunted by the knowledge that until Lucais let her go, she'd be forced to live here with these angry, vengeful people.

"'Tis all right, Beth. Trust me. I'll keep you safe."

As they mounted the stairs, Elspeth wondered if she could trust a man. Especially one who had every reason to want to hurt her as she'd hurt him.

Chapter Eight

"What do ye mean, ye lost her?" Alain shouted.

Seamus looked up from the stew he'd been shoveling into his mouth. "Sutherlands jumped us. They've got her at Kinduin."

"Bloody hell." Alain threw his helmet onto the floor, heedless of the way it slid through the slimy rushes before coming to rest against the scarred leg of Seamus's chair. "I knew I shouldna ha' gone raidin' and left ye to watch the broch."

"We were outnumbered. I'd no' wish to get meself killed for a wench who's as good to me dead as alive."

"Shut up!" Alain threw himself into the small chair that sat beside the thronelike one Seamus had had made in London. Seeing the storm had abated, a servant crept forward to set ale and stew before him on the filthy trestle table.

"So..." Seamus pushed his grease-coated bowl away and wiped his mouth on a sleeve crusted with the remnants of his last meal. "I oft wondered what 'twould take to light a fire in the whey that runs in yer veins. Fancy it bein' Raebert's skinny widow."

Careful, Alain warned himself. 'Twould not do for Seamus to learn how much he wanted Elspeth. His elder half brother took perverse delight in making certain Alain did not get what he wanted. Raebert had inherited his sire's twisted ways, plunged them to depths Seamus had not even approached. King's champion, Alain scoffed, wondering if David II had known that, away from the field of honor, his knight enjoyed torturing small, helpless things. Especially women. Elspeth had fought back... in the end. Pray God Seamus never found out what part she'd played in his son's death. "'Tis the deed I'm thinkin' of," Alain said quietly.

"Is it?" Seamus drained his cup, slammed it on the table and bellowed for more. "And I've been thinkin' we dinna need a scrap of paper to get us in yon broch."

Alain sighed and set the unappealing stew aside. When he was laird here, he'd hire a French cook such as King David kept at Edinburgh. "And how do ye plan to get inside the damn thing if we dinna own it? We havena enough men to fight a pitched battle outside the broch whilst the rest of us search for this treasure. And Lucais Sutherland'll never stand aside..."

"I'll go through him, then, as I should ha' when we first learned what was in the bloody broch. This damned peace between us is ruinin' my livelihood. Why I let ye talk me into—"

"I didna talk ye into it. Lucais did...at the point of a sword, if memory serves."

Recalling the day Lucais had trapped him turned Seamus's fleshy face crimson. "He got lucky."

Alain leaned back, enjoying himself now. 'Twasn't often he got the best of his brute of a half brother. "Ye were lucky he proposed peace instead of runnin' ye through." Personally Alain had hoped Lucais would kill Seamus and do him a favor."

He hadna choice," Seamus snarled. "We had him surrounded."

"But he had ye beneath his blade. Checkmate, I believe were Lucais's exact words," Alain said with a grin.

Seamus grunted and snatched the refilled cup from a servant. "What took ye so long?" He backhanded the hapless wretch, tumbling him down the two stairs that raised the dais above the grimy floor. The man's head hit the leg of the nearest table with a thud, and there he lay, sprawled like a broken doll. None of the men wolfing down their own dinners even looked up. It did not pay to cross Seamus Munro.

"'Twill give me great pleasure to make young Lucais eat his words...and a few inches of me sharp steel, to boot," Seamus muttered. He drained half the ale, then leaned toward Alain. "After I've looted his precious broch."

"How do ye propose gettin' in? The Sutherlands are watchin' the place closer than a hen with one chick." This had been the problem from the first. How to buy enough time to get inside and find the treasure without becoming trapped within.

"And Lucais'll likely double the patrols now that he kens we're interested in the place." Seamus cursed and glared out over the smoky hall, his expression so fierce even the most hardened of his henchmen slumped lower in their seats.

Alain sat back in his, absently rubbing his lean belly. "I'm thinkin' we should try deception instead of force. We could split the men in two groups. One will decoy the Sutherlands away with a raid while the others go to the broch, hide their horses and climb into the fort. They'll pull the rope ladders up after them, so when the Sutherlands return, they willna know we're inside."

Seamus's lip curled. "And we'll be trapped inside."

"The first group can return for us several hours later, near dawn, mayhap. That should give us enough time to dig up the gold. If the Sutherland scouts spot us leavin' and send word to Lucais, we'll be back at Scourie with the treasure before their reinforcements can arrive."

"Why did ye nae suggest this before?" Seamus demanded.

Tempted as he was to point out that he *had* proposed a similar plan when the gold was first discovered but had been shouted down, Alain merely shrugged. He had what he wanted for now... Seamus's cooperation. 'Twas a short step from there to his goal, leadership of Clan Munro *and* the Sutherlands' gold with which to finance his future. His and Elspeth's. "Let me see the coins."

"'Tisna wise to flash the gold about," Seamus whispered, casting a wary eye over his clansmen. Rough and greedy as the man who led them, they'd stick their own mothers if there was profit in it. "The less they know about what we're after, the better."

"No one will see if ye pass me one under cover of the table," Alain snapped, irritated that Seamus had kept all five coins for himself. Besides, the men had finished their meal and were hunched over draughts and dice as they steadily worked their way through the nightly keg of ale.

"Just a peek, mind," Seamus grumbled as he reached for the leather pouch that hung from his belt. "Bloody hell!"

"What's happened?"

"Me pouch's been nicked." Seamus stuck his finger into the jagged tear and spilled the contents into his hand. Two ancient gold coins winked dully in the hollow of his grubby hand.

"Where are the rest of them?" Alain snarled.

"Keep yer voice down." Lowering his own to a gravelly rumble, Seamus added, "Must have happened when I tried to seize Elspeth. The wee man who rode with her leapt at me. Savage as a wolf, he was. Nearly did me in before I got my sword up."

"Never mind that. What if the Sutherlands find them?"

Seamus shrugged and tucked the gold away. "Unlikely. They're either ground into the mud near the broch or scattered somewheres on the trail twixt there and Scourie. 'Tis a bit of bad luck, but we willna miss them when we've got the rest," he said firmly.

Alain nodded, but his mind was far from easy. "Mayhap it was the curse of the broch, not ill luck, that took the coins."

"A pox on that fool curse." Seamus's lip curled. "'Twas a tale the ancients put about to keep those who came after them from searchin' the broch and findin' their gold."

"The tale says no man who invades the broch will live to tell of it," Alain warned.

"Well, Duncan got in, found the treasure and told us."

"Aye, but he didna long survive the experience."

"He fell down the stairs the next day and broke his neck."

"Duncan was surefooted as a cat," Alain pointed out.

"And he drank like a fish. Besides, 'tis our good fortune he died before he could slip and tell anyone else about his find." Seamus's lips split in a twisted parody of a smile.

Alain nodded slowly. "But how do we ken there's enough gold there to make it worth breakin' the peace wi' the Sutherlands?"

"Peace," Seamus scoffed. "Ye've gone soft and daft." Then he saw a way to light a fire under his brother. "I near forgot to mention . . . seems Elspeth's a widow no longer."

Alain started, spilling his ale. "What?"

"Lucais claims she handfasted wi' him last night."

Dreams of gold fled, replaced by the craving to go after the flesh-and-blood prize he coveted even more. Damn, he'd kept her secret, lied to the king and his brother about Raebert's death. Elspeth was his. "She'll be a widow soon as I can arrange it."

Seamus grinned. "Thought that'd make ye see reason."

Tired as he was, Lucais found sleep impossible. No matter how he tried to relax, his mind ran in tight circles, going over and over the events of the past two days. Events that had turned his well-ordered world upside down. Elspeth's unexpected arrival. The Munros' interest in the broch. The confrontation with them that had ended in the handfasting with Elspeth.

He exhaled, rolled his head on the pillow so he could see her . . . the woman who was his wife but shunned his touch.

Pale light from the night candle slanted in through the bed curtains she'd insisted remain open. Because she feared the dark . . . among other things. Back to him, drawn into a tight ball, she lay as far from him as she could without tumbling off the bed. Further proof of her distaste for him. She'd wanted— nay, demanded—to sleep in the counting room.

"I ordered the camp bed taken down," he'd informed her, and braced himself for yet another battle. Nor did she disappoint.

"I willna sleep with you," she'd shot back, hands on hips, eyes shooting purple sparks of defiance that were strangely at odds with the quiver in her lower lip. *Vulnerable.* 'Twas a word he'd never associated with feisty, willful Elspeth. At their first meeting he'd learned the only thing she respected was strength, the only way to deal with her was to meet fire with fire. So he had, touching off many an argument. But now . . .

She feared him. The realization seared Lucais like hot steel . . . blinding pain that nearly sent him to his knees before her. Nearly. Only the sure knowledge that she'd despise him for such weakness kept him upright, kept him probing for a chink in her defenses. She reminded him of a wild, frightened thing backed into a corner, claws bared. Why had he not seen it before? Because she was exhausted now, her armor rent by the same events that stretched his own patience to the breaking point.

Digging deep inside himself, Lucais had sought the gentleness she'd never wanted from him. "We must share a bed, Elspeth, else my people willna think us truly wed," he'd crooned in the same voice he'd used when he'd trained Jock. "I want no man to think you fair game." Her eyes had widened with fear as the reminder of the scene in the hall struck home.

After that, she'd offered no further resistance, but it had hurt to watch his brave Beth scuttle about the room like a mouse who expected the cat to pounce at any moment. She'd refused to bathe or change her clothes, merely washed her hands and face in the cooling buckets of water and slid beneath the blankets in the tunic and split skirt she'd donned this morn. Not until he was certain she slept had Lucais joined her in bed.

Their marriage bed. Their wedding night, but he'd have no joy of her this night, nor likely any other, for not only did she despise him, she feared him. Had ever Fate played a crueler jest than this?

A soft moan jerked Lucais from his troubled thoughts. On the far side of the bed, Elspeth shifted, her movements swift, abrupt as she struggled against something. Another nightmare? Her agonized whimpers made him instinctively seek to comfort her.

"Shh. Elspeth, I'm here." Lucais reached beneath the blankets to stroke her shoulder.

"Nay!" She came off the bed like a scalded cat and rounded on him. From the corner of his eye, he caught the glint of steel as a blade arched down toward his throat. Only the lightning reflexes honed in countless battles over the years saved him.

Lucais dodged left, grunted as the blade raked his shoulder, leaving a trail of fire in its wake. "Damn." He grabbed for the arm that wielded the dirk and rolled with her so their positions were reversed. She lay still beneath him for a heartbeat, then tried to buck him off. "Hellcat," he rasped, anchoring her hands with both of his, scissoring his legs to catch hers.

"Lucais?" Elspeth opened her eyes. "What . . . ?" Belatedly she realized she lay beneath him, arms stretched above her head, legs spread, torso pinned by his hard warrior's body. *Sweet Mary, 'twas her worst nightmare come true.* "Nay. Dinna hurt me," she whispered, hating the pleading tone but afraid, so afraid of the pain and degradation to come.

"You're the one with the dirk, lass."

"Dirk?"

"Aye." He smiled, but his eyes held such sadness. "If you vow you willna try to stick me again, I'll release you."

"Aye. Anything to get you off me." As he rolled away, she slowly filled her lungs with air, wary lest this was some trick. But he made no move toward her, merely lay on his right side, head supported in his hand, inscrutable eyes locked on her face. "You . . . you tried to rape me."

Lucais winced, the pain her words brought worse than the agony in his shoulder. "Nay, I said I wouldna bed you and I keep my promises. I was tryin' to protect myself from you. Ross always did say you were far too handy with a dirk."

Dirk? Elspeth lowered her arms, stunned to find the knife she'd tucked beneath her pillow clenched in her right hand, the blade wet with blood. "Oh my God." Her horror grew when she saw the crimson line on his collarbone. "What . . . what happened?"

"Nightmare would be my guess. You cried out. I touched your arm to wake you. . . ." He shrugged, heedless of the blood that trickled down across his chest.

Elspeth's conscience pinched. In defending herself against Raebert's memory, she'd hurt the man who'd twice saved her life. "I'm sorry. I . . . I'll bind it." She sat up, swayed dizzily.

"Easy." Lucais offered his hand but didn't touch her.

For that reason alone, Elspeth took a chance and laid her left hand on his right one. To her surprise, he didn't grab her; his fingers remained open, his palm providing support without caging her. Though he steadied her, there was something about the feel of his callused palm pressed against her smooth one, something about the intensity of his gaze that made her pulse falter. "I . . . I'll see to your wound."

"You dinna need to." The husky edge of his voice slid across her skin like a caress. Had he always sounded like that? Or was it the lateness of the hour, the golden glow of candlelight that softened the angles of his face and made him seem . . . gentle.

"Aye, I do." Elspeth bolted from the bed, craving space between them as much as an outlet for the restlessness that suddenly invaded her body. "You saved my life twice today," she added as she dipped water from one of the buckets into the washbowl. "And look how I repaid you." She grabbed a bar of strong soap and two of the linen towels Ena had laid out by the hearth.

"'Twas an accident," he said from close behind her.

Elspeth jumped and turned around. "Sweet Mary, you move quietly for so big a ma..." Her voice trailed off as her gaze took in the breadth of his shoulders, the thick slabs of muscles rippling beneath the red gold pelt that covered his chest. "You're naked!"

"I left my braises on."

Her glance skittered to the short linen pants riding low on his hips. Heart-stoppingly low. Elspeth spun back to the hearth, cheeks burning as though she'd thrust her face in the coals. She should have been repulsed by the sight of so much bare bronzed flesh. That she was more intrigued than disgusted terrified her, made her snap out, "Sit if you want me to tend your wound."

"I want, Elspeth, never doubt it." Ordinary words, yet the purr underlying them vibrated with possibilities she dared not even consider. "'Tis safe to turn round, lass."

Nay, 'twas not. Never mind that his voice was beguiling enough to coax birds from the trees, she didn't feel safe at all. She felt anxious, confused, uncertain about this man she'd thought she knew so well. She hid behind the haughty rage that had served her so well in the past. She'd snipe, he'd fire back, and the ensuing argument would burn away these uneasy feelings. She whirled on him. "I willna be made sport of."

"Laughter is the last thing on my mind at the moment." His smile rocked her so she nearly dropped the soap.

Strike back. "You mock me."

"Never." The smile broadened to carve a dimple in his cheek.

A warrior with a dimple? Impossible. Engaging. Elspeth stomped her foot to break its spell. "You make me so angry."

"Thinkin' of carving up my other shoulder?"

"Lucias," she shouted.

He raised both hands in surrender, that maddening, entrancing grin firmly in place. "Easy, lass. God knows we're both exhausted and—"

"Why are you acting thus?"

To dilute your fear. And 'twas working. "Actin' how?"

"Like a man bent on seduction." The word hung between them, making the air sizzle. She trembled, shocked by the heat that suddenly blazed in his eyes, frightened by the answering spark that kindled deep inside her. Nay, she couldn't want him. " 'Tis a waste of time. I am impervious to your romantic claptrap."

Aye, Elspeth had always thought his gentleness a weakness and reviled him for it, Lucais recalled. But things had changed, they'd changed...she more so than he. Now she needed all the gentleness he could muster. "What need have I to woo a woman who is already my wife?" That stopped her. Lucais could almost see her clever brain working behind her warily narrowed eyes.

"How like a man," she snapped. "You think because we are wed I am your slave, to bind and beat as you see fit. Well, think again. I am nae man's possession . . . nae ever again."

The fear that darkened her eyes even as she challenged him confirmed the suspicions raised by her nightmares. Raebert *had* abused her. Just as he had Jean so many years ago. Bloody hell, if the bastard weren't already dead, Lucais would have taken great pleasure in killing him. Twice. Once for each of the two black-haired women the bastard had tormented. "Easy, little hedgehog, you've naught to fear from me," he murmured.

"Hedgehog!"

"You remind me of a hedgehog I once found." The poor wounded creature had shown Lucais naught but teeth and spines until patience had taught it to trust him enough to open its underbelly for his caress. Lucais had no doubt Elspeth would bite him did he try to stroke *her* soft belly, but one day...

"Being compared to a hedgehog is scarce flattering to a lady's vanity," she grumbled.

"You are the least vain lass I know," Lucais replied. "In fact, you said flowery compliments made you sick."

"Aye. They did . . . do, but . . ." Her voice trailed off in indecision. Poor hedgehog. She might be confused, but to Lucais the course seemed obvious, the objective clear, so when she straightened her spine and said, "Do you want your shoulder bandaged or not?" he knew just how to reply.

Settling back in the chair, Lucais spread his arms wide. "I am all yours, lass." In more ways than one.

"I'm a lady, not a lass." She briskly crossed the few feet separating them, then hesitated, casting about for some place to put the basin, soap and toweling.

"You can set them in my lap," he murmured, and felt his body rise to the suggestion.

"In your lap?" She looked down and immediately up, her face crimson with embarrassment. The linen underdrawers covering him from waist to midthigh were not sufficiently thick to hide his response to her. "But..."

Lucais shrugged and forced a lazy grin. "I seem to have an, er, strong affinity for hedgehogs. Mayhap if you set the bowl down in my lap, it will conceal the, er, problem."

Elspeth all but dropped the bowl on him in her haste to comply. Lucais sucked in air as the water slopped over the edge, subduing his problem. Temporarily. 'Twould take more cold water than there was in Loch Shin to douse the feelings time and circumstances had not diminished. Still he flinched when she touched the wet cloth to his wounded shoulder.

"Sorry. Did I hurt you?" Her eyes were wide and anxious, her face so close he saw the salty path tears had left on her cheeks.

Aye, she'd hurt him... years ago with her rejection, tonight when she repudiated him yet again. But he suspected her pain went deeper even than his. *What did Raebert do to you?* he longed to ask, but did not. Proud creature that she was, she'd shun his pity, curl inward like the hedgehog and prick him with her spines. 'Twas a fine line he walked 'twixt care and desire.

He desired her. That thought stayed foremost in Elspeth's mind as she washed the blood from Lucais's chest. Small wonder she couldn't forget, for the heat and tension that radiated from him seemed to seep into her body, making her hot and jumpy.

"I have never forced a woman in my life, Beth," he murmured. "And I sure as hell wouldna start with you."

"Why?" she asked, though Raebert had told her time and again she was unwomanly, a loathsome creature who deserved to be beaten.

"Because I canna take pleasure from another's pain."

"You used to enjoy taunting me."

"'Twas a game we both excelled at when we were young, but we are bairns nae longer. 'Tis time to put aside such things."

And do what? The question burned in her mind, caught in her throat as their gazes tangled, locked. The sticks she'd tossed onto the fireplace embers ignited then, the flames picking out the golden flecks in his hazel eyes. They glowed with a life all their own, vibrating with a silent message. *Trust me.*

Nay. She dared not, but deep inside her something stirred. A yearning so strong she swayed where she stood.

"You're exhausted. We'd best get back to bed." His voice sounded as choked as her own tumbling emotions.

"Nay, I . . . I couldna sleep a wink knowing . . . knowing . . ."

"Knowin' that I desire you?"

Elspeth nodded and licked her lips, not at all reassured by the hungry glint in his eyes as he followed the path her tongue had taken. "I . . ." Panicked, she backed up a step.

"'Tis nothin' new, Beth. I've wanted you from the first moment I saw you." Lucais stifled a sigh when his admission made her gasp and clutch her tunic closer. Did she expect he'd try to tear her clothes off? Probably. "In all that time, have I ever tried to corner you and have my wicked way with you?"

Elspeth shook her head, wary as a doe poised for flight. "But . . . but my family was near."

"And I wasna your husband then," he guessed, hurt anew by her shaky nod. Damned Raebert, he hoped he was roasting in hell. "It makes nae difference," he quietly assured her. "I wouldna take what you dinna give willingly."

"I'll never be willing." But she wanted to be. And that scared her most of all, because if she let down her guard, gave in to these strange urges, he'd . . . he'd want to do *that.*

"Get into bed, lass. Dinna fret about my joinin' you. I've a notion to sit up and have a cup of wine."

Elspeth wasted no time complying. As she crawled beneath the covers she looked over to where he sat by the fire. The sight of his bent head and bandaged shoulder made her feel like . . . like comforting him. Sweet Mary, had he cast some spell that made her disregard the lessons Raebert had taught her?

Flopping back on the bed, Elspeth squeezed her eyes shut, but Lucais's image was etched into her lids.

Lucais, snatching her from Seamus's evil clutches.

Lucais, defending her from his vengeful clansmen.
Lucais, denying his own base urges to spare her.
What kind of man was he?

One worthy of your trust, her heart cried, but her mind rebelled. Raebert had treated her kindly before their marriage and turned rabid the moment they were wed. But Lucais hadn't hurt her . . . so far. He'd confused her. Naught new there. He'd always tied her in knots, attracting her despite her vow to wed a warrior. Now he was one. So where did that leave her? Bah! All she could do was wait and watch and keep her guard up.

Chapter Nine

"'M'lady! M'lady!" Ena cried, bursting into the sickroom.

Elspeth leapt from the stool where she'd been sitting vigil at Wee Wat's bedside. "Shh. You'll wake him," she admonished. 'Twas a miracle Wee Wat had survived the night, and he needed all the healing sleep he could get.

"'Tis sorry I am to be disturbin' ye." The woman's voice dropped from a shout to a whisper. "Ye're needed in the hall."

"I doubt that." The Sutherlands had made their hatred clear again this morn, their damning glances following Elspeth as she'd crossed the hall on her way to check on Wee Wat. Cringing inside her hastily donned garments, she'd regretted refusing Lucais's suggestion that she remain in their rooms with him.

"'Tis Lucais." Ena's face was pale as new snow, and her plump hands fluttered nervously. "He's . . . he's gone mad."

Mad. Elspeth's hand rose to her throat, images of Raebert's towering rages ripping through her mind. "Why come to me?" she croaked. "Surely Niall would know better how to deflect—"

"Nay. He willna listen to anyone. I . . . I've never seen him take on so. He's stompin' about the hall, shoutin' fit to raise the dead and threatenin' to punish Gillie."

"Gillie?" Elspeth forgot her own fears. "Why?"

"Somehow Gillie got into the chest where he keeps the ledgers and tally sticks. She's ruined them and Lucais—"

Elspeth didn't wait to hear more. Gathering the skirts of her borrowed woolen gown, she ran from the room. The corridor seemed darker and longer than it had last night. But the sight that greeted her when she threw open the door to the hall made her long to cower in the passageway until the danger had passed.

Lucais's curses echoed like thunder off the old stone walls, holding in thrall the scores of Sutherlands assembled for the morning meal. Still as images carved from alabaster, they watched their laird pace before the dais where his quarry had taken refuge. Crouched under the high table, the lass clutched a broken tally stick and torn parchment pages to her heaving chest.

That grim evidence of her own part in the crime, coupled with the tears coursing down Gillie's cheeks, prodded Elspeth forward. "Hold," she cried as she waded in to do battle. The sea of stunned Sutherlands parted for her, and all too soon she stood before Lucais. A Lucais who bore no resemblance to the man who'd been so gentle with her last night.

Elspeth had not understood Lucais, but she had vast experience in dealing with large, enraged males. Her first objective was to soothe him and deflect his anger. "M'lord. If you'll come away, I'll fix—"

"Fix! Fix?" Lucais's voice rose along with the color that turned his face crimson as a Highland sunset. "Years' worth of records smashed and hopelessly scrambled. The little sneak is always pokin' into my things, but by God, there'll be no fixin' the mess she's made this time." The convulsive way he clenched his fists made Elspeth want to flee before he flattened her with one, but 'twas worth a few bruises to ensure Gillie's safety.

"Hit me if 'twill ease your anger," Elspeth said calmly, though her knees were knocking. "But spare the bairn."

If anything, this seemed to make him angrier. He drew himself up so he filled her vision. The vein throbbing at his temple looked fit to burst. "You think I'd beat her? Or you?"

Raebert would have done so without hesitation. He'd beaten his poor page senseless for not properly cleaning his boots. And when he'd discovered Elspeth had hidden some of her jewelry from him he'd... Despite the heat in the hall, the memory made her shiver. *Nay, dinna think of it.* "I deserve the punishment." She took a deep breath, but it did nothing to steady her hammering heart. "I broke the sticks and ripped up your ledgers."

Lucais snorted. "Proud Elspeth surrenderin' herself for punishment to spare a bairn she scarcely knows."

"How little you know *me*," Elspeth said slowly, but then, she understood him even less. Once she'd decried his gentleness; now she wondered how to reach it beneath the tough layers the years had added. The Lucais of long ago had valued the truth. She hoped he still did. "I am the guilty one." Elspeth looked at the broken sticks clenched in Lucais's fist. "Think you she's strong enough to rent the sturdy oak made to last for generations?"

He glanced down at the sticks. "Well..."

"It took all my strength to break them," Elspeth quickly added. "But they say anger fortifies the muscles, and I was furious enough with your high-handed ways that first night to bend iron...had there been any about. Unfortunately the only thing I found on which to vent my wrath was the contents of the chest in which you stored your estate records."

The gasp of the assembled Sutherlands filled the awkward silence that followed her confession. No less stunned, Lucais slowly raised his gaze from the ruined wood to Elspeth. Her eyes were purple bruises in a face gone white with misery and fear. That she obviously expected him to beat her made his belly knot tighter. That she faced him and her punishment with a stiff spine and quiet dignity made his heart contract, as well.

She had grown into a braw lass, was his first thought. His lass. His wife. If he could keep her.

Someone in the crowd shifted, making Lucais aware he had an avid audience just when he wished himself alone to sort this out. Elspeth's spite had shattered a portion of his clan's heritage, and they'd expect him to punish her accordingly. Even though she was a well-born lady. Especially because she'd once been Raebert Munro's lady. How to do that and not doom his marriage, not smash the fragile bond he'd begun to forge last night?

Lucais swallowed, but it didn't ease the constriction in his throat and chest. "Do you still write a fair hand?" he asked.

"Aye, but what does that have to do—"

"Beatin' you would be too easy, the punishment too quickly over." He pitched his voice for his clansmen's ears. "Instead, you shall remain above stairs in my countin' room until you've pieced together every page from the ledger and recopied it. When you've finished with that, you'll glue the tally sticks together, as well," he added, pleased with himself. In one neat stroke, he'd avoided beating Elspeth, assured she'd be apart from Cathal and the others who wished her harm, *and* his clan's records would be restored. Everyone would be happy with the solution.

Elspeth looked anything but. "That could take days..."

Weeks, if he was lucky. Weeks in which his people would grow used to the idea of her as his wife. Weeks in which he could sort out the business of the broch and woo his prickly little wife. "Then you'd best make a start." Anxious to get her out of the hall while he still had the advantage, he took her arm and herded her toward the stairwell.

"Fiend!" she snapped, and tried to jerk free.

He maintained his grip, firmly but painlessly...a symbol of things to come. She was his, and he was keeping her. "But a clever one." And patient. Aye, with gentleness and patience, he'd win his brave, wary little hedgehog.

"I would prefer any other punishment to being locked up," Elspeth said as they mounted the stairs.

"Would you?" Lucais stopped in the stairwell, his body blocking the light from below so she couldn't see his face. "The penalty for treason against the clan is death." If he felt her tremble in his grasp, it didn't soften his tone as he continued, "Since you are my lady wife, I might have commuted that to fifty lashes, but I doubt you'd prefer being stripped and whipped."

"You are cruel and sadistic."

"Life in the Highlands is harsh, Elspeth. We live surrounded by our enemies, with only our kin for support. Any man...or woman...who isna with us is against us. Some of my people already see you as an enemy and question my wisdom in having wed you. Surely you must realize I couldna let your deed pass unnoticed."

Elspeth shuddered, feeling so small, alone and helpless she wanted to throw herself into his arms and weep. Appalled by the longing to have him hold her as he had last night, she leaned away from him. "I understand, but to lock me up..."

Now it was he who trembled, his hand tensing on her arm. "'Tis the second time you've said that. Who locked you away?"

Raebert! she wanted to shout, but pride kept the words inside. "Nae one. I am just used to being able to come and go as I please." Now that Raebert's gone. "Come, we waste time standing here. The sooner I begin, the sooner I'll be done and free of you." She tugged on her arm and was startled when he released it, but as she hurried up the stairs, she thought she heard him say, "You'll never be free of me, Elspeth." Which was ridiculous. He'd vowed not to bed her until she was willing. Once he realized she never could be willing, he'd grow bored and let her go home.

Last night's storm had blown itself out, leaving the world clean and wet under a cloudless blue sky. Lucais drew in a lungful of damp air and let it out slowly as he guided Black Jock through the woods that bordered the broch.

Leaving Niall in charge of the keep and his prisoner, he'd taken a score of men, including Cathal, and ridden north. The brisk pace he'd set owed as much to the need to work off his restlessness as his determination to be back at Kinduin by dark.

A Sutherland scout suddenly materialized from the thick foliage. "Ye're up and about early, Lucais."

"Aye." Lucais stretched his weary muscles. "Aught stirrin'?"

"Naught but the creatures of the forest."

Lucais nodded. "Cathal, will you ride around and pass the new orders to the rest of the lads on watch?"

"I'd stay behind here and lead them in battle when the Munros return," the older man grumbled, his mouth a sullen line.

Doubtless. But Lucais was after more than revenge. He wanted answers to the questions that had been roused by the Munros' renewed raids and deepened with yesterday's confrontation. "You're the fiercest fighter I have, Cathal," he said honestly. "I need you at Kinduin if the village or the keep are attacked."

Cathal grudgingly accepted the praise and rode off with the others to spread Lucais's orders regarding the Munros. When the last of his men disappeared, Lucais turned his own mount toward the broch. At the edge of the woods, he hesitated, studying the weathered building from beneath a canopy of dripping leaves.

Though the old stone fort had provided his ancestors with a safe haven against marauding Vikings, it guarded no strategic pass or vital bridge or supply road. So why were the Munros suddenly interested in it? And their interest was sudden. Up until a few weeks ago, reports of Munros in this area had been practically nonexistent. Then a group of Sutherland hunters had come across a band of marauding Munros.

The Munros had insisted the loot they carried was lifted from the Gunns beyond the mountain, but the suspicious Sutherlands had been unconvinced. According to reports, the Munros had stampeded the stolen Gunn sheep at the Sutherlands and fled in the ensuing confusion. As was the way of the Highlanders, the Munros had split up, each man forging his own trail home and forcing the pursuing Sutherlands to do the same. 'Twas Cathal himself who tracked a Munro close to the broch, but the man had seemed to vanish into thin air. Cathal had found a riderless horse cropping grass at the base of the fortress and combed the woods for his enemy, only to come up empty-handed. 'Twas Cathal's opinion that his quarry had fallen victim to the broch's curse.

Lucais didn't believe in curses, he believed in facts. What if the Munro had somehow gotten inside the broch and waited there for Cathal to leave? Possible, but not probable . . . unless the Munro could fly, Lucais thought, eyeing the sheer rock face of the broch. Or had a ladder with him. Not a ladder, a rope.

Lucais straightened in the saddle. A man going a-raiding in the Highlands would likely take along a sturdy rope and grappling hook with which to scale his victim's walls. His blood quickening with excitement, Lucais nudged Jock forward. The air grew colder as they rode into the long, dark shadow cast by the broch, and a shiver worked its way down his spine.

"'Tis just the loss of the sun's heat," he murmured, but Jock felt something, too, and shied away from the old gray stone. "Easy, lad," he whispered, as much to soothe his own wariness. "There's naught here to harm us."

Chafing the gooseflesh from his arms, he stared up at the gaping maw a story above him. A man with a good eye and arm might throw a hook high enough to catch the edge of the opening, then climb up the attached rope and into the broch. Lucais's own muscles twitched with the urge to give it a try. He'd wanted to explore the fort from the day old Daibidh, guardian of the clan legends, had brought him here to see this part of his legacy.

Forbidden.

The word whispered all around him, raspy as some warning from the crypt. The hairs at Lucais's nape rose and his skin crawled as though it had been touched by unseen eyes. He whipped his head around, scanning the clearing with a practiced eye. Empty. As was what he could see of the forest. Still he couldn't shake the feeling that someone . . . or something . . . watched him.

Munros was his first thought, but not his only one. The Scottish legends of old were filled with tales of spirits and such. While he enjoyed the stories, the practical side of Lucais's nature insisted they were just that. There was no such thing as ghosts or curses.

Munros, then.

Instinctively Lucais's hand slid down to grip the hilt of his sword. The familiar feel of leather-wrapped steel against his palm steadied his pulse, chased out the last lingering fantasies. With them went the vague sense of unease. 'Twas the wind stirring in the trees that had chilled him, naught more. Still, there was no getting around the fact that 'twas forbidden to enter the broch. As chief of his clan, 'twas his sworn duty to uphold that ancient edict, not flaunt it out of idle curiosity.

"Lucais! What do ye there?"

He looked up to see Cathal and the others filing out of the woods. The distance separating them did not conceal the looks of disapproval on their faces. Further proof, if he needed any, that now was not the time to test their loyalty by breaking one of the clan's cardinal rules. "Looking for Wee Wat's dirk." 'Twas true enough. When he'd gone to check on him this morn, the little man had roused himself enough to ask for his knife.

"Must have dropped it durin' the fight," Wee Wat had whispered. "My da gave it to me. If ye happen across it . . ."

"Anythin' for the man who so gallantly defended Elspeth," Lucais had readily promised. "Though next time, you should think twice about attackin' a man who's twice your size."

"I'd do it again in a trice...and so would ye." Wee Wat scowled up at Lucais. "Giles says ye've handfasted wi' her."

"Aye," Lucais said, bracing for another fight.

"Hurt her, and I'll ha' yer heart on a skewer."

Lucais had smiled ruefully, thinking of his bandaged shoulder. "If history's anythin' to go by, she's far more likely to wound me."

"I'll grant that was so in the past, but she's..."

"Changed," Lucais put in, seeing Wee Wat's lids droop with pain and fatigue. "Though you may have cause to question my methods, I want only what's best for her."

"Do ye love her, lad?" Wee Wat had asked.

"Mayhap... but if you tell her so, I'll have *your* heart on a skewer," Lucais had replied, drawing a wan smile from Elspeth's dour little champion.

"Ye willna find the dirk here," Cathal snapped, jerking Lucais back to the present. "The fight was yonder."

Lucais nodded and cantered away from the broch, oddly relieved to leave the cold shadows for the warm sunshine. Dismounting, he walked the torn earth and bloodied grass, mute testimony to yesterday's brief, savage struggle. Though Cathal sat his horse and watched, the other men climbed down to aid in the search. A ripped mantle and a dented helmet were recovered, but there was no sign of Wee Wat's knife.

Resigned to returning without it, Lucais gave the order to mount, but as he put his foot in Jock's stirrup, he saw something glint on the ground. "Step aside, lad."

Jock balked, refusing to budge until Lucais stroked his nose and coaxed him into moving out of the way. "I seem to be cursed with stubborn creatures," Lucais murmured as he hunkered down to examine the ground. But he supposed it was a good lesson in cultivating the kind of patience he'd need to win Elspeth.

For his reward, the glint turned out to be the tip of a dirk. Digging into the hard-packed mud, Lucais drew it forth and wiped it clean on a patch of grass. The blade was long and curved, the hilt etched with Pictish symbols. "'Tis Wee Wat's,"

Lucais called. Pleased with his find, he stood, but the sun caught on a bright bit in the hole that had yielded up the knife.

"Damn. It must have broken." But when Lucais reached into the soil, he found not the expected fragment of the dirk but two round shapes lying side by side. Coins. Gold coins by their heft, he thought as he straightened. A quick wipe on the edge of his plaid confirmed they were thick gold coins with strange markings the likes of which Lucais had never seen before.

"What did ye find?" Cathal called.

"Something else of Wee Wat's, I warrant." Lucais slipped the coins into the pouch at his waist, tucked the dirk into the top of his boot and swung into the saddle. "Come, I'd make Kinduin by nightfall," he shouted, thinking how like a Scot to place more value on an old dirk than on two gold coins twice its worth. Doubtless Wee Wat would be pleased to have them back, though.

Something had happened to Lucais, Elspeth fretted, pacing the length of the laird's chamber.

For the tenth time in the quarter hour, she stopped and peered down into the courtyard through the slats of the wooden shutters covering the window. Still no sign of Lucais and the men who'd left with him hours ago. Around the tower, the wind moaned, making the torches in the bailey leap and twist. 'Twas an eerie sound, desolate and mournful. How many generations of Sutherland wives had stood at this same window, waiting, praying their men would return safely from a dangerous raid? Shivering, she turned away, arms wrapped about her waist to still the trembling.

"Ye'll wear a path in the fine carpet Lucais bought in Edinburgh," Ena admonished from her stool by the hearth, mending in hand, Gillie sprawled on a nest of fur at her feet.

"The confinement's made me restless, that's all," Elspeth lied, tossing her head to clear it of concern for Lucais.

Ena saw through her. "I'm certain Lucais is fine."

"But he left right after breakfast," Elspeth cried. Barely had Lucais left her in his chamber with the torn ledgers and a pile of fresh parchment before a commotion in the courtyard drew her from the task. She'd seen ten men readying their mounts for travel. Her eyes had focused on Lucais as he swung into the saddle. The wind had caught his plaid, whipping it back to reveal the heavy claymore at his side. "How could he be so foolish as to go raiding with only nine men?" she asked Ena.

"What makes ye think he's on a raid?"

"His expression," Elspeth murmured. As he'd wheeled his horse to leave, Lucais had glanced up long enough to give her a glimpse of the fierce determination etched into his features. "Sweet Mary, he looked so ruthless my blood fair ran cold."

Ena smiled. "'Tis a face he puts on for the men."

Intrigued, Elspeth drifted over to the fire. "Tell me more," she demanded, sitting cross-legged on the furs with Gillie.

"I dunno." The old woman cocked her head, wrinkled lips pursed. "I'm nae one to gossip, mind. But ye are his wife."

"Aye." For the present. Even though this was only a temporary marriage, Elspeth felt oddly compelled to learn more about the man she thought she'd known full well.

"Lucais was only seventeen when he came here eight years ago. Old Angus's son and heir had been killed fightin' the Munros and we all thought the laird had gone daft, namin' as his heir a boy who'd been groomed to be a bard, not a warrior. Little did we know Angus had asked Laird Eammon to see to Lucais's knightly trainin'." Ena chuckled. "Showed the lads of Kinduin a thing or two about fightin', Lucais did. 'Twas him taught the Sutherlands the skills needed to keep the Munros from wipin' us out."

"And turned himself into a ruthless Highlander in the process," Elspeth said sadly.

"Nay. Oh, never doubt he's the best man wi' a sword these hills have ever seen," Ena said quickly. "But he doesna enjoy the killin', that's sure. There's a gentleness deep inside him that hasna been tainted by the hard things he's been forced to do as our chief, though he shows that side of him to very few... for fear of being thought weak, ye ken?"

Elspeth knew only too well, for she had hurled that insult at his head more times than she cared to recall. Obviously there was more to Lucais than the quick tongue and razor-sharp intelligence she'd recognized from the first because they'd complemented her own. He was strong enough to face down Seamus and win, yet he'd treated her with tenderness and sensitivity last night. Aye, there was more to Lucais than she'd ever suspected, things that drew on her, made her long for his presence when past experience warned her away from all men.

"He's lonely, m'lady. So lonely it fair breaks my heart."

Loneliness. Elspeth gasped, suddenly realizing 'twas loneliness that shadowed his gaze. A loneliness deep and profound as the ache in her own soul. *Oh, Lucais . . .*

"Wi' all he's done for us, he hasna found anyone for himself. Till now," Ena added, glancing slyly at Elspeth.

Elspeth turned away from the old woman's speculation and her gaze fell on Gillie, asleep beside her, rumpled black head cradled in her wee arms. "What of her mother?" she asked, dismayed to find her throat tight with jealousy.

"A sad business, that." Ena shook her head, lips pursing as she studied Gillie's face by firelight. "We were that surprised when Lucais went to Edinburgh seekin' a bride four years ago and brought Jean back. She werena very bright, for one thing, though she was pretty, all shiny black hair and soft skin."

He hadn't wasted even a day getting over her rejection of his suit, Elspeth thought sourly. "They wed quickly."

"Oh, he didna marry Jean...even when it became known she was carryin' Gillie."

"How like a man to use a woman and then discard her when he's done with her," Elspeth snapped, and Lucais tumbled from the pedestal Ena's words had built beneath him.

"I wouldna judge him too harshly. I dinna ken why he didna wed her, but when Jean up and ran away, Lucais went after her."

"What did he do to make Jean leave?" When Ena averted her gaze, Elspeth leapt to her own conclusions. "He ignored her. Just as he does Gillie." His coldness to his daughter mocked the things Elspeth was coming to feel for Lucais. How could she respect a man who treated his own bairn so cruelly?

"Lucais was busy tryin' to keep the Munros from swallowin' up our clan," Ena said stoutly. "He had no time to coddle a silly lass. But when he returned from a raid and learned she'd taken off, he rode straight out, found her and brought her back. Had to fight off the Munros who'd caught her on the road."

"Sweet Mary, she's lucky they didna kill her." Or worse.

"Lucais said as much, but he was furious wi' her for runnin' in the first place. We lost six men in the battle to free her."

"Did Lucais punish her?" Elspeth tried not to think of the price she'd paid for trying to escape Raebert.

"Well, he locked her up, of course, so she couldna get out again and get hurt again, or cause more trouble."

Just as he's locked me away. Elspeth's heart went out to poor Jean, alone in a strange castle, pregnant by a man who ignored her. Lucais did not rant and hit, but his methods were as cruel as Raebert's. It did not bode well for her own future, she thought, for her crimes were more serious than Jean's.

A loud noise from without had them both turning toward the window. Elspeth leapt to her feet, threw open the shutters just as the portcullis rumbled up to admit a troop of men. The pipes began to wail, drowning out the barking dogs and clattering hooves of the new arrivals. Men tumbled into the courtyard from the barracks across the way. "Lion, Lion," they chanted.

Their shouts pierced Elspeth to the quick, ripped open a scar that had never healed. "Of whom do they speak?"

"Lucais. The Sutherlands gave him the byname Lion of the North for his fierceness in battle." Ena's face glowed.

"My brother was called Lion." Elspeth's eyes narrowed on Lucais as he drew off his helmet and tossed it to Niall. "He canna steal Lion's name nor lock me in his damned tower." Ignoring Ena's shout of dismay, Elspeth dashed from the room.

Her anger grew apace with every step she took, down the stairs, across the now deserted hall, through the entryway and out into the crowded bailey. "Make way," she commanded, shoving men aside in her haste to reach the object of her ire.

Lucais stood talking with Niall, his back to her, an empty cup dangling from his left hand.

"Name stealer!" Elspeth grabbed his arm, fury lending her the strength to turn him about. "How dare you style yourself after Lion? How dare you steal my brother's name and leave me here to rot, you—" The sight of his torn, bloody tunic and grimy face stopped her cold. "Sweet Mary! You're wounded!" Fear drove out every thought save the need to help him. "Niall! Quick, carry him within so I may tend him. Ena...Ena, I need water, linens..."

"Beth." Lucais's arm closed around her with a strength no dying man could muster. "The blood isna mine."

"What?" Elspeth looked at the gore, then at his face.

"'Tis the boar's." As she gaped at him in stunned silence he went on, "It charged out of the woods but three miles from Kinduin, slashed Jock's leg before I'd even realized what was happening. Jock went down and I rolled free. I barely managed to get my sword out when the beast came at me again."

"Y-you werena hurt?"

"If I hadna had Wee Wat's dirk tucked in my boot, I'd likely be dead. I thrust my sword in the boar's chest, but it kept bucking and slashing. I saved myself by slitting its throat."

"Oh." Conscious of the milling Sutherlands, Elspeth felt like a fool. Stiffening, she pushed at his chest. "Let me go."

"Nay. Just now, I need your help."

"You lock me up and expect *me* to help *you?*" She kicked him.

Lucais swore, moved his leg out of range but did not release her. "'Tis Jock who needs your healing skills." That stopped Elspeth's struggles, but her eyes were still hostile. "He has several wicked cuts on his chest and legs. We bound them up best we could on the trail, but I recall you've a way with such..."

"Aye. I'll help *Jock,*" Elspeth allowed.

Despite his concern for Jock, Lucais couldn't help smiling to himself as he escorted Elspeth to the stables. She cared for him, else the idea of his being wounded wouldn't have upset her. Once Jock was seen to, he'd address her other accusations. He understood well enough why she resented being confined to their room, but the name-stealing charge confused him.

"Poor thing," Elspeth crooned, kneeling in the straw at Jock's head. The horse lay on his right side, soulful eyes glazed with pain, body racked with great, shuddering sighs. The jagged wounds torn open by the boar's sharp tusks were bound in strips ripped from Lucais's plaid. Though the dressing had stopped the worst of the bleeding, the gaping flesh needed stitching and there was no telling whether Jock would ever walk again. *So like her da,* Elspeth thought, cringing inside.

"Might's well slit its throat and be done wi' it," Cathal commented from the front of the stall.

Elspeth's head came up, but it was to Lucais she looked, not Cathal. "Nay. Where's there's life, there's hope." Still, she feared this new, harsher Lucais might not agree. "Besides, the stallion's too valuable to kill when he might be saved."

To her relief, both men nodded. "True enough," Cathal said, grudging respect in his tone. "I've a mare I'd like bred to Jock. Tell me what ye need, and I'll fetch it myself."

"You are wise in the ways of dealin' with men," Lucais said when Elspeth had sent Cathal off to raid Ena's healing supplies.

"If I were, I wouldna have made such a hash of my life."

Did she speak of Raebert or himself? He struggled against the urge to blurt out the question. Afraid of what she'd say, Lucais stood and stripped off his ruined tunic and chain mail lest the smell of the boar's blood upset the stallion.

"I do know that men such as Cathal brook nae weakness."

Nor did she, Lucais thought, though there were times when she looked sorely in need of tenderness. Jesu, but she was a contrary lass, prickly one moment, vulnerable the next. Winning her was like crossing a marsh...one misstep and he'd sink from sight. For now, he'd stick to an impersonal path. "Cathal has the clan's best interests at heart," he said slowly. "Dinna mind his wariness of you . . . old prejudices die hard."

"But I was raised a Carmichael," Elspeth protested.

"You wed a Munro. To some, that makes you one of them."

Elspeth raised troubled eyes to his. "What do you think?"

That I never stopped loving you. But such an admission was fraught with danger . . . for himself and his clan. Before Lucais could dredge up a safe answer, Cathal returned.

"Thank you," Elspeth murmured as she accepted the medicine chest and other supplies, half-wishing he'd taken longer. She sensed Lucais had been about to reveal something startling. Something that had darkened his eyes, softened his lips. *What was it?* Absently wetting a cloth, she touched it to Jock's hide. The horse screamed and erupted into a welter of thrashing limbs.

"Get back!" Lucais threw himself between Elspeth and the deadly, steel-shod hooves, shoving her aside.

Elspeth landed against the wooden side of the stall. Stunned, she lay there, one hand over her thudding heart as she watched the battle Lucais waged to calm the panicked animal while Cathal and two of the grooms dived in to help.

"Dinna hurt him," Lucais cautioned. Wrapping both arms around the horse's head, he anchored it to the ground.

"Nay, he's more likely to kill us," the old man snarled, but the trio moved in slowly. Grunting and swearing, they used their combined weight to pin the hindquarters to the straw. Moments later, Jock subsided into a mass of quivering horse-flesh.

Tempted as she was to go to the frightened horse, Elspeth saw Lucais had the situation in hand. And a gentle hand it was. Lying on his stomach in the straw, he gently stroked Jock's head. "Easy, lad." Lucais crooned soft Gaelic phrases that Elspeth recognized as an ancient ode to a comrade injured in battle. How appropriate. Though it was doubtful Jock understood the praise being heaped on him, his panic gradually eased. His eyes ceased to roll; his snorts trailed off to an equine whimper.

"Amazing," Elspeth whispered, touched by the glimpse of this strong man's gentleness. Mayhap Ena was right and he hadn't totally lost his compassionate side. The idea drew her.

"Beth," Lucais said, low and harsh as he sat up. "It may be hopeless, but . . . but I'd have you try."

"Of course." Elspeth crawled forward, laid a hand on Lucais's chest. Though a week ago, she'd not have willingly touched a man, tonight it seemed the most natural thing in the world. Her fingers splayed, drawing strength from the warm wall of rock-hard muscles, the beat of his heart against her palm steadying her for the ordeal ahead. "I'll do all I can."

"I know you will." As he watched Elspeth with Jock, Lucais let go the breath he'd been holding. She treated the horse with as much concern as she had Wee Wat. After giving him a dose of poppy for the pain, Elspeth cleaned the wounds, sprinkled them with ground herbs and stitched them closed. Moldy bread on the top to draw infection, she explained, then asked for help in the difficult task of wrapping the deeper cuts with linen bandages.

"I've done all I can," Elspeth said at last. Sitting back on her heels in the straw, she arched her neck against the stiffness that hunching over Jock had put there. Warm hands came up to rub the tight muscles. Lucais's hands. She should move away, but his touch beguiled where another's had terrified. Sighing, she leaned into his caress. The sigh became a moan as his fingers strayed beneath the neckline of her gown, kneading her shoulders, drawing her back into the curve of his body. It fit her perfectly.

Heated tendrils radiated out from the lazy circles traced by his fingers. The heady tingling spread, warming her in the places where they touched, making her ache in the places where they did not. Alive. Tired as she was, she felt more alive than she had in years. Yet she felt safe, too . . . safe and cherished.

"Thank you for savin' Jock," Lucais whispered, daring to brush a kiss across her temple, glorying in her soft sigh.

"I hope I have. I wouldna see him a cripple, too."

"You're thinkin' of your da?"

"Aye." So sadly he hugged her tighter.

What was it about Laird Lionel's wounding that continued to trouble her so? " 'Twasna your fault he was hurt."

"If only that were true."

"What are you sayin'?" When she didn't reply, he tucked his fingers under her chin and turned her face toward his.

"Naught. I'm merely tired." A lie. Yet her expression was so anguished that instead of pressing for an answer, he kissed her down-turned mouth. It trembled, echoing the shudder that swept her in the instant before her lips melted, molding to his.

Sweet. The feel of her turning into him, moaning as she returned his kiss, was the sweetest pleasure he'd ever known. He wanted to drown in it and take her with him. Desire swept him with the savagery of a Highland storm, wild and elemental. She was his. She was his. Growling her name, he deepened the kiss. Or tried to. The tongue that had been following his lead suddenly retreated. *Too soon.*

Wrenching his mouth away, Lucais buried his face in her hair, gulping air, shuddering with the effort it took to pull back from the brink of fulfillment. "Beth. Dinna be afraid," he crooned, much as he had to Jock an hour before.

"I . . . I'm nae afraid." Her voice shook a little, but she didn't try to pull free of his embrace. "J-just confused."

"Why? You know I desire you." And she'd wanted him. For a few precious moments her passion had matched his own.

"But how can I feel so...so..." She pressed her hot face into his neck. *His Beth shy?* "How can I welcome your kisses when so much is unsettled between us?"

Lucais slowly released his pent-up breath. She *did* want him. "Mayhap we are closer than you realize."

"How can we be when you hold me prisoner?" Bitterly.

Lucais sighed. "Beth, we've been through the reasons why—"

"What reasons did you give Jean?" she asked, sitting back.

"Jean? What has she to do with—"

"Ena said you ignored her." *As you do Gillie,* but she didn't want to dig up that old chestnut tonight. "She said Jean tried to run away and you locked her in the tower. As you have me."

"'Tisna the same." He dragged a weary hand through his hair. "Jean was..." *Bent on killing herself.* But he couldn't say why without spilling the whole, ugly story. A secret he'd sworn never to reveal. Vowed it on Jean's grave. "She was unbalanced."

Elspeth frowned. "Really? Then why did you...?"

"Take up with her?" Lucais asked, pleased by the glint of jealousy in her eyes. *Because she looked like you.* But that, too, gave away more than was safe right now. "She was beautiful."

"Ah." Elspeth looked away. She *was* jealous.

Lucais nearly crowed with joy. But knowing he'd won one wee skirmish in the most important war of his life, he changed the subject. "Why did you accuse me of stealin' your brother's name?"

Elspeth blinked, remembered and welcomed the rekindling of her anger. 'Twas better than jealousy. "I heard you called Lion."

"Aye, well... Niall dubbed me that on the day I backed Seamus into a corner and forced him to cry peace," he mumbled.

He was embarrassed, Elspeth realized, charmed against her will. Still the fact remained. "There can only ever be one Lion. Doubtless you encouraged your clan to call you by his name, thinking 'twould make you as great a warrior as he was."

"'Twas a welcome change from the whispers of 'outsider' and 'misfit,'" he admitted with an engaging half smile that faded quickly. "But it takes more than a name to make a man a warrior."

It took strength, courage and skill to be a warrior and, though she'd not realized it till recently, it took compassion to make that warrior a good leader. Lucais had all four. Still, part of her begrudged him the use of her beloved brother's name.

"Come, I'll escort you to our chamber," he said, as though he knew further discussion would not change her mind.

"I'd stay here. Jock might need me in the night." And she needed to teach Lucais she couldn't be shut up or ordered about.

"We'll both sleep here, then," he said, neatly turning the tables on her.

Chapter Ten

Come morning, both of Elspeth's patients were on the mend. Black Jock was resting comfortably under young Danny's watchful eye; Wee Wat was sitting up in bed.

"Ah, thought ye'd forgot all about me," the little man chided as Elspeth entered his room with Lucais beside her.

"Silly man." Still, she fairly flew to his side, fussed with the blankets and bandage. "You're doing well enough. The wound seems to have stopped seeping."

"Good. I'll be up and about, then. 'Tis bloody borin'—"

"You'll do nae such thing," Elspeth said, hands on hips.

Wee Wat snorted. "Ye'll need an army to keep me here."

Elspeth turned immediately to Lucais. "Oh, I think one man'll do. Lucais is strong enough to keep six of you down."

The approval dancing in her eyes made Lucais feel ten feet tall. "For you, I'd slay dragons, m'lady," he teased, bowing with a flourish. But he meant every word of it.

"I appreciate your gallant offer." The ready smile, so evident in her youth but missing lately, made her face glow in the soft light. "But as you see, 'tis only one daft old man."

"Daft, is it?" Wee Wat exclaimed, his wan features lightened by tolerant amusement. Clearly he'd sensed the change between them and approved, Lucais thought, pleased that, though he'd not been able to secure her father's permission to wed, he had the blessing of this shrewd old bird. And Elspeth's?

Mayhap. Lucais smiled faintly. Though he deeply regretted Black Jock's wounding, he was pleased with the ground he'd gained in his quest to win Elspeth. She'd slept the night in his arms, smiled when he'd awakened her with a kiss at dawn. A kiss and nothing more, despite the desire that had raged inside him.

Cradled in the curve of his body, she'd felt his response. Eyes widening, fear evident even in the dimness of the stables, she'd tensed to repel the attack she obviously expected. *Oh, Beth.* "Easy, lass, you're safe in my arms," he'd crooned.

She'd blinked rapidly. "I—I'm . . ."

"Frightened. Confused," he'd replied for her. "I know." He stroked back the tendrils that had come free from her braid and touched his mouth to her temple.

"How can you when I barely know myself?" she asked, voice shaky as the pulse beating against his lips. "Nor do I know you."

"Me?" He drew back to study her face, pale and stripped bare of guards and pretense. "I'm the same man I've always been."

"Nay. You're harder now. Colder. More ruthless."

And that troubled her? Curious. "Just the sort of man you admire. Like Raebert." The old bitterness made his chest ache.

"Raebert wasna what he seemed. To others, he was the king's champion, but in private, he changed. He wasna . . . honorable."

Amen to that, Lucais thought, pricked by the necessity to keep secret from Elspeth Raebert's most dishonorable act. "I'm nae like that," Lucais whispered, but he could see she didn't believe him. "If I seem hard, 'tis because the Sutherlands need a strong chief, but deep down inside, I'm still the lad who . . ." Who what? The answer came so swiftly he laughed. "Still the lad who tickled you breathless." And he proceeded to do just that.

Laughter had lightened the mood and awakened Jock, shifting Elspeth's thoughts from herself to her patient. The shy, searching glances she had sent Lucais's way since leaving the stables proved she was puzzled by what was happening between them. At least she no longer seemed afraid of him, Lucais thought as he moved to stand behind her, one hand resting lightly but possessively on her shoulder.

She smiled faintly at him, then turned back to Wee Wat. "Aye, you're daft if you dinna do as you're told," she warned.

Wee Wat cocked his head and winked at Lucais. "Ye dinna think it daft when ye take a mind to do somethin' ye aught not."

"Are you saying I'm stubborn?"

"Aye, ye're that, and ye've Laird Lionel's temper."

Lucais felt Elspeth flinch. Over her head, he and Wat exchanged frowns. What was it about her father that made her jump every time his name was mentioned? But before Lucais could voice his concern, she stepped from under his hand.

"I'd best take a look at your wound, Wat," she said briskly.

Probing her mysterious reaction must wait till they were in private. "I found your dirk." Moving around the other side of the bed, Lucais handed over the knife he'd cleaned this morning.

"Ah." Wee Wat's smile ended in a grimace as Elspeth removed the bandage. "Careful . . . I'm armed now."

No cheeky rejoinder followed and Elspeth's expression as she went back to work held too much sorrow for Lucais's liking. *What ails her?* he silently asked of Wee Wat.

The little man shrugged, sighed, then laid the dirk on the blanket. "'Tis all I have left from me da," he said quietly, eyes boring into Elspeth's bent head. "It belonged to him and to his father before him, and so on back as far as I know."

Lucais saw her fingers tremble, longed to go to her, wrap his arms around her and demand answers. *Patience,* an inner voice counseled. "He was a Highlander?" he asked of Wat instead.

"Aye, from the frozen north of the Orkneys. Came south, he did, met me ma and stayed a time." He turned the dirk, sending light from the flame on the bedside table licking over the dull metal. Though it was dark and worn with age, the symbols carved into the hilt stood out in bold relief.

"Wait, I've somethin' else of yours, as well." Lucais reached into the pouch at his waist, drew out the pair of old coins and laid them beside the knife. Washed clean of the mud from the battlefield, they glowed in the flickering light.

"I agree the markin's are kin to those on my dirk," Wee Wat allowed, nudging one with his finger. "But they're nae mine."

"I found them directly beneath your blade."

Wee Wat frowned. "They could ha' lain there for years, I suppose, and been unearthed by my scuffle wi' Seamus Munro."

"Mayhap he dropped them," Lucais exclaimed, gaze narrowing.

"Could be." Wee Wat frowned. "But these coins are old, and from what I've heard of Seamus, he doesna hold on to gold longer than it takes to spend it on ale and horses."

"That's so." Uneasy, Lucais retrieved one of the coins. 'Twas thick and heavy, with strange symbols cut into either side. Had Seamus dropped this? Where had he gotten it?

"Could be somethin' the Vikings left behind," Wee Wat mused.

"Vikings!" Lucais and Elspeth exclaimed in unison.

"Or the Picts."

"Picts," Elspeth breathed. The legends Megan had taught them both were full of tales of the fierce Pictish ancestors from whom the Scots were descended. "Oh, Lucais, do you suppose these were made by the Picts who built Broch Tower?" she asked, eyes aglow.

"Possibly, but why do you find that so excitin'?"

"They could have been dropped there by those ancient people and lain there all these countless years waiting for you to rescue them." She looked at Lucais as though he'd saved them from extinction, but Lucais knew better.

A thousand horses and beasts of the forest had walked through that glen in the generations since the broch was last used. The coins would have been either discovered or ground into the dirt long since. Nay, they'd come there recently. But how? The fine hairs at his nape rose as he turned the possibilities over in his mind, not daring to voice them. 'Twas not that he didn't trust these two, he thought, gaze skipping from Wee Wat's pursed lips to Elspeth's reverent expression. He respected the man, was halfway in love with the woman.

And therein lay the problem. Lucais didn't trust himself or his instincts where she was concerned. He'd fallen under her spell again so swiftly it fair took his breath away every time he looked at her. But she'd lied to him about her reasons for coming to Kinduin. And then there was her claim on the broch.

Lion of the North

"Best keep quiet about findin' these, or ye'll ha' every greedy bastard for miles about trompin' through yon glen wi' a shovel in hand diggin' for treasure," Wee Wat muttered ominously.

Lucais grasped the excuse quicker than a drowning man would a lifeline. An apt description, for if Elspeth was betraying him with the Munros... He didn't think he could survive that. "Aye. I'll just tuck them away," he said, pleased his steady voice didn't betray the quaking inside him. After the noon meal, he'd take them to the village to show Daibidh. The self-proclaimed wizard of the Sutherlands of Kinduin might recognize the markings on these coins, and Daibidh would cut out his own tongue before he told a soul of their existence.

If only he was as certain of Elspeth's loyalties, Lucais thought with a pang, watching her as she expertly rebandaged Wee Wat's wound. He wished he'd waited until she was gone to show Wat the coins and felt disloyal in the thinking. He loved her. He did. And with love came trust. But the simple truth was that even though they'd grown a step closer since last night, they neither one trusted the other.

"Could I see one of the coins?" Elspeth asked as Lucais pulled shut the door to Wee Wat's room.

The comforting warmth of his hand dropped from the small of her back. "Why?" So curt, so suspicious. Torches flickering in the wall brackets threw light and shadow over his face. In its harsh wash, he seemed a grim stranger.

"I meant naught by it," Elspeth said slowly. What had happened to the rapport they'd shared last night? Where was the man who'd kissed her this morn, his gentleness easing her fears even as passion sent her senses spinning? How could the man who'd tickled her then look so severe? "Do you think I'd steal them?"

"Would you?"

Ah, so he was back to being the cold, calculating knight who'd seized her on the banks of Loch Shin. "Fine. Keep the damn things." Exasperated, nerves on edge from trying to deal with the situation she found herself in and the man who'd thrown her whole being into turmoil, she spun away and stomped down the length of the corridor. Temper pounded against her ears so she couldn't hear if he followed or nae. Nor did she care.

Elspeth pushed open the door and was momentarily stunned. The dazzle of a hundred torches turned the hall beyond bright as a meadow at midday. Blinking, she saw the room was filled to capacity, Sutherlands packing the trestle tables like herring in a barrel, all dressed in their feast-day best.

"See, I told ye she'd be along directly," Ena called out, stilling the murmurings, turning hundreds of eyes toward where Elspeth stood on the threshold. "And Lucais wi' her."

"What is this?" Lucais asked in the same wary voice he'd used on Elspeth only moments before.

"I promised ye a feast in honor of yer weddin'," the old woman promptly replied. "And this is it."

Elspeth's frown deepened as she looked down at her clothes. When she'd returned to their room this morn, she'd been so anxious to check on Wee Wat that she'd torn off her rumpled gown, washed hastily and dressed in the first thing pulled from the travel pack Lucais had returned to her. The peacock blue silk gown was a favorite of hers, but 'twas old and unadorned. "I should wear something special," she said in dismay.

"Your gown is fine." Lucais took her arm and led her to the high table with every pretense of gallantry.

How like a man to dismiss her costume as unimportant, Elspeth thought as she plopped down into the chair he held for her. "Just because you dinna give a fig for the way you're dressed doesna mean I must wear old sacking," she grumbled.

"No one has asked you to," he retorted.

"L-Lucais," Danny asked, coming to stand between them. "Would ye like wine?" The lad had a pitcher clasped in both hands. His eyes darted nervously between the two of them.

Lucais's expression gentled for his squire. "Aye, thank you."

"First that business with the coins, now this," Elspeth said when the lad had filled the cup they'd share and fled. "If you regret we are wed, 'tis simple enough to dissolve the union."

"You'd go back on your word?" Lucais gazed at her intently, eyes more green now than brown. Piercing. Probing. Looking for a weakness she was determined not to show.

Elspeth lifted her chin. "I am your wife for a year, but I needna pass it here, since my greedy presence so offends you."

"Bloody hell," Lucais snapped, raking a hand through his hair. That they were back to where they'd started was his own fault for letting his suspicions color his attitude. And her inbred prickliness didn't help. "I didna think you meant to steal the coin." Exactly. "But 'tis wisest to keep it a secret."

She scowled, and he could almost see her weighing his words, measuring her own response. This hesitancy was new in one who used to sling words back at him, quick and wild as arrows on a battlefield. "And you dinna trust me to do that."

Damn. "I want to, Beth," he replied, taking her hand and looking deep into her troubled eyes, willing her to understand, to bend, to trust. "But you lied about your reasons for coming here, and I dinna think you understand about the broch."

She stiffened, and he could practically see his hedgehog bristle. "Broch Tower was deeded to me by the Munros."

"It wasna theirs to give."

"But I have the paper, signed by the king."

"A map isna proof of ownership," Lucais argued, ignoring a frisson of unease. Harder to ignore was the way she suddenly pressed her hand to her mouth and looked away, as though she'd said something she regretted. "What is it?"

"Naught," she said quickly. Too quickly.

"Elspeth. Tell me what's wrong."

"The meal is served, Lucais. Elspeth," Ena chirped.

"Oh, thank you." Elspeth sagged with relief at the reprieve, but afraid to face Lucais, she looked out over the hall. And right into a sea of disapproving Sutherlands. *Damn.* Bad enough she'd quarreled with Lucais after thinking they'd reached an understanding *and* hinted she had a deed to Broch Tower. How could she eat with his kin watching her as though she hid a band of Munros under her skirts? "I dinna feel very hungry."

"Nor do I," Lucais said in a terse undertone. "But we'll eat because Ena has gone to the trouble of preparin' this feast. And we'll smile because my clansmen have come to wish us well."

"I doubt that," Elspeth replied, eyeing Cathal and the sullen men grouped around him. Last night the old man had unbent to help her for the stallion's sake, but clearly he did not welcome her as Lucais's wife. The only friendly faces were those of Niall, who'd just taken a seat to her left, and the Carmichaels, who sat together at a table near the dais.

The meal went downhill from there. Knowing that the boar Ena's helpers so proudly carried into the hall was the very beast that had gored Black Jock made the sauced bits stick in Elspeth's throat. The pottage lacked salt, the rabbit stew lacked pepper, and the bread had been made with something that tasted like... "Barley and water," Lucais murmured.

"Why?" Elspeth choked on a bite, forced it down with a swallow of wine from the cup they shared. Sour. She gagged and set the cup down with a thump, longing to spit into the rushes.

"We've run out of flour and the wine's left over from last year," he supplied, gaze steady, unreadable.

"You could send to Curthill town for more supplies."

He shook his head. "I dinna have the coin to pay for it."

"Surely Laird Eammon would extend you credit."

"I willna eat what I canna pay for."

"And you call me stubborn." Elspeth gazed about the crowded hall. People who'd looked hale to her moments ago now seemed gaunt and hollow-eyed. "You'd starve them for your pride?"

"They've food enough to fill their bellies. And if it isna of the best quality..." He shrugged his shoulders. "We eat it anyway, for we canna afford to waste anything."

Elspeth shuddered, suddenly assailed by images of the Sutherlands starving to death. "But when this is gone..."

"'Twill last another two weeks till we can take the winter's harvest of marten pelts and salted salmon to market. Then we'll replenish our stores." Lucais's spirits plunged further as he watched revulsion steal the color from her face. *Fool,* he thought. Buoyed by the heady notion of having her to wife at long last, he'd hoped they could work out their problems, forgetting that they came from two different worlds. She'd been doted on by her wealthy, loving parents and given every luxury.

While he was far from poor, he could not afford to keep her in such style without taking from his kinsmen. And that he'd not do...even for Elspeth. Best she understand that now. "But our funds willna stretch to more fancy gowns," he growled, casting a jaundiced eye at her clothes. The peacock blue silk surcoat oversewn with gold thread likely cost enough to finance a suit of chain mail. "Such delicate stuff isna warm enough for our clime, and 'tis impractical, besides. 'Twillna stand up to our rugged life." Nor would she, he feared.

Elspeth sighed. Though not half as fine as the garments she'd worn at court, 'twas her favorite. But he was right, the wretch. Even in summer, the Highlands were colder than home, she'd noted, Kinduin damper and draftier than Carmichael Castle. "This is the plainest of the gowns I brought with me."

"I guessed as much."

That got Elspeth's back up. "Wearing silks and such doesna make me an evil, greedy person," she snapped.

"I think she looks beautiful," Niall put in, earning a sharp look from his cousin.

"So does a lily, but 'twouldna survive a Highland winter," Lucais muttered, his expression growing bleaker by the minute.

"Are ye tryin' to frighten her?" Niall asked.

An interesting question. Elspeth wondered what went on behind Lucais's shuttered, hazel eyes. Earlier he'd made it plain he wanted her to stay, even though he didn't trust her. Now he seemed bent on driving her away. Truly men were confusing beasts.

"I want her to understand that life here is harsh."

He thought her too weak to survive. Ha! "I'll ask Ena to help me find or make something more suitable to my new life."

"But for how long will you be content wearin' rough wool and eatin' barley bread?" His voice held no censure, only a challenge that made Elspeth sit up a little straighter. *Perverse must be yer middle name,* her mother had often chided. *The moment ye're denied a thing, 'tis exactly what ye want most.* 'Twas certainly true in this case. No sooner had Lucais said she was too soft for Highland life than she was determined to prove him wrong.

Lucais regretted his harsh words the moment he felt Elspeth stiffen beside him. Damn, he'd only wanted to point out to her the differences between life at Carmichael Castle and the life she could expect here. Mayhap if he'd been more honest with Jean from the beginning, her life might not have ended so tragically. "Elspeth, I am sorry that I canna provide the things you are used to, but I felt it only fair to warn you..."

"I understand." The face she turned to him looked not at all downcast, it positively glowed. And the light that gleamed in the depths of her wide purple eyes was one he'd seen before... and learned to dread. Bloody hell! What was she up to now?

The stable door creaked open, letting in a wedge of early afternoon light. "Lady Elspeth?" Sir Giles called, eyes narrowing as he scanned the dark interior of the building.

"Here," she whispered, materializing from the gloom.

"Why ever did ye want me to meet ye here?" he exclaimed.

"Shh." Grabbing his hand, Elspeth fairly dragged the knight into the stall next to Black Jock's. "I want you to assemble the men and prepare to return to Curthill."

"Curthill? But what of yer marriage to Laird Lucais?"

"I'll remain here, but I've an errand I'd have you see to."

"I canna go hyin' off on some errand," he grumbled. "Lord Ross charged me with seein' to yer welfare, m'lady."

"Think you I'm nae safe here, wed to Lucais and sequestered behind Kinduin's stout walls?" No need to tell the man she didn't intend to stay behind them. He'd only fret.

Sir Giles frowned and toyed with the ends of his mustache. "Aye, the keep's sound enough, but—"

"Good. Here is what I'd have you do," she said briskly, before the man could argue further. "Take my clothes with you." She stepped aside to indicate the large travel pack.

"What will ye wear?" he demanded.

Elspeth threw aside the edges of her cloak to reveal a plain woolen gown. "Ena has found me garments more suitable to my new life here at Kinduin."

The knight's eyes rounded in horror. "Laird Lionel'd have a fit if he saw ye in that. Why, they're scarce good enough for—"

"The silks I wore before are nae sturdy enough for the life of a lady of a Highland laird... which is what I am."

"But why are ye doin' this?"

To prove a point. But she doubted Sir Giles would understand. He'd lived most of his life at Carmichael Castle, first as a page, then a squire and finally a knight. To him, ladies were soft, gentle things garbed in silks. "Besides—" Elspeth smoothed the wool over her hips "—they're really quite soft and much warmer than my...my former clothes. I want you to take these to Curthill and sell them."

"Sell them?" Sir Giles gasped.

"Aye." A bit of peacock blue silk stuck out of the neck of the pack. Suppressing a wistful sigh, Elspeth bent and tucked it out of sight. She had loved that gown. Mayhap Ena could dye some wool that color, she thought as she straightened to face Sir Giles's outraged expression. "Sell them, and with the money, you're to buy supplies for Kinduin. I've written a list." She pulled a roll of parchment from her sleeve. "Give this to Lady Mary at Curthill. She'll know exactly what I need."

"If ye say so, m'lady," Sir Giles grumbled, years of taking orders from Carmichaels ingrained in his nature.

"Aye." She'd show Lucais she wasn't greedy or weak. She was made of sterner stuff than he could possibly imagine, else she'd not have endured four years with Raebert. She'd come to the Highlands to make a home, and that's what she'd do. She'd vowed to be Lucais's wife for a year and a day, and she'd do that, too.

Apprehension gnawed at her confidence. 'Twas one thing to turn Kinduin into a fine home and reign as chatelaine. Quite another to perform the more private duties Lucais would expect of his lady wife. Could she bring herself to be intimate with him?

Chapter Eleven

Daibidh Sutherland's hut was made of stone and sat apart from the others in the village. Squat and dark, it crouched at the edge of the forest where the ferns and mushrooms grew. An appropriate dwelling for the man who guarded the Sutherland legends—a man who was nearly a legend himself.

As Lucais strode up the path toward the hut, the sounds of the village faded to a hum. Even the stink of drying fish lessened, held at bay by the breeze from the trees. Pausing, he lifted his face to savor the sweet smell of pine, the tang of wood smoke and damp earth. Mysteriously the troubles that plagued him seemed to ease. Aye, there was magic here, the same sort of hushed beauty that pervaded the broch in the glen. Small wonder. Local lore had it that the same people who had built it had built this old hut to shelter the soothsayers of Clan Sutherland.

Hopefully Daibidh would be willing to share a few of his secrets, Lucais thought. Closing the distance to the building, he knocked on the weathered door, then stepped back a respectful distance to wait. With any luck, the old man wasn't out wandering the woods or whatever it was wizards did with their time.

"Come in, Lucais," called a faint, raspy voice.

'Twas the same greeting he always got, but it still sent a shiver down Lucais's spine. Daibidh was a hermit. Even his own kin were not welcome, yet he not only tolerated Lucais's visits, he seemed to anticipate them.

The door opened to his touch, creaking back on thick leather hinges. Inside 'twas dark and gloomy, the air heavy with the smoke that rose from a small hearth in the center of the hut's only room and escaped out the hole in the roof. It smelled faintly of spice and earth and alchemy. Lucais tensed.

There were no windows. The only light came from the tiny fire and a sputtering candle set in a wall sconce in the far corner of the room. Beneath it sat a table strewn with parchment rolls so old they were cracked and yellow. Wooden chests banded with iron lined the smoke-stained walls. Above them hung shelves crowded with a jumble of crockery jars and stoppered flasks. How old Daibidh found a thing in here was beyond Lucais.

"I manage right well." The crisp words, spoken in Gaelic, jerked Lucais's gaze to the figure sitting cross-legged on a pallet at the far side of the fire.

"Doubtless because most of the knowledge is in your head," Lucais replied. He lifted a brow in a silent request for an audience, received a regal nod in return. Rounding the hearth, Lucais dropped down at Daibidh's right. The earthen floor was packed hard as stone and just as cold. He suppressed a second shiver and wondered how Daibidh managed to stay warm.

The ancient one was thin as a wraith, clad only in scuffed leather boots and a long black robe so threadbare even the most pious monk would have disdained it. His face, what little of it Lucais could see in the shadows cast by the cowl, was smooth and creaseless, ageless. Stretched tight over high cheekbones and the prominent Sutherland nose, his skin was as yellowed as his old scrolls. His teeth were gone, giving his mouth a sunken look, but the eyes that gazed out from beneath sparse white brows were a bright, clear gold, merciless and piercing as the noon sun.

"Ye've somethin' to show me." The old man held out his hand.

Without question, Lucais reached into his pouch, brought out the two coins and set them gently into the bony brown palm.

Daibidh jerked as though he'd been burned, clawlike fingers snapping shut. "Where did ye get these?"

So, the old man was not all-seeing. Lucais drew in a steadying breath, then let it out and related the events of the last few days, beginning with the arrival of Elspeth and her men, ending with his trip to the glen to look for Wee Wat's dirk. "You recognize the coins." A statement, not a question.

Daibidh did not respond. He sat motionless, the hand holding the coins pressed to his breast, his strange eyes fixed on the leaping flames. Reflecting back the reds and oranges, they glowed as hotly as the fire. The silence deepened, grew around them; the smell of the smoke changed, sweetened so Lucais fancied it smelled of lavender. Of Elspeth.

"She is the one I've been expectin'," the old man muttered.

Lucais jumped. "She is?" Was that good, or bad?

Daibidh slowly turned his head, focusing his too bright gaze on Lucais. "I foresaw this, but I didna ken 'twould be so soon."

"What is it? What do you see?"

"Death."

Oh God. "Elspeth's?" Lucais croaked, dying inside.

"What I see is more important than one woman. 'Tis the death of what once was." He paused. "The broch has been violated."

"By Elspeth?"

"Nay. Not yet."

"Meanin' she does intend to." He knew it. "I'll...I'll send her away." Though the idea nearly killed him. "I'll..."

"'Tis too late for that. Forces ha' already been set in motion. Evil forces."

Lucais shuddered. "The Munros." Please let it be his enemy and not his wife.

"Aye. The Munros are our enemy," the old man said, and Lucais breathed a sigh of relief. 'Twas short-lived. "But there's something else at work. Ye felt it when ye were at the broch."

Lucais felt it again, like an icy finger drawn down his spine. "What is it?"

"A power beyond our imaginin'." Daibidh looked into the fire, then quickly back at Lucais. "They should ha' heeded the warnings. They never should ha' entered the broch."

"The Munros got inside and stole those coins," Lucais guessed. "Durin' the battle with Wee Wat, Seamus dropped them."

"The coins belonged to the ancient ones."

Air hissed through Lucais's teeth as the pieces fell into place. According to legend, the broch contained the bones of the Sutherlands. 'Twas what made the place sacred to his clan. Given the fact that the ancients had often buried their dead dressed in fine garments and accompanied by all their worldly goods, Seamus's sudden interest in the broch now came horribly clear. Wee Wat had not been far off the mark this morn when he'd warned of treasure hunters. "How did they get inside?" he murmured.

"Does it matter?"

"Nay. But I'd wager my soul they havena found more than these coins, or they wouldna be hanging about the place like scavengers at a kill." Too angry and frustrated to sit still, Lucais jumped up to pace the narrow confines of the hut. "I'll step up the patrols in the area."

"It might be wise."

"Shall I try to put the coins back?"

Daibidh shook his head. "I wouldna ha' ye risk runnin' afoul of the curse that guards the broch."

"Aye, the curse," Lucais said softly, his thoughts on Elspeth, so determined to get inside the broch. When he returned to Kinduin, he'd assign a guard to follow her. She'd be furious with him, of course, but that was nothing new. It crossed his mind again that it might be best to send her home. 'Twas a measure of how much he wanted her that he rejected the idea. Besides, he did not truly believe in curses and such. Only in evil, greedy men. "If there is a curse, why didna it seek revenge against the Munros?"

"Who's to say it didna?" Daibidh retorted. "'Tis been my experience that curses work in mysterious ways."

"No instant hail of ghostly arrows?" Lucais quipped.

Daibidh smiled faintly. "I warned yer grandsire that ye had an irreverent streak."

"I prefer to call it reason and logic."

"Aye, ye've that, Lion of the Sutherlands. And a stout heart, as well, else ye wouldna ha' done so well by our clan. Take care yer heart doesna lead ye astray."

"What do you mean? Is Elspeth a threat?"

"Keep her close to ye," the old man muttered, then he turned back to the fire and shut his eyes, ending the discussion.

The cryptic words echoed in Lucais's head as he left for the keep, pounded in time with his horse's hooves. Keep her close. Why? Was she threatened, or a threat? By the time Kinduin's walls came in sight, his nerves were pulled tighter than a drawn bow.

Daibidh's way of speaking in riddles had never annoyed or frightened him more. The old man had obviously foreseen Elspeth's coming...a fact he'd not mentioned before, damn his hide...and clearly he feared trouble. Death, to be precise. But whose? The possibilities made Lucais's blood run cold despite the warmth of the sun. Was Elspeth in danger? Or was she a danger to the clan?

Nay, he rejected the idea instantly. Elspeth was not bad; she was imperious, impatient and hot-tempered. Those same passions that fired his love for her could also be her downfall. He needed to take steps to keep her safe, even from her own schemes. Which reminded him of her hints that she had a deed to the broch. Later tonight, he'd search her belongings again.

As he waited for Kinduin's drawbridge to be lowered, Lucais lifted his gaze to the tower visible over the walls, and to one window in particular. Was Elspeth in their chamber?

Their chamber. The words conjured up the hopes and dreams he'd held so long they were part of his blood. Dreams of forging a life with the only woman he'd ever loved. Hopes that she'd someday come to love him, too. A foolish hope that had not seemed so foolish last night when she'd fought to save Black Jock, then slept peacefully in his arms. But the harsh lights of the hall this noon had opened his eyes, made him see Kinduin as she must.

The walls were rough, the furnishings old and plain, the timbers of the vaulted ceiling black with smoke. Ena and the maids did their best to keep things clean, but they needed a woman to guide them as his grandmother had. Was Elspeth that woman? He desperately wanted her to be, providing she wasn't a Munro spy—and in his heart of hearts, he sincerely believed she couldn't be. But could she be happy here?

He must find a way to make it so, Lucais thought as he urged his mount over the drawbridge. Barely had he cantered into the bailey when he met a party of clansmen charging out.

"Lucais!" Cathal's horse reared as he reined in. "There's another boar been sighted in the woods. We're off to get it." That Cathal and some of the men with him had spent the hours since the feast polishing off the keg of ale was evident from their flushed faces and unfocused eyes.

Normally Lucais would not have interfered, trusting the sober ones to keep the rest from harm. But Daibidh's talk of death had made him edgy. "Leave the boar for now. I've another task I'd set you to."

"I'm huntin' boar," Cathal growled.

"What if I order you to stay?"

Cathal stiffened. "Ye'd do that?" The Sutherlands milling around them exchanged uneasy glances. Even the horses sensed the tension, tossing their heads and snorting.

"Do I have to?" Lucais met the older man's glare levelly, silently reminding him they'd had this out once before. The confrontation had begun the day old Angus died and Lucais assumed command; it had ended on the training field below the keep with Cathal on his back, Lucais's blade pressed to his throat.

"Mayhap the woman has softened ye," Cathal grumbled.

"Leave it, Da," said Cathal's younger son. " 'Tis too hot to hunt boar." Obviously Harry was smarter than his sire.

"What about huntin' Munros?" Lucais asked, hiding a smile as Cathal's expression altered from sullen to avid.

"Ye've a mind to break that cursed truce?" he asked.

"I'm thinkin' on it." Of bending it at least. "But we've plans to make first, and I'll send out no drunkards."

"Aye, we'll need our wits about us to fight those bastards," someone shouted, evoking a chorus of agreement. The crowd broke up, men talking excitedly as they turned back toward the stables.

"I'd speak with Sir Giles," Lucais said as Cathal made to follow the others. Setting the Carmichaels to guard Elspeth would free up more Sutherlands to watch the broch. "Have you seen him?"

Cathal's mouth twisted into a parody of a smile. "Oh, aye. They packed up their things and rode out just after ye left."

"Elspeth, too?"

"Dunno. I've better things to do than watch that bitch—"

Lucais didn't wait to hear more. Spurring his mount to the keep, he leapt from the saddle and raced up the steps to the entryway. *She couldn't be gone. She couldn't.* Chest heaving, hands clenched into fists, he tore through the hall, took the steep, winding stairs to the second floor at breakneck speed and flung open the door to his chamber.

It crashed back against the wall, the sound echoing through the room, drawing a startled gasp from Gillie, who stood atop a stool in front of the window. She had a length of material draped over one shoulder, and all he could think was that she'd been into his things again.

"Gillie. You've been warned a hundred times not to sneak in here where you dinna belong," he shouted, advancing on her. Before he'd gone two steps, Elspeth leapt up from where she'd been crouching beside the stool. The sight of her here, when he'd feared she'd left him, transfixed Lucais to the spot.

Elspeth had no such difficulty. "Gillie's your daughter," she cried, and flew at him like an avenging angel. "She has as much right to be here as I do." To emphasize the point, she hit him in the chest. He barely felt it.

"You are still here. You didna leave," he murmured.

"I wouldna go back on my word," she snapped. "I promised to be your wife for a year and a day."

He wanted more, so much more. "Aye, so you did," he said hoarsely, goaded by the fears and distrust that had been building all day. To hell with patience. The only one way to bind her to him was with passion. "But I've yet to see any wifely devotion."

The face she raised to him was so white he feared she might faint. "What...what do you mean?" she whispered.

"You know full well what I mean."

Elspeth gasped. Despite her wariness, the heat of his gaze ignited an answering spark deep inside her. Memories of the kiss they'd shared, the warmth, the heady excitement, warred with logic. Once she'd trusted Raebert, and look where that had gotten her. "Nay, I canna..." She swayed, would have collapsed if he hadn't grabbed hold of her upper arms to steady her.

Gillie cried out and squeezed between them.

Elspeth looked down at the lass they'd forgotten in the heat of battle. Touched by the concern in the small lass she'd come to love, she soothed, "He willna harm me." 'Twas true, she realized. In spite of his anger and the threatening way he towered over her, Lucais's grip on her arms was surprisingly gentle. No matter what she'd done to him, he had never hurt her physically.

"If you believe that, then why do you deny me?" he asked.

The pain underlying his words brought Elspeth's head up. The anguish in his eyes took her breath away. *What do you want from me?* But she already knew the answer, knew he wanted more than she could give him or any other man. Yet part of her longed to try, to reach for the things his kisses had promised. That was what frightened her. "I . . . I need time."

Her eyes met his and were caught, trapped by the desire glittering there. The air backed up in her lungs as she suddenly became aware of how close he stood. She shivered, trying to ignore the insidious way his warmth stole into her chilled body.

But he knew. The tautness in his mouth eased, replaced by a slow, lazy smile that made her heart leap. "Time? I've waited years for you already, Beth."

Had he really wanted her that long, that desperately? Elspeth's mouth went dry. She licked her lips, had her answer in the hungry way his eyes followed the path her tongue had taken. Mayhap he had not wed her just to save her from Seamus. Mayhap, despite her rejection and his obvious distrust, he still cared for her. Inside her, the tiny flame grew, feeding off the heat in his gaze, in the hand he raised to gently caress her cheek.

"What about my new gown, Mama?" Gillie interjected.

Mama? Elspeth blinked, but was distracted from responding to this startling development by the tremor that shook Lucais.

"Sh-she spoke," Lucais exclaimed.

"Aye." Smugly. Elspeth expected him to hug his bairn or say something profound. If he'd avoided Gillie in part because of her supposed idiocy, here was proof the lass could speak.

Some tortured emotion darkened his eyes, deepened the furrows bracketing his mouth. "Lady Elspeth isna your mama," he said, raw and anguished. "Go find Ena."

"Lucais!" Elspeth exclaimed, shocked by his outburst, angered by the pain that crumpled Gillie's features.

"I've things to say and need no audience," he replied.

"Surely there are kinder ways—"

Lucais sighed. "There are things you dinna understand. Reasons why 'tis best she isna underfoot."

"Underfoot! You barely tolerate her presence."

Nor did he deny it. "I have my reasons."

"None that can possibly justify being cruel to your own bairn." Elspeth wrenched free of his grasp, but Gillie had gone, vanishing quietly, as was her custom. Cursing under her breath, Elspeth started for the door, only to be stopped by Lucais's voice.

"Let her go. I've something we must discuss."

"Her feelings are more important than anything you could say to me," Elspeth shot back, in no mood to listen.

"I know you think me harsh and cruel, but I can barely look at her without seein' Jean and rememberin'..."

Elspeth sucked in air, feeling as though the ground had been pulled from beneath her feet. *He still loved Jean.* Loved her so fiercely he could not bear to be in the same room with the bairn they'd created. *Sweet Mary, what must it be like to be loved so deeply, so strongly?* She wanted to know. Wanted desperately...

He sighed and rubbed the back of his neck. "Speak with me now, I'll make amends to her later."

Elspeth stared at him, too numb with longing to reply.

"I'd have peace between us," he added.

"Aye," she managed to reply. She wanted peace, craved it after her terrible marriage to Raebert. "But how can you think of... of bedding me when you still... love Jean?"

Lucais blinked. How could she think he loved Jean? Because of what he'd said about Gillie. He started to disagree, but knew admitting he'd never loved Jean would spawn questions he couldn't answer. "Jean and Raebert are both dead," he said slowly, weighing every word. "'Tis time we got on with our lives."

"I suppose." God knew 'twas part of the reason she'd come north, but could she lie with him? The thought of being touched by him, kissed by him, seduced by him, was heady and frightening. She shivered as he gestured her into one of the chairs that flanked the fireplace. Nervous, she perched on the edge.

Lucais lifted a flask from the nearby table, filled two cups with wine and handed her one. As she grasped the cool metal, his fingers moved to lightly clasp her wrist. "What of you, Beth? I need to know what you want." His low, husky voice slid across her skin like a caress, leaving gooseflesh behind.

Trembling, she struggled to collect her scattered thoughts. She, who'd always rushed headlong after what she wanted, even when 'twas a mistake, felt shy, uncertain. "To stay here at Kinduin and to have peace between us."

"I want that, too." And more. The sensual promise darkening his eyes frightened her, but she was more afraid of the things it stirred to life deep inside her. Wild things. Sweet things. Things she longed to explore but didn't dare, for 'twould mean trusting this strong, mercurial man.

"Does—does my being here mean so much to you?" she stammered.

"You must know it does." His voice was tight and raspy as her breathing. Yet he made no move to act on the desire simmering in his eyes, just continued to stare down at her.

The tension between them coiled tighter so it seemed to suck the air from the room. She was drowning, and it didn't help matters when his thumb moved to caress the back of her hand. Gentle as his touch was, it made her whole body vibrate. Tiny ripples radiated out from the spot where he lazily stroked her skin, flooding her with unexpected heat. She swayed, buffeted by conflicting urges. Lean closer. Run. Something had to give, she thought, but not her, not yet. Not till she was sure she'd be safe. Slipping free of his grasp, she looked away, sought distance in words. "I-it didna seem so at dinner. You were bent on making it seem I wasna suited to be lady of Kinduin."

She was surprised—and disappointed—when he didn't try to recapture her hand, but dropped into the other chair instead. " 'Tis Kinduin that isna good enough for you."

"I agree it has a few rough edges. After you'd gone to the village, I asked Ena for a tour of the keep. I dinna see aught that canna be set to rights with time and—"

He frowned. "I dinna have the coin to spend on expensive tapestries and fine wines from France."

"I was going to say hard work," Elspeth retorted. "We can make our own tapestries, if your heart is set on them. Personally, I didna think men cared for such things."

"But women do. You do. 'Tis what you're used to." He sighed, turning the cup in his hands. "I only visited Carmichael Castle once with Laird Eammon, but I still recall 'twas like being wrapped in silk and sunlight."

"And 'tis run as efficiently as a monastery. Boring," Elspeth said flatly, drawing an exclamation of surprise from him. She hadn't understood it herself until 'twas too late. The monotony of life at home had been one reason she'd been so enchanted with life at court. Too late she'd learned that beneath the glitter and laughter lurked an evil that would nearly cost her her life. "I hadna realized how boring until we left Curthill and began to climb into the Highlands," she went on, shaking off the memories of the past, looking to the future. "The air was so crisp, the land so wild, so untamed. I knew this was where I wanted to live." Then she'd had her sights set on Broch Tower as a home. Now she readily admitted the place was not habitable. But it still fascinated her, and she still intended to see what it was like inside. After all, 'twas hers. "You, of all people, should know how much I relish a challenge."

Indeed he did. 'Twas part of the reason he'd opposed her whenever they met...to prevent her from walking all over him or, worse, dismissing him as spineless. Still, he wanted to be more than her latest crusade. "So, you'll stay here until the task is completed, then be off?"

Indecision flickered in her gaze, terrifying him. "We're handfasted for a year and a day. I'll stay that long."

Her announcement chilled him, nearly sent him to his knees to beg her not to go. Nearly. Dredging deep, he found the strength to hide his pain. "It may take longer than that, since I've no coin to spare for fripperies like—"

"I promise to buy no wine or tapestries . . . if you'll give me leave to make improvements."

That she asked instead of demanded was another mark of this new maturity of hers. He masked his growing love behind a scowl. "What of the ledgers and tally sticks?"

She sighed, looked toward the counting room. The door stood open, revealing a table covered with piles of parchment scraps. "I've matched up the pieces of each page and begun the task of recopying them...."

"But. With you, there is always a but."

She scowled right back at him. "Surely you canna expect me to spend all my time working on them. I'd go blind."

"And you canna bear to be cooped up inside."

"Nay." Her mouth pursed into a pout he longed to kiss.

"In that we are much alike," he reasoned. Though from her puzzled look, he knew she didn't yet recognize it. "I would make you a bargain," he said before she could voice the difference she had always harped on—she'd been born a lady, he the son of a tailor. "You have free run inside Kinduin's walls if you promise not to leave unescorted or to visit the broch."

Her chin came up. "What makes you think I'd try?"

"Because you are curious as a cat." And possessive. Unless he missed his guess, she thought of it as hers. "This morn you said something about havin' a deed to the broch," he slipped in.

Elspeth blanched, her eyes darting to her boots, where they sat by the hearth. "I...I have the map, which you've seen."

Not a lie, exactly, but Lucais was saddened to realize she withheld the truth. "Elspeth, I'd have honesty between us."

"And I, too, but—"

Just then, Ena burst into the room. "Gillie's run off."

'Twas full dark by the time the search party left to look for Gillie. A quarter moon peeked down through the leaves as they raced along the narrow, rutted road toward the village. They couldn't ride fast enough to suit Elspeth.

Gillie had been seen near the wagon of the village smithy, and it seemed likely she'd crawled inside his wagon for the trip to the village. But once there, there was no telling what sort of trouble the lively, inquisitive lass would get into.

"How much farther?" Elspeth asked, leaning over the neck of Lucais's mount as it strained ahead of the twenty clansmen who accompanied them.

"Sit still or you'll fall off," he growled, hauling her back against his chest. "Damn, I shouldna have brought you along."

"I'd have followed will you, nill you." That threat was the only reason he had grudgingly agreed to bring her. Even so, he'd insisted she ride with him, for safety's sake. Elspeth didn't know whether to be outraged over his high-handedness or flattered by his protectiveness. Typical. The man confounded her at every turn, she thought, straightening as the village came into view.

They were challenged by a pair of mounted men as they left the woods. Nor was this the first patrol they'd run into since leaving Kinduin, testimony to Lucais's vigilance against the threat of a Munro attack.

Though she hated Raebert and feared Seamus, it seemed strange to think of Alain as an enemy. More like another brother. And, too, he hadn't been with Seamus at the broch.

Elspeth had a brief impression of whitewashed huts set in orderly rows as they swept into the village and drew rein before a timber building she assumed was the stables. Her guess was confirmed as the door of the building opened and a muscular giant stepped into the torchlit yard.

"Is aught amiss, Lucais?" the smith asked.

"My daughter's missin'." Though Elspeth swore he hadn't a care for the poor lass, Lucais didn't stumble over claiming her as he told the smith she'd been seen near his wagon.

"I havena seen the lass runnin' about," the smith said. "But my wagon is within, and I've yet to unpack it."

"Mayhap Gillie fell asleep," Elspeth said. "I'll go wake her so she isna startled by so many fierce men."

"By me, you mean," Lucais said, voice low and tight. "I drove her away. And if she's hurt, I'll never forgive myself."

Elspeth laid a hand on his stubbled cheek. "I'm certain she's fine. We'll sort out the rest later." He loved the lass; that was all that mattered. Once they were back at Kinduin, she would heal the breach between father and daughter, as she longed to ease the estrangement with her own sire.

"Come, I'll walk you partway." Lucais swung down, lifted her from the saddle and escorted her to the open doorway.

Walking in the pool of light cast by the smith's torch, Elspeth crossed the tiny stables and lifted the tarp at the back of the wagon. The sight of Gillie curled up in a pile of rope, her finger in her mouth, made Elspeth smile.

"Is she all right?" Lucais whispered, and she turned to find him peering anxiously over her shoulder.

Gillie chose that moment to wake up. Blinking owlishly, she rubbed her eyes, then smiled. "Mama. Ye came for me."

The pang that went through Elspeth was intensified by the unhappiness that crossed Lucais's features. Was he thinking of Jean? "Nay, I'm nae your mama," she said as gently as she could.

"We need to get back," Lucais muttered. Reaching past Elspeth, he plucked Gillie from the wagon. The girl cried out and reached for Elspeth, but Lucais kept walking.

Elspeth rushed after them. "I can take her."

"She's heavy and you're tired," Lucais said as they reached the doorway. Before Elspeth could argue, a rider galloped up.

Sawing on the reins of his mount, he yelled, "Munros!"

"Where?" Lucais cried.

"On the ridge, comin' this way."

"Mount up," Lucais growled, expression fierce, eyes blazing. The men who'd come with them leapt into the saddle as he thrust Gillie into Elspeth's arms. "Stay in the stables. Dinna come out until I return for you."

Easier said than done. Oh, Elspeth dutifully crouched in the darkened building, a terrified Gillie clinging to her neck. But when the doors Lucais had closed behind him were suddenly wrenched open and a flaming torch thrust inside to ignite the straw, she knew she couldn't stay put another moment.

Clutching Gillie to her, Elspeth dashed from the building...and ran straight into a hard, mailed body. "Lucais?"

"Nay, 'tis me," came a voice she'd heard at another fire. Looking up, Elspeth found herself facing Alain Munro.

"Alain? Sweet Mary, what do you here?"

"I've come to take ye home wi' me," Alain replied.

"Are you mad? What if the Sutherlands find you?"

He shrugged. "They're right busy." Too true. Flames shot up from several burning huts. By that terrible light, knots of men writhed in mortal combat. Gruesome sounds filled the night, the shouts of the attackers, the shrieks of the defenders, the screams of the wounded. "I'd hoped to create a diversion and lure the Sutherlands from the keep so I could look for ye."

His grin turned wolfish. "'Tis sheer luck to find ye here in the village."

"You . . . you started this to get me?" At his nod, Elspeth's fears grew. This wasn't the quiet, gentle Alain she knew. Moving cautiously, she put Gillie down and tucked the crying bairn behind her. No telling what he'd do if he learned Gillie was Lucais's. "Why are you doing this?"

"To save you from makin' another mistake. Lucais isna the man for ye."

And he was? Elspeth shivered, but, conscious of Gillie behind her, asked, "If I go with you now, will you call off the attack?"

"A moot point." Lucais stepped from darkness into light. "Since I willna let you go." Bathed in the glow of the burning stables, his face looked fierce, terrifying. "It seemed I underestimated your eagerness to leave, Elspeth. I wouldna have thought you'd stoop to killin' innocents to get your way."

"I had no part in this," Elspeth cried, but even as she spoke, Lucais pushed her aside and raised his sword.

"En garde, Munro!" Lucais shouted.

"Nay!" Alain was no swordsman. Much as she deplored his actions, Elspeth couldn't stand by and see him slaughtered. She owed him her life. Acting on instinct, she leapt between the two men, throwing herself on Lucais's sword arm and momentarily immobilizing it. "Run!" she called to Alain.

Chapter Twelve

"I wasna running away," Elspeth said wearily. 'Twas the hundredth time she'd repeated the words, but Lucais didn't answer. He just sat in the high-backed chair before the hearth in their chamber, his stony gaze fixed on the flickering fire.

'Twas late, way past midnight. Alain had escaped. The Munros had been driven off, the fires in the village extinguished and Gillie brought back to bed. Through the open window, Elspeth heard the faint sounds of the Sutherlands in the hall below, licking their wounds and plotting their revenge. Doubtless they schemed to be rid of her, as well, she thought, heart heavy with sorrow and remorse. Why could she not make Lucais believe her?

Slowly, Elspeth approached him. While she'd seen to Gillie and changed clothes, he'd removed his armor. Clad in a bed robe lined with marten fur, he sat with bare feet extended toward the dwindling embers, a cup dangling nearly forgotten in his right hand. His face was cold and remote as chiseled granite. He'd not looked at her since she'd aided Alain in escaping, not even when he'd set her before him on his horse and ridden back to Kinduin.

Elspeth had never been one to care much what others thought, but Lucais's censure pierced her to the quick. Something precious had blossomed between them in the stables last night. She'd not let Alain's actions kill that fragile flower. "I couldna let you kill him," she whispered, willing him to listen.

A muscle in his cheek leapt as he flexed his jaw. "What of the villagers? Do you care how many of them died?"

"Died?" Elspeth's legs went weak and she sank onto the carpet beside the chair, a hand on his knee. "H-how many?"

"None," he spat, fury blazing in the gaze he turned on her. "But 'twas only because the lads and I were close by when the bastards struck. Still there's three huts burned down, three families going without because Alain Munro thought to free you."

"I didna ask him to come for me. I deplore his actions," she said stoutly. "But neither could I let you kill him."

Lucais's eyes narrowed. "Why?"

"Because he saved my life."

He raised a skeptical brow. "When?"

"The night Raebert died." Though she'd sworn never to speak of what had happened, she knew 'twas the only way to make him understand. "Raebert came to my room. This time he didna want money. He'd come to tell me he was going to Stourie in the morn. He said he no longer needed me or the money I brought him."

"Oh, Elspeth . . ."

"Dinna pity me," she snapped, but she didn't argue when he lifted her to sit on his lap. "The day we were wed, he made it brutally clear he'd wed me for my dowry." Held safe in Lucais's embrace, she found the words surprisingly easy to say. "That last night I was glad he no longer needed it or me. But when I wanted to return to my family, he said he had other plans." She shivered, recalling his ugly sneer, his cruel laughter.

Lucais folded her closer, his hand stroking her back through her bed robe. "You dinna have to tell me if it upsets you."

Elspeth put her hand on his chest, left bare by the open vee of his robe and drew strength from the steady beat of his heart. "I want you to understand. He . . . he intended to marry his mistress when he returned. For that he needed to . . . to . . ."

"To kill you," Lucais said in an appalled whisper.

She swallowed and nodded. "He had the knife out before I suspected his evil intent, but a Carmichael doesna go down without a fight. I grabbed up the iron candle stand from beside the chair where I'd been reading. All I wanted to do was drive him off." Her nails sank into Lucais's flesh, her eyes dilated with remembered horror. "He . . . he dodged. I lashed out..." She drew in a ragged breath. "The edge of the metal struck him in the temple. He went down like a felled oak."

Lucais ached for her. "You have no cause to regret killin' him, Beth. You were defendin' yourself."

"Aye, but I didna kill him. He was breathing. I saw his chest rise and fall." Her eyes beseeched Lucais to believe. "But the drapes caught fire from the candle. I...I tried to rouse him, but couldna. I tried to move him, but he was too heavy. By the time I returned with the servants, the whole room was in flames. Alain arrived then. He said 'twas hopeless, dragged me back just as the beams collapsed. He saved my life."

Lucais nodded, feeling rage eat at his soul. Fury for what she'd endured, regret that he hadn't been there to help. But he was here now. Swallowing his hatred of the Munros, he said, "I can see why you aided Alain." Though he didn't like it. His reward was in her sigh of relief, the way she sagged against him. He smoothed back the tendrils of hair that had worked loose from her thick braid. Cradling her head in his palm, he pressed it into the hollow of his shoulder. "You're safe now, lass."

"I know." She snuggled deeper into his embrace, her hand idly stroking his chest. An innocent gesture, but her touch made his skin heat and tingle. His pulse raced with possibilities he could not act on. Not with all she'd been through tonight.

But he wanted to. God, how he wanted to. His lower body tightened in response to that need. Seated on his lap, she had to feel the changes taking place in him, yet she made no move to flee. Glancing down, he saw her eyes were closed, her profile relaxed, pale and delicate in contrast to his tanned hand. 'Twas heaven to sit here with his arms around her, his fingers tangled in her silky black hair, her thigh pressed against the growing proof of his desire. 'Twas hell to know he could not, in all honor, take what he so desperately craved.

He wanted her. Even knowing that a man's lust caused a woman pain and degradation, Elspeth didn't leap up and run. Her mouth went dry, but 'twasn't wholly fear. 'Twas her inbred curiosity that made her pulse quicken in time to the beat of his heart as she splayed her fingers over his warm resilient flesh. Raebert had been a big man, too. But a beast with shaggy black hair and a bulky body he'd used to ruthlessly subdue her. Lucais was more leanly built, his chest a broad expanse of bronzed skin stretched over sleek muscles. The way red gold hair curled around her fingers fascinated her.

"Beth?" He said, low and husky.

"Mmm?" She shifted her head to meet his gaze. The raw sensuality glittering in his hazel eyes took her breath away, sent a shiver of dread racing down her spine. It took a heartbeat for her to realize his passion was held carefully in check by the iron will she'd both admired and resented. "You should be abed."

"With you?" she asked, and found the idea more intriguing than frightening.

His big body trembled. "Nay. I'll sit here awhile."

Elspeth frowned, perversely piqued by his gallantry. Challenged by it. "Is it because of Jean or because I was wed to your enemy that you dinna want me in your bed?"

"What?" He looked stunned; she felt better. "If you dinna know how you affect me, you're the most innocent—"

"I know what happens between a man and a woman," she said stiffly. Raebert had raped her four times before she'd managed to get a dirk and use the blade to forge an uneasy truce. She coaxed money from her family and in exchange he did not bed her.

Seeing the spasm of loathing that curdled her features, Lucais guessed the experience had been as vile as the other glimpses she'd given him into her marriage. Damn, he should have kidnapped her four years ago and forced her to wed him. Of course, that's what he'd done this time, he thought uneasily. "What happens in bed differs from couple to couple," he said to reassure her. "For two people who love one another, it can bring great joy."

"Is that how it was with you and Jean?" Bitterness filled Elspeth's mouth. Surprising, since she'd never been jealous of Raebert's mistress. That Lucais flinched and looked away made the gnawing in her chest worse. "I ... I shouldna have asked."

Lucais sighed. "To my everlasting shame, there was little pleasure and no joy in our joinin'."

"But ... but she bore you Gillie."

"Aye." The pain in that single word made Elspeth shiver, but Lucais misunderstood the cause. "You're chilled," he growled. Tightening his grip on her with reassuring possessiveness, he added, "You'll be warmer in bed."

"Nay, I'd be cold without you," Elspeth said, knowing he'd put her to bed alone and unwilling to be parted from him. Sitting with him like this was exhilarating. A little like dancing too close to the edge of a cliff—one misstep and she'd fall. But when he looked at her the way he was now, as if she were a ripe peach and he a starving man, she felt so dizzy she feared she already was falling...under his spell.

"Jesu, Beth," Lucais groaned. "When you look at me like that, 'tis damned difficult for me to keep my wits about me."

The little minx cocked her head. "How am I looking?"

"Like you were wishin' I'd kiss you."

"What if I am?" Elspeth asked, aware from the darkening of his eyes that she danced closer to the edge.

"Are you sure?" When she nodded, he captured her chin, tilted her face up to bind her gaze with his. "I know Raebert hurt you, gave you a fear of men. Did he use you ill in bed as well as out? God knows I'd rather forget you were ever wed to him, Beth, but I have to know what he did, because I'd sooner die than frighten you somehow in my ignorance."

Elspeth trembled like a rabbit in a trap, but there was no escaping his piercing gaze. "He...he raped me."

Lucais groaned and squeezed his eyes shut. The shudder that rippled through his body touched her. He cared. He really cared. "Too bad he's dead. I'd take great pleasure killin' him."

"What he did matters less and less the longer I'm with you."

Lucais's eyes flew open, bright with surprise and hope. "Truly?" At her nod, he dipped his head to brush a fleeting kiss across her mouth. Too fleeting. "I'd never hurt you."

"I know." Elspeth smiled, conscious of the battle he waged between desire and protectiveness. His gentleness had never been more evident than at this moment, or more welcome. Here was a man worth trusting...worth loving. It hurt immeasurably that although he'd said he understood why she'd let Alain escape, Lucais did not trust her. She knew of no other way to gain his trust than by giving him hers. Reaching up, she framed his face with her hands and drew it down.

Lucais moaned as Elspeth's mouth closed over his, making up for lack of expertise with an enthusiasm that drove the rest of the air from his lungs and every thought from his head save one. Kissing her back. Loving her.

He tasted of wine and passion, Elspeth thought as the firm line of Lucais's lips softened, slanted to give her better access. He tempered her desperation with the silent assurance that he'd deny her nothing. She opened to him, welcoming the sensual thrust of his tongue, her own turning greedy in return.

As it had the night before, something deep inside her broke free, something wild and sweet that drove out fear. She had no past, only this moment and this man who made her whole body come alive. Tight as he held her, 'twasn't enough to ease the ache building low in her belly. Craving more, instinctively knowing he held the cure for the fever in her blood, she strained against him in time to the rhythm of their kiss.

Elspeth's frenzied response ripped at Lucais's control. After years of wanting her, she was here, burning and twisting in his arms. He ran his hands over her, pushing aside her woolen bed robe to cup the sweet swell of her breast. Her groan was like a cold plunge into the icy loch, dragging him back to reality. Wrenching his mouth free, he rasped, "Did I hurt you?"

"You will if you stop." She clutched at his shoulders, cheeks flushed, eyes glittering with passion. "I've never felt this way. 'Tis a little like racing the wind atop a fast horse . . . scary, but exciting. I dinna want it to end."

"Neither do I," Lucais said huskily. "But . . ."

Elspeth smiled. "I'm nae afraid in the least." How could she be when there was no similarity between what Raebert had done and what Lucais was doing? "Take me to bed. Show me all the things you would have done if I hadna been so foolish four years ago."

"Beth," Lucais whispered, marveling that she could trust him after what Raebert had put her through, humbled by the fear that in his overwhelming need for her he'd betray that trust. His legs shook as he stood with her in his arms and crossed to lay her on the sheets Ena had turned down hours ago. Though she smiled up at him, her face was pale against her dark hair, bound still in a loose braid. Another time he'd see it free, flowing across the pillows as it had in his dreams. For now all he wanted was to sink down beside her and fashion a sweet memory to drive out the vile ones Raebert had thrust on her.

"Lucais," Elspeth murmured. His name ended on a sigh as he joined her under the covers, drawing her close and aligning the hard planes of his body with her softer curves. The layers of wool separating them were suddenly unbearable. She tore at them with trembling haste.

Lucais growled in agreement and finished what she had begun, stripping off their robes, glorying in the feel of her smooth, slender body eagerly pressing against him. Slowly. Dimly he realized he must go slowly or he'd frighten her, but his good intentions turned to ashes when her lips parted beneath his. She tasted of honey and passion as his tongue slipped in to parry and thrust in perfect imitation of the more intimate joining to come. Her soft whimpers fired the desire coiling tight in his belly. She was burning him alive, Lucais thought, wrenching his mouth free before her untutored passion led him to madness.

Elspeth moaned as Lucais stitched a trail of fiery kisses from her mouth to the swell of her breasts. His mouth closed over one sensitized peak, drawing down with such devastating sweetness that she arched off the bed. Threading her fingers into his thick hair, she cried his name over and over in a litany of pleasure. 'Twas too much, 'twasn't nearly enough, she dimly thought, glorying in the feel of his hands stroking her heated skin. Her whole body throbbed with a dark, compelling need he seemed to understand, his fingers unerringly drifting to the juncture of her thighs, where the craving was the sharpest.

"Oh," she gasped when he touched her layered softness.

Lucais lifted his head from her breast. "Did I hurt you?"

"Nay," Elspeth gasped, staring up into gold-flecked eyes so filled with concern they cast out any lingering doubts.

"I can stop," Lucais said, and wondered how he could.

"If you do, I'll kill you," she growled.

"Imperious little witch." He laughed, the low, husky sound so at odds with those she was used to hearing in the bedchamber that her heart soared. "Very well, then, have your way with me."

Despite her demands, Elspeth knew a moment of fear as he rose over her. Instinctively she closed her eyes to that part of a man she knew dealt pain. But there was naught save pleasure in the gentle probing of hot, blunt flesh. His slow, patient thrust filled her with wonder, not revulsion. Opening her eyes, she saw him poised above her. The muscles in his throat were corded with the effort it took to control the passion blazing down at her from his hooded gaze.

"Beth?" he whispered, and she knew that if she told him how uncertain she felt he'd somehow find the strength to pull back.

"Oh, Lucais." Heart too full to say more, she lifted her hips to welcome the hard, plunging edge of his hunger. He stretched her body to the limits, yet made her feel complete, heart and soul. A groan of pure pleasure escaped her as she moved with him. He echoed it, setting a pace that carried them higher and higher until the coil inside her splintered.

The sounds of her breathless cries, the feel of her coming apart in his arms, convulsing around him, burned away the last of Lucais's control. Burying himself deep in the core of the sensual explosion, he gave himself up to her, poured into her all the love he dared not express in words.

Elspeth woke to pale dawn light and the stunning realization that she wasn't alone in bed. A large male body was pressed close against her back; his hand stroked her hip. Raebert? she thought, and died a little inside.

"Sorry I woke you," growled a welcome voice.

"Lucais!" Glancing over her shoulder, she saw he lay on his side, his head propped in one hand. "I—I feared last night was a dream," she said shakily.

"Oh, 'twas real enough, and I've the claw marks to prove it," he cheerfully replied.

"Claw marks?"

He grinned lazily, smug and supremely male. "You're a very demandin' lass," he drawled.

Memories of the hot, wild things they'd done last night singed her mind. Elspeth felt the heat creep up from her breasts, decently covered by the sheet, fortunately, to her face. "You make me out a wanton."

"Never that. You are a lovely, passionate woman." He kissed her shoulder, his mouth sliding up her neck, leaving fire in its wake. "What we do together is beautiful," he whispered.

"Aye," Elspeth answered in kind. "I never imagined . . ."

"I did." His tongue darted into the shell of her ear, making her shiver with longing and regret. "None of that," he murmured, reading her thoughts as easily as ever. "There isna any sense in lookin' back when we've the rest of our lives ahead of us."

A beautiful sentiment. Sighing, Elspeth rolled onto her back and stared up at the enigmatic man who was her husband. He grinned, looking unbearably handsome in the pearly light filtering in through the open drapes. His tousled chestnut mane brushed his tanned shoulders; his eyes glowed with carefully banked desire. "What happens now?"

"That depends on you, lass." He lightly caressed her belly with those long, clever fingers that had taught her so much, made her yearn and burn and cry out with the joy she'd found in his arms. She closed her eyes, shivering as sensations spilled through her like molten honey.

Lucais smiled as he felt her muscles contract beneath the warm, satiny skin. She was a very passionate woman. His woman. His wife. His heart expanded so it felt as though it might burst from his chest. *God, how he loved her*. The words sang in his blood, crowded his throat. He held back, sensing she wasn't yet ready to hear them. Prickly as she was, the little minx might see his love as a trap. Still, the primitive need to bind her to him was nearly an obsession. If passion was all she'd accept from him for the moment, he'd use that. With the skill of a master strategist, Lucais set out to reinforce his claim.

Elspeth gasped, eyes flying open as his warm hand slid up to capture her breast. "Oh, Lucais." Arching off the bed, she pressed the hardened peak into his palm and dragged his mouth down for a burning kiss. He tasted of desperation and a hunger that matched the one building inside her. Yet his tongue was oddly elusive, coaxing and beguiling, withholding the mating she sought until greed forced her to turn aggressor. Shoving with all her might, she forced him onto his back and pinned him there. "You are the most maddening man," she snapped.

Lucais laughed, his passion-darkened eyes crinkling at the corners, his hands lightly circling her hips. "Am I now? And here I thought you were a lass who enjoyed takin' charge."

"What I'd like is a little cooperation," she huffed.

He spread his arms wide. "Your eager servant, madam."

Belatedly she became aware of his eagerness throbbing against her thigh. She glanced down his bronzed chest, following the pelt of coppery hair as it veed in at his narrow waist, then flared out again in a nest of bright red curls from which rose the proof of his desire. "Lucais," she whispered, eyes widening.

"See something that interests you?"

"Your hair is very bright . . . there," she said lamely, knowing she should look away but frozen in place, awed, fascinated.

"As the flames of hell," Lucais quipped, looking not the least embarrassed to have her staring at him so. "Though I swear 'twas you who scorched me last night," he added, waggling his sun-kissed brows so wickedly she laughed. "That's better. Now that you're assured of my, er, cooperation, what will you do?"

Elspeth frowned, knowing where she wanted to end up, but not how to begin. He roused her so easily, with a look, a caress, while remaining in complete control. "I dinna know how to start."

"Touch me," he rasped.

Close as they'd been last night, the daylight made her shy. Hesitantly, she laid a hand on his chest, startled by the tremor that shook him as she flexed her fingers, enjoying the textures of crisp hair and warm skin. "Did I do aught wrong?" At the shake of his head she set out to explore, glorying in his deep groan, the way his back arched when she dipped her fingers into his navel.

"Ah, Beth," he gasped. His eyes were closed, his head thrown back on the pillow. Sensual tension corded his chest and arms, had him clutching at the sheet, mute testimony to the effect her touch had on him. The realization that she held such power over this strong, arrogant knight sang in her veins, increased her desire tenfold. 'Twas exhilarating, humbling.

Bold beyond her wildest imagining, Elspeth moved her hand down to catch and hold him. Hot as fire, smooth as satin were the fleeting impressions she got in the instant before her husband cried her name and shifted her onto her back.

"You will be the death of me," Lucais growled, then proceeded to prove they were both very much alive.

And glad of it, Elspeth thought later, much later, when they lay tangled together, sweaty and smugly happy with themselves and each other. But as her breathing slowed, reality intruded, grim and cold. "What will we do now?" she forced herself to ask.

Lucais groaned. "I've created a monster. Give me a few minutes to recover my strength, at least."

"I didna mean *that*," Elspeth said, pinching him on the arm to keep things light, because suddenly the future seemed dark.

Alarmed by the edge in her voice, he raised his head from the haven of her soft throat. "What is it? What troubles you?"

"Everything." Elspeth gripped his neck a little tighter. "Your clan. The Munros." He stiffened, putting space between them, and she was sorry she'd raised these specters, but . . .

"Once my kinsmen come to know you, they'll come around," Lucais said bluntly. They had to. Heavy as the burden of leadership was, he could not bear the added weight of being forced to choose between his people and his wife. The matter of the Munros was a different breed of fish altogether. A fish that stank more foully with every passing day.

"Do you think the Munros will be back?" she asked.

"Likely," he temporized. Greedy as they were, the Munros wouldn't stop until they'd taken the broch apart stone by stone and carted off everything of value. Preventing that was tricky. An all-out war was out of the question. Equal as their numbers were, 'twas likely both clans would be wiped out.

"What will you do to protect your people?"

Lucais glanced down. Her head rested on his shoulder, hair a tumbled black cloud, eyes dark with concern. *Your people,* she'd called the Sutherlands. Too true. Much as he loved her, Elspeth was an outsider here, and it troubled him more than a little to admit he didn't totally trust her. Not where the matter of the Munros and the broch was concerned. Conscious of her watchful gaze and the sharp mind behind it, he launched into the expected litany of increased patrols, extra guards and the like.

Elspeth nodded, but her thoughts had already skipped on to a problem she had a chance of solving. "What of Gillie?" she interjected when he paused for breath. The shock and horror that twisted his handsome features made her heart drop. "Oh, Lucais." She laid her hand on his heart, wishing she could draw out whatever poison lay there. "How can you be so kind to me, after all I've done to hurt you, and be cruel to an innocent bairn?''

The air hissed out between Lucais's teeth and he looked toward the window, doubtless wishing himself anyplace but here. "She's well treated, has everything she needs . . ."

"Except her father's love."

"Elspeth." He raked an exasperated hand through his hair, tried to stand, but she clung to him. "You dinna understand."

"I know she's a reminder of the love you bore her mother." Sweet Mary, it hurt to think of Lucais loving another. "You must put the past behind you, for Gillie's sake."

Lucais closed his eyes to the sight of Elspeth's pale, anxious face. Elspeth might not love him, but she cared deeply for Gillie. Much as he wanted to tell her the truth, the whole truth, he feared 'twould change her concern to loathing. "I will try to be more . . . of a father to her."

"Thank you. I'm certain 'tis what Jean would want," Elspeth whispered, flayed by the whip of her own youthful folly. She'd rejected Lucais, who was worth ten of Raebert any day, and lost him to Jean. Permanently, it seemed. For though he'd said they should forget the past and look to the future, Lucais was still haunted by Jean's memory. What if he never got over his first love? Elspeth wondered, peeking at his proud profile through lowered lashes.

Even in repose, his eyes closed, he was ruggedly handsome, from his arrogant beak of a nose to his stubbornly square chin. Lucais Sutherland was a strong man. Her man. But would he ever truly be hers? Pain welled up inside her, a longing so sharp it nearly choked her. She wanted him to love her.

As she loved him?

Elspeth tensed at the notion, had her answer as Lucais drew her closer, murmuring a sleepy reassurance. Sweet Mary, she did love him. She was challenged by his wit, respected his code of honor, enjoyed his teasing humor and admired his strength. But it was his gentleness, the tender way he'd wooed her last night—despite his mistrust—that had thawed her long-frozen heart.

Surely 'twas the cruelest twist of fate that he yet loved another woman.

But Elspeth was not one to let fate direct her course. She'd refused to give in and let Raebert kill her. She refused to give in and let Jean keep Lucais's heart. Trust. That was the key. Lucais valued trust above all things. If she could find a way to make him trust her, then he just might come to love her.

"Of all the lame, stupid . . ." Seamus threw his cup into the fire, the remaining ale making the flames hiss and jump. Nothing else in the gloomy, crowded hall moved.

"I couldna leave Elspeth wi' him," Alain said.

"Rut on one of the castle wenches if ye've an itch," Seamus snapped. "But dinna waste my men and horseflesh."

Alain let the slight to Elspeth pass. Seamus had no idea how to treat a lady. " 'Tisna a waste. Lucais'll be forced to double the watch on the village now, in case I return."

"But ye willna." Seamus grabbed Alain by the tunic and shook him as a dog would a rat. "I'll slit yer throat from ear from ear if ye do." Dropping Alain, he shouted for more ale.

Alain shrugged his clothes back into place, fists clenched at his sides. He'd have loved to plant one in Seamus's fleshy face, but that luxury would have to wait. "While in Kinduin village, I found something interestin'." He went on to tell his brother about the storage sheds full of fish. "If we'd had more time, we'd ha' relieved the Sutherlands of their bounty, but 'tis my guess they'll soon be takin' the lot to market."

Seamus's eyes gleamed. "Ah. A chance to rob them of their profit and line our pockets." He rubbed his hands together, cackling in gleeful greed. "We'll post a lookout."

"Already done," Alain said smugly. When the maid sidled out of the gloom with two cups of ale, he drank deep of his. "Are we ready to get inside the broch?"

"Aye. The ropes and hooks ha' been fashioned as I ordered."

To *his* specifications, but Alain didn't quibble. 'Twas enough that plans were moving forward. His failure to get Elspeth still rankled, but he was a patient man. Soon he'd have it all. The gold, the lairdship of Clan Munro and Elspeth.

Chapter Thirteen

Elspeth's spirits were high as she and Lucais descended the stairs to break their fast. The horrors of the past four years were behind her. She felt bright and clean as a new penny, warmed by the tenderness gleaming in his eyes, dressed in a plain gown she just knew would help her fit in with his clan.

"Where did you get that gown?" Lucais had asked, head just emerging from a fresh tunic as she stepped from behind the wooden screen she'd had set in one corner to give a measure of privacy to washing. "Surely that isna something you brought with you?"

"Ena said it belonged to your grandmother," she'd replied, turning in a swirl of blue wool that smelled of the rosemary sprinkled on it when it had been packed away. "'Tis soft, warm and fits right well." Best of all, 'twasn't one of Jean's.

"'Tis older than hell." He crossed the room to tower over her, scowling darkly. "Where are your things?"

Sold to some prosperous merchant, by now, she'd hoped. "You said they werena suitable, and I agree," she'd said with a shrug. When asked about her men, she'd told Lucais she'd sent them to Curthill to assure Lord Eammon and Lady Mary she was all right. Not for the world would she tell him she'd asked Sir Giles to sell her clothes. Men, even one as logical as her Lucais, were prickly about women taking control of things. Her father would have shouted down the castle, she thought with a pang, wondering how he was, if there'd ever come a time when she'd feel easy with him.

"Why, there's Wee Wat, up and about," Lucais said, drawing her from her musings to find they'd entered the hall.

"Where?" Spotting the little man at one of the trestle tables, hunched over an ale cup, Elspeth squeaked in dismay and dashed over to scold, "You shouldna be out of bed."

"Leave off," he grumbled. "That Ena's already torn a strip out o' my hide." He looked up at her and his frown vanished. "Well, ye're perky as a cat in fresh cream. Seems Highland livin' agrees wi' ye right well after all."

"Aye." Instinctively Elspeth sought Lucais. He stood a few paces away, deep in conversation with Niall, but his eyes were on her. Their gazes met. Held. The crowd of laughing, bickering Sutherlands faded away, until it seemed they were alone. Even across the distance separating them, she saw his eyes gleam with memories of last night, felt her body quicken in response beneath the wool. Sweet Mary, he was so handsome, so tall and straight, not only of limb but of soul, too. Her heart swelled with love.

"So that's the way of it," Wee Wat crowed, breaking the spell. Good thing, too, because in another minute she'd have gone to Lucais and embarrassed them both.

"Aye, 'tis," Elspeth snapped, defiantly tossing her head so the black braid Lucais had fashioned with those exquisitely nimble fingers of his slapped against her defiant backbone. "Doubtless my family willna approve of my wedding him, but—"

"Approve? Ross'll take credit for the whole damn thing."

Elspeth started. "My brother knew this would happen?"

"He knew ye'd be passin' through Sutherland territory on yer way to that broch. Always fancied havin' young Lucais in the family." Wat shrugged. "Looks like he got his wish." At Elspeth's disgruntled snort, he grinned. "Just like yer da, hate doin' what ye think was someone else's idea, but Ross had yer best interests at heart. Knew ye'd prosper well here."

"How could he know Kinduin wasna some crumbling ruin?"

"Who do ye think bought young Lucais's first shipment of furs and smoked fish?"

"Ross," she murmured, thinking of the many balls her brother juggled to bring revenue into the Carmichael coffers...farming, shipping, the wool trade. Lucais could not have asked for a more knowledgeable partner. "Why did Ross never tell me?"

Wee Wat raised a grizzled brow. "Seem to recall ye refused to hear a word about the lad. Guilt, I always thought."

Elspeth felt her face go hot. "Aye." She looked down at her knotted fingers. " 'Twas a mistake."

"One ye've taken steps to mend, by the signs," he replied, awkwardly patting her arm.

"I'm trying," she murmured, thinking of her efforts to mend the breach between Lucais and Gillie.

"The lad seems to have forgiven ye for turnin' him down once before, but his clansmen willna be so easy won over," Wat warned. "Especially after the trouble in the village last night."

Elspeth nodded grimly. Her skin crawled with the awareness that Cathal and his cohorts sat two tables away, their malevolent glances shooting daggers into her back. "If they'd only give me half a chance, I'd prove I'm worthy of being wife to their laird." She brightened on a happy thought. "I sent Sir Giles on an errand. When he returns, the Sutherlands will change their—"

"What mischief are ye up to now?" Wee Wat asked warily.

Elspeth bristled. "I'm a woman grown, not some impetuous ninny. I gave him my clothes to sell for food to—"

"What?" Wee Wat exclaimed.

"Shh," she hissed, aware of the many curious eyes turned on them, Lucais's chief among them. " 'Tis a surprise."

"Shock, more like," Wee Wat grumbled. "He willna thank ye for meddlin' in his business, lass."

Before Elspeth could contradict him, Ena slapped a bowl of barley gruel down on the table and bade her eat. Elspeth looked down her nose at the gluey mass and shuddered.

"What is it, lass?" Lucais's hand was warm on her waist.

Twisting to look up at him, Elspeth forced a smile. " 'Tis naught. I was about to break my fast. Will you join me?" His grimace of distaste pleased her, and she cast Wee Wat a superior smirk. *See, he'll be glad of the food,* she silently said.

"Nay, I'm bound for the village," Lucais replied tightly. His people were used to making do with slim rations during the early summer, but that Elspeth should be reduced to eating such poor fare grated on his pride.

"I'm coming with you," Elspeth announced.

Much as he hated being parted from her, Lucais shook his head. "Nay, I've much to see to, and—"

"As your lady, 'tis my duty to see to the welfare of those whose homes were burned last eve," she earnestly replied. And she was right, damn her. His clansmen would not learn to know her did he keep her locked in their room as he'd have liked.

"She'll lead ye a merry chase," Niall commented as Elspeth ran off to fetch her cloak.

"Aye." Watching the gentle sway of her hips as she wove her way between the trestle tables, Lucais felt raw desire ripple through his body. Nay, 'twas more than that, 'twas love that made his chest expand, wonder that lifted his soul. Dealing with Elspeth was like trying to mold hot metal. "But the prize is well worth the effort."

"Is it wise to take her wi' us?" Niall asked, drawing Lucais away from the tables to the privacy of the large hearth.

Lucais propped his shoulder against the mantel and stared into the small fire needed to chase the chill from the cold stones even though it was summer. Did Elspeth miss the warmer clime of the Lowlands? If so, she'd never once complained. "I see no harm in it," he said at last, matching his cousin stare for stare. "'Tis what Grandma would have done, and if our clansmen are to accept her as their lady, Elspeth can do no less."

"Will ye tell her ye've decided to take the furs and fish to market this week instead of a fortnight hence?" Niall asked.

"Nay. 'Tisna because I think she's in league with the Munros," Lucais quickly put in, glad that no one besides himself had seen her aid in Alain's escape. He believed the tale she'd told him, but his clansmen would not be as understanding. "The fewer who know of our plans, the better."

Last night, as Elspeth lay sleeping in his arms, he'd decided to market what goods they had now and make a second shipment later in the month. 'Twas blind luck that the Munros had not burned the village to the ground and carried off the Sutherlands' harvest. Lucais did not believe in tempting fate. If the Munros came again, they'd find the village nearly stripped of wealth and armed to the teeth. "Elspeth can help with the cleanup…suitably guarded, of course…while I quietly see the goods gotten ready for market."

* * *

Nothing was worse than the aftermath of a fire.

The air stank. The ground was littered with charred wood. Pools of black water stood everywhere, reflecting the bleak faces of the villagers as they went about the task of resurrecting order from chaos and misery.

Blowing a tendril of hair from her sweaty face, Elspeth arched her back against the cramp put there by bending over a caldron of hot soapy water set over a fire in the center of the village. With a stick, she poked at the last of the grimy, soot-streaked clothes in her tub. Had this been Carmichael, her mother would have ordered the grubby rags thrown out and new made from the stores of wool. But Kinduin could ill afford such luxury.

"We dinna have any cloth, and we're nae like to get any till after market day," Hylda, wife of the headman, had informed her.

"If then," her sister had pointed out. "There'll be marten traps to buy and nets and such. And now we've the added cost of replacin' three roofs." Both women had curled their lips as they ran hostile eyes over Elspeth, making her face burn with shame and frustration.

I'm nae a Munro, she'd wanted to scream. Instead, she'd taken on the most disagreeable task and kept at it for hours, accepting load after load of filthy garments without complaint, though she suspected this last batch were the rags used to clean what furniture had been salvaged from the three burned out huts.

"Are ye done yet?" Hylda demanded, coming to stand beside the big iron pot.

The woman's tone made Elspeth's blood boil faster than the scummy water. *Did you speak so disrespectfully to Lucais's grandame?* But Elspeth knew the answer to that. Though dead these five years, Lady Nessa Sutherland was still revered as a near saint by her people. Swallowing her anger, Elspeth used the stick to lift out the clothes, plopping them into a bucket of cold water so they could be wrung dry. "Is that the last of them, then? Or should I start on the horse blankets?"

Hylda had the grace to flush. "Ye've done right well." Grudging praise, but welcome nonetheless.

"Much to your surprise, I'm certain," Elspeth tartly replied. "My mama insisted we learn by doing." She had chafed over every lesson, not realizing she'd ever put such knowledge to use, or be filled with such a feeling of accomplishment as when she looked at the clothes flapping on the rope tied between two huts.

"Aye, well . . . we were glad of yer help."

"I wanted to, especially since you all doubtless blame me for the Munros' attack last eve," Elspeth said to clear the air.

"Ye were wed to one of the devils."

"For four miserable years." Elspeth let all the pain and regret she felt show in her face, absurdly happy when Hylda's wrinkled features softened in return.

"H-he mistreated ye?"

Elspeth nodded but said no more, aware that a gush of horrible details would ill aid her cause. 'Twas enough that she'd planted the seed in Hylda's mind.

The older woman nodded once, as though coming to a decision. "We've ale and barley cakes in my hut, if ye'd deign to join us."

Would she. Elspeth wasted no time in pulling off the soggy linen towel that had served as an apron and following the older woman. The two hard-faced Sutherland guards who trailed after her didn't seem nearly as offensive as they had when Lucais set them to watch over her. For her protection, he'd said, but she feared he didn't truly trust her.

Sad. But then, she'd not been totally honest with him, either, Elspeth thought. As she entered Hylda's tiny hut, she weighed the idea of showing him the deed. A woman's property became her husband's when she wed, unless otherwise spelled out in a marriage contract. None had been drawn up between them, so by law Broch Tower now belonged to Lucais. Sweet Mary, but that rankled, no matter that she was half in love with him.

"I'm sorry we've naught finer," Hylda said, handing Elspeth a small wooden cup.

Elspeth shook away her unsettling thoughts. "'Tis what's within that matters." She took a long, cooling sip, made a point to praise the ale, though 'twas sour from storage over the winter. When Sir Giles returned, she'd make certain the villagers got a share of the ale she'd asked him to buy. That decided, she turned her attentions to charming her hostess and the six wary women who'd crowded into the main room of the hut.

Lucais had brought her here that first night, but Elspeth saw it now through different eyes. Sparsely furnished, but neat and tidy, lit by a smoky candle in the middle of the table. The wooden chest in one corner doubtless held the family's clothes. Their sleeping pallets were rolled up against the far wall. Conscious of the seven pairs of watchful eyes, Elspeth picked out the finest object in the room, a pair of metal candlesticks displayed on a shelf with the wooden dishes.

"What lovely workmanship," she exclaimed honestly. There was a simple beauty to them that reminded her of Wee Wat's dirk.

Hylda rushed forward to explain they'd been a wedding gift from her husband. "They've been in his family for generations."

"Who made them?"

"The ancient ones," Hylda said reverently.

"May I touch them?" Elspeth asked, and felt some of the tension leach from the room. Hylda smiled as she got down one of the candlesticks; the other women looked less hostile. 'Twas a long way from the acceptance Elspeth craved, but 'twas a start.

The door opened and Lucais looked in. "Here you are."

"Did my watchdogs nae tell you?" she asked tartly.

"I willna apologize for protectin' you," he muttered. Ducking his head to clear the doorframe, he entered the hut, bringing in the stink of smoke and the tang of freshly cut wood. "We've finished reroofin' the three huts, if you've . . . Jesu!" he cried. "What have you done to yourself?" His incredulous gaze roved from her tangled hair to her wet, filthy gown.

"Helping out. I doubt I look much worse than you do," she replied. His face and hands were streaked with black grime, his tunic and hose covered with bits of thatch.

"But . . . but 'tis my duty to—"

"And mine, as well," Elspeth insisted, afraid he'd undermine her efforts to win his people. "There were clothes to wash."

"To hell with the— Look at your hands!" He grabbed one despite her efforts to evade his grasp, gaping at the red, wrinkly skin. "Your flesh's been near boiled off. And you're tremblin' with exhaustion."

"My skin's been too long in water but will recover anon. And if I'm trembling, 'tis with anger over your silliness," she said crisply, drawing a gasp from their forgotten audience. "Men." She rolled her eyes for the onlookers' benefit, drawing several smirks of agreement.

"Women," Lucais countered. He scowled, clearly not pleased she'd gained ground with the women at the expense of his dignity. Personally, Elspeth was thrilled, not only with the progress she had made at winning over the Sutherlands, but with the possessiveness with which her new husband swept her into his arms moment later and carried her back to the castle.

Nor did he release her once they'd reached the courtyard. Swinging his leg over the saddle, he slid to the ground and bounded up the steps to the tower. Once inside the hall, they were pounced on by Ena and Wee Wat. "She's fine," Lucais said in response to their concern. "Just tired and in need of a bath."

"I'm perfectly capable of walking," Elspeth said, her enchantment with the novelty wearing thin.

"You've done enough for one day." The arrogant wretch had her upstairs and seated in a chair with a blanket tucked around her before she could draw breath. "You're unused to such labor." He tsked, cradling her hands in his larger ones.

"I'm nae as soft as you think. I've worked harder taking care of Ross and Megan's pack of wild bairns," she scoffed. "It felt good to be useful. I—I needed to help, to make amends . . ."

"It wasna your fault Alain raided the village."

Wasn't it? Elspeth looked up at him, debated telling him the whole truth, then gave in. Trust had to start somewhere. "Alain admitted he'd attacked the village to draw you away from the castle so he could get me. Rescue me, he said."

Lucais straightened. With his back to the fire he'd rebuilt in the hearth, she couldn't read his expression. "Why didna you tell me this last night?"

"Because I knew you'd be angry." And she'd needed the closeness they'd found in bed to help make him believe in her.

He was furious, but his anger was tempered by the memory of her sweet response to him. "I heard you offer to go with him."

"If he'd withdraw his men and leave." Craving the physical contact, she snagged one of his hands. He let her keep it, but made no effort to grip hers in return. "Please believe me. I want to be here, with you. Had I wanted to go with Alain, I wouldna have stood there arguing with him."

"I believe you," he said, but before he could vent the tension shuddering through him, Ena and the maids arrived with the hot water. They took one look at his dark scowl, set the buckets and fresh linen by the wooden tub and fled. "You'd better bathe while the water's hot," he growled when they were alone.

Elspeth had no intention of making herself even more vulnerable by taking off her clothes. But needing to put space between them, she stood and crossed to the tub. He was right behind her, the muffled tread of his boots on the carpet making her pulse race, her skin tingle.

"I willna let you go." He wrapped his arms around her, dragging her back against his muscular body. The blatant length of his arousal nudged her bottom, and she instinctively pressed closer, eyes drifting shut on a wave of pure joy.

"Oh, Lucais. I dinna want to leave you. Not now, not ever." She felt an anguished groan rumble through him as his hands swept up to cup her breasts, bringing the nipples to aching prominence.

"Beth. Beth." His breath was warm on her neck, his teeth enticing as they nibbled at her ear. "You're mine. Mine." His rough, husky voice slid down her spine, leaving fire in its wake, making her burn. Turning in his embrace, she dragged his head down for a kiss she needed more than her next breath.

He kissed her with a desperation she fully understood, reveled in as he lifted her, fitting them together. Soft to hard. Female to male. It felt so good, so right to be with him like this. She twisted against him, glorying in the growl that rose from his throat. Closer, she had to get closer, find the center of the storm raging through her. Through them.

Elspeth's passion, unfettered and wild as a Highland storm, tore at Lucais's control. He wanted to rip away the layers of cloth separating them and plunge into her. He wanted her body and soul, craved the essence of her to the depths of his being. Desire had never built so swiftly, ached so sharply. Now. It had to be now. Murmuring her name, he lowered her to the carpet and began tugging at the laces on the back of her gown.

Dimly Elspeth felt her clothes fall away. The cool air made her shiver, then Lucais was back, the light furring on his chest making her quiver for a different reason. "Aye," she whispered, drawing him down, needing his weight as an antidote to the ache coiled deep in her belly. "Now," she murmured, half plea, half demand, nails digging into his shoulders.

Poised above her, he shuddered, eyes glowing in the pale sunlight slanting in through the open window. "I've never wanted anyone as I do you," he growled. "But I'd nae hurt you..."

"I'm ready for you...waiting for you."

Her name came out a feral growl in the instant before his mouth slanted across hers, hungry, devouring her in a sensual prelude that only whetted her appetite for what was yet to come. The fiery conclusion to the passion that had begun building between them before they were even out of bed this morning.

Elspeth groaned in pure pleasure, lifting her hips to meet the blunt thrust she'd been craving. He filled her, stretched her, completed her in ways she was only coming to understand.

"Beth." Her name was an anguished rasp, his face taut with suppressed passion, eyes shadowed with concern. "I should stop...go slowly at least..." Wrapped tight around her, buried deep inside her, his big body trembled with conflicting urges. Never had another's sacrifice touched her more.

"If you do, I'll die with the wanting," she whispered, and moved her hips to the cadence he'd taught her last night. His groan of surrender as he followed her lead went to her head like strong wine. But her heady sense of power was short-lived.

Cradling her hips in his hands, he brought her closer, plunged deeper. With swift, sure strokes he silently challenged her to let go, to lower her shields and meet him on equal terms. No winners. No losers. Only the two of them burning together until they were consumed by the wildfire they'd kindled. She gave herself up to it, to him, without fear or reservation, holding back nothing and getting everything he was in return.

Drowning, he was drowning in the scent of her, the feel of her coming apart in his arms. Her body tightened around him, drawing him into the heart of the conflagration. "Beth," Lucais rasped as he poured himself into her. She echoed his ecstasy, crying his name over and over again.

So, this was love, Elspeth thought as she drifted back to earth a bit later. Groaning, Lucais stirred and made to leave her. "Nay." She clung to him, unwilling to face reality.

"I'm too heavy." He rolled them onto their sides. His fingers trembled as he stroked the hair from her eyes. "Jesu, Beth, I'm sorry. I dinna know what happened . . ."

"I do." She walked two fingers up his sweaty chest and touched his mouth, wet and swollen from their kisses. " 'Twas me."

Lucais let out the breath he'd been holding and nipped at her fingers. "Minx," he teased in lieu of the "I love you" that filled his heart. They'd come so far together, he from a gangling lad, she from a rebellious brat, but he'd not chance driving her back into her shell by threatening to cage her. And he had no doubts that his Beth would see love as a cage. "At least let us get up from the floor. I must have squashed you flat."

"Aye," Elspeth said cheerfully. Was that love she saw gleaming in his eyes? Or merely a reflection of the noonday sun? Nay, he must care for her, else he'd not have found it in his heart to treat her so tenderly after her cruel rejection. "And you smell like a goat . . . a smoky goat," she teased, enchanted by the lightness between them. It felt so good to laugh. His gift to her, more stirring even than the desire he kindled in her.

"Fine talk from a lass who smells like a lye pit."

Elspeth cocked her head. "Doubtless the bathwater's cold."

"We'll see if we canna warm it up, then."

She grinned, he chuckled, and the game was on. Amid much tickling and laughing, they washed each other. But scrubbing soon gave way to caresses of a different sort, and they both discovered their earlier joining had but blown the froth from their passion. By the time Lucais lifted her from the tub and carried her to the bed, there was more water on the floor than in the tub.

"This time, we'll go slowly," he said as he turned back the blankets and laid her damp body on the sheets. They did, but only because Lucais tempered Elspeth's impetuous greed with a tenderness she couldn't refuse. Tangled with him in the sweet aftermath, she quickly fell asleep.

Lucais found sleep elusive. Tired as he was in body, his mind refused to quiet. Instead it raced over the events of the past several days since Elspeth had burst back into his life. Thinking of how quickly and satisfactorily their relationship had changed, he hugged her closer, delighted by the way she snuggled into his embrace.

He supposed he had the Munros to thank for this, he grudgingly admitted. If not for Seamus's attempt to capture Elspeth, he would not have handfasted with her. But that brought up the thorny problem of the broch. And the deed. Did it exist?

Turning his head, Lucais spotted her boots by the tub.

Elspeth woke with a start as warm lips closed over hers. "What is it?" she mumbled when Lucais ended the quick kiss.

"I have things to do." Lucais stood beside the bed, naked but looking surprisingly alert.

"How long have you been up?" she asked sleepily.

He looked away. "Just a few moments." Leaning over her, he tucked the covers under her chin. "You stay here and sleep. God knows you got little enough last night...." His brows waggled wickedly. "And you're nae like to get much more anytime soon."

Elspeth giggled and looped her arms around his neck. "I never knew it could be like this." She sighed. "'Tis like . . . like racing the wind. Dizzying and exciting," she whispered, awed by what he made her feel. Fresh things that drove out the pain. "After what Raebert did I never thought to laugh with a man."

Lucais frowned. "I'd have spared you that."

"I know. 'Twas my own stupidity...."

"That's behind us now." He kissed her and straightened. "Rest now. I've things to do. I'll see you at supper."

"What things?" Her mother was involved in all aspects of life at Carmichael, and she'd settle for no less in her marriage.

"Oh, this and that." Seemingly unconcerned with his nudity, he padded over to the clothes chest. How finely made he was, she thought, eyes greedily skimming his broad shoulders, strong back and long legs as he bent to pull out fresh tunic and hose. 'Twas easy to see why he'd been dubbed Lion. She was surprised that the comparison no longer hurt as much. With his brave heart and golden red hair, Lucais much resembled a lion. Her lion. Suddenly she didn't want to be parted from him. "I'm nae sleepy."

"Work on the ledgers," he said, voice muffled as he tugged on a dark brown tunic over his hose.

"They're nearly done."

His expression grave, he crossed and sat beside her on the bed. "I fear you'll be bored with life at Kinduin."

"Never. There's plenty to do, but you willna let me out to do it. You canna keep me locked in this room forever."

"Just till things with the Munros calm down." His words confirmed her fears, grated on her independent spirit.

"Lucais," she exclaimed. He silenced her with a kiss.

"I know this is akin to clippin' a falcon's wings, but . . ." He couldn't risk having her or the deed fall into Munro hands. He shuddered, thinking of the damned paper, pried from her boot and hidden in a chest in the counting room. He'd resealed the boot heel with the glue used to repair the tally sticks and felt dishonest all the while. The urge to confront her with it had been strong, but not as strong as the need to know why she'd kept it a secret . . . especially after last night. "Have patience."

The door creaked open and Gillie stuck her head in. Her eyes widened as she spotted Lucais and she started to retreat.

"Gillie, come hither," he called, seeing a way to occupy Elspeth and right a wrong he'd not knowingly committed. The lass's bowed head, the way her feet dragged as she crossed the room made his heart cramp. Jesu, he'd thought to do right by her, but his own guilt had blinded him to the wee bairn's pain.

Elspeth squeezed his hand. "She's young yet. There's plenty of time to make it up to her."

"Thanks to you." Knowing he'd been right to withhold the truth about Gillie, Lucais engulfed Elspeth's hand with his and together they waited for the lass to cross to them.

"I didna ken ye were in here," Gillie whispered.

"'Tis all right, Gillie." His voice caught. No matter that she reminded him of his worst sin, he'd no call to hurt her so. "I want you here." He tugged gently on an untidy black braid. The eyes she raised to him were not gray as Jean's had been. They were a pale brown easily mistaken for his hazel ones. But he knew where she'd gotten those eyes. Pray God Elspeth never found out.

"Ye made a mess," Gillie lisped.

Lucais started, followed Gillie's gaze to the pools of water surrounding the tub. "Aye." He tried to keep a straight face, but 'twas difficult to ignore Elspeth's muffled giggles.

"Ena'll be mad," Gillie warned. "I clean it."

"I have a more important task for you," Lucais said.

"Ye do?" Gillie's mouth rounded at his nod. "What?"

"I have to go out for a bit, and I'd appreciate it if you entertained Lady Elspeth for me."

Gillie frowned. "Ye mean Mama?"

Lucais jerked his head around to meet Elspeth's tear-filled eyes. "She is my wife, Gillie, but—"

"Gently," Elspeth advised. "Time enough for explanations when she's older. She seems to think our black hair relates us in some way, and I dinna mind. Megan and Ross are called Mama and Papa by all their adopted bairns."

Gillie tugged on Lucais's sleeve. "Mama wants to look at yer books." Her earnest little face shone with innocence.

"Does she?" Lucais saw through that ploy at once. From the time she could walk, the lass had been obsessed with putting her grimy hands all over his prized books. "And here I thought she was simple," he murmured to Elspeth.

"I'd say she has her sire's ability when it comes to manipulating people," Elspeth whispered. She wondered at the pained expression that crossed Lucais's face, but she sent him on his way with a kiss, well pleased with the way things had turned out. He'd kept his word about taking a gentler tone with Gillie, and the lass had fairly sparkled at his few kind words.

An excellent start, indeed. A portent of good things to come, Elspeth thought.

Chapter Fourteen

"Books," Gillie demanded, stretching her thin arms toward the shelves. Afternoon sun poured in through the bedroom window, glinting on her raven black hair, gilding her wide brow, high cheekbones and tipped-up nose with its sprinkling of freckles.

Thankfully she hadn't inherited Lucais's nose, Elspeth thought. Then it occurred to her that she actually saw very little of him in Gillie. Except mayhap around the eyes. Gillie's were a clear, pale brown without a trace of Lucais's greenish hazel, but there was something familiar about those eyes.

"My papa said I could, 'long as my paws werena grubby." The cheeky lass held out two pink palms for inspection.

"So he did." Whether from guilt or affection, Lucais had given in to his tiny daughter's demands. Grinning, Elspeth found what she hoped was the least costly book and settled Gillie at the table with it. For a few moments, she stood close by while the wee lass reverently traced the drawings made by some long-dead monk. In that strange way that children have, Gillie seemed to have forgiven her father for ignoring her. Watching them together earlier, Elspeth had felt a strange tugging deep inside, a longing to bear a child of her own.

Mayhap she already was with child. Her hand strayed to her flat belly, lingered protectively. Each time Raebert had bedded her, she'd spent the next weeks on her knees praying his foul seed hadn't caught. Now she sent an ever more fervent appeal skyward…for a son. Lucais already had a daughter. She'd give him a son. A strong lad who'd be the next laird of Kinduin.

Restlessness drove Elspeth into the counting room in search of something to occupy a mind that raced with all that had happened since yesterday. The last remaining pages of the ledger didn't hold her interest long. Standing, she stretched, relishing the slight twinges in private places that reminded her of how greatly her life had changed. Lucais had awakened in her a sensuality that was as stunning as it was unexpected. Even more touching was the way he seemed to read her thoughts. 'Twas the same sort of wordless communication she'd seen pass between her parents and between Megan and Ross. Seen and envied.

But no more. Though there were problems to be faced, she felt confident that she and Lucais would conquer them together. So confident, in fact, that she'd decided to tell him about the deed. Tonight, when they were alone, she'd pry it from her boot heel and show it to him.

Truly, she felt wonderful, Elspeth mused, hugging herself. As she spun in a slow circle, her eyes fell on the chest she'd been unable to unlock that first day. Curiosity stirred as she drew closer and knelt to examine the symbols etched into the thick metal banding it. They reminded her of Wee Wat's dirk and Hylda's candlesticks. What was inside? More finely wrought metal? Or mayhap more of Lucais's grandmother's clothes.

Curiosity became obsession. Surely Lucais would not mind if his wife looked inside. Likely he'd have opened it for her ere now had he not been so busy. With that thought to salve her conscience, Elspeth drew the eating knife from her belt and went to work on the old lock. It was tricky and recalcitrant; she was steady and tenacious. Finally, the metal gave way. The hinges creaked in grudging surrender as she lifted the lid.

The first thing she found was a *bldag*. The hilt of the huge Highland dirk was covered with more of the ancient carvings. Likely it had been handed down from laird to laird for many generations, she thought, and her heart beat a little faster. One day, her son, their son, would carry this very knife.

Beneath the *bldag* lay a velvet cloak wrapped in linen. His grandsire's, she decided, judging by the tarnish on the intricate gold fastenings. 'Twas like delving back in time. Mayhap back to a time when people had lived in Broch Tower. Were there things like this inside the stone fortress? she wondered. Old things, special things, waiting to be discovered and brought forth into the light again. The idea intrigued her, made her itch with the urge to get inside the broch and see for herself. The tingle became a shriek when she found the chest.

No bigger than a loaf of bread, it was very old and made entirely of wood, all except for the lock, which yielded easily to the point of her blade. Inside she found three pages of some sort, made of hide stretched over a metal frame. She marveled at the ingenuity of these ancient people. The drawings had faded over time, but there was no mistaking the silhouette of Broch Tower on the first one. The second was a thick circle, its interior divided up into small cells, each marked with a symbol. A map of the inside of the broch? Her hands shook with excitement as she examined the third. It showed the same circle and a walkway leading away from it to a grouping of three rocks. Nay, not a walkway, a tunnel.

The air hissed between Elspeth's teeth. Of course, these people were too smart to seek sanctuary in a fortress with only one entrance. They had an escape route, a way to bring in fresh supplies while their besiegers watched the front door.

Did Lucais know? Nay, he'd told her there was no way in. Mayhap he hadn't gotten around to going through his grandsire's things. Suddenly she couldn't wait to tell him of her find.

Elspeth hastily put the pages into the chest and replaced it and the *bldag* in the trunk. As she lifted the cloak back on top of them, she dislodged a square of parchment that had been caught in the linen. It fluttered into her lap and lay there staring at her. One word had been scrawled across it. Her name.

Her hands trembled as she picked it up and unfolded it, for she knew what was written on that scrap of paper. It was the deed to Broch Tower. Her deed. Not only did Lucais know about the deed, he had taken it from her. The pain of his betrayal was so great that for a moment she couldn't think, couldn't move.

"Why are ye cryin', Mama?"

Elspeth started and brushed the tears from her cheeks. "'Tis naught." Naught but her heart breaking, her life ending just when she'd thought... A ragged sob tore from her throat as the enormity of her loss sank in. Just when she thought she'd finally found a place where she belonged, a challenge worth facing, a man worth facing it for and with, all had been snatched away.

By a man's greed.

He must have found the deed that first night and taken it. She should have known when he suddenly seized the opportunity to handfast with her that he'd had an ulterior motive. He hadn't wanted her, only the broch and revenge. How it must have pleased him to have the woman who'd refused him tremble and beg for his touch. Her stomach clenched, nauseated now by the things they'd done. The ache in her chest grew so she could scarcely breathe.

Fists balling, she fought to stay strong, to find a way out of the mess. She couldn't stay here, that was certain.

The urge to run clawed at her insides. *Flee now, before he locks you up as he did Jean,* an inner voice shrieked.

"Mama, where are ye goin'?" Gillie demanded, clutching at her skirts as Elspeth stood and moved toward the door.

Oh, Gillie. If only things had been different, I'd have loved you, cared for you like my very own. "I dinna know yet, dearling," she choked out. But she did. Already her brain raced in tight circles, plotting, scheming. A horse. Food. Water. A weapon and sufficient time to reach the broch.

"Elspeth, where are you?" Lucais threw open the chamber door and strode in, a man atop his world and pleased with everything and everyone in it. Even Cathal's sullenness this afternoon had not been able to dampen his happiness.

"I'd rather raid the Munros than guard the shipment all the way to Curthill," the older man had grumbled.

"Cheer up, mayhap the Munros will attack you," Lucais had retorted, knowing there was little chance the enemy knew they'd advanced the timing of their trip to market. Doubtless they were licking their wounds and trying to figure a way into the broch. Lucais's next objective as soon as the men returned from Curthill was to set a trap to capture his enemies. Not to kill them, for that would only touch off a blood feud. Nay, he'd throw the lot of them in the dungeon till he could negotiate a settlement.

"Papa!" Gillie stood in the doorway of the counting chamber, hair untidy as ever, face red and puffed from crying.

"What is it, lass?" But even as he voiced the question, apprehension slid an icy finger down his spine. Elspeth. Something had happened to Elspeth. Gut knotting, he started for her, and she flew to meet him, throwing her arms around his legs and sobbing for him to help. "Easy, lass." He hunkered down to take her in his arms. "I canna understand you when you greet so."

"She took the dirk and runned away," Gillie choked out.

"What?" Fear drove him the few steps to the counting room. "Elspeth?" Lucais stopped in the doorway, taking in the open trunk, his grandsire's cloak trailing on the floor. *Oh God, she'd found the deed.* Stark terror drove him to his knees before the trunk. His hands shook as he frantically rifled through the items passed down by generations of Sutherland lairds.

Gone. The deed was gone.

Lucais rocked back on his heels, eyes squeezing shut. What must Beth be thinking? The worst, knowing her propensity for jumping to conclusions. He groaned aloud, wondering how he'd ever make her understand that he'd taken the deed not to cheat her but to protect his clan. Given her temper, he was surprised she hadn't been here, lying in wait behind the door to brain him with a pot. "Where is she?"

"I dunno," Gillie said. "She took the big knife and the things from the wee box. She told me to stay here till ye came."

"What?" Lucais's eyes flew open. He snatched up the small chest entrusted to him by Daibidh.

"This chest is never to be opened," the old bard had bade him. "My time draws short, and I wouldna risk havin' it fall into the wrong hands. Keep it. Pass it on to the one who follows me."

Lucais had been touched by the old man's trust. Now he was appalled to discover that the lock had been forced and whatever had rattled about inside when Daibidh had given it to him was gone, too. "Bloody hell," he whispered, snatching it open. The inside smelled of incense and alchemy, of dark secrets and ancient rites. A secret Elspeth had stolen.

Why? To spite him because of the deed? Or for some deeper, more sinister purpose? Doubt tinged the fear that had hounded Lucais from the moment he'd realized Elspeth had found the deed. Suspicion bit deep into his brain. Nay, he did not want to think ill of her, especially after the happiness they had found in each other's arms. Still, there was no escaping the facts.

The moment he'd let down his guard, Elspeth had violated his trust. For greed, for revenge, he didn't know what drove her. But he did know where she'd gone.

To the broch.

* * *

The broch was even larger than she'd remembered.

Elspeth peered out from around a massive oak at the edge of the woods and squinted up at the point where the tower blended with the treetops far above. A ray of late afternoon sun pierced the leafy canopy, bathing the weathered stone in pale, ethereal light. The hushed, brooding silence that pervaded the glen made her skin crawl. Riding through the forests that bordered the loch, her horse had kicked up all manner of small game. Here it seemed not a creature stirred, not bird, not beast, not man.

Glad as she was for the last, having no wish to run into either the Munros or the Sutherlands set to patrol here, Elspeth felt the first frisson of disquiet low in her belly.

Getting away from Kinduin had proved easier than she'd feared. The kitchen building just outside the tower had been empty when she'd sneaked down for provisions. Through the open window she'd heard the maids quarreling and laughing as they tended the herbs in the small kitchen garden. She'd wasted no time in loading a sack with enough bread, cheese and dried fish to last her a couple of days and in filling two skins, one with water, the other with wine. Sir Giles would return soon with food and drink aplenty, so what little she took would not deprive the Sutherlands of a meal.

Clad in hose, boots and one of Lucais's tunics, far too loose, but cinched tight at the waist with the wide leather belt into which she'd stuck the unwieldy *bldag* and her eating knife, Elspeth had crept into the stables, stolen the first likely horse she'd come upon and ridden to the gate. With her enveloping cloak spread to conceal her woman's form and purloined food, she'd bluffed her way out by convincing the guard she had something of import to bring to Lucais.

Now, tired from the journey, nerves jangled by the constant need to ride with one eye over her shoulder and the other peeled for signs of trouble ahead, she wished she'd waited for Sir Giles to return. Or at least brought Wee Wat along.

Nay. Wat's injuries were not sufficiently healed, and waiting for Sir Giles would have entailed confronting Lucais. 'Twas a prospect too gut-wrenching to contemplate. One look at his face and the memory of his treachery would have broken her into a thousand sharp, aching pieces. Not that he wouldn't eventually trace her here, but by that time she planned to be inside . . . inaccessible. Did he put a ladder up to the door, she'd . . . she'd hack it to bits with his grandsire's *bldag*.

The trick now was getting inside, and quickly, for night would come early to these deep, dark woods. Reaching into her pack, she drew out the ancient drawing of the tunnel leading away from the broch. From the position of the door, she gauged she was on the correct side of the tower. All she had to do was ride away from the building and find the three large stones shown on the map. And keep a sharp eye out for Sutherlands. Curious she'd not seen any when Lucais had made a point of doubling the guards after the incident three days ago.

Elspeth rode slowly, grateful for the damp leaves that muffled her horse's hooves . . . till she realized 'twould make it that much easier for someone to sneak up on *her*. A nervous glance back revealed naught moving save the branch she'd pushed out of her way. Here the sun barely penetrated, and every black tree trunk became an enemy skulking in the shadows, waiting to leap out. Indeed, the forest suddenly seemed to wrap her in its verdant arms, cutting her off from the familiar . . . the safe. Suddenly she was sorry she'd left Kinduin.

"Impetuous fool," she muttered. Her breath misted in the dense, cold air, hung before her, then faded like a ghost. *Sweet Mary, why did she have to think of that?* Because the ghosts of the past were everywhere. Biting her lip, she urged her mount to pick up the pace. Leaves and pine needles slapped wetly at her cheeks; the thorny brush tugged at her cloak.

Elspeth lost control of her reason and her mount, giving the beast its head. Mayhap it could get her out of the mess she'd gotten herself into. No sooner had she thought that . . . prayed that . . . than the horse shied and skidded to a halt.

A great wall of stone rose up from the forest floor, blocking their way. Heart pounding so she could scarcely breathe, desperate to be away from here, Elspeth urged the horse around it. On the other side, the wall resolved into three huge boulders. Half as tall as the broch, black beneath a fringe of green moss, they leaned into one another like weary travelers. Or warriors who'd stood guard for centuries.

Excitement chased the fear away; Elspeth's fingers trembled with it as she took out the map. Crude as the drawing was, there was no mistaking that the formation was the same one depicted there. She'd found it. But unless the builders of the broch were stupid or overly confident, she doubted that the entrance to the tunnel would be so easily discovered.

"What a time to be right," Elspeth grumbled a futile hour later. 'Twas getting late; she was running out of time and the gloom that passed for daylight in this grim place. Her hands were filthy, the nails chipped from running them over the unforgiving crevices in the rock. Cold, hungry and more than a little intimidated by the thought of spending the night in the open, she plopped down on a stool-size rock at the foot of the largest boulder. "If there's a door here, 'tis sealed over for all time."

"What? Given up already?" called a reedy voice, and an old man hobbled out of the shadows, his dark clothes blending with the coming night so his face seemed to hover in the air.

Not a reassuring sight. Elspeth scrambled to her feet, backed up till she crashed into the cold, unyielding boulder. "Wh-who are you?"

"I am Daibidh of the South Land," he replied. "And no' threat to ye, lass."

South Land. Elspeth knew from Megan's stories that was the name by which the Vikings had once called this place. So, he was a Sutherland. Frantically searching for normalcy, she studied the face staring back at her from the depths of his cowl. Old. Nay, ancient, his skin yellowed as parchment, smooth over high cheekbones and a wide forehead. But it was the eyes that caught her attention, held it. They glowed, bright as the sun, twice as piercing. Hard to forget. "Did I see you in the village yesterday?" From a distance, indistinct, a withered black crow among the bustling Sutherlands bent on cleaning and rebuilding.

"Aye." His voice rustled, like wind through dry leaves.

"You were standing by a tree." Watching her, she recalled. Wariness became alarm. She eyed the distance to the *bldag*, which she'd leaned against the boulder because it interfered with her search for the door. Too far. "Wh-what are you doing here?" she asked to distract him. They were nearly of a height, and he was old. If he attacked, she'd shove him . . .

" 'Tis my duty to be here." He rested both gnarled hands on his twisted walking staff, looking very much like a pilgrim.

A comforting thought. Mayhap he was a priest of the old religion. "Is this your post, then?"

"Ye might say that."

Elspeth frowned. Surely Lucais would not set so frail a man to guard the broch. "There must be others with you."

"Aye, young Lucais takes his responsibilities seriously. He's posted guards about the place."

Hearing her formidable husband referred to as one might a wee lad made Elspeth feel like smiling for the first time in many a long, weary, frightening hour. "Where are they?"

"I set them to watch the high road twixt here and Munro land. That's where the real threat lies."

"Do you think they'll come again?"

"Aye, greedy as wolves after a herd of prime cattle, they be." His golden eyes narrowed. "Ye were wed to one," he added, and Elspeth braced herself for the slur. "So ye know how they are."

Relieved by the compassion in his gaze, she nodded. "I dinna know what 'tis they want here, but they willna stop till they have it." A notion stirred. "Is it to do with the coins?"

Daibidh nodded. "Have ye come lookin' for more coins?"

"Nay. I've come because..." Because this place is mine. My hope, my destiny. She didn't know how that could be, only that 'twas true. It went beyond the deed signed by Seamus and Raebert, 'twas...elusive. A feeling just outside her grasp. Mayhap when she was inside, that feeling would be clearer. She squared her shoulders, tilted her chin at the strange old man. "I'm going to get inside. And I'm going to stay there. I've brought a rope, and I'll scale the rocks if I have to."

"Can ye really do such a thing?"

"Aye. My brothers taught me to climb like a sailor."

"Ye're an unusual lass." He tapped his shrunken mouth with a long finger. "I'm glad I lived long enough to meet ye at last."

"You make it sound as though you were expecting me."

"Perceptive, too. I've come to let ye in."

Take care what you wish for, her mother used to say. "Lucais believes no one is allowed to enter the broch."

"So our old legends say. Do ye believe in such things?"

The stillness was so complete Elspeth fancied she could hear the blood pumping through her veins. "Before her marriage, Megan, my brother's wife, was bard of the Sutherlands of Curthill. I aided her in setting many of the old tales to parchment. So they wouldna be lost." He nodded. In encouragement or understanding, she didn't know which. She felt compelled to go on, to fill the yawning silence. "So I know most of the legends, but I fear I've too practical a mind to believe in curses and spirits."

"When ye've lived as long as I have, ye'll learn there's much defies *practical* comprehension." His eyes glittered with a strange light as he cocked his head toward the smaller of the three rocks. "Come, I'll show ye the way in."

"Even though I'm an outsider?"

"Is that how ye see yerself?" he slyly inquired.

Elspeth frowned. "Must you answer a question with another?"

"If we dinna ask, how can we learn?"

Point taken. "I want to fit in here," Elspeth said. "But the Sutherlands are wary of me because I was wed to a Munro."

"Ye can change that," he said, and turned away to the rocks, leaving her alone in the growing darkness. The wind had picked up, moaning through the trees, lifting the hair on her arms.

Shivering, Elspeth wrapped them around her waist and studied Daibidh's cloaked figure. With his back to her, she couldn't tell if he was praying to the rocks or prying at them. Suddenly he turned, motioning her forward. She stumbled in the dark, would have fallen had he not grabbed her arm. There was surprising strength in the bony fingers that tugged her forward, flattening her against the cold stone. *Sweet Mary! He meant to kill her!*

"Dinna stiffen up like that," he grumbled. "I mean ye no harm. I'd show ye how to work the mechanism." Guiding her hand with his, he thrust deep in a shoulder-high cleft in the stone. The space was cramped, the angle awkward, and then she felt it. A thick metal lever. "Pull down," he commanded.

The rock she leaned against shuddered to life, began to move. The ground shook beneath her feet. Elspeth squealed and jumped back, careening into Daibidh. He steadied her with a gentle hand and a quiet word that didn't quell the panicked thudding of her heart as the earth slowly opened up, releasing a long sigh of pent-up air. 'Twas dry and fresh, where she'd been expecting damp and dank. But the passage was even darker than she'd anticipated. "Good thing I thought to bring candles."

"No need." Daibidh stepped into the yawning black maw with the confidence of a man who could see in the dark. She'd not put it past him. Flint struck, a flame leapt to life, and her strange mentor returned bearing a torch.

"You've been inside before." She tried to see more of his face to gauge his purpose in helping her. But it had retreated into the depths of his cowl, away from the flickering light.

"Does that surprise ye?"

"I suppose not."

"I'm the guardian of the Sutherland legends. 'Tis my duty to make certain their heritage is kept safe."

"Then why are you helping me?"

"Because those secrets are threatened."

"How will letting me into the broch change that?"

"Only time will tell."

"That isna an answer."

He rolled his eyes, making them gleam in the darkness. "They were right. Ye are a most curious and forward lass."

"They?" Elspeth prompted, but he handed her the torch and moved past her to collect the meager supplies she'd brought. He stuck the *bldag* back in her belt, hung the skins over one shoulder, the food sack over the other. "Now I know what my packhorse feels like," she grumbled.

"'Tis only a short distance through the tunnels. The footin' is firm, the steps up into the main chamber of the broch wide and evenly spaced. Ye'll encounter no difficulties."

She hoped not. Elspeth stared into the inky blackness. Burdened as she was, if she fell, she'd never get up. "Can you at least carry the torch?" When he failed to answer, she looked around and her heart plunged. *He was gone.*

"Daibidh?" she called, The wind whipped his name back at her in chilly denial of her plea. He was gone. She was alone. Shoulders slumping with more than the weight of her provisions, Elspeth swiftly reviewed her options. Tempted as she was to crouch here in the opening till daybreak, then return to Kinduin, pride and the inbred stubbornness that had been both boon and curse made that impossible. She would *not* crawl back there to the man who had wed her under false pretenses, led her to believe he truly wanted her when all the while 'twas the broch he wanted.

Nay, she'd go on as planned, shut herself up in the broch for a year and a day, if necessary, till she was free of Lucais. That decided, Elspeth squared her shoulders and stepped into the tunnel. After all, she had Daibidh's blessing. He'd showed her how to open the stone door. She paused midstep. The notion that he'd likely had an ulterior motive turned her stomach queasy, had her looking back over her shoulder.

The little glade was empty; nothing moved in the fading light save the branches twisting in the wind. It tugged at her hair and cloak like greedy fingers bent on keeping her back from the tunnel. The prospect of entering the inky bowels of the earth sent a chill down her spine, yet she sensed no evil here.

Murmuring a prayer, Elspeth stepped into the tunnel, kicked a large rock into the threshold and nudged the door with her shoulder. It moved like a well-oiled cog, sighing just short of closing when it met her makeshift stop. If she had to beat a hasty retreat, she didn't want to waste time looking for the lever on this side of the door. Satisfied she'd done the prudent thing in an imprudent situation, she started forward.

Given the dampness of the forest, the tunnel was surprisingly dry, the hard-packed dirt level beneath her feet. Moving cautiously but steadily, she held her dirk in one hand, the torch in the other, senses alert for any sign of danger. The circle of light was nearly lost in the blackness that wrapped around her like a cloak, blanketing sight and sound. Nothing stirred, not bat, not rodent, not bug. Either Daibidh was an exemplary housekeeper or the threat of the curse had reached the ears of even the lower orders.

Not a comforting thought.

You dinna believe in curses, she reminded herself. Still her heart beat much too quickly, jarring against her ribs like a trapped bird. It faltered altogether when she ran up against the blank stone wall.

Trapped!

Elspeth turned, flight her first reaction. But where would she run to? Nay, there was no going back. Remembering how Daibidh had opened the door to the tunnel, she took hope. The ancient ones would not have left their secret entrance standing open to unwanted company. Unburdening herself of her provisions, she held the torch aloft in one hand and felt with the other along the deep-set edges of the stone door. At the bottom, on the left-hand side, she found a lever.

With a soft groan that was becoming familiar, the stone swung away from her. Elspeth flattened herself against the wall, heart quaking, free hand going to the dirk at her waist. Long moments after the door had stopped moving she remained there, waiting for something to swoop in from the darkness beyond her circle of torchlight. When nothing happened, she slowly forced her stiff body away from the wall, crept to the opening and thrust the torch into the unknown.

'Twas a small, empty room. Leaving her provisions on the threshold as a doorstop, Elspeth slipped into a short corridor. Several chambers similar to the first one opened off it. Storage rooms, she decided, empty now, save for shards of pottery and baskets that should have long since rotted away to dust, yet were intact. Truly the broch seemed a place where time stood suspended.

The stone stairs at the end of the corridor posed another dilemma. Should she hide in one of the storage rooms and wait for daybreak? Nay, she'd not gotten this far by being faint-hearted. Squaring her shoulders, she mounted the stairs to face whatever new challenge awaited. 'Twas a short hallway, and beyond that...

Elspeth gasped. Turning in a slow circle, she tried to take in the enormity of the room she'd entered. Nay, room was too small a word for this... this structure. 'Twas like standing inside an enormous chimney, for when she looked up, she could see a patch of gray sky some forty feet above her. The sheer walls were pocked with openings. Not windows to the outside, but to rooms, mayhap. Four doors were ranged around the base of this central hall. Three were dark; one of them, reached by a flight of several steps, opened to the outside. Clearly, this was the door visible from the ground. But where did the others lead?

To a staircase, Elspeth discovered when she peered into the nearest one. She climbed up far enough to discover that the massive walls of the broch were actually hollow, honeycombed with small chambers that opened off the spiral staircase. They were windowless, but pale light entered them through chinks in the layers of stone that comprised the outer wall. The windows she'd seen from the hall were openings in the inner wall of the stairs, from which she could look down into that central room.

Ingenious. Her father and brothers would have marveled at this example of early defensive engineering. Doubtless the builders of the broch had kept the storage rooms filled with provisions and water to see them through a siege. When threatened by marauding Vikings, they had only to gather their livestock and dependents and retreat inside their shell like turtles.

As she wandered back down the stairs, Elspeth smiled, imagining families sleeping together in the wall chambers, gathering in the hall to take their meals and entertain the bairns as best they could. All the while they'd laugh up the sleeves of their rough tunics while their would-be attackers raged ineffectually in the glen below. From the second-floor doorway, a few men with bows and arrows could easily pick off the more daring of the raiders with little risk to themselves.

Her smile broadened as she imagined Lucais Sutherland cast in the role of besieger. Aye, she'd take great delight in listening to him fume and plead with her to come down from her impregnable stone tower.

Never!

Suddenly she didn't feel the least bit tired or hungry, and she certainly didn't feel afraid. She felt calm, welcome, at peace with herself. There was a spring to her step as she started down the stairs. Her mind whirled with the things that must be done before she slept. A fire would be nice, though the inside of the broch was warm enough so she'd probably be comfortable wrapped in her cloak and blanket.

The thought of going outside to search for firewood was unappealing and she decided to wait until tomorrow. But she'd go and close the far door tonight to ensure her privacy, Elspeth thought as she rounded the curve in the stairwell.

A crunch of dirt and movement in the air were all the warning she had before a bulky figure swooped in from the darkness below. The torch fell as two strong hands grabbed her by the upper arms. She was wrenched off her feet and slammed against a hard wall of muscles with enough force to drive the air from her lungs.

"I thought I'd find you here," rasped a deep male voice.

Chapter Fifteen

Ghosts! was Elspeth's first thought. But the steely muscles wrapped round her belonged to no vaporous being.

Munros! The thought was almost more terrifying. She fought back instinctively, lashing out with her feet. Her boot cracked against a shinbone, drew a satisfying groan of pain, but the hold on her did not lessen.

"Stop that, you witch," her captor hissed, giving her a little shake. The deep timbre of his voice penetrated her panic.

She stilled. "L-Lucais?"

"Aye. Nae quite the man you were expectin', I'll warrant."

"What?" She whipped her head up, startled by his cynicism. The torch had fallen when he grabbed her and lay sputtering on the next step. In its wavering light, his face was an angry mask of red and black. She'd never seen him like this, not even when she'd refused him. "I wasna expecting any—"

"Hah!" Lucais snorted, but her nearness, the bewildered frown creasing her brow threatened to weaken his rage. He set her from him but retained a grip on her wrist. Her pulse fluttered frantically. "Where are your friends?" he demanded.

Sorrow flickered in her eyes. "I have none here."

"I meant the Munros," Lucais snapped, angered anew that with a look she could actually make him feel sorry for her. "Where are they? And where is the property you stole from my countin' room?"

"The deed to Broch Tower is mine."

"That isna what I meant. You opened the chest Daibidh entrusted to my care and took what was inside it."

The little witch had the nerve to raise her chin. "*Borrowing* the old maps was nothing. You stole my deed and kept silent about it. You let me think . . . you let me hope . . ." Her voice trailed off and she looked away, but not before he caught the glint of tears seeping through her lashes.

Oh, Beth. I didna mean to hurt you, his heart cried out, but he dared not soften toward her. "Where are these maps? Have you already given them to your Munro kin?"

She stiffened as though he'd slapped her, head swinging back around, face flushed with a fury that dried her tears. "The Munros are nae kin of mine, and 'twas your precious Daibidh himself who showed me how to open the door to the tunnel."

"Daibidh was here?" Suspiciously.

"Aye. Close as you followed me, you must have seen him."

Lucais shook his head, his eyes locked on hers, probing with an intensity that made her glad she had naught to hide. "Why would he let you into our sacred place?"

"He didna say, except that 'twas fated to be. How did you happen to come after me so quickly?"

"Fool that I am, I was impatient to be with you. I left Niall to finish preparations in the village and rode back to Kinduin. When I realized you'd found the deed . . ." His voice caught on some deep emotion. Regret or suspicion? She couldn't tell. "I knew you'd come here."

"Aye, to claim what is mine."

"To turn it over to my enemies," he growled.

"Never." Elspeth clutched at his tunic, willing him to believe her . . . to believe in her. "This place is too beautiful to be defiled by the likes of them."

Lucais's eyes narrowed as he studied her upturned face. Pale in the uncertain light, it glowed with a sincerity the shadows couldn't hide. "Why did you come here, then?"

Elspeth let out a pent-up breath. He believed, a little. Given his betrayal, it shouldn't have mattered, but it did. "Because I wanted to see inside. I have from the first moment I saw it. And, too, I wanted to get away from you."

Lucais flushed. "I took the deed only this morn. I was goin' to tell you—"

"When? On the day a convenient accident took my life and left you with a deed to the disputed property?"

"What?" His hand shook as he took her wrist. "Elspeth, you canna think I'd do that." He looked so shocked she reconsidered.

"Mayhap not, but you canna deny 'twas why you—"

"Beth!" He grasped her shoulders and gave her another little shake, then groaned and dragged her into his embrace. "Jesu, Beth, even furious as I was with you, I died a hundred deaths when I came upon your bundles in the tunnel and couldna find you. I thought . . ." He squeezed her so hard her ribs creaked in protest. It felt wonderful. His unguarded reaction convinced her of his sincerity more surely than a dozen practiced explanations.

"I believe you." Nose buried in his chest, she dragged in the scent that was uniquely Lucais. His chain mail bit into her skin through the layers of wool separating them, but the hurt was nothing to the pain in her heart. "Why did you take the deed?"

Lucais sighed, his grip on her easing fractionally. "I was afraid it might fall into the wrong hands. The Munros had no right to give you land that wasna theirs, but the king's seal on the damned paper worried me, for it seemed to add legitimacy to the claim. I decided to hang on to the bloody thing till I knew exactly why they were interested in the place."

"So, you handfasted with me to make certain the broch stayed in Sutherland hands," she said slowly, sadly. Lucais denied it, but his words didn't make a dent in her conviction.

"You canna believe that," Lucais growled. When she didn't look up, he knew she did. *Little fool.* He put his fingers beneath her stubborn chin and lifted it till their gazes met. The misery in her violet eyes pierced him to the quick, nearly drove him to admit he'd wed her for love. But unsettled as things were, he dared not give her that hold over him. "I could have burned it."

She jerked as though his words had burned *her.* "Aye, you'd do that, destroy the only thing I own. Think you I've forgotten your parting words four years ago? You said you'd make me sorry I'd refused your suit."

"Be reasonable, Beth," Lucais pleaded, voice raw, eyes anguished. His arms tightened around her. "I spoke in anger and pain. I was young, proud, and you'd hurt me beyond belief."

Elspeth trembled, wanting desperately to believe, but afraid to. Lucais was a clever man with a silver-edged tongue when it came to molding others to his will. "Mayhap tonight you speak out of determination to save your clan's land."

"Bloody hell." He raked an exasperated hand through his hair. " 'Tis like doin' battle in a bog. No matter which way I turn, I find myself sinking deeper into the hellish morass."

'Twas that, Elspeth thought sadly. They had had one night and one morn together, a time filled with incredible joy and beauty, a taste of the happiness that could be theirs. Now it seemed they had no future together. "'Tis why I left Kinduin."

Tension vibrated through Lucais, cording the muscles of his neck. His jaw flexed as he clenched his teeth over a ripe oath. "Nay, you are my wife and you'll live with me," he shot back, eyes filled with a possessiveness she'd have welcomed under different circumstances.

Instead her own temper caught fire from his. "How can we live together without trust?" she asked again.

Her words pierced Lucais to the quick, reality making a mockery of his hopes and dreams. In the near darkness of the stairway, they glared at each other from opposite sides of the issues that divided them. Aye, there was more than anger in the heat they generated. Passion smoldered close to the surface, a wanting that defied betrayal and mistrust. She was headstrong and impetuous, but once won, she'd be unswerving in her loyalty. The question was, how did they resolve their differences?

"Did ye get all of them?" demanded a muffled voice from somewhere below them.

Someone was in the broch! Elspeth gasped, looked at Lucais as he swung his gaze to the gallery window two steps below them.

"Aye," replied another rough voice. "There were six guards. We killed them all."

"Be sure," grumbled the first speaker. "We canna risk havin' even one escape and ride to Kinduin to raise the alarm."

"Seamus?" Elspeth hissed, nails digging into Lucais's arm.

"Aye." Curtly. Nor did she like the hard look he gave her before he released her to extinguish the torch and creep down to the opening. One glance through it and he was back beside her. "I dinna see anyone in the hall. They must be outside."

"Or in the tunnels," Elspeth said shakily.

"Nay, the voices dinna come from that direction."

The clang of metal on stone sent both of them scrambling back to the small aperture. Elspeth bristled when Lucais insisted she remain behind him, but she found she could see over his shoulder. The moon must have risen to its zenith while they were arguing, for its pale, eerie light filtered in through the narrow opening in the roof. She had barely finished sweeping the shadowy interior of the hall with anxious eyes when a dark shape thrust itself through the broch's only outer doorway.

For a moment the man crouched there, a weapon gleaming dully in his hand as he scanned his surroundings. Seamus? she wondered, not realizing she whispered the fear aloud till Lucais replied, "Nay. He'd send another in to take the risks."

"What are we going to do?" Elspeth murmured.

"Stay here for the moment." He asked her about the layout of the broch, and she described the small chambers above. Lucais swore when he heard this stairway was the only way down.

"If we go now, mayhap we could make it to the tunnel."

Lucais shook his head. Already four of the Munros had climbed up the rope ladder and fanned out from the doorway. Two of the men held torches aloft. "Nay, we canna cross the hall without being seen. We'll wait till they separate to explore the place..." He let the words trail off, not wanting to frighten her further with the hopelessness of their situation.

The six men he'd sent to patrol the broch were dead. Their deaths weighed heavily on his conscience, but he dared not dwell on them while he and Elspeth were yet in danger. His hand tightened reflexively on the hilt of his sword as he considered their options. *Few.* And prospects for survival. *Even fewer.*

Keeping well back from the opening so his pale face wouldn't be picked out by the torchlight, Lucais watched the enemy pour into the Sutherlands' sacred broch. Alain was the fourth man up, Seamus the tenth and final intruder. Ten men against one.

"I can wield a dirk," Elspeth whispered in his ear.

Very handily, if memory served. Still, "I pray it willna come to that," he replied in kind. He felt her tremble against his back, wished he could turn and wrap his arms around her. "If we hear them comin' up these stairs, we'll hide in one of the chambers and deal with them one by one."

"Providing they dinna come up in a group. Oh, Lucais..."

He looked down into the hall just as three men approached the doorway that led to the very stairs where they now crouched. Elspeth's stifled groan of horror echoed his own fears. The curve of the stairwell would conceal them until the enemy was only a few steps away, but he was taking no chances with Elspeth's welfare. "Go up to the nearest chamber and hide as best you can." She tugged at his arm, turning him to face her. He saw a protest brewing in her stormy eyes. "You can

help me best by stayin' clear. 'Twill distract me if I must look
to your safety.'' Jesu, he wished they were on better terms. If
anything happened to him, she'd never believe he'd truly loved
her. "Beth, I—"

"I'm sorry, too." Elspeth cupped his jaw, seeking to ease the
tautness there. He turned his head to plant a kiss on her palm.
It burned her flesh, made her ache for what could not be...for
the faith and trust that had withered in the face of betrayal...his, hers, theirs.

"Go quickly and quietly as a mouse," he said, his voice savage and sharp as the ache in her chest.

"Not that way, ye dolts," Seamus called out, dragging Lucais's attention back to the hall. "Duncan said the treasure
room lay opposite the outer door."

The men who'd been about to enter the stairwell turned to
their laird. "Alain said we should look around," one replied.

"We dinna have time for that," Seamus snarled. "We've
other business to be about tonight, and there's no tellin' when
the Sutherlands'll send men to relieve those we've done in."

Not till morn, Lucais thought with a pang of regret for the
good men lost. Sending men to their deaths was one thing he'd
never get used to. Nor did it sit well to crouch here in the dark
whilst his enemies raided the broch. He was swept by an in-
sane urge to rush down the stairs and attack, kill as many of
them as he could. *And leave Elspeth at the mercy of the Munros?*

What if she had been meeting them here? asked a traitorous
little voice. Lucais stiffened, whipped his head around to look
for her. Mercifully empty, the stairs above were dappled by the
gray wash filtering in through the stones. She'd done as he
asked—for once. Still, he couldn't help wondering if mere coincidence had brought her here on the night Seamus chose to
raid. He didn't want to believe that. It killed him even to *think*
her capable of treachery. Still, the facts were damning.

Nay. Shoving aside his doubts, Lucais looked down in time
to see eight of the men, including Seamus and Alain, leave the
hall. The remaining two guards found old metal rings in the
walls and stuck their torches into them. All hope of creeping
down the stairs and surprising them vanished when they took
up posts in full view of the exit he must use.

Time hung heavy, punctuated by the occasional muffled thud
that marked the Munros' progress in their dastardly theft. It

sounded to Lucais as if they were tearing the place down. A restless wind moaned around the tower, seeped in through the cracks in the stone to whip the flames into unearthly shapes.

"They say the place's haunted," the younger guard said.

"Aye." The older man shifted closer to the outer door and the iron claws fastening the rope ladder to the threshold. Suddenly a new sound intruded, a low sigh that grew and swelled, rising above the night wind. Shrill and wild as a banshee's wail, it echoed through the old broch.

"Holy Mother!" Drawing his sword, the older guard scrambled backward, missed his footing and tumbled through the opening. His startled shriek rent the air, then was cut short by an ominous thud.

"My God, he's dead," someone called from outside.

One less enemy to deal with, Lucais thought, but he was more concerned to learn that Seamus had men posted on the ground, as well. A strangled gasp from behind had him whirling about to discover Elspeth crouched on the step above him, her face ashen, her eyes round with horror. "What is it?"

"I . . . I didna mean for him to die," she whispered. "I . . . I just thought to frighten them into leaving so we could . . ."

Lucais went to her, hugged her. A wave of protectiveness swept him as she slumped against him, trembling so her teeth chattered. "Shh. It isna your fault," he murmured, stroking her back, trying to absorb her guilt. He pressed her face into his neck to muffle her ragged sobs. Her suffering tore at him, but a distant part of his mind registered relief. If she'd been in league with the Munros, one shout from her would have brought the lot of them pounding up the steps to capture him.

The sound of the young guard shouting for Seamus jerked Lucais from his reverie. Holding the shivering Elspeth close to his side, he crept to the aperture in time to see the man dash from the hall in search of his laird. This was their chance. "Beth, we have to go," he said gently but urgently.

She stirred in his arms, shuddered once, then raised her head. Moonlight silvered the twin tracks the tears had taken down her ashen face. Her eyes were sad but calm. "I know."

"That's my brave lass," Lucais murmured as he rose and helped Elspeth to her feet. He groaned as the blood rushed back into his cramped legs, a sound that Elspeth softly echoed as they started down the stairs. With his sword in one hand, the other arm wrapped around Elspeth to steady her, Lucais got them to the bottom with more speed than stealth. If the Munros heard footsteps in the hall, he hoped they'd put them off to ghosts.

Pausing only long enough to make certain the Munros weren't on their way back into the hall, he hustled Elspeth across the deserted chamber toward the passageway that led to the tunnel, all the while cursing the torches. If 'twas full dark, he might have lain in wait and picked a few of them off. He had barely gotten Elspeth into the inky safety of the corridor when Seamus charged out from another doorway.

"Curse be damned," he bellowed, glaring at the guard who trotted along beside him. "If Sim fell, 'twas his own stupidity. The only thing cursed here is our luck. All this waitin' and plannin', and we've naught to show but a few more coins."

So, they had robbed the broch. Blood boiling with anger and frustration, Lucais hid in the shadows and listened.

"I still say that was just an anteroom," from Alain. "If we break down the wall, we're likely to find the burial chamber."

Grave robbers! Indignation drove Lucais from the wall. Elspeth's hand caught his arm, holding him back. In her eyes, he read a silent plea for sanity, acknowledged it with a curt nod.

"Oh, aye, and ye'd be the expert in such things," Seamus scoffed. "Still and all, I'm no' givin' up. Once Lucais discovers we've done in his guards, we willna get in again so easy."

"What of the shipment?" Alain asked.

"Ye can see to that. They'll be travelin' slow, so ye can easily overtake them at Orkel Pass as we'd planned."

"Me?" Alain stuck his face in his brother's. They were of a height, but Seamus outweighed him by several stone. "Ye expect me to ride off after a few wagonloads of furs and dried fish whilst ye stay here and grab all the gold?"

Seamus shoved his brother back, features twisted with rage and contempt. "I expect ye to follow orders." Another shove. "We mayna find more gold here, but those goods are a sure thing. The coin they'll bring us at market is almost as welcome as the notion of deprivin' young Lucais of them. The Sutherlands willna follow him so eagerly when their bellies are knockin' again' their backbones." A third shove had Alain teetering on the edge of the precipice that had already claimed one Munro.

Lucais hoped Alain would be the next victim. Elspeth's soft gasp of dismay reminded him of yet another cross between them. She gave Alain Munro the loyalty she wouldn't give him.

"That's when we'll move in for the kill," Seamus went on, rubbing his hands together. "This time, we willna stop till we've wiped the Sutherlands out for good and all. Damn, I should ha' done this years ago, but nay, ye..." He poked a fat finger into Alain's chest. "Ye urged me to sign that damned peace pact."

"Lucais did ha' a dirk at yer throat," Alain pointed out. If he sensed the perilous emptiness yawning behind him, he gave no indication. Such bravery in a Munro surprised Lucais.

Seamus snorted and wheeled away. "That's in the past. This time, I'll come out on top. Get ye gone." He waved a dismissive hand at his brother. "I'll stay here till dawn, then meet ye at Scourie. See ye dinna return empty-handed," he snarled.

"The same to ye, dear brother," Alain taunted. He escaped the beefy paw Seamus aimed at him and scrambled down the rope.

"That young pup'll get his." Seamus motioned for the Munros to follow and left the hall, no doubt to continue the plundering.

As the sound of their footfalls died away, Lucais exhaled and slumped against the wall, scarcely feeling the stone against his back. "Jesu, they're goin' to attack the caravan."

"What caravan?" Elspeth murmured.

"The goods bound for market at Curthill. Niall left with the wagons near dusk. That's where I was earlier today, in the village makin' certain all was packed and the list of goods accurate." Lucais straightened so quickly Elspeth gasped. "I've got to go after them," he announced.

"After the Munros?" Elspeth clutched at his arm. "But... but there's too many of them."

"I've got to warn Niall and the others, else the Munros will ambush them, slaughter them like sheep in a pen."

They rode over some of the roughest terrain Elspeth had ever seen. After picking up their mounts at the mouth of the tunnel and sealing the stone door, they'd left the broch and headed straight up a mountain. 'Twas a steep climb, over a twisting, barbaric trail choked with boulders and made even more treacherous by the brutal pace Lucais set.

Elspeth was grateful for the men's clothes she wore, which made riding astride possible. Otherwise she'd have toppled off at the first of many jolts. She ached in every muscle; her body shivered beneath the cloak wrapped close against the bitter cold. The wind brought tears to her eyes and harried a string of black clouds across the moon, plunging the landscape from light to dark at perilously unpredictable intervals.

Following along in Lucais's wake, Elspeth wondered how he could stay on the trail, how he even knew his way through these dark, wild hills. Yet it seemed he did, for they eventually reached the rocky spine of the mountain and began to descend. Finally the ground leveled off and they entered a wooded glen. Night mist eddied around the black tree trunks; the leaves dripped water to soak through her clothes.

"Damn, I should have left you behind," Lucais said, startling Elspeth from her misery to realize they'd stopped. He'd dismounted and stood beside her. "Come, we'll rest a moment." He caught her around the waist and swung her to the ground. Her numbed muscles gave way, and she stumbled against him. "Easy, lass," he murmured, steadying her.

She swayed in his loose embrace, less afraid of toppling on her nose than of bursting into tears. *Damn.* She despised such weakness in herself. "I—I'm f-fine," she managed.

Damn. She was one nudge shy of collapse, held together by sheer stubbornness. What if 'twasn't enough? He couldn't leave her here, couldn't spare the time she needed to rest. Tipping up the visor on his helm, Lucais forced a grin and prodded her with the only weapons at hand . . . his tongue and her temper. "You're done in, but I'd expected nae better of a weak Lowland lass."

Elspeth stiffened away from him, anger sending a welcome shaft of warmth through her body, lending strength to her flagging muscles. "I'd like to see the man who'd last as well."

"I'm feelin' right fresh," he lied. "We *lions* have the endurance of huntin' cats," he taunted to goad her further.

"My brother would have made two of you any day." She wavered over to a wet boulder and sat with a huff . . . and a wince. But her color was up and her shoulders were square.

That's my lass. Fondly. He slipped the wineskin from his saddle and brought it to her, gratified to see her hands were steady as she lifted it to her mouth and drank deep. The curve of her throat glowed in the dimness, slender and vulnerable. He relented. "I'm sorry there wasna time to take you to Kinduin."

Elspeth lowered the skin and glared at him. "I can keep up. If you've any regrets, save them for the fact that you werena able to gather an army to help you fight. You'll need it."

"Likely," Lucais allowed. He took the wine, sated his thirst and handed her a hunk of bread from the provisions she'd brought to the broch. They ate in silence while the weary horses drank from the nearby burn, their breath misting like dragon's smoke above the dark, rushing water.

Her belly full, her blood warmed by the wine, Elspeth felt considerably better. "You did that apurpose."

"Did what?"

"Made me angry at you so I'd forget about being tired."

Lucais's faint smile was her answer. "Did it work?"

"Aye. Thank you." Her words broadened his smile, but his eyes remained alert, watchful. Tonight he was the rough Highland warrior, the Lion of the Sutherlands, sitting by the burn, his plaid flung back to reveal the sword at the ready.

Sweet Mary, how she loved him. Even now, with her heart still aching over the fact that he'd wed her for the broch, not for herself. More important, somehow, she'd come to respect him as she did few men. But could they ever come to trust each other?

"Why are you frownin', Elspeth?" he asked.

"I—I wondered how far it was to the pass," she hedged.

He scowled, but didn't press. "An hour. The trail is easier, but we must ride flat out to reach Orkel before the convoy does."

"How did Seamus know when it left? I thought you werena planning to make the shipment for another fortnight."

"He either has a spy in the village or someone watching it." Not a comfortable thought. 'Twas twice in as many days the enemy had gotten close to the village. The lack of raids over the past few years had obviously dulled his men's senses. He'd see them cured of such laxness when he got back...if he got back.

Elspeth groaned aloud when Lucais announced it was time to ride. It took everything she had not to crumple into a heap when he tugged her to her feet. Accepting his boost onto her horse grated on her pride, but was preferable to falling on her face.

After that, things seemed easier. The tall shoulder of the mountain shielded them from the wind; the ground beneath their horses' thundering hooves was more even. On and on they rode, following no trail she could see in the uncertain light and leaving none behind. They wove around the hills, cutting through gorges and gullies, fording streams, invading wooded glens. As her surefooted mount followed Lucais's lead, Elspeth grew drowsy, lulled by the motion and the wine sloshing in her head.

Had it not been for the danger to the Sutherlands, she might have actually enjoyed herself. There was something ... exciting about riding through the night, racing through the wild hills with a braw Highlander for company, the two of them bent on an urgent mission. It harkened back to the old legends Megan had related. Glancing ahead at the man she followed, his back straight despite the hour, his shoulders unbowed despite the burden placed on them, Elspeth knew her slurs on his valor for a lie. Lucais truly deserved the byname Niall had given him.

Lucais stopped atop a high rise. As she drew rein beside him, he muttered, "There's the road to the pass. But 'tis empty, and I canna tell if we're too early ... or too late." The illusion this was some fanciful tale shattered.

Straightening in the saddle, Elspeth gazed down the long, steep hill to the dark ribbon that wound through the valley below. The trees edging the trail obscured much of it from view, but as far as she could tell, nothing stirred on the road. Still, apprehension skittered down her spine. Silent and peaceful as the scene was, something was not right. Something she couldna ...

"What could have roused the cattle?" Lucais murmured.

Elspeth swung her head and took a second look at the familiar black shapes she'd dismissed at first glance. A shaggy Highland bull stood guard halfway down the hill, flanked by his harem of twenty or so. "Mayhap they heard us ride up."

"Nay. The bull isna lookin' this way. 'Tis the road he's starin' at. See how he's placed himself between it and the cows?"

The moon chose that moment to shake free of the clouds, and in the sudden wash of light, Elspeth saw something move. "Look there ..." She pointed to a gap in the line of trees.

"Wagons. I see them."

"Oh, Lucais! We're in time." Giddy with relief, Elspeth made to spur down the hill, but Lucais grabbed her horse's bridle.

"Wait. The wagons are too far off to have startled the cattle." He stood in his stirrups, visor tipped up, eyes narrowed as he scanned the moon-drenched landscape.

"Bother the stupid cattle," Elspeth grumbled.

"Ambush!" The word hissed between Lucais's teeth, drawing her horrified gaze to the trees at the base of the hill. She saw it then, the glint of light on metal. A sword, a dozen, unsheathed and waiting with restless eagerness.

"Quick, we have to ride down and warn your men," she cried.

"They're too far off to hear our cries, and the Munros could put an arrow in my throat ere I got close enough."

Elspeth shivered at the thought. "Wh-what will you do?"

"I'll improvise."

Chapter Sixteen

Alain Munro could taste victory, see it in the dust raised by the Sutherland wagons as they moved slowly into view. A wedge of five men rode at the fore, swords unsheathed and at the ready. Behind them, he counted at least thirty more men strung along the route of march, and they likely had a rear guard, as well. Beside him, a man shifted, eager to be up and at their prey.

"Easy," Alain murmured. "They outnumber us. We'll need the element of surprise to carry the day. Pass the word to wait for my signal." He wanted to make this as bloodless as possible in hopes of making peace with the Sutherlands when he was laird.

His hand clenched tight on his sword hilt, Alain watched the Sutherlands advance, each step they took measured in the quickening of his pulse. Soon. Soon. He fancied the earth shook with the refrain, then realized the earth *was* shaking.

"'Tis the bloody cattle," exclaimed the man beside him.

Spinning, Alain saw a wall of burly black shapes hurtling down the hillside, running straight at their hiding spot. Behind them rode a single man, sword held aloft, gleaming like a torch in the moonlight, cloak flowing out behind him like the wings of a dark, vengeful angel.

"Get him. Cut him down before he ruins everything." Alain's hoarse whisper sent men scrambling through the trees.

Too late. "Munros!" shouted the avenging angel, and then he followed it up with the Sutherland battle cry.

Alain's blood ran cold as the words were bellowed back from the road. The guards deserted the wagons and poured into the woods, their war cry swelling to a roar that heralded doom. "Retreat," Alain shrieked, and set spurs to his horse.

Trapped as they were between the sharp horns of the enraged cattle and the swinging swords of the furious Sutherlands, the Munros didn't stand a chance.

Even knowing they'd brought this on themselves, Elspeth felt
her stomach roll. She wanted to turn away, wanted to block out
the knots of men writhing together in mortal combat, but she
was afraid that if she took her eyes off Lucais, even for a second, something dreadful would happen to him. So she stood
atop the hill where he'd bade her wait, arms wrapped around
her trembling body, throat clogged with tears.

Lucais fought with an economy of movement, a tireless flu-
idity that was both beautiful and terrible to watch. Studying his
arching thrusts as he put away one opponent, his lightning
parries as he whirled to face yet another, Elspeth was haunted
by the slurs she'd cast on his knightly skills. As a child, she'd
often sneaked down to the tiltyard to watch her brothers practice with sword and lance. Lion had been the best, the stron-
gest, the most aggressive—the standard against which she'd
measured all men, and found them sadly lacking. Until now.
Aye, Lucais would have tested Lion's mettle, she thought.

The sight of a man breaking away from the battle and
charging up the hill jerked her from her reverie. Was he Munro?
Or Sutherland? That she couldn't tell sent her scrambling back
for her horse, tied to a nearby tree. Barely had she taken the
reins in her chilled hands when the man was upon her. She
whirled as he pulled his mount to a halt, reaching for her dirk,
her back pressed to the rough bark of the tree.

"Elspeth! What good fortune to find ye here," he rasped
out.

"Alain?" Elspeth asked, trying to identify the red-rimmed
eyes staring at her from the sockets of his helmet.

"Aye. 'Tis me." He was breathing hard, and there was a
bloody rent in his left forearm, but otherwise he seemed unhurt.

"I'm glad you survived," she said honestly. "Let me bind
your wound, then you must be off before Lucais—"

"I'm fine," he growled. "Mount up. I'll take ye wi' me."

Elspeth sighed and came closer, laying a hand on his boot to
take the sting from her rejection. "We've been all through this,
Alain. I'm Lucais's wife now, and I'm well pleased—"

"Pleased!" he exclaimed, raking her from tangled hair to the mud-splattered hose visible beneath her cloak. "How can ye be? Every time I see ye, ye look worse."

"Thank you very much," she snapped back.

His expression softened. "Ye're as beautiful as ever, love, but ye deserve to be dressed in the finest silks, not coarse castoffs. 'Tis obvious Lucais willna keep ye in the manner ye deserve, despite the fact that he's wealthy enough to do so."

"Lucais's first concern is his people's welfare," Elspeth said defensively. "I understand that—"

"Aye, ye've a lovin' heart, but 'tis wasted on him," Alain said firmly. "He has a way of usin' up women and discardin' them. Jean found that out... to her sorrow."

Elspeth started. "What do you know of her?"

"Like ye, she wasna happy at Kinduin, so she ran from Lucais... straight into trouble."

"Trouble? What kind of trouble? What are you saying?"

Alain shrugged. "'Tis in the past. Come now." He seized her hand. "I'll take ye away from all this. I'll see ye ha' whatever ye want...even another house in Edinburgh, if ye've a mind."

"I've a mind—" *For you to let me go,* she would have added, but just then Lucais walked out of the trees, his horse's reins in his left hand, his bloodied sword in the right.

"So, wife, we replay this drama," he growled in a voice nearly as terrible as the contempt burning in his eyes.

Elspeth blinked and tried to step back, but Alain's gauntleted fist held her fast. "Lucais, it isna what you—"

"Oh, I think I have a pretty fair idea what's goin' on, but it willna work, Munro. Not this time."

Alain's hand tightened painfully on hers. "Ye've uncommon luck attractin' the lasses, but ye canna hold on to one."

"The only way you Munros can get a woman is to poach one of mine," Lucais said, low and tight. "But I willna give up Elspeth."

"What are you talking about?" Elspeth demanded.

"We'll see about that." Alain reached for his sword, but in unsheathing it had to let go of Elspeth.

Lucais leapt forward, shoving her aside. She hit the ground with enough force to drive the air from her body. Over the ringing in her ears, she heard the clash of steel on steel, the grunts of two men bent on killing each other. Nay. She could not let that happen. Both men were precious to her, each in his own way. Shoving the hair from her eyes, Elspeth scrambled to her feet and swayed there as she studied the battle.

Lucais had the edge in reach and weight, but Alain was mounted and used his horse as a weapon, drawing the beast in tight circles to block his opponent's blows. Did he realize, as she did, that Lucais would hesitate to cut down the hapless horse unless all else failed?

Oh, Lucais! her heart cried, yet she dared not voice her fears lest she distract him. A distraction! That's what she needed. Something to make both of them draw back long enough for her to reason with them, make them understand she had no intention of going with Alain. Getting Lucais to allow his sworn enemy to ride off into the night might be trickier, but...

The wind whipped across the bleak hilltop, tugging at her hair, lifting her cloak.... Her cloak. Elspeth tore at the fastenings, ripped off the garment and advanced on the battle. "Stop!" she cried, and tossed the cloak over their crossed swords. Dark wool settled over deadly steel, enveloping it in a mire of thick, damp cloth. The sharp tips of the blades poked through the fabric, snaring them even more deeply in her trap.

"Elspeth! You fool!" Lucais bellowed. He wrenched at his sword, cursing as he tried to free it. Atop his horse, Alain did the same. The cloth bobbed back and forth between them, like a rag caught in a tussle between two large, angry dogs.

"You're the fools." Elspeth grabbed the edge of the tattered cloak and pulled down. Hard. The wool rent, then wrapped tight around their sword hilts. Actually, this was a very effective means of stopping a fight, she thought, pleased with herself. Of course, it helped that neither of these men truly wanted to kill her... yet. One look at Lucais's enraged expression and she wondered if she'd gone too far. "Listen to me, both of you. I—"

Lucais spat a vile oath, let go of his sword and pulled the dirk from his belt. "Stay back, Elspeth," he shouted, and would have leapt at Alain had she not thrown herself between them.

Wrapping both arms around Lucais's waist, Elspeth grabbed hold of his thick leather belt and clung for dear life. His, Alain's and their clansmen's. "Be reasonable, Lucais," she begged, wishing she could see beneath the metal mask he wore.

"Reasonable!" he exploded. His left hand grabbed her upper arm, not gentle and tender as she knew he could be, but hard, hurtful, desperate to shake her off and get on with the business of killing his sworn enemy. She was out of time and miracles.

"Run, Alain," she screamed.

"Damn you," Lucais shouted over the scramble of hooves on loose stone as Alain seized the opportunity and escaped.

"You shouldna have done that." Lucais thrust her from him.

"I know," Elspeth said, dizzy with misery. She'd likely lost her chance for a life with him. "But I owed it to Alain. He isna like Raebert and Seamus. There's good in him."

"You love him," he said in a dead, dull voice.

"Nay!" But Elspeth saw from the tight set of his jaw and the bitterness in his eyes that he didn't believe her. And then there was no more time for pleading or explanation, for the victorious Sutherlands swept up the hill to congratulate their laird on the brilliant ploy that had saved their lives.

She'd lost, Elspeth thought as the laughing men swirled around her. She'd tried to save two men and lost both of them. There must be something she could do to salvage the situation, some way to convince Lucais that gratitude, not love, had motivated her to save Alain. But right now she was too exhausted, too numb with cold and misery to think of a way out of this twisted labyrinth of pain and half-truth.

It was midafternoon before Lucais got Elspeth and the two wounded Sutherlands back to Kinduin. In defiance of his bleak mood, the sun had shone the whole way. With the harvest safely on its way to market and the Munros sent back to Scourie with their bloodied tails between their legs, he should have felt victorious. He felt hollow, instead. Achingly empty. As though Elspeth's betrayal had ripped a great hole in his chest.

If he hadn't gone in search of her, would she have run off with Alain? Munro's taunts came back to haunt him, made him wonder if there was something lacking in him that caused his women to flee from him. Was he too harsh? Too gentle? How did he know what a woman wanted from a man? What Elspeth wanted?

The ache became a sharp pain that twisted deep in his gut. Even during the heat of battle, the part of him not concentrating on staying alive had been afraid for her, alone and unprotected on the hilltop. When he'd seen Alain break away from the fighting and spur up the slope, his first thought had been saving her. Quickly dispatching his current opponent, he'd given chase, circling around through the copse of trees so Alain wouldn't see him coming, panic and harm Elspeth.

Never in his most tortured nightmares had Lucais expected to find them talking together like old friends . . . or like lovers. Jesu, that had hurt. The sight of Elspeth's hand resting on his enemy's leg, her lips curved in a warm smile as she looked up at the bastard, had roused such a black fury in Lucais he'd flown at Alain with a ferocity that shocked him. Only to be thwarted by Elspeth and her damned cloak.

Lucais trembled with renewed rage. That was twice she'd dashed in and saved Alain. Proof Munro was more than a friend to her. White-hot agony ripped through Lucais, nearly doubling him over in the saddle.

"Lucais?" Elspeth said gently, pulling him from his tortured reverie. "The drawbridge is down. We should get Harry within."

Trembling with the will it took to master his turbulent emotions, Lucais glanced back at young Harry, riding double with Cathal. The lad had taken a sword thrust to the shoulder and would have bled to death on the road had Elspeth not stepped in and cobbled together a thick bandage strapped on tight with Cathal's belt. At her insistence, they'd stopped every hour so she could loosen the binding and replace the padding. Though he hadn't uttered a word of complaint, Harry listed to one side in his father's arms, face ashen and dotted with sweat.

"Lead the way," Lucais said gruffly to Elspeth, wary that she'd bolt from Kinduin's gates.

Elspeth sighed and bowed her head to the inevitable. He hated her. That scene on the hilltop had been the final straw, shattering whatever chance they'd had at happiness into a thousand bitter shards. Yet she was not sorry she'd saved Alain. He was a decent man. If only she could make Lucais see that past his hatred of all Munros. A sidelong glance at his closed profile made her doubt he'd ever speak to her again, much less listen.

She reluctantly nudged her weary horse into motion, her shoulders slumped beneath the plaid Lucais had loaned her. Despite the hours she'd worn it, the scent rising from the sun-warmed wool was Lucais's own. The unique smell of sunshine and man filled her nostrils as she clattered across the wooden drawbridge, mocked her with memories of their single night together. Doubtless this was as close as she'd get to him again.

The whole of Kinduin had turned out to welcome them home. The throng lined the road from the outer wall, through the bailey and into the inner ward. Lucais rode like a man carved from granite. Looking neither right nor left, he ignored the questions hurled at him by his worried clansmen. It was left to the two troopers who'd been detailed to guard their miserable little party to shout back a brief description of the night's events.

A moan swept the crowd when they heard the wagons had been set upon by Munros. The moan became a gasp of wonder at Lucais's daring ploy to foil their scheme, rose to a jubilant roar as they learned the enemy had been routed. "Lion! Lion!" they chanted.

The hero of the day seemed unmoved by their cries of adoration, Elspeth noted as she glanced over her shoulder at him. He'd removed his helmet and tucked it under his arm, but his scowl was grim, foreboding.

What would he do now? she wondered as she pulled her mount to a halt before the keep. Kinduin tower glared down at her, dark and disapproving as its laird, chilling her so she trembled despite the warmth of the sun. In a few moments, she'd dismount, walk up those steps and be swallowed up by the black maw of the open doorway. And then what? Would Lucais once again lock her in the counting room? The shivering increased. She set her teeth together to still their chattering.

"Thank God ye've been returned safe to us," Ena called. She stood by Elspeth's stirrup, tears of gratitude running down her cheeks. Behind her stood Wee Wat, grinning nearly as broadly as wee Gillie, held high in his arms.

"Aye. Thank God," Elspeth murmured, but 'twas to Lucais she turned her troubled eyes, for at the moment, he controlled her destiny. The hard look he gave her in return was as cold and impenetrable as those of the tower's open windows. It sent another shiver down the spine she'd kept stiff by sheer will alone. Her skin crawled. At any moment, she expected him to turn to the boisterous Sutherlands and denounce her as a spy, and worse, a despoiler of their sacred place.

In her mind echoed the terrible sounds of Seamus and his men tearing at the walls of the broch, debauching its sanctity, grinding its precious history beneath their greedy boot heels.

Even now, they could be riding off with their ill-gotten plunder. *Someone must go and stop them,* she thought. As she opened her mouth to tell Lucais, he turned away and started issuing orders.

None of them concerned throwing her in the dungeon and tossing away the key, Elspeth realized with a giddiness that bordered on hysteria. That he had not forgiven her was obvious from the intensity of his stare. Dazed as much by apprehension as exhaustion, she gratefully accepted Wee Wat's help in dismounting and climbing the stairs.

"Are ye certain ye're unhurt?" the old man muttered as they entered the hall. "Yer color's none too good and ye're tremblin' like a newborn foal."

"I . . . I'm fine," she whispered. "Just tired."

He snorted. "No wonder. More than four and twenty hours ha' passed since ye left Kinduin, and from those great circles under yer eyes, I'd say ye've no' slept. Where did ye tear off to? Ye went to yon broch, did ye?" he added when she didn't answer.

"Keep your voice down." Elspeth looked around nervously, but Ena and Lucais were bent over Harry and everyone else was clustered around the other wounded trooper, plying him with bread and ale in exchange for the details of the battle.

"Something is wrong," Wee Wat growled.

Elspeth bowed her head. "Naught that can be fixed."

"What is it?" His fingers tightened on her arm. "If he's done aught to harm ye, I'll get ye away so quick—"

"Nay. Lucais has done naught." Except to refuse to believe in me. For Elspeth, raised on honor and honesty, 'twas the cruelest cut of all. If only there was some way she could reach past the barricades he'd erected. She'd done it once, they'd made a start two nights ago, but how to recapture those feelings? How to break through his icy reserve and kindle the fire that had burned so hotly between them?

Wee Wat's sigh of exasperation echoed her own aching frustration. "Ye'll tell me in time, I suppose. And there's naught to be gained by standin' here shiverin'."

Elspeth pulled her arm free when he tried to lead her from the room. "I have to tend young Harry."

"You've done enough already," Lucais growled, spinning her in her tracks to face his chiseled features, hard and unrelenting as the mountains they'd traveled in their desperate race

to save his clansmen. Didn't their shared adventure count for
anything? Apparently not. "Take her above," he said to Wee
Wat, then he turned his back on them and walked away, spine
stiff, shoulders square. With him went Elspeth's heart and her
hope. He hated her.

And yet... There had been something in his eyes, something briefly glimpsed in that instant before he moved. Pain.
Pain and a yearning as deep and profound as her own. He hated
what she'd done but was not immune to the sensual bond
they'd forged.

How could she build on that tenuous link? was Elspeth's only
thought as she followed Wee Wat from the hall.

'Twas dark and supper long since over when Lucais dragged
himself up the stairs toward his chamber. Exhausted as he was,
he probably could have slept on the floor, would have preferred it to being cooped up with Elspeth, but he'd be damned
if he'd air their differences before Cathal and the others. Pride
was part of it. After the debacle with Jean, he wanted no one
whispering about his inability to hold a woman.

His other concerns were more practical. If his clansmen
learned that Elspeth had stolen Daibidh's chest, gone to the
broch and *twice* aided Alain in escaping, their fury might lead
them to do something destructive. Bitter as he felt toward her,
the thought of her being hurt was insupportable. 'Twas the
need to protect her until he could decide what must be done
with her that had driven Lucais from the hall full of celebrat-
ing Sutherlands to face his own private demons. His prickly,
lying little witch of a wife.

Lucais's hand hesitated on the latch. Likely Elspeth was
asleep. It had been hours since the servants had come down
with her dirty bathwater and the remains of her meal. Untouched for the most part. Like the food Ena had tried to force
on him. Though he'd not eaten since last night, the fish stew
and barley bread had caught on the lump in his throat.

Aye, if she was half as exhausted and disheartened as he was,
she'd likely sought oblivion in sleep. Praying 'twas so, Lucais
opened the door and slipped in, then wished he'd stayed below
when the scent of lavender and Elspeth wrapped itself around
him. His knees went weak on a wash of bittersweet memories.
Elspeth defying him. Elspeth challenging him. Elspeth laugh-

ing with him. Elspeth loving him. Shuddering with the force of his emotions, he leaned against the door.

Oh, Beth, his heart cried out. *Why did you do it? Why can' you not see what we could have together?*

A sigh, a rustle of bed linens from across the room had him straightening away from the door. Fists clenched, breath bated, he watched the tightly closed drapes, waited for some sign that she was awake. Raw and ragged as he felt, he knew he couldn't bandy words with her. Not without saying or doing something he'd regret later on. But whether he'd send her away, flee from her or beg her to love him, even he didn't know. He only knew that he was wound so tight that something had to give.

If he could only make it through tonight, get the rest he so badly needed, mayhap he'd be stronger tomorrow, more able to cope with the question of what to do with Elspeth.

When no further sound issued from the curtained bed, Lucais crept across the room like a thief. He parted the velvet bed hangings, letting in light from the single candle burning on a pike beside the fireplace. To his relief, Elspeth lay on her side facing him, eyes closed, hands tucked under her chin. Seeing the tears dried on her pale cheeks made him sigh with regret. He set his teeth against the urge to touch her, to soothe away the pain.

Lucais had washed up downstairs and put on old hose and a tunic that were languishing in Ena's mending basket. Conscious of the tenuousness of his control, he left the clothes on and crawled into bed. The straw mattress rustled, the ropes supporting it creaked beneath his weight as he gingerly stretched out on the very edge of the bed, his back to temptation.

It did no good. Her scent moved over him like a physical caress, beckoned him to turn and bury his aching flesh in the warm haven of hers. He wanted her as never before, the craving sharpened by the memories they'd built in each other's arms.

Tomorrow he'd find some plausible excuse to send Elspeth home. Without the deed and whatever else she'd stolen.

Elspeth stirred in her sleep. Chilled and seeking warmth, she rolled closer to the only nearby source.

Lucais. She'd recognize his scent anywhere. More asleep than awake, she buried her nose in his chest, disappointed to meet wool instead of flesh. Her fingers drifted down, searching until they found skin, then diving under the wool to pet and explore.

"Beth," he whispered, his strong arms enfolding her, his hands moving up and down her back, making her tingle with anticipation. Needing more, she pushed his tunic up, groaning as the hairs on his chest abraded the tips of her breasts.

"Aye." She lifted her mouth, moaning as his lips slanted across hers, hot, hungry, urgent as her own growing passion. Eagerly she followed his lead. Her hands tangled in his hair as he deepened the kiss, his hands moving over her, steadily, provocatively building the fire inside her.

He growled his approval when she arched up, offering herself. His mouth slid down her neck to close over one turgid peak, suckling her so lushly she cried out, twisting against him, wanting more, wanting everything. Her blood coursed like molten honey, the coil inside her drawing tighter and tighter with each caress, every taste and touch.

"Please," she breathed, the sound ending in a sigh as his clever fingers slid over her belly to stroke her there, where the need was sharpest. But she wanted more, so much more. "I need you," she cried. "Now, inside me, filling the emptiness."

His response was low and guttural, a mingling of desire and urgency as he ripped away the woolen barrier separating her milling legs from his. A growl of satisfaction rumbled through him as he lifted her for the plunging edge of his invasion. She welcomed it with a purr of pure pleasure, wrapped herself around him as the storm built higher. The tempest quickened, took on a life of its own and carried them with it. Higher. Higher.

"I love you," she cried in the instant before the sweet, hot whirlwind crested, shattering in its intensity. Dimly she heard him shout her name, felt him shudder in her arms, but sleep reclaimed her before she could say more.

What have I done? Lucais thought, dazed, appalled.

He'd made love with his wife. His treacherous wife. No matter that his senses had been dulled by exhaustion, the fact remained that he'd coupled with her.

Shaken, weak and drained by more than just physical exertion, Lucais rolled onto his side, one arm thrown over his eyes

in a vain attempt to ward off the recriminations flashing
through his brain. Even then, Elspeth wouldn't let him go.
Sighing softly, she cuddled against him, one leg sliding across
his, her head nestling into the curve of his shoulder. Just as
though she had every right to be there.

Had she planned this? Seduced him to circumvent his anger?

Well, it wouldn't work.

Elspeth forced herself to stay limp despite the tension radiating from Lucais. It saddened her to realize that their loving
had solved naught. He still doubted her. She'd just have to find
a way to make him see reason.

Chapter Seventeen

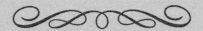

Lucais slowly crawled out of a deep, exhausted slumber, sensations gradually registering as he awoke. He lay on his back. In bed. His own, he thought, for Elspeth's lavender scent filled his nostrils when he moved his head on the pillow. Moving the rest of his body was more difficult. He tried his legs first. Couldn't budge them. His arms were stretched above his head. He attempted to lower them, but got no farther than waist-level when something tightened around his wrists, held him fast....

"Bloody hell!"

Lucais's eyes flew open and he leapt up. Or tried to. He was tied to the bed at hand and ankle. *The Munros had somehow taken Kinduin whilst he slept!* Perversely, his first thought was for Elspeth. He had to get free and find her, save her. Swearing under his breath, he tugged at his bindings, bucking and twisting...to no effect. He lay back, panting with exertion and dread, thwarted but undefeated. He'd find a way. He'd—

"Ah, you're awake at last," called a cheery voice. The bed hangings were wrenched aside, drenching his darkened little cave of horrors in bright sunshine.

Lucais squinted against the sudden light. "Elspeth, what is goin' on?" he demanded of the figure silhouetted in the opening.

"I've tied you up. Now, will you have the chamber pot first, or food?" she inquired, hands on hips, head cocked like a pert sparrow's. When he didn't reply, she repeated the question as though to a small, backward bairn.

"Untie me!" His enraged bellow drove her back a step. The minx squared her shoulders and advanced again.

"I canna do that. Not until you listen—"

"You can tell me whatever you want . . . after you've untied me," Lucais snarled, tugging at the ropes.

Her face gentled. "You'll only hurt yourself. I'm afraid those silken cords are really quite strong, and Lion taught me to tie a very efficient knot. You willna get free till I say so."

"They'll miss me below and come lookin'."

"I told them you were exhausted and like to sleep all day."

He lunged against the cords. "I'll shout the place down."

"I'll stick a rag in your mouth."

"Witch!"

"Fool!"

He slumped back and glared at her. "Only for trustin' you."

"The point is, you *dinna* trust me." Elspeth sighed heavily. " 'Tis hurting me, and 'tis tearing us apart."

Her pain was reflected in his eyes. "I want to trust you. Three nights ago I thought everything would work out. Then . . ."

"And then I discovered that you'd stolen my deed, and I got angry. Angry enough to teach you a lesson and take what was mine. Or what I thought was mine," she added softly. Once inside the broch, she'd realized it belonged to the ages. "I'd never have found the tunnel entrance if Daibidh hadn't helped me."

"*When* you untie me, I'll go and ask him about it."

Elspeth stomped her foot. "Why is it you canna believe *me?*"

"Because . . . because there is no logical reason for Daibidh to defy tradition and let you inside our sacred place."

"Trust ofttimes defies logic. Considering our history, it wasna logical for me to agree to handfast with you."

" 'Twas either me or Seamus Munro," he pointed out.

"You're contradicting yourself, m'lord. Had I been in league with the evil old bastard, I'd have ridden off with him straight away. The truth is . . ." Elspeth shivered. "The truth is, I have much to fear from Seamus. If he ever learned I played a part in Raebert's death, he'd move heaven and hell to see I died slowly and painfully. Or mayhap you think I lied about my marriage."

Now 'twas Lucais's turn to flinch. "Nay. I heard you cry out in your sleep. I saw the fear in your face when you awoke and thought I was him." And he knew Raebert was capable of cruelty.

"Thank you for that much, at least," she muttered.

"Good. Then untie me."

Elspeth shook her head. "Not till you believe . . . truly believe . . . I dinna plan to run off with Alain."

"You two certainly seemed cozy yesterday," Lucais said in a cold voice that nearly killed Elspeth's hope. Nearly.

"Stupid man." She thrust her face in his. "I was trying to make Alain understand I didna need or want his help."

"Why would he keep comin' back if you didna encourage him?"

"Because he's as thickheaded as any man. He's a good man, though, or would be if he were strong enough to get out from under Seamus's thumb." This drew a pithy oath from Lucais. Elspeth threw up her hands and began to pace. "Fine. Dinna believe me. I think Alain persists in trying to rescue me now because he lacked the courage to confront Raebert when he learned I was being abused. Alain feels . . . protective of me."

"Protective, hell! He wants you in his bed." That Lucais looked fit to do murder made Elspeth smile. He still cared.

"That may be. Coupling seems much on men's minds . . . even when they are angry with someone," she said slyly. Smugly.

"I was asleep last night," he grumbled.

"Oh? You seemed right . . . lively for a sleeping man." Her gaze turned speculative as it swept down his sheet-covered body. "Are you saying that if I touched you now, you'd *sleep* through it?" Her head was thrown back, her hair a black river flowing over her shoulders and down to the waist of her blue bed robe. Her eyes gleamed with a sensual challenge as old as Adam and Eve.

Lucais swore silently as his traitorous body stirred to meet it, quickened to match the erratic beat of her pulse in the pale hollow of her throat. Gritting his teeth, he tried to subdue his rising passion, but it was a losing game. And she knew it. *Witch.* "Do what you will, then untie me," he growled.

"I want more than that from you, Lucais."

"I know what you want." Eyes narrowed, he stared at her. He was tied down but by no means defeated. Above the sheet, his chest rose and fell in counterpoint to her own ragged pulse. His mouth was tightly clenched, his expression grim and distrustful.

She considered punching his stubbled jaw, decided the blow wouldn't dent his stubbornness. "You havena the faintest idea what I want," she said instead. "I came looking for Broch

Tower because I didna have anywhere else to go. I'd wed the wrong man and suffered for it. Glad as I was to be reunited with my family, there was no place for me at Carmichael Castle ... little for me to do but be daughter to my parents, sister to my siblings and aunt to Ross and Megan's adopted brood. It wasna enough. Nor could I bear to watch Da struggling to walk again." She drew in a ragged breath, let it out slowly as she prepared to bare her battered soul. "I felt guilty every time I looked at him."

That got his attention. "Why should you blame yourself? I understood from Ross's message that 'twas an ambush."

"I could have prevented it." Elspeth looked away, unable to bear his scrutiny and his censure. "Raebert said he'd hurt Da if I didna tell him where I'd hidden the last of my jewelry so he could sell it." She bowed her head. "I didna think he'd do it."

"Bloody hell," Lucais breathed. "Did you tell Lionel?"

Elspeth shook her head. "Raebert said that if I told anyone, he'd deny it, then he'd order his men to maim Ross next."

"It isna your fault. I know only too well Raebert was a cruel, evil man who delighted in rapin' and killin'."

"I should have been stronger. I should have done some—"

"Oh, Beth. Come here," Lucais said gently.

Glancing sidelong at him, Elspeth saw her confession had turned his hatred to pity. She wanted neither from him. "Nay, I have to tell you all of it. Though I didna know it when first I arrived, I needed this." She swung in a slow circle, arms outstretched to encompass the room and all of Kinduin, as well. "I want to live out my days here, working shoulder to shoulder with you during the day, sleeping in your arms at night. I want to read all your books and mayhap work on a book of legends like the one Megan wrote. I want to be wife to you, mother to your daughter ... and any others God gives us. I want to be the lady of Kinduin. Your lady." *Your love.* Through the blur of tears, she stared at Lucais, willing him to believe.

"Why?" His voice was as raw as her nerves. His eyes filled with such anguish it hurt to look at them. Worse still was the realization that if she had any hope of making him understand, she'd have to lay her heart open and risk even greater pain.

Elspeth trembled. "I ... I've always been drawn to you. I fought it and you because you were a bard, not the warrior I wanted. It seems mad, I know, but I rejected you so cruelly because I was afraid...afraid of my secret desire for you, afraid to wed a man I wanted but didna respect and doom us both to misery. Now I respect you, Lucais, and I...I love you.''

Lucais's mouth dropped open; the shutters fell away from his eyes, revealing the emotions they'd been guarding. Loneliness, longing and a vulnerability that nearly matched her own. All three paled in comparison to the love shining there. Mesmerizing in its intensity, his love stole her breath, healed her heart.

"Untie me, Beth," he whispered.

Do you believe in me? she wanted to ask. But she knew that if she wanted his trust, she'd have to give hers first. Because she'd rejected his love once, and he would not offer it a second time and risk being refused again. She understood that. But...

Slowly he unclenched his left fist, bound still by the loop of fabric. The palm was rough and callused as the rest of his exterior; the gesture was as tender as his soul. "If you canna free me, at least bring your lips closer. A declaration of love should be sealed with a kiss.''

Elspeth sank onto the bed. Tangling her fingers in his thick hair, she brought her mouth down to his. She parted her lips to the persistent pressure of his, shivered as his tongue swept in to tantalize and explore. *He loved her.* Sweet Mary, 'twas so joyous a thing she couldn't kiss him hard enough or deeply enough. Groaning, she gave herself up to the wonder of it all, scarcely feeling the tug at her waist till he let her up for air and she found he'd somehow taken the dirk from her belt.

"Your knots are stout, lass, but you didna tie my wrists nearly close enough to the posts. Gives a man too much maneuverin' room.'' He waggled the hand holding the knife.

"I'll remember that next time," she snapped.

"Easy, little hedgehog. I'm hopin' there willna be a next time.'' Smiling, he flipped the dirk and offered her the hilt. "Cut my bonds, will you?''

"And then what?'' Warily.

His grin grew, deepening the fine lines around his mouth, making his eyes twinkle. "Well, since you've cleverly arranged things so we willna be disturbed, I thought we'd *sleep* in a bit longer this morn.'' Sensual promise softened his features.

Elspeth's bones melted with longing. "You believe me?''

"Aye," he murmured, deeply touched by her revelation. "I only wished you'd shared your thoughts with me then." It might have saved them years of heartache if he'd only known, but he'd not flay her with that now. "If I've been distrustful, 'twas because I couldna believe you finally wanted me, too."

"Oh, Lucais. I've always wanted you, I was just too stupid to trust my heart." As blind to Lucais's good points as to Ross's. She attacked his bindings with more zeal than care.

"'Tis in the past, love. Mind you dinna nick me."

The task complete, Elspeth sat back and smiled cheekily. "I promise I willna cut off anything important, m'lord."

"Minx." He tackled her, rolled her onto her back and began tickling her mercilessly. Her struggles to evade his nimble fingers loosened the tie on her bed robe. The sight of her naked breasts and rosy nipples distracted him instantly. "Ah, Beth." The hands that had so recently tormented her slipped beneath the fine wool garment and began a torture of a more refined nature. His gentle touch, so at odds with the fierce hunger blazing in his eyes, melted away any remaining doubts.

Twining her arms around his neck, she whispered, "Love me, Lucais. Let me show you how much I love you." His murmur of assent went to her head like warm wine; her senses spun as he drew her against the hard planes of his body. Her lips parted eagerly for his deep, hungry kiss, her belly shivering in anticipation of the more intimate invasion yet to come.

"Beth." Wrenching his mouth away, he buried it in the curve of her neck. "I want to go slowly, to savor every precious moment." He trailed stinging kisses down to the swell of her breast. "But seeing you like this, knowing you love me . . ."

"I love you." Her words ended in a gasp as his mouth closed over one sensitized nipple and suckled it with devastating thoroughness. Pleasure spilled through her. Arching closer, she unleashed all the love pent up inside her, received back her gift twelvefold. He stroked her, cherished her with touches more potent and poignant than any words.

There was an urgency to the pace he set, as though he sought to bind them together for all time. Yet when he finally gave in to her whispered pleas and made them one, it was he who groaned in surrender. "You'll be the death of me," he rasped.

"But we'll die happy." Filled with a sense of power, of freedom, she rose above him, determined to explore the sensual skills he'd taught her. Her hair flowed over them like thick black silk; her heart soared on a wave of pure bliss. She cried his name as the wave crested and ecstasy rippled through her. Gloried to hear her own name shouted as he followed after.

"You'll never know how much I love you," Lucais whispered, cuddling her close in the sweet aftermath.

"I think you just showed me," Elspeth murmured, fiercely happy, terribly pleased with herself and with him. He was everything she'd dreamed of and more. A valiant knight, a kind man, a tender lover. With him, she'd found a home and a mate.

"Nay." His fingers trembled as he stroked the damp hair from her cheek. "You showed me." He kissed her temple and sighed. "God help me, if anything happened to tear you from me now, I'd die."

"I'm afraid you are stuck with me for all eternity, husband." But even as she snuggled deeper into his embrace, his words jogged her memory. "Is it because Jean left you? Was that what Alain meant when he said you'd lost another woman?"

He tensed. "'Tis in the past and best forgotten."

Elspeth didn't want to threaten their newfound harmony, but... "I told you about my father. Can you nae tell me about Jean?"

"Jean wasna happy at Kinduin," Lucais said cautiously.

"How is that possible?" Elspeth asked so sincerely that he began to believe she really did like his home.

"She wanted things I couldna give her." She'd wanted his love, but he'd given that to Elspeth years ago.

"Ah, 'twas because of Jean you feared I wouldna think Kinduin grand enough." Taking his silence for agreement, Elspeth burrowed closer. "I wish you could see inside me, read my thoughts and know what pleasure I take in being here. Partly 'tis because I love you." She kissed his throat, her fingers splayed over his heart. "So very much."

"And I love you, too, Beth," he said quickly, honestly.

Still she heard the slight hesitation in his voice. "What must I do to get it through your thick skull that I prevented you from killing Alain because I owe him my life?"

"I understand that, but..."

"What if you'd killed Alain and touched off a feud? Bad enough I must live with the knowledge that my cowardice was responsible for Da's crippling injury. Think you I want more blood staining my conscience?"

"'Twasna your fault Raebert ambushed Lionel," Lucais said gently, sidestepping the issue of Alain.

Elspeth sighed, her pain eased by the feel of his large hand caressing her spine. "Nor yours that Jean ran off. Ena says you went after Jean and brought her back. At least you were able to do something to help her. I didna even know Da had been wounded till 'twas over, and Raebert wouldna let me go to him."

"It took me four days to trace her to Bonar, a village loyal to Clan Ross," he began. "'Twas neutral territory for the Munros and Sutherlands, but by the time I arrived, 'twas too late."

"Too late? What happened?"

"She'd been ill-used, by Munros, accordin' to the landlord of the inn where she'd sought work as a maid. She was lyin' in an upstairs room, all bruised and battered when we got there. Six of my men died in the battle to rescue her." But the man who'd beaten and ravished Jean had escaped. "She didn't want to live, but I brought her back here to heal."

"Oh, Lucais." In vain she searched for words to ease their mutual guilt. "You did the best you could for her."

"But 'twasna enough."

"Fortunately the beating didna cause her to lose Gillie."

Lucais flinched as her words pierced more tender flesh than she could possibly know. Must never know. An old wound, a scar he would carry to his grave. He dredged up a smile to ease the scowl creasing her brow. "There is that."

Elspeth cupped his cheek with her hand, wishing she could absorb his pain. "Lucais, the bairn is blameless in this and Jean is dead. The only way we can make it up to them is by raising Gillie with love and kindness."

He kissed her palm. "Your capacity for lovin' and givin' amazes me. With your help, I'll try to be a good father to her."

"And I will be the best mother." Sighing, Elspeth buried her nose in his chest. "I love you so."

"And I love you," Lucais echoed, but his eyes were bleak as they stared blindly out over the sun-drenched chamber and his heart was heavy with the lie he'd told. The lie he must live for the rest of their lives. But he dared not stray from the path he'd trod these four years. He owed it to Jean and to Gillie.

* * *

'Twas afternoon by the time Lucais and Elspeth walked up the path from the village to Daibidh's hut. The wind whispered through the trees, making them bow and sway, and tugging at the tendrils that had come loose from Elspeth's braids.

Sniffing appreciatively, she lifted her face, drawing in the tang of pine and damp earth. "I love it here."

"Aye." Lucais paused, his arm tightening around her waist as he looked down at her flushed cheeks and bright eyes. "You fit in at Kinduin more completely than I'd dared hope."

"'Tis the clothes," she retorted with a saucy grin.

Lucais frowned as his glance swept her borrowed wool gown. "I'd sooner see you clad in silk. What happened to your—"

"Impractical. Thank you for bringing me with you," she said hurriedly before he could ask again about her silk gowns.

"You should have stayed at Kinduin, in bed," Lucais grumbled. "God knows you got little enough sleep."

"I canna sleep without you holding me."

That brought a twinkle to his eyes. "And when I do, you dinna let me get much real sleep."

Elspeth's cheeks flamed. "Am I too bold?" she asked, but without the defensiveness that had once marked their exchanges.

"Never." Lucais kissed the tip of her nose, delighted by the changes in her. Not that they wouldn't quarrel. They were both far too strong-willed to live in perfect harmony, but their arguments were tempered by mutual respect. Aye, beneath her fiery temper he'd found a bright, witty, brave woman, one who could incite his passions in bed and challenge his mind out of it. "I love you just as you are."

"And I've discovered that you are so much more than I'd ever dreamed," she whispered, remorse darkening her eyes.

"I thought we'd agreed to look forward, instead of back."

Elspeth swallowed and nodded. "Most men wouldna so easily put aside such a blow to their pride."

'Twasna his pride that had suffered when she refused him; 'twas his heart she'd broken. And now mended. "I'll let you make it up to me . . . tonight." His leer made her giggle. "We could go back now, forget this visit to Daibidh."

"Nay. You said you believed me, but I willna rest easy till he's told you he let me into the broch. And why." Mayhap then he'd truly know she wasn't in league with the Munros.

Lucais nodded, stepped up to Daibidh's hut and knocked, but there was no response from inside the small stone building.

"Do you think Daibidh's still at the broch?"

"Ena said he was seen in the village yesterday."

"But you said Daibidh didna have a horse. How could he have gotten back here so quickly? How did he get to the broch?"

"Daibidh defies reason. Still, I think we'd better take a look." Lucais lifted the latch and pushed the door open. It was black as pitch inside and cold, but the tingling that crawled down Lucais's spine owed more to dread than chill. "Wait here." Using the wedge of pale light from the open doorway, he crossed to the worktable, took flint from the pouch at his waist and lit the candle in the tall iron pike.

"Oh, my God," Elspeth exclaimed.

Lucais whipped around, found her kneeling over the pallet where Daibidh lay, a huddle of humanity wrapped in a tattered blanket. "He's alive," she whispered as Lucais crouched down beside her. "But barely."

"We'll take him back to the castle." But as Lucais made to slip his arms under the old man, Daibidh roused.

"I knew ye'd come," he rasped, his gaze on Elspeth's pale, worried face. "The Munros got inside the broch, then?"

"Aye," Elspeth said sorrowfully, guiltily. "But you mustna fret about that now. Lucais will see that they pay. Now, we need to get you someplace warm and—"

"I'm nae sick, just old and past my time. Ye were late gettin' here," he chided.

Elspeth nibbled on her lip. "We...we returned to Kinduin late last night and slept in."

"I expected ye four years ago."

Elspeth's gaze flew to Lucais, found her own shock reflected in his eyes. "But how could you have known...?"

"It doesna matter. What's important is that ye're here." A clawlike hand emerged from the blanket to cover her knotted ones, clenched uselessly in her lap. "Look at me, daughter." She did, surprised by the intensity of his stare. 'Twas as though he sought to see inside her, uncover her deepest secrets. "Ah. Ye've found the man ye were lookin' for, then."

"Aye. I've found him." Her eyes drifted to Lucais. She smiled faintly, then shook herself, suddenly all brisk efficiency as she ordered him to build up the fire, heat water and...

Daibidh's raspy chuckle filled the tiny room. "I can see ye'll ha' yer hands full managin' this one, lad."

"Life willna be dull, that's sure," Lucais replied, his words robbed of their sting by the kiss he brushed over her indignant frown before he rose to do her bidding.

"Was the broch all ye'd expected?" Daibidh asked her.

Elspeth sat back on her heels and smiled as she thought of those first moments when she'd stood in the central hall and looked up at the patch of evening sky. "It was so...so beautiful. So peaceful. I...I imagined I could see them." She closed her eyes. "The ancient ones inside the fort, warm, dry, well fed, safe from the hordes of Norsemen raging through the glens."

"They've chosen wisely, then," Daibidh said.

"Who has?" Elspeth blinked away the images of the broch and stared down at the bewildering little man.

"It doesna matter. Ye'll understand soon enough." He patted her arm, his hand surprisingly warm despite the chill of the room. He smiled as Elspeth touched his forehead. "I dinna ha' a fever. I'm just an old man who doesna feel the cold any longer." He amazed her anew by sitting up as Lucais approached with a cup of wine laced with herbs and heated with an iron poker.

As the old man drank, Elspeth looked at Lucais. "We'll take him back to Kinduin with us," she murmured.

"Nay." Daibidh lowered the cup and shook his head. "My place is here, where I can come and go as the spirits will."

Surely he meant "spirit," Elspeth thought, but a niggle of doubt raised gooseflesh on her arms. Who was Daibidh, really?

Hunkered down on the other side of the pallet, Lucais voiced the question that had brought them here. "I'd like to return to the broch and ascertain how much damage the cursed Munros did."

"Not as much as they could ha'." Daibidh set the cup aside but refused Elspeth's suggestion to lie down. "They havena found the treasure in the chief's crypt, but they willna give up."

Lucais swore and surged to his feet in a lithe movement. He paced to the table piled high with parchment and pots, then turned. "Where is this crypt?" That he could ask the question with her present was proof he trusted her, and Elspeth knew she'd never loved him more.

"Ask the lass," Daibidh replied.

"Me? But I dinna know—"

"Ye've seen the maps."

"Aye, but I didna understand the markings on them." And yet... She'd felt something. A stirring of her mind, a quickening of her blood when she'd passed the doorway next to the tunnel. "How did the Munros find out about the treasure?"

"From Duncan Munro," Daibidh said. "He was returnin' from a raid when he was chased by Sutherlands. Ill fortune led him to the broch. He had with him the rope he'd used to scale the walls of the tower he and his cohorts had attacked. It took him three tries, but he got the hook over the threshold of the outer door and climbed inside before our clansmen arrived on the scene."

"You should have told me this," Lucais said.

"I didna know until ye brought me the coins ye found in the glen. When I studied them, I saw it all." The thin lids dropped over Daibidh's dazzling eyes. "Watched Duncan explore the broch lookin' for another way out. He didna discover the secret tunnel, but he stumbled upon the entryway to one of the lesser tombs."

"Damn him," Lucais spat out. "He took the bloody coins back and fired Seamus's greed for gold. The bastard willna stop till he's torn the broch down and carted off what's inside."

"Duncan paid a high price for his trespass. He died in pain and terrible fear." Pale, icy triumph glittered in Daibidh's eyes as his lashes lifted. "As will any others who violate—"

"What of Lucais?" Elspeth blurted out. "I swear he only entered the broch because of me."

"Never mind me." Lucais scowled at the old man. "Why did you risk Elspeth's life by lettin' her into the broch?"

Daibidh shrugged, but the intensity of his stare was anything but casual. "She'd have found the lever sooner or later. She was clever enough to decipher the secret maps."

"I didna know 'twas forbidden to see them." She picked up the sack she'd brought with her, removed the maps and laid them on the old man's lap. "Take them back, please. Is there someone you can tell the fault was mine? Some way to save Lucais from—"

"Nay." Lucais thrust her behind him. "The blame is mine. I'd locked the chest away as you instructed, but I hadna found time to warn Elspeth about it. Punish me, but let her go."

"Dinna listen to him. I'm the one at fault!" Elspeth cried.

"Yer concern for each other does ye both credit," Daibidh murmured. The cowl of his robe had fallen back, revealing the sharp angles of his face. In the merciless wash of candlelight, he looked frail and unutterably weary. Except for his eyes, which glowed with pride. "Dinna worry about assignin' blame. If the spirits had wanted ye dead, ye wouldna be here now. As a matter of fact, I've a task I'd set ye to."

"Anything," they cried in unison.

Extracting the ancient coins from the depths of his robe, Daibidh placed them in Lucais's hand. "On the morrow, return these to their proper place. Elspeth will describe it for ye."

"But what of the curse?" Lucais asked.

"Ye willna be in danger so long as ye're puttin' something back, but ye must take care ye dinna disturb anything or take aught out wi' ye," the old man warned.

"Of course." Lucais looked at Elspeth, pleased by her quick nod of agreement. "I'll post a guard around the broch. As soon as Niall and the others come back from Curthill, we'll plan our revenge against the Munros. I willna rest till they've—"

"But, Lucais. 'Twill reignite the feud." Elspeth grabbed hold of his arm. "Only think of the cost. The hills and glens would run with blood. And for what? Surely there must be another way."

"Justice must be served," Lucais said in a hard voice.

"'Twill," Daibidh replied quietly, ominously. "But mayhap nae in the way ye think." Nor would he say more. He stared at the fire, his mind drifting to a place theirs couldn't reach.

Sunk deep in his own thoughts, Lucais nonetheless kept a sharp eye peeled for Munros as he and Elspeth rode back to Kinduin. As though sensing his change in mood, the sun that had brightened their ride to the village was swallowed up by a black cloud. Just so did the Munros seek to obliterate the Sutherlands.

The broch was just the beginning. Never mind that its violation would be a blow to their pride and their history, if Seamus found the treasure, he'd use it to buy weapons, armor, an army with which to sweep down from the north and wipe them out.

Lucais shifted in the saddle, his mind scrambling for a solution. But with every passing day, the noose around him seemed to tighten, choking off option after option till he could see no way save war to free his clan from the menacing Munros.

War. His blood chilled as the images formed in his mind. Death, destruction, burning huts, murdered men, weeping women and orphaned bairns. That had been the way of things when he'd arrived, and he'd sworn to give his people a better life.

"Oh, Lucais. What are we going to do?" Elspeth cried.

Lucais stopped on the trail. "We'll find a way out of this," he promised. Somehow. He had to, for there was more at stake now than there'd ever been before. If it actually came to war, he'd send Elspeth back to her family.

She must have read his mind, for her frown deepened. "I'm staying here," she said softly. "I willna leave you."

"Nor would I want you to go," he said hoarsely.

But he'd do what he had to to protect her. Elspeth read the determination in his taut jaw, his bleak gaze. "Lucais, I—"

"Something's amiss at the castle," called one of the guards who'd ridden with them. "See, the drawbridge is down and there are wagons movin' over it."

"Elspeth! Behind me!" Lucais ordered. He had his sword out and was ready to spur forward when he realized the wagons were going *into* Kinduin, not raiding Munros making off with their plunder. "'Tis too soon for Niall to be back...."

"They wear the Carmichael red and black," Elspeth said, standing in her stirrups. "'Tis Sir Giles." Before Lucais could stop her, she'd set her heels to her mount and was galloping up the rocky path toward Kinduin.

"Slow down. You'll break your fool neck." Lucais launched himself after her, managed to catch her just shy of the gatehouse. Grabbing her horse's bridle, he pulled her to a stop. "Elspeth. What in hell possessed you to—"

"Come and see." She flashed him a cheeky grin, broke free of his grasp and clattered over the wooden bridge, leaving him no choice but to trot along behind.

In the bailey, chaos reigned. All of Kinduin had turned out to unload the wagons. Amid much laughter and shouting, the men and women exclaimed over the wonders they'd uncovered . . . barrels of ale, sacks of flour, fresh vegetables from farms in warmer climes. The bairns had gotten into the seeded cakes and were stuffing their faces while the dogs noisily vied for the crumbs.

"What is all this?" Lucais asked, his eyes darting from one group to another, his face a mix of pleasure and doubt.

"I had Sir Giles buy a few things in Curthill."

"What? Did you defy my wishes and send him to beg credit of Laird Eammon?" Lucais exclaimed.

Elspeth knew a bellow of outraged male pride when she heard it, and set about to soothe it as she'd seen her mother do with her father. "I wouldna go against your wishes, my love," she said gently, her face a mask of subdued femininity.

"You'd flaunt the king's will if it suited you." His eyes narrowed to angry slits. "What have you done?"

"Well." Either she was not as skilled at this as her mama, or Lucais was less manageable even than her temperamental sire. Elspeth took a deep breath and plunged in. "I knew you hated seeing our people go without, so when I realized how impractical my gowns were, I—"

"What have your gowns to do with this?"

"I sold them. Traded actually," she amended as his face turned scarlet and his mouth dropped open. *Oh, please don't be angry.* There'd been enough strife these past few days to last her a lifetime, with things likely to get worse before they got better. "Lucais. Say something." *Say you approve.*

Lucais exhaled sharply, outraged that she'd sacrificed her beautiful things, touched that she'd been moved to do so. Then he recalled the last order he'd given to Niall before his men had left for market and decided that things had a way of evening out. "I love you" was all he could say.

It was exactly the right thing. Tears welled in Elspeth's eyes and her lower lip trembled. "Thank you," she whispered.

"Nay, 'tis I who thank you . . . on behalf of my people." Swinging down from his saddle, he went to lift her from hers.

"Our people," Elspeth murmured, and leaned up to kiss him.

"Wine, lass?" he asked when she let him up for air.

"Only if you'll share my cup."

"Done." He laughed and swung her into his arms, much to the amusement of the Sutherlands who trailed them inside the castle. As they crowded into the hall, Lucais told them to whom they owed thanks for this bounty, and their laughter turned to cheers.

Elspeth's heart soared as her name rose from every Sutherland throat to ring off the rafters. Instinctively she looked to Lucais, her eyes brimming with tears of joy. "I think they just might come to like me," she whispered.

"I know they will, love," Lucais replied, his throat clogged with emotion. If they got the chance, he thought bleakly, his happiest hour tainted by apprehension. They'd come so far, he and Elspeth, but their greatest trials lay ahead. How the hell was he going to save the broch without risking all-out war?

Chapter Eighteen

Alain shivered and drew his cloak closer. Despite the sun riding high in the sky, 'twas dark and cold in the woods edging Loch Shin. Uncomfortable so far into Sutherland territory, he kept his ears cocked for trouble. The only thing that disturbed the silence was the rush of wind through the pines and the lap of water against the shore. His thoughts were far less tranquil.

Seamus was up to something. Something more than just returning to the broch and locating the treasure.

Alain had crawled back to Scourie yesterday, sorely bruised in body and soul, wanting nothing more than to drown himself in ale and forget the horror of the ambush gone wrong. Predictably Seamus hadn't given him a moment's peace or an ounce of mercy.

"Ye canna do anything right," Seamus had snarled. "Ten men lost and twice that many horses." Alain knew he begrudged the loss of the latter more than the former.

"At least we managed to bring their bodies back for a proper burial," Alain had said. Telling the new widows and grieving parents had wrung his heart out. He'd felt inept as a commander. Worse, he knew that the lads, some of them scarce old enough to shave, had died for naught but Seamus's greed. And then there was Elspeth. Jesu, he'd hated leaving her on that bleak hill with Lucais looking fit to do murder. *Coward,* his conscience chided. *Weakling.* He'd failed to protect her from Raebert; now he'd abandoned her to Lucais. Seamus was right; he was spineless.

Alain shifted in the saddle and looked at his brother with loathing. Older by ten years, more burly of build and aggressive of temperament, Seamus had started bullying him when

Alain was still in the cradle. With Alain's mother dead, and their sire too busy killing Sutherlands to care, the pattern had been set. Seamus led; Alain followed, or suffered the consequences. But a new element had been added...fear for Elspeth. "I hear ye had a visitor from Edinburgh," Alain said with feigned nonchalance.

Seamus turned his head, lip curling. "What's it to ye?"

"Naught." He hoped. If Seamus had somehow learned the truth about Raebert's death, Elspeth would be in grave danger. Apprehensive, Alain looked away from Seamus's hostile gaze and changed the subject. "I dinna think Lucais is comin'. We should go back to Scourie and forget this mad scheme of yers."

"Never!" Seamus screeched. "That gold is mine."

"What gold? Ye searched the broch for most of the night and found naught but a few old weapons and some jewelry."

"Tearin' down those stone walls is slow work. We only had time to break into three small burial chambers."

Alain shuddered. Over the years, Seamus had forced him to do things that pricked his conscience, but violating the dead made his hair stand on end. There was something about the broch that reminded him of a graveyard at midnight. And then there was the way Duncan had died...screaming and ranting about demons.

"I havena the time to pull the whole broch down lookin' for the room where the high chief's likely laid out wi' all his wealth." Seamus smacked his lips in anticipation. "Lucais is goin' to show me where 'tis."

Alain sighed and looked toward the trail that led from Kinduin to the broch. It was barely visible through the thick underbrush that shielded the Munros from sight. "He willna do that. Even if he does come lookin' for the guards ye had killed, Lucais would never betray—"

"He will if he values his clansmen," Seamus snarled. "For I'll kill as many of them as it takes to persuade Lucais—"

"Hark, someone comes," whispered the lookout.

Seamus gestured his men down. Their black capes blended into the inky shadows on the forest floor. "Wait till they've passed," he hissed. "We'll fall on them from behind."

* * *

Elspeth rode near the back of the column of Sutherlands, her head down, her chin buried in the folds of her purloined cloak, only too aware of Lucais's fury should he discover she'd defied his orders...again. Glancing through her lashes, she caught a glimpse of his metal helmet and broad shoulders through the shifting line of riders up ahead.

How stiffly he held himself, his head swiveling this way and that as he scanned the woods bordering the trail. The wind had risen, tossing the branches and brush so she wondered how he could tell the sounds of encroaching foe from those of the swiftly approaching storm. Did Lucais really expect the Munros to attack forty well-armed men after their rout at Orkel Pass? Apparently, else he'd not have forbidden her to go with him.

"You're to stay here, safe inside Kinduin's walls," Lucais had commanded. Leaving Sir Giles and the Carmichaels in charge of the castle, he'd stripped the place of every man who could bear arms and set out on this bleak mission...to bring the murdered guards back for burial and return the coins to their rightful place. Providing the broch was even standing after a night and a day of Seamus's rapacious greed.

Elspeth's hands tightened on the reins, her nerves taut with dread. Despite Daibidh's assurances they'd be safe, she was afraid to let Lucais enter the fortress alone. The spirits that guarded the site might be willing to overlook one trespass, but that was before Seamus and his fiends had started tearing it apart. God alone knew what they'd find when they arrived.

A battle, most likely. And Lucais would wade in, determined to do his duty no matter whether he was threatened by ghosts or Munros. She'd come to make certain her brave warrior didn't do anything foolish...or dangerous. With any luck, Lucais would never even know she'd come along.

Elspeth had just realized they were nearly to the trail that led from the loch to the broch when something erupted out of the stand of pines she'd just passed.

Boar! she thought. But a quick glance over her shoulder showed an even more deadly enemy. *Munros!*

"'Ware!" she cried. "Munros!"

Up the line, her shout was echoed. Lucais thundered back down the trail, followed by the rest of his men. Too late. Cathal and the three men guarding the rear were already surrounded.

"Hold, Sutherland!" Seamus bellowed above the din. "Or we'll slit their gullets." Indeed, four Munros had leapt on behind the four Sutherlands and pressed dirks to their throats.

Sweet Mary aid them! Safely hidden by the bulk of Lucais's men, Elspeth looked to her husband. What would he do now?

Lucais sat still as a statue, his blazing gaze fixed on Seamus Munro. A dozen equally grim Sutherlands flanked him, swords at the ready. "What do you think you are doin', Munro?"

"I've a little project I need yer help wi'."

"Release my people."

"All in good time." Seamus smiled smugly, clearly relishing his advantage. "First ye'll give me the gold from yon broch."

A mutter of outrage rustled through the assembled Sutherlands, and they edged closer, only to be brought up short by Seamus's renewed threat to slit the throats of their kin.

"Rush them," Cathal called out, but Lucais shook his head.

"There isna any gold in the broch," he told Seamus.

"I know differently." Reaching into the pouch at his waist, Seamus withdrew a handful of coins. They gleamed seductively in the light, drawing gasps from Munro and Sutherland alike.

Lucais straightened, eyes narrowed, body shaking with the urge to leap at his enemy and knock the purloined coins free of that grimy, rapacious paw. Only the sight of the thin red line at Cathal's throat and the knowledge that all their lives hung in the balance restrained him. "Grave robber," he snarled, fighting back with the only weapon at his disposal. "The spirits of our dead ancestors willna rest till you're dead." A rumble of thunder punctuated his threat, and the wind turned chill.

The Munros shifted in their saddles, eyeing one another nervously, but Seamus only snorted. "Your curse is naught but a tale made up to frighten bairns. I took these and got away clean enough." He leaned forward. "And now ye'll take me to the rest."

And then Seamus would kill him. Lucais read his own death in the predatory gleam in his enemy's hard eyes. Whether they found the treasure or not, Seamus would not pass up this opportunity to eliminate him. And then there'd be naught to prevent Munros from wiping out the Sutherlands.

Elspeth. God, what would happen to Elspeth? She'd suffered so much at Raebert's hands; she mustn't be allowed to fall into Seamus's. Fear for her steadied Lucais's pulse, stopped his brain from racing in frantic circles. Though his hands were tied at the moment, he'd play for time. He'd go with Seamus . . . there was no choice there . . . but once inside the broch, he'd find a way to reach the secret tunnel and escape.

Seamus was planning to kill Lucais! The knowledge pierced Elspeth to the quick. She swayed in the saddle, her heart racing with fear. Why didn't Lucais fight back? Because he'd save his kin with nary a care for his own skin. Well, she cared, dammit, and she'd not give him up without a fight.

"I'll go with you," Lucais said grimly.

"Nay!" Elspeth shouted. Heads turned as she nudged her horse through the circle of Sutherlands and drew rein before Seamus.

"Well, well. What ha' we here?" the old man purred in a tone that drove her fear up another notch.

"Elspeth!" Lucais spurred toward her, but the Munros raised a wall of swords to keep him at bay. He looked furious enough and anxious enough to brave even sharp steel to get at her.

"I had to come to make certain you were safe," she said to Lucais, willing him to understand, to forgive her.

"I dinna need your help." Lucais's voice rose to rival the wind that whipped her hair about her face, making her eyes sting. Nay, 'twas the anguish in Lucais's face that brought the tears. That and the fear he'd hate her after this.

He'd forgiven her much, but she doubted his love was strong enough to withstand what he'd surely see as her final betrayal. And yet, she couldn't back down.

"Ride away, Elspeth," Lucais ordered tersely.

She swallowed. "I canna." *Trust me. I do this for you, and I'll be safe.* Alain would protect her. 'Twas the sight of her friend's shocked face in the crowd that had given Elspeth the courage to act. "Seamus only wants the gold. He willna harm me."

"Nay, I'm very glad to see ye here," Seamus said. His smile revealed sharp, twisted teeth, and his eyes glittered with an odd intensity that tightened the coil in her belly.

"Let her go," Lucais said. "Or I willna show you the gold."

"You have nae idea where it is," she countered. "But I do."

Seamus's parody of a smile deepened. "Then I'm a doubly lucky man. Ye'll take me to it." An order, not a question.

Sweet Mary, she feared him. But she had to see this through. Hands braced on the pommel of her saddle, Elspeth nodded. Once inside the broch, she'd find a way to escape through the secret tunnel. "But only if you let everyone else go," she said, praying Seamus's greed outweighed his hatred of Lucais.

"Very well," the old man said more quickly and easily than she'd have expected. "Tie them up and leave them here."

Elspeth let out the breath she'd been holding, but Lucais wasn't grateful. Nay, he roared in outrage and spurred his horse toward her in defiance of the Munro swords. His charge took them by surprise . . . all save Seamus, who raised his weapon, clipping the side of Lucais's helmet with the edge of his blade.

The ring of steel on steel echoed off the trees. Lucais grunted in pain, wavered, then slumped forward in the saddle.

Elspeth cried his name as Lucais slid onto the ground, would have gone to him had Alain not grabbed her horse's reins and dragged her back. "Ye can do naught to help him," he growled.

I did it for him, Elspeth longed to cry, but she doubted Alain would believe her any more than the Sutherlands did. Eyes colder and harder than the flinty soil, they stared at her as the Munros trussed them up like pigs bound for market.

"Leave their weapons and horses nearby," Elspeth choked out past the lump in her throat. Wonder of wonders, Seamus agreed to that, too. As he led her from the glade, Elspeth looked back for one last glimpse of Lucais. He lay on his side, a bright stream of blood running from beneath his helmet, his face turned away from her. And so it would be even if she managed to elude Seamus and return to Kinduin. In saving him, she'd lost him for good.

"Ye were a fool to place yerself in Seamus's hands," Alain said in a low whisper.

Elspeth looked away from the men trying to hook a rope on the broch's threshold. "Better me than Lucais."

"I wish I were certain of that," Alain said cryptically. But when she pressed him for details, he glanced over to where Seamus stood watching them. "'Tis likely naught. I take it Lucais didna beat ye for lettin' me escape?"

"Nay, he didna," Elspeth said absently, worried she'd placed too much faith in Alain. Though he was a good man, he was weak.

"Ye're certain?" At her nod, he sighed. "Thank God for that. But why, then, are ye helpin' Seamus?"

"I'm doing it for Lucais, though I doubt he sees it so. I knew if he went with Seamus, your brother would kill him."

"If ye're loyal to Lucais, why did ye twice help me escape?"

"Because you are my friend."

His lips tightened. "'Tisna what I'd have from ye, Elspeth."

"I know." Sadly. "I owe you my life, Alain, but . . ."

"I dinna want yer gratitude, either," he snapped.

Now it was her turn to sigh. Carefully. Because he fancied himself in love with her, she needed to tread carefully so as not to wound his heart more than she already had. Or prick his pride. "I would that I could give you what you want, Alain, for you are a good man." At his snort of disbelief, she smiled faintly. "You've been a good friend to me, and I need one just now."

"That's true." He looked over to where Seamus paced before the broch, cursing his men's slowness in getting a hook into the sill of the door two stories above. "He's determined to have yon treasure. Are ye sure ye can find it?" he asked anxiously.

If she wanted to, which she didn't. Daibidh's maps made clear the location of a large chamber. It lay between the corridor Seamus had been exploring two nights ago and the one next to the tunnel, buffered on either side by three smaller rooms. Mayhap the final resting place of the chief's wives or of other, lesser leaders. "I know the most likely spot, but 'twill take time to reach it." Long enough for her to sneak away and get through the tunnel. And then what? If Lucais got free and came here, 'twould be to fight Seamus, not save her. Nay, if he'd regained consciousness, Lucais well and truly hated her.

Sweet Mary, she had never felt so cold, so alone.

"Ye're shiverin'," Alain said. "Here, take my cloak."

"Never mind that," Seamus roughly interjected. "She canna climb wearin' that thing."

Elspeth looked over, saw a pair of Munros scrambling up the ropes to disappear into the broch's dark mouth. Her spirits and her options plunged, yet she dared not defy Seamus when he ordered her up the ropes after them. The climb was more arduous than those she'd made as a bairn, or mayhap 'twas because her hands were numb with despair, slick with fear.

When at last she heaved herself over the sill and accepted Alain's help to stand, she noted that though it was warmer outside than it had been two nights ago, inside the broch it was colder and damper. It reminded Elspeth of the crypt below the chapel at Carmichael where her ancestors were buried. Nay, there was a subtle difference, for here the souls were...restless.

Alain felt it, too. He paled as he joined her in looking about the central room. Black shadows crept out from the corners to meet in the middle of the stone floor. The stark gray walls towered above them, the openings of the gallery windows glowering down on them like malevolent eyes, unblinking, unfriendly.

Seamus wasn't nearly as sensitive. "Well, where is it?" His booming voice was swallowed up in the soaring height of the room, and Elspeth suddenly knew what was different. Last time, the broch had welcomed her. Today it seemed to swallow them up.

"Quit stallin'," Seamus growled. "Even if Lucais and his men get free, they willna be comin' to rescue ye."

Dread clenched in her belly. "What have you done?"

Seamus's fleshy lips twisted into a cruel smile. "I sent a few of the lads back to...check on them."

To kill them. Elspeth's blood ran cold, then hot. "Damn you. You said you'd spare them if I helped you." Fingers curling into talons of retribution, she flew at him. Her nails found the side of his cheek, dug a long bloody furrow before he backhanded her into Alain's waiting arms.

"Bitch," Seamus snapped. "Ye'll pay for that, too."

Vision blurred by tears of pain and anguish, Elspeth trembled in Alain's embrace. *Lucais! Oh, Lucais!* She had to get out of here, had to save him somehow. But as she roused herself to run, Alain held her back.

"Ye canna help Lucais now," he whispered, and gave her a little shake. "Be reasonable. Save yerself."

Save herself? With Lucais dead, she didn't care if she lived, but she couldn't give up. Somehow she had to thwart Seamus. "Seamus canna afford to kill me if he wants the gold." She tasted blood in her mouth and spat it at him.

Eyes glinting evilly, Seamus wiped his chin. "'Tis true enough, but I taught Raebert all he knew about causin' pain.

Shall I prove I can loosen yer tongue wi'out takin' yer life?''
Ignoring her gasp and Alain's, he continued, ''After ye've told
me where the gold is, ye'll tell me how my son *really* died.''

He knew. Somehow he knew she'd killed Raebert. Elspeth
sagged back against Alain. ''He . . . he died in the fire.''

''He was bludgeoned to death,'' Seamus snarled. ''And the
servants heard the two of ye quarrelin' before the place
burned.''

Sweet Mary! Elspeth read a long, slow, painful death in her
enemy's twisted, hate-filled features.

''A rafter fell on Raebert,'' Alain said with a calm that belied the tension Elspeth felt in the arms he kept around her. ''I
lifted it from him myself when I entered the burnin' room, but
'twas too late to save him. He was already dead.''

A lie. Dazed as she'd been that night, Elspeth knew Alain
had only gone partway into the blazing inferno, far enough to
see Raebert's body, mayhap, but not touch it.

Seamus grunted. ''I heard there was a candle stand lyin'
nearby. Someone said it looked like he'd been struck wi' it.''

''Likely there was a candle stand, but 'twas the rafter that did
poor Raebert in,'' Alain replied so sincerely Elspeth nearly believed him herself.

Seamus scowled. ''Ye know better than to lie to me.''

''Nor do I have reason to.'' But Elspeth felt Alain tremble,
saw the fear in his honey brown eyes as he let go of her and
stepped away. For a brief instant, he looked just the way Gillie
did when she was afraid. ''Show us where the gold is, Elspeth,
I dinna relish stayin' here longer than necessary.''

Elspeth blinked, surprised by Alain's forcefulness but grateful for his timely support. Much as she hated leading Seamus
to the treasure, defiance would earn her a beating and would
not save Lucais and the others. Her only hope lay in the fact
that Seamus had apparently thought Lucais powerless and
hadn't ordered him bound. If Lucais somehow managed to re-
gain consciousness before the Munros reached him . . .

''Very well,'' she murmured through numb lips. Knees
knocking together, she walked toward the nearest doorway.

''We searched that tunnel already,'' Seamus snarled.

''Then you didna look far enough. The chief's burial chamber lies beyond three smaller ones.''

Seamus's wary scowl eased some. ''We did breach those. But
how do ye know the next chamber's the one we seek?''

"I saw an old map of the place. There was a crown of sorts in the largest room." Elspeth shrugged. "It could mean naught."

"Nay. Nay, 'tis likely the one we want." Rubbing his hands together, Seamus bellowed for men with shovels and axes.

That both tools had already been employed to devastating effect was clear once they reached the first tomb. Rocks tumbled out into the corridor as though cast by a careless giant. The first cell was choked with stone and pottery shards. As Elspeth picked her way through the rubble, she spotted the box upended in one corner. 'Twas a wooden coffin, she noted as she hurried past it, decorated with intricate carvings and miraculously intact . . . except that the cover had been torn off.

Elspeth avoided looking at the shadowed interior, afraid of what she might see. Instead, she concentrated on the outside. 'Twas a miracle the wood casket had not disintegrated over the ages. Further proof the broch was impervious to the ravages of time . . . if not those of greed and evil, she thought, glaring at Seamus as he stepped through the doorway into the second cell.

It was a duplicate of the first, but in the third, which was slightly larger, the signs of destruction were more evident. The floor was knee-deep in stones torn down in an attempt to broach the next wall. Amid the piles of rock, Elspeth identified the remains of weapons and household goods destined to accompany the departed on his journey to whatever these people called paradise. Someone—likely Seamus, crazed at being stymied in his quest for treasure—had hacked the coffin to bits and flung the pieces over the broken bows, wooden lances and smashed pottery.

"How could he?" she breathed when she saw the tumble of cloth-wrapped bones slung ignominiously in one corner.

"Seamus believes he's above even God," Alain mumbled, and crossed himself before turning Elspeth toward the far wall where Seamus awaited them with barely leashed patience.

"Is this the wall?" his greedy brother snarled.

Elspeth nodded. *Forgive me,* she silently cried to those who'd departed long ago. Her soul weighed down by despair and dread, she turned to leave, unable to watch the rape of this sacred place, but Seamus refused to let her out of his sight.

"I'll keep watch over her," Alain vowed.

"Hah. She's already got ye wound round her finger. I want her where I can see her," Seamus snapped. And that was that.

The Munros set to work at once. Urged on by Seamus, they groaned and cursed over the difficult task of demolishing a wall that had doubtless taken the ancient ones months to build by hand with primitive tools. The air was soon so thick with dirt and stone dust that she could scarcely draw breath.

Nay, more like 'twas sorrow and fear that clogged her throat, Elspeth thought. To her, the sounds of the stones being torn from one another and tossed aside were like the sharp thrusts of a lance into her body. She stood in the doorway of the third room, as far from Seamus as he'd permit, her back to the ugly sight, only dimly aware of Alain hovering anxiously nearby. All her thoughts were turned inward. On her own stupidity.

How could she have been incredibly stupid enough to believe she could save Lucais and the Sutherlands from Seamus? Every second that passed without Lucais's arrival made it clear she'd failed. Failed to save their lives, failed to save the broch. She leaned against the old building for support, scarcely feeling the cold stone for the block of ice lodged in her chest.

Oh, Lucais. I tried to help. I really did. Yet for all her grief, Elspeth knew she'd do the same thing all over again. Better to be here, in the thick of things, than home pacing Kinduin's walls, waiting for the men to ride back with news that Lucais had perished at Seamus's hands. At least she'd tried, which was more than she'd done when her father's life had been threatened. Small consolation.

A shout from behind her had Elspeth spinning to find the Munros had poked the first hole in the wall. Bellowing for everyone to stand aside, Seamus thrust the torch he'd been holding through the breach. A second later, he swung back around and grinned triumphantly.

"'Tis a chamber so vast I canna see it all from here."

Elspeth sagged against the doorframe, wishing the earth would open and swallow her. When that didn't happen, she looked around and realized Alain had abandoned his post beside her. Drawn to the crypt by greed or curiosity, he'd crossed the room and stood watching the workers tear stones from the wall, enlarging the opening at an alarming rate.

This was her chance to escape. The only one she was likely to get. One hand pressed against her thudding heart, Elspeth stepped from the hazy circle of torchlight and into the dark of the adjoining chamber. If she could just reach the tun—

An arm came out of the dust-choked gloom to snag her around the waist and drag her back. "Lucais!"

"Nay, 'tis me." Alain's grimy face peered down at her.

"Let me go," she said, hating the pleading tone in her voice but afraid. So afraid. "Seamus will kill me."

"Ye'll be safe enough wi' me," Alain assured her. "I saw Raebert's wound. I know ye must ha' hit him, but I dinna blame ye. He deserved to die. I only wish I'd had the courage to—"

"Bring her back here," Seamus commanded.

"Alain, please. If you care anything for me at all..."

"I love ye, Elspeth," Alain said, his pale brown eyes holding hers steadily. Odd, she'd never realized Alain's eyes were the same color as Raebert's had been. "And now that Lucais is dead, ye're a free woman again. I'll wed ye and keep ye safe till I can find a way to be rid of Seamus."

"Oh, Alain," Elspeth gasped, horrified at the thought of Lucais's death, but Alain misunderstood.

"Dinna think too harshly of me for plannin' my brother's downfall, Elspeth. 'Tisna only yer good at stake. Seamus ha' been a terrible chief to our clan, brought us naught but death and misery." He swallowed convulsively. "I should ha' challenged Seamus years ago but wasna certain I could best him, nor that the men would follow me if I did. But I canna let him harm ye."

"Then help me get away from him."

"Nay. Ye'll be safe wi' me. I willna let him hurt ye."

"What are ye whisperin' about?" Seamus roared. "Could ye nae hear me shoutin' for ye to bring her over yonder?"

"The whole world could hear ye," Alain snapped. "The lass is done in. She's brought us this far, let her be."

"Nay. I want her to go in first." Seamus pointed to the wall. His men had torn a four-foot hole in it and now stood back, eyeing it warily. "Just in case there's some... trouble."

Alain frowned. "I thought ye didna believe in the curse."

"Nor do I," Seamus assured him. "But I've heard tell about other's who've tried to rob these old burial places. Some of them have been killed in traps set about to catch the unsuspectin'."

Elspeth trembled. She'd heard a few such tales herself, but assumed there was more myth than substance to them.

"I'll go in her place," Alain said.

"How gallant," Seamus sneered. "But I canna afford to lose ye. The wench is naught to me now that we've found the chamber. If ye go in her place, I swear I'll kill her whilst ye're gone."

"'Tis all right, Alain." Elspeth laid a hand on his shoulder and looked up at him. Once again his expression . . . a mix of fear, vulnerability and frustration . . . reminded her of Gillie. Poor Gillie. Motherless and now fatherless, as well. But she couldn't think of that now. She had to stay strong. Had to find a way out of this horrible mess. "I dinna mind going, really," she added. "If Lucais is gone . . ."

Alain's hand tightened on her arm. "Ye really do love him."

"With all my heart. I only wish I'd realized it sooner. I threw away four years. Precious time we could have spent together." Gillie could have been their daughter, she thought, and her empty womb ached with longing. But the pain in her heart was sharper, ran deeper. "I let Raebert make me a prisoner, when I should have swallowed my pride and run home to my family the first time he abused me." Elspeth brushed the hair from her sticky face, conscious that part of the moisture came from the lone tear sliding down her cheek. One was all she could afford to shed, for if she gave in, she might never stop crying. For the time lost. For the love that had been doomed from the start. "Dinna let your fears keep you from doing what's necessary."

With that, Elspeth turned to do Seamus's bidding. Surprisingly Alain stuck by her, his hand at her back to guide her through the mounds of debris. When they reached the hole in the wall, Elspeth stopped and glared up at Seamus, letting all the disgust and loathing she felt show in her eyes.

Seamus rubbed a filthy paw over his stubbled chin. "Quit gawkin' and get movin'." He thrust a torch at her.

Somehow, Elspeth managed to unclench her frozen fingers and accept the light. The rough wooden rod felt solid in her hand. A dose of reality in the nightmare world into which she'd been plunged. *Sweet Mary, she did not want to do this.* But Seamus grabbed hold of her arm and shoved her toward the black opening. It was walk or sprawl facedown in the dirt. Elspeth walked.

As she stepped through the breach, the cold hit her, sharp as a physical blow. It seemed to penetrate to her very bones. *Cold as the grave.* Elspeth shivered, partly from fear, mostly from the stream of frigid air that leaked out through the gash in the wall, like blood seeping from a mortal wound. Why had she thought that? Why did the Munros' violation of the broch seem so...so personal? Because from the first, she'd felt in tune with the old fort, she realized, startled by the notion.

The back of her neck crawled as though ants roamed it...or unfriendly eyes. In the darkness beyond the reach of her torch, she sensed something stirring, building with an intensity that mirrored the storm outside, rivaled it.

"Move," Seamus snarled.

She was on her own, without hope of aid or reprieve.

Chapter Nineteen

Sprawled facedown on the ground, Lucais regained consciousness slowly. His mouth was full of dirt; his head rang like a kirk bell at Easter mass.

"Lucais? Rouse yerself." The words were harsh, urgent, punctuated by a sharp poke in the side.

White-hot agony slashed through Lucais, wrenched a raw groan from his throat. The command and the shove were repeated. "Go away," he rasped, raising his head to confront his tormentor. The movement set the world spinning dizzily; nausea roiled in his gut. He swallowed hard. "Cathal?" he croaked.

"Aye." The older man lay on his side, his arms behind him. "The bastards tied us up and took the Lady Elspeth wi' them."

Elspeth. Memory returned in quick flashes, stunning as a dozen vicious blows to his battered brain. "She *went* with them. Elspeth's takin' Seamus to the treasure."

"Aye." Cathal snarled the word and more besides, a stinging condemnation of the woman who'd won Lucais's trust, then betrayed it. His assessment was echoed by the other trussed-up Sutherlands.

Nor could Lucais dispute their reasoning. Every time he turned around, Elspeth did something that stretched his faith in her to the breaking point. But this time his trust didn't waver. He knew she'd gone with Seamus to save *him.* Battling the spinning in his brain, he crawled to his knees. "I'll cut you loose, then we're goin' after her." Before he could say more, a new sound mixed with the rumble of distant thunder. The thud of horses' hooves, coming fast from the direction of the broch.

"Munros!" Lucais wasted no time in using the dirk in his boot to free Cathal. Between them, they managed to cut the bindings on the other men before their enemy charged into view. Lucais spotted their weapons piled against the base of a sprawling oak and tossed them to his clansmen just as the Munros reined in and fell on them like raging wolves.

Shouting at his men to close ranks and protect one another's backs, Lucais reached deep inside his battered body for the strength to face the enemy. Guided by instinct and reflexes honed by years of fighting, he parried and thrust ... intent on ending this in the shortest amount of time. Aye, time was precious, for the longer Elspeth was in Seamus's hands ...

Nay. He dared not think of that. Instead, he concentrated on what was surely the most important battle of his life. Curiously, he felt neither fear nor pain. Fury drove him to lash his way through wave after wave of attackers. Fury at his own stupidity in not guessing Seamus was desperate enough to make another attempt to steal the treasure. He should have killed Seamus and Alain when he'd had the chance. Did God grant him another, he'd not hesitate to cut them both down.

The sounds of battle rose above the wail of the wind as the storm drew nearer. Lucais lost track of the number of men he faced, the number of times his sword sliced through mail and muscle. Then suddenly the wind fell away and all was quiet save for a few pitiful moans and the hard rasp of his own breathing.

"Ah, lad. We've carried the day." A grin split Cathal's blood-spattered face. "Jesu, but ye fought like a man possessed."

Elspeth. He had to get to Elspeth, but first, "How did we fare?" Lucais rasped, wiping his sword and sheathing it.

A quick check revealed only one Sutherland dead, though several were sorely hurt. Despite their early advantage, the Munros were not as fortunate. Six of the thirty men were dead; all of the survivors were wounded. Cathal "persuaded" one of them to admit that Seamus, Alain and five others were in the broch.

"Do we put them to the sword?" Cathal asked eagerly.

Lucais eyed the Munros, knowing such hard, Highland-bred men would neither ask for nor expect mercy. But he'd had enough bloodshed. "Nay. I wouldna make them pay for Seamus's crimes."

Surprisingly, Cathal nodded. "Do we go to after Seamus?"

Pulling the helmet from his aching head, Lucais wiped the sweat and blood on his sleeve while he considered his options. Not many. And none of them good. The very defensive structure that had saved his ancestors so many years ago was now turned against him. Seamus could hole up inside the broch until he had what he wanted, then buy safe conduct out by threatening Elspeth.

Lucais bowed his head. Damn. Why couldn't she have stayed safely at Kinduin? Knowing his brave, impetuous love, 'twas because she'd had some mad notion of helping him. Damn. When he got her back, he'd chain her to his wrist. If he got her back.

Lucais's fury drained away, replaced by steely determination. "I'm going to the broch to rescue Elspeth."

"Ye'll never get inside."

"I know a way," Lucais replied, and prayed he could find the mechanism that opened the tunnel entrance.

Cathal swept the crowd of weary, bloodied Sutherlands, then said, "We're wi' ye, Lucais."

"You'd risk your lives for a woman you dinna trust?"

"Well..." Cathal stared at his boots. "Now I think on it, 'twas Elspeth insisted Seamus leave our weapons behind."

Clever lass. How he loved her, feared for her. But thunder boomed in the distance, reminding Lucais there were other forces besides the Munros lurking inside the broch. "Cathal, pick ten men and ride with me as far as the glen. The rest of you see to the wounded...ours and theirs."

Sweet Mary, she was so afraid. Elspeth took a step forward, then another. The cold wrapped itself around her, a choking, numbing blanket. The darkness pressed all around her, so complete it nearly swallowed up the puny light from her torch.

Somewhere in the distance, thunder boomed, but deep in the heart of the broch, 'twas deathly quiet. Her breathing sounded unnaturally harsh in the silence. Warily she placed one foot in front of the other, tensed to flee at the first sign...

Her toe caught on something and she looked down, startled to see the floor wasn't smooth like the others in the fort, but made from large stone blocks three paces wide. A symbol had been cut into the one she stood on. She'd seen the shape on the map next to the tunnel entrance. The block before her was marked, too, but to the side she saw plain ones. What did it mean? The tunnel was a means of escape. Could these marks indicate which stones to step on in order to escape a trap of the sort Seamus feared?

Feeling it could do no harm to assume so, Elspeth changed course, keeping to the carved blocks. The "safe" stones did not always abut one another, and it was not easy to leap from one to the other, but Elspeth persisted. A dozen stones into the room, she caught a glimmer of something crouching in the black void just ahead. She hesitated staring hard....

'Twas a beast! Its eyes gleamed red in the torchlight, its forked tongue spearing out between huge white fangs.

Elspeth's heart stopped. Too terrified even to breathe, she waited for it to swoop in and gobble her up. Several anguished seconds later she realized the monster had not moved or made a sound. Squinting, she made out a long neck curving down to become the front of a structure. A boat.

The relief was so great Elspeth swayed. The pulse thundered in her ears. Dimly she heard Seamus order her forward. One hand pressed to her heart, she walked the path until she was six squares from a ship twice the size of any that fished the loch.

"It looks like a Norseman's boat," Seamus called. "What do ye see inside it?" His voice echoed off the unseen rafters far above the dragon's head, and again Elspeth felt something stir in the cold, stale air around her.

Something dark and threatening.

It soaked the remaining heat from her body, the air from her lungs. If the ancient myths were true, she knew what she'd find laid out within ... the laird of these people in his battle regalia, surrounded by the plate, jewels and costly trappings he'd need to ease his way in the next world.

She crept closer, stopped when she realized *all* the stones on the floor surrounding the ship were smooth and unmarked. Holding the torch aloft, she let the glowing circle of light spill over the inside of the funeral barge.

Jesu, 'twas magnificent. Awed, she studied the warrior laid out in all his finery. Of his face she could see naught, thank God. A helmet covered his head, topped off with a snarling lion whose jeweled red eyes glittered in the torchlight. More red stones decorated the large round shield embossed with two huge boars locked in combat. He wore a leather tunic that fell past his knees to meet the tops of fur-lined boots laced up with thick thongs. In his right gauntlet he held a long, iron-tipped spear.

Around the warrior were hanging bronze bowls filled with grain and dried meat and skins that had likely contained water or ale. Elspeth was amazed that these things hadn't disintegrated over the years. Of more interest to Seamus would be the silver spoons and bowls and the three small chests overflowing with gold coins and jewelry. The amount and diversity of the horde struck her instantly. No local craftsmen could have fashioned such fine things. Either the goods had been taken from the very Vikings who'd come here to plunder, or Lucais's ancestors had been traders, mayhap exchanging pelts and fish for goods even as the Sutherlands did today.

"What ha' ye found?" Seamus demanded yet again.

She couldn't let him have these things. Elspeth whirled, saw his bull-like body blocking the doorway his men had rent in the wall. "There's naught here," she quickly replied.

"Lyin' bitch." Seamus glared at her. "I'll come see fer meself." Over his shoulder, he told Alain to guard the entrance and ordered the rest of the men into the crypt.

They looked terrified, their eyes rolling this way and that so the whites gleamed in the light of the torches each held high above his head. Seeming oblivious to the cold and the ominous heaviness in the air, Seamus snapped, "Get a move on, ye stupid louts. I want everythin' of value out of this ship and onto our animals before 'tis full dark."

"Have a care for the floor," Elspeth called.

"The dead willna mind what I track in," Seamus replied, and lumbered into the tomb. His feet landed randomly on plain square and marked, with no ill effect, making Elspeth think she had misjudged the situation, but when he stepped onto the smooth stone beside the boat, a low rumble pierced the silence.

Elspeth felt the ground tremble beneath her feet. The Munros felt it, too. Grabbing hold of one another for support, they clung together, heads swiveling toward the dragon figurehead on the ship as though they expected it to come alive and eat them.

"Fools! 'Tis naught but the storm." Seamus slapped the nearest man and ordered them all onward.

Elspeth *knew* 'twas nothing as safe and ordinary as a storm. The moment Seamus had entered the room, she'd been aware of a change in the atmosphere. The sense of something rousing, gathering itself, was growing out of all proportion. Gooseflesh rippled across her skin; the hair stood out at her nape.

"Jesu, will ye look at that," Seamus exclaimed. He stood beside the boat, his eyes bright with unholy greed, lips pulled back in a predatory grin. "There's a fortune here." His hands shook as he reached for the nearest chest.

"Wh-what if 'tis a trap?" one of the Munros stammered.

Seamus drew his fingers back as though they'd been singed. Scowling, he turned on Elspeth. "Fetch me those gold coins."

Elspeth lifted her chin. "I willna rob this grave for you."

"Ye'll do as I say." He grabbed Elspeth by the upper arms, shook her so hard she dropped the torch she'd been carrying. It hit a smooth block, sputtering and sparking as it rolled onto a cluster of three marked ones. "Get that ches—"

"Let her go!" The command boomed through the chamber, rang off the stone walls, drawing all eyes to the hole in the wall. Hazy light spilled through the opening. It crept only a few feet into the black crypt, silhouetting two figures whose faces were shrouded by the long inky shadows.

"Alain?" Seamus queried, head cocked, eyes narrowed.

"Aye." Shakily. The pair walked forward, slowly entering the pool of light cast by the Munros' torches. Alain's arms were extended in a gesture of surrender. Something gleamed at his throat . . . the curved edge of a dirk.

Elspeth looked up, past Alain's strained expression and frightened eyes to the man who stood behind him.

Lucais.

"Sutherland!" Seamus exclaimed.

"Aye. Back from the dead to protect what's mine." Helmetless, his hair matted with blood, his face streaked with gore and grime, Lucais did look like a specter from the grave.

He's alive! Elspeth thought. Lucais was alive and he'd come for her. Her heart soared like a bird on the wing, then faltered. He was alive, but Lucais had not once looked at her as he stalked across the crypt. His piercing gaze was focused on Seamus and the funeral barge. Mayhap he hadn't come for her at all. Mayhap 'twas only the treasure he sought to protect.

"Leave this place or I'll kill your brother," Lucais commanded, halting a few feet away, gaze riveted on Seamus.

Seamus snorted. "I dinna give a fig for Alain's life, but I wager ye dinna feel the same about the wench." He hooked his arm around Elspeth's neck and dragged her back against him, the keen edge of his dirk flirting with the underside of her chin.

Checkmate. Lucais fancied the floor shifted beneath him, but knew it must be caused by his throbbing head. The pain was naught compared to the sight of Elspeth, alone and vulnerable to his enemy. Damn. He nearly wished he hadn't bid his clansmen wait outside the broch. Nearly. None of them had been keen to violate the ban against entering the old fort, and in truth, not even an army could stop Seamus while he held hostage the one thing Lucais valued more than his own life. "Let her go and I will—" God forgive me "—loot the ship for you."

"Nay," Elspeth cried, but her plea fell on deaf ears.

"Done." Seamus chuckled, the sound low and ugly. "Place yer weapons on the floor, kick them away and come here." Elspeth tried to protest, but his arm choked off her words before they could reach her lips.

Lucais set his sword and knife down, but left the one hidden in his boot. 'Twas not an honorable act, but Seamus Munro was a dishonorable man. Lucais stepped away from Alain, but the fool stuck close by, crossed the room with him.

"Dinna trust my brother," he said for Lucais's ears alone.

"I trust neither of you." Lucais stopped in front of Seamus, his eyes locked on the bastard's smug face. If he looked at Elspeth, he feared he'd go mad. *Oh, Beth. Why did it have to end like this?* "Let Elspeth leave."

Seamus's smirk became a sneer. "Think ye I'm daft? She stays till I ha' every last bit of yon treasure. Guard her," he growled, and shoved Elspeth at his brother.

Lucais turned his head, locked eyes with Alain. "Keep her safe, Munro, or I vow I'll come back to haunt you."

Elspeth cried his name, straining to escape Alain's grip, but he held her fast. "I'll see she comes to nae harm." Alain's words rang with sincerity and determination.

Unable to resist one last look at the woman he loved, Lucais let his gaze stray to her face, wished he hadn't when he saw the pain darkening her violet eyes. And the love. An answering burst of emotion lanced through his chest, sharp and bittersweet as the smile he gave her. "I love you, Beth," he mouthed.

"Oh, Lucais. I love you, too," Elspeth whispered, his anguished features blurring as tears filled her eyes. It couldn't end like this. It couldn't. But what could she do, a lone woman against six armed men? Sweet Mary, she'd not felt so weak and helpless since her da had been wounded. Nay, she was not weak. Weaponless she might be, but she could create a diversion, give Lucais time to seize his sword and, mayhap, the moment.

Silently begging her friend's forgiveness, she kicked Alain hard in the shin with the heel of her riding boot. Alain yelped and loosened his hold on her arms. 'Twas all the opening Elspeth needed. Wrenching free, she leapt at Seamus. "Fiend," she cried, fingers curved into claws to scratch out his eyes.

She never got close.

Seamus roared an obscenity, raised a beefy arm and backhanded her. She flew through the air, landed with a thud that drove the air from her lungs and made stars dance in her head. Around her, all hell broke loose. Shouts and curses filled the tomb. Battling dizziness, she sat up, pushed the hair from her eyes and saw that her ploy had worked . . . to an extent.

Lucais crouched in a fighter's stance. His jaw set, his eyes blazing to rival the gleam of the dirk clenched in his right hand. But he'd need more than righteous fury to best the lethal reach and killing strength of Seamus's double-edged claymore.

Seamus knew it, too. His smile was evil, ugly as he advanced. Holding the sword with both hands, he swung it like a scythe, intent on cutting Lucais's legs from under him. Once, twice, three times Lucais managed to leap over the wickedly gleaming length of steel.

Dimly aware of Elspeth's strangled whimpers, of his own ragged breathing and flagging stamina, Lucais focused his energies on thwarting his brawny adversary. Seamus was surprisingly quick for a man of his years and girth, but his pale brown eyes betrayed his intentions in the instant before he struck. Lucais kept his gaze riveted to Seamus's, waiting, watching for an opening . . .

Seamus brought his weapon around, a lethal streak of silver taking deadly aim at Lucais's belly. A stroke Lucais could not leap over. Nor did he try. Instead, he tucked and rolled like a tumbler at a fair. Seamus's blade whistled harmlessly through the air over his head. The sound was drowned out by the old man's bellow of rage as Lucais reached up and buried his knife in Seamus's thigh.

The tip of the dirk bit through chain mail, drawing blood and a satisfactory grunt of pain. But 'twasna enough, Lucais knew, for Seamus twisted free and brought his own weapon to bear.

Steel shrieked on steel as Lucais leapt up and countered the downward arc of the claymore with the puny force of his dirk. For an instant, the sword caught on the hilt of the knife and he thought he'd done it. Then the brute strength of the superior weapon won out, sundering the dirk just above the hilt.

Lucais dropped the useless handle and scrambled backward, Elspeth's screams echoing in his ears. Off-balance, disoriented from the blow on the head, he felt his feet slip on the smooth stone, realized he was going down.

Seamus knew it, too. "I've waited four years for this," he crowed, moving in for the kill.

"Run, Lucais!" Elspeth cried, but 'twas too late. Already Seamus had sent his sword on an arc that would sever Lucais in two even as he fell to the floor. She started forward, willing to take the blow herself. But Alain was quicker.

Lunging across the few feet that separated them from the battle, Alain shoved Lucais out of the way, taking the sword stroke in his midsection. The metal links of his mail parted, leaving an ominous red trail. For an instant, everyone froze, staring at the blood that dripped from between the fingers Alain had pressed to his side. "I didna think ye'd do it," he whispered, looking at Seamus with wounded eyes. Then his eyes rolled back and he started to fall. Would have, if Lucais hadn't caught him and lowered him to the ground.

"Y-ye killed him," gasped the youngest Munro clansman, a round-faced lad whose eyes were wide with horror.

"Shut up, John," Seamus snarled, glaring at his appalled clansmen. "I didna do it apurpose. He should ha' known better than to get in my way. Idiot," he added, yet Elspeth could have sworn she saw a glimmer of remorse in his expression before he turned away. But 'twas gone quickly, replaced by his usual sneer. "See Sutherland doesna move," he growled at the nearest of his men. "The rest of ye help me get the treasure out of yon boat," he ordered, and stomped over to claim his ill-gotten plunder.

His words freed the others from their stupor. Elspeth darted forward and knelt beside her fallen friend. "Oh, Alain," she whispered when she saw how pale his face was, how red the tiles beneath his body. "Lucais. We have to help him."

Lucais stared at Alain. "Why did he save me?"

"Because he is a good man." But he'd be a dead one if they did not stanch the bleeding. "I need light and cloth to bind the wound. A shirt, a cloak, anything." She raised troubled eyes to Lucais, touched by the swiftness with which he began to strip off his woolen surcoat under the watchful stare of John Munro. Dimly she was aware of the four Munros filing past them on their way to the bier.

"Will he die?" young John asked, his feet shifting nervously. The movement drew Elspeth's glance to the floor. One look at his shuffling boots and dread joined the concern roiling in Elspeth's stomach.

They were all on the smooth floor stones.

Elspeth grabbed hold of Lucais's arm. "We must move Alain over to those tiles." She pointed to the island of three carved blocks, where the torch she'd dropped yet flickered.

"I'll bring you the light," Lucais said, and started to go.

"Nay." Speaking low and urgently, Elspeth told him her theory about the floor.

Lucais arched one skeptical brow. "I doubt such ancient people would have the tools to build an elaborate trap."

"I know it seems farfetched, but..." He wasn't listening to her. His narrowed gaze was focused on Seamus and the bier. Her dread became stark terror. "Lucais. What are you planning?"

He swiveled back, features taut. A muscle in his cheek jumped as he flexed his jaw. When he spoke, 'twas not to her. "John. If you value Alain's life, help my wife get him from here."

"Lucais." Elspeth caught at his arm. He covered her hand with his, squeezed it briefly, then lifted it to his lips for a kiss that chilled her nearly as much as the grim determination stamped on his face.

"I love you, Beth. But I canna stand aside and let Seamus steal my people's heritage." When he rose, he had Alain's sword in his grip. He turned toward the funeral barge in time to see Seamus reach into it and lift out a chest. There was a distinct click as the jewel-filled box cleared the rail. The ship shuddered in its huge wooden stand. Nay, 'twas the whole room that moved as though rocked by some unseen hand.

Elspeth surged to her feet. "We have to get out of here...now!" A sound like thunder punctuated her words. It came not from outside, but from deep within the broch.

"Bloody hell! What was that?" Seamus's question was echoed by the four Munros huddled beside the bier.

The noise came again. Louder this time. And the floor shook as though something stirred in the bowels of the broch. Something big and powerful and angry. The rumbling grew louder, became a constant din, the grating sound of stone against stone.

"'Tis the curse!" shouted the Munros at Seamus's side. Abandoning their leader, they ran for the exit, got no more than two steps before the floor in front of them suddenly shifted, opening to reveal a great, yawning cavity. Unable to stop in time, they crashed into one another, then fell headlong into the abyss. Their hoarse screams were drowned out by a hideous grinding as the rest of the floor began to crumble.

Nay, 'twasn't crumbling, 'twas sliding...each unmarked square of rock slipping under a marked one.

"Run!" Lucais shouted.

"Nay! We have to get to the marked squares," Elspeth cried above the din of shifting rock.

This time, Lucais didn't question her. "Make haste. I'll follow with Alain." He scooped up Alain's limp body, then jumped from the plain stone he'd been occupying onto the wedge of three safe ones where Elspeth waited. John Munro followed hard on his heels. By the dim light of the torch shaking in John's hand, Elspeth vaguely made out the shadowed shapes of pillars supporting the marked flooring.

"Bloody hell!" Seamus shrieked as the destruction rippled toward him, more and more of the floor disappearing. "The ship's the only secure place," he cried. "They wouldna want it harmed." He leapt toward the barge just as the rows of smooth stones around it slid away. Unable to stop in time, he teetered on the edge of the abyss, then toppled over, still clutching the cask of Sutherland gold to his chest. If he screamed, they didn't hear him over the grinding of the stone.

"Oh God." Elspeth hid her face in her hands.

To Lucais, it seemed a fitting end, but he said nothing.

The shuddering and rumbling stopped as abruptly as it had started. The floor on which they sat seemed secure, but they were trapped on an island of stone, surrounded by a black, bottomless pit. In the middle of the room, supported by a stone column, the funeral barge seemed to float on that same sea of nothing.

"Oh God. H-how do we get out of here?" Elspeth stammered.

"Easy, love." Lucais wrapped an arm around her trembling body and silently weighed their options, grateful to be alive, yet conscious they might yet die. A trail of standing stones led toward the hole in the wall, but the distance between them was too great to leap with any safety. "We'll wait," he said with a calm he didn't feel. "Cathal and the others will come lookin' for us ere long." How they'd get them out was another matter.

Elspeth nodded. "Meantime, I—I'll bind Alain's wound." She picked up Lucais's discarded surcoat and tore it into strips.

Lucais sighed and bent to help her. Close by, John Munro was quietly praying. It seemed like a good idea, so Lucais followed suit, giving thanks to a God he'd nearly stopped believing in four years ago. Giving thanks for their lives and for one in particular. For Elspeth Carmichael Sutherland. His impetuous wife, who'd been brave enough to face Seamus, and wise enough to fathom the mystery that had saved their lives.

While he was at it, Lucais gave thanks to Alain Munro for his unexpected sacrifice. "Why do you think he did it?" Lucais asked, glancing down at the still, ashen features of the man who'd been his enemy and was now his . . . what?

"Because he's a good man," Elspeth said steadfastly.

Alain groaned and his lashes fluttered up. "Fool, more like," he croaked. "I should ha' let ye die, Sutherland, and kept Elspeth for myself."

"Why did you save me?" Lucais had to know. The man's selflessness went against everything he'd been taught to believe about the enemy that had harassed his clan for years.

"I did it for her. She loves ye." Alain turned his head and smiled up at Elspeth. "I couldna bear to see ye lose the man ye loved, not after what Raebert did to ye." He looked over at Lucais. "Ye've both suffered hurts at Munro hands. I was sorry about what happened to Jean."

"What do you mean?" Elspeth asked, frowning.

'Twas Lucais who replied. "We'd best get this wound bound up ere he bleeds to death," he said gruffly.

Elspeth's curiosity soared, but she knew he was right. Still, as she bent to bandage Alain's wound, she was caught by how much his golden brown eyes reminded her of Gillie. *Oh, my God!* Elspeth sucked in air as she looked...really looked...at Alain. But it wasn't his face she saw gazing up at her in the torchlight, it was Gillie's. The color of the eyes. The shape of the mouth...

Sweet Mary. Could Alain have sired Gillie, and not Lucais? Elspeth shuffled through all the things she'd been told about Jean's flight from Kinduin. Lucais said he'd found her in an inn. She'd been badly treated by Munros. 'Twas...'twas unthinkable that Alain could have raped and beaten poor Jean, but...

What had Alain just said? *Ye've both suffered hurts at Munro hands. I was sorry about what happened to Jean.*

Incredible as it seemed, Gillie must be Alain's daughter.

"Beth, why have you stopped workin'?" Lucais asked. "Do you need more cloth for bindin' the wound?"

Elspeth started and raised her gaze to his. Anxiety clouded his eyes, his face was a mask of dirt and blood. Did Lucais know? Did he know that the bairn he'd claimed as his own—the daughter he could scarcely bear to look at because she reminded him of the woman he'd loved and lost—had been sired by his enemy?

"Beth? We canna let him die. There must be something we can do." Lucais glanced down at Alain, and she had her answer in her husband's expression. There was no hatred there, only distress for a fallen man. He didn't know.

"Oh, Alain isna like to die." Elspeth pasted on a smile to reassure both men. "The mail kept the blade from biting too deep. He should recover...providing we can get out of here."

Lucais nodded. A smile of relief curved his lips as he laid a hand on Alain's shoulder. Relief on two fronts. Despite Alain's outburst, Elspeth had not guessed the truth about Gillie, and Munro was like to live. "I thank you for what you did."

"Mayhap this will mark the beginnin' of a new and lastin' peace twixt our clans." Alain's face was free of the twisted greed that had marked his evil half brother and ruthless nephew.

"I would like that, too," Lucais said from the heart. Providing they got out of here.

"Ho, Lucais! Are ye all right?" a voice called, echoing hollowly in the silent tomb.

Lucais spun toward the ruined wall, expecting to find Cathal had somehow managed to locate them. 'Twas Daibidh who stood in the opening, torch in hand. "Jesu, but you are well come. We—"

"I know," the old man muttered. "Patience whilst I contact the spirits and persuade them to raise the floor."

Spirits? Elspeth heard John whimper, saw him hide his eyes. Hers were focused on Daibidh, who looked suspiciously as if he searched the wall for a release mechanism, not otherworldly assistance. Suddenly the floor shook and began to move again.

"We're doomed," John cried.

Lucais winked at Elspeth. "Nay, we're saved."

To Elspeth, it seemed the squares took far longer to grind back into place than they had to open and gobble up the enemy. Only when Daibidh had walked out to them did she judge the floor safe. "Ye can lower the wounded man through the doorway to the Sutherlands waitin' in the glen," the old man said, and she knew he'd ordered it done so as to keep the tunnel a secret.

While Lucais and John carried Alain on ahead, Elspeth lagged behind, matching her steps to the old wizard's. "I... I wish I could have prevented this," she said softly, tears welling as they passed from the crypt into the ruined chambers beyond.

"Ye did what was intended, daughter. Thanks to ye, the guilty were punished, the guiltless spared."

"B-but I led Seamus here." Her own guilt pierced her soul.

Daibidh took her hand in his gnarled one. "This was the only way to stop him...and others like him. Times are changin', men dinna respect the old legends nor fear the ancient curses as they used to. They require proof...a proof written in blood and fear. Yon Munros willna soon forget this lesson."

"But the destruction, the desecration."

"I will stay and put things right," Daibidh murmured.

Elspeth started. "How?" One look at the light sizzling in his strange eyes and she said, "Can I stay and watch?"

Daibidh chuckled. "Brave and curious. If ye'd been born a man, ye'd ha' made a fine soothsayer." Even before she had time to bristle, he added, "Ye've a far more important task ahead of ye. Yer second son will take up my staff."

"Second son? I dinna even have a first one yet. 'Twill be years before a second one's born and grown." And he was so old.

"By then, I should be just about finished here."

A dozen questions swirled in Elspeth's mind, but they'd reached the central room by then, and Lucais had set Alain down near the doorway, left John with him and come back for her.

"My thanks for your help, Daibidh. The men are below riggin' a sling for Alain." Lucais put his arm around Elspeth. "I wish I could make up for what happened, repair the damage."

"That's my task." Daibidh reached into his robe and removed a chain from which hung a hunk of amber as bright as his eyes. "Yer first son will wear the mantle of Clan Sutherland. This is for yer second." He handed the chain to Elspeth. "Wear it next to yer skin, guard it till yer son is old enough."

Elspeth's hand trembled as she accepted the amulet. "How old is old enough?" But when she looked up, Daibidh was gone and she stood alone with Lucais. "He is the most confusing man."

"But an excellent judge of women. Come, my little soothsayeress, I'll take you home."

"Females canna be wizards," Elspeth said, leaning against him as they crossed the central chamber.

"Well, the way you saved our lives in the tomb was naught short of magic." His grip tightened. "I feared I'd lost you."

"And I you," Elspeth whispered.

"Never. We've got two sons to breed up." He waggled his filthy brows. "I canna think of more pleasant duty."

Nor could she.

Chapter Twenty

Elspeth leaned out the window of her bedchamber and took a deep breath. Though 'twas only mid-September, already there was a chill to the early morning air. Lucais had warned her that winter came to the Highlands far sooner than it did to the Lowlands. Still, the sky was blue and cloudless, promising good weather for the annual Gathering of Clan Sutherland.

A thrill of pride went through her as she gazed over the castle wall to the green field beyond, crowded now with tents. Each flew the Sutherland pennant—three gold stars on a red background—and a smaller one bearing each family's insignia.

"I thought you'd be wearin' the peacock blue silk I had Niall fetch you from Curthill," said a deep voice.

Elspeth spun to find Lucais advancing on her. In place of his usual tunic and hose, he'd put on the traditional Highland saffron shirt. Belted at the waist, it covered him to midthigh, leaving his legs bare to the tops of ankle-high leather boots. His plaid was draped over one broad shoulder and pinned there with the badge that had been his grandsire's. A thong held his hair back from his tanned face, flushed now with an excitement and anticipation that matched her own.

"You look every inch the wild Highland laird," she murmured, heart swelling with love, pride and a profound sense of wonder that this most special of men was her husband.

"Look at me like that much longer, lass, and you'll be ruinin' the fit of my fine garments," Lucais drawled.

Elspeth's gaze dropped to the yellow wool below his belt. The stirring there roused both her pulse and her curiosity. "What do you have on under your shirt?"

"I'll show you...later." Sensual promise glittered in his eyes as his mouth swooped down to kiss her breathless.

Elspeth groaned and twined her arms around his, lips parting as she melted into his embrace. Two months wed and they still couldn't get enough of each other. All too soon, he wrenched his mouth away and nuzzled her ear.

"Jesu, now I really am in trouble," he growled.

"So I note." Giggling, she pressed her hips against the source of the problem, drawing from him a moan that curled her toes. " 'Tis a malady that keeps croppin' up, though I do my best to cure it whenever it arises," she purred, drunk on pure feminine delight in her power over him. In his power over her.

"Cheeky wench." Lucais's answering groan was part laughter, part regret as he struggled to master the passion she so easily roused in him. There was no time for the kind of loving she deserved, and he'd be damned if he'd take her in haste...today of all days. Nay, if his plans went awry, he wanted her in charity with him. He reluctantly took her arms from around his neck and placed a kiss in each palm to take the sting from his withdrawal. "Our clansmen await us below. Will you be wearin' the silk?"

Elspeth hesitated, not wanting to tell him she could no longer fit into the beautiful cotehardie he'd had Niall purchase at Curthill. The problem was temporary, but explaining it would entail divulging a secret she wanted to share later. Much later, when they had the whole night to savor it. "The woolen gown I have on is far more practical for a day spent in the fields watchin' the competition and seein' to our guests."

She was hiding something. Close as they'd become these past two months, there was still a part of Elspeth he couldn't reach, not with words, not with actions. He thought it concerned Gillie, for Elspeth tensed whenever he was with the bairn. Redoubling his efforts to play the part of Gillie's father only made matters worse. Now she refused to wear the gown he bought to replace the ones she'd sold. What ailed her? "Are you happy here, Beth?"

"Of course," she exclaimed. "Why would you think I wasna?"

"You've been distant and preoccupied of late."

She started, then bristled. "If I've been busy, 'tis only because there's been that much to see to, what with the harvest to bring in and the stores to replenish before winter. Or would you rather our clansmen starved?''

"Nay," he said quickly, truthfully. She had been working hard. Too hard. Suddenly she looked fragile, her skin nearly translucent in the sunlight. The mauve circles under her eyes bespoke too little sleep. His fault for loving her far into the night. What if she was sickening with something? Dimly he recalled she'd refused food these past two mornings, preferring to lie abed. Which wasn't like her at all.

Fear twisted deep in his gut, had him dragging her close again, hugging her so tightly she squeaked. "Curse me for a fool, love. I've been that busy seein' to preparation for the Games that I've ignored all else. Are you all right? Do you need—"

"You are all I need." She wrapped her arms around his waist, her smile warm and reassuring.

"Ah, Beth." He rubbed his cheek against her silky hair. "You've worked wonders here. The hall sparkles and the food's so good we've all put on a few pounds. You spoil us rotten . . . Gillie and me especially."

She flushed with pride. "I must write to Mama and thank her for forcing me to learn housewifely things when I'd rather have been on the tiltyard crossing swords with my brothers."

"Would you like to go home for a visit?" he asked softly.

She flinched. "Nay. I . . . I . . . Kinduin is my home now. I dinna want to leave . . . ever."

" 'Tis all right," Lucais said, knowing it was not, knowing, too, that she lied. She did miss her family, especially the sire she'd always idolized. But thanks to Raebert's ruthless act, guilt would keep her estranged from the Carmichaels, mayhap forever. Unless something was done. Something drastic. He only hoped what he'd done wasn't so drastic as to turn her against him. "I love you, Beth. Whatever happens, remember that."

He was up to something. Apprehension sizzled down Elspeth's spine. "What do you mean?" she asked, but he only smiled faintly, took her cold hand in one of his warm ones and led her from the room. All the way down the stairs, she fretted over his cryptic comment. Had he guessed the truth about Gillie's parentage?

Nay. She'd taken care to keep the bairn away from Lucais, though it nearly killed her to see the hurt and bewilderment in both his face and Gillie's every time she came between them.

Lucais was willing to be a father to Gillie, and the lass needed him. Sweet Mary, her heart ached for all three of them, for the sins of the past that yet tainted their future. So many secrets. So many lies. Could they ever live together happily and openly?

"'Tis the laird and his lady," someone shouted as they entered the hall. Immediately they were swept up by a crowd of boisterous Sutherlands, and Elspeth put aside her troubles. Most of the men were dressed as Lucais was in saffron shirt and low boots. The women provided a contrasting swirl of color, garbed in bright red and blue, some with a gold broach or necklet winking against the wool of their gowns.

Beneath her clothes, nestled against her heart, Elspeth felt the amber amulet heat. It did that sometimes. A subtle reminder of Daibidh, absent but not forgotten? she wondered.

"All is in readiness wi'out," Cathal told Lucais. The older man's eyes flicked to Elspeth, accompanied by a nod of greeting and respect that warmed her more than the amulet.

The other Sutherlands were more effusive in their welcome. They engulfed her, hugging her and praising her so heartily her ribs soon ached and her head swelled from their compliments. Nay, 'twas her heart that swelled . . . with love. This was where she belonged. At Kinduin, where life was a constant challenge made well worth the effort because 'twas a burden shared with those she loved and who loved her in return. If 'twas not perfect, 'twas as close as she was like to get in this lifetime.

"I'm very proud of you, love," Lucais murmured in her ear.

Elspeth grinned back. "And well you should be" came her cheeky reply, but her eyes were still ghosted by a pain he was so frantic to ease he'd resorted to a desperate ploy.

"I'll prove it by giftin' you with every prize I win today," Lucais said solemnly, knowing that the most crucial contest was one she wasn't even aware of. Pray God his plans didn't go awry, he thought as he led the way from the tower.

Accompanied by yapping dogs, capering bairns and shrilling pipes, the people of Clan Sutherland marched through the courtyard and out over the drawbridge to the grassy knoll below the castle. A large square twice the size of Kinduin's hall had been roped off to contain the Games. While the spectators lined up behind the ropes, Lucais made his way to the center of the field, still holding Elspeth by the hand.

"When I set the date for this Gatherin' of the Clan, I told you 'twould be different than in past years," Lucais began.

"This is no *wappenschawing,* no testin' of our weapons and the battle skills we'd need to face the Munros. We've made peace with our enemy." A low rumbling of disagreement came from some quarters.

Lucais stifled it with an upraised hand. "I understand your wariness ... even share it," he added, turning in a slow circle, letting his gaze sweep over the crowd. "But Alain Munro leads them now, and he isna greedy or evil. If he were, I wouldna be here today. Alain risked his own life to save mine, takin' the sword thrust Seamus had aimed at my heart."

"Are we supposed to forget about the Sutherlands killed and the crofts burned by the Munros?" a rough voice called out.

Surprisingly 'twas Cathal who replied. "Nay. We'll never forget, but there's been blood spilled on both sides ... all for Seamus's greed. He's dead and his evil spawn, Raebert, too. I say we gi' thanks to God that their line died wi' them and gi' this peace a chance. More killin' willna bring back our dead, 'twill only make more women widows, more bairns orphans."

But their line had not died. Despite the warmth of the sun, a shiver worked its way down Lucais's spine.

Elspeth tightened her grip on his hand. "I love you," she said softly, but would she still if she knew the truth?

Lucais forced the problem from his mind and looked around at his waiting clansmen. "What say you we give this peace a chance?" he shouted. The response was a resounding, if not a unanimous, aye. As the sound fell away, he let out a sigh of relief. One hurdle vaulted, but the most vital one was yet to come. "A keg of heather ale to the man who wins the first footrace."

His offer was greeted by a raucous cheer that set the tone for the rest of the day. Niall won the ale, dashing across the finish line a whisker ahead of Cathal's Bran, a pack of panting clansmen on their heels. Laughing and pounding one another on the back, they broached the ale, quenched their thirst and moved on to the next event. Tossing the caber.

Loud. Boisterous and rowdy as a bunch of lads let out to play after a week's rain, Elspeth thought as she watched each man struggle to lift and toss the ten-foot, twelve-inch-thick tree trunk into the air, then squabble with the others over who had thrown it the farthest and the straightest. Lucais was in the middle of things, coming in second to Cathal in the toss.

"Where's Papa?" Gillie asked, catching Elspeth's hand.

"You were supposed to stay inside," she scolded, then relented when the lass teared up. Kneeling, Elspeth put an arm around the small, slumped shoulders. "'Tis just that you're so small and there are so many people about you could be trampled."

"I want to see Papa win." Tears magnified the size and color of Gillie's golden brown eyes. Alain's eyes. At least he was a gentle man, Elspeth thought, despite his one act of violence that had resulted in Gillie's creation. Lucais had explained to her, when she'd one day worked up the courage to ask the question in a casual, general way, that men were sometimes carried away by drink to do what would normally be abhorrent to them. Not that that excused Alain, but mayhap it explained what had happened.

"Ah, here are my two favorite lasses." Lucais strolled up, grinning hugely, his hands clasped behind his back.

Elspeth leapt up, fought the urge to stuff Gillie behind her back. She hadn't realized she'd moved between them until she heard Lucais sigh. "Wh-what is it?"

"I can hardly be a proper father to her with you shiftin' her out of the way whenever I'm about."

Elspeth went hot with shame, then cold with fear. He'd turn Gillie out of Kinduin if he knew the truth. Mayhap after a few years of peace between the two clans she could tell him. "Now isna the time to talk about this." She cast a meaningful glance at the puzzled but alert little face staring up at them.

To her relief, he nodded. "We'll discuss it later, then," he muttered, and the coil in her stomach tightened.

"What's behind yer back, Papa?" Gillie asked. Her eyes and mouth both rounded with awe when he brought out two pieces of gundy and handed one to each of his favorite lasses.

Elspeth popped hers into her mouth. The toffee was doubtless delicious, but all she tasted was dread. How long could she keep this up? What if Gillie grew to look more like Alain, not less?

"Will you walk apart with me?" Lucais asked, and the day, which had been so warm and sunny, turned cold and dark.

"I . . . I have to watch Gillie," Elspeth hedged, and averted her eyes from his piercing gaze.

"Beth," Lucais began, but just then one of the lookouts galloped up to say they had visitors.

Munros! Elspeth stiffened. Much as she welcomed peace with the Munros, she was terrified that Alain would come visiting and Lucais would see the resemblance between him and Gillie. But the troop that trotted toward them across the grassy knoll carried a familiar red-and-black banner.

"They're Carmichaels," she exclaimed, scanning the tall knights in the lead. Encased as they were in gleaming armor, their faces hidden by their visors, their identity eluded her. "Mayhap 'tis Sir Giles with news that Megan has given birth." Lifting her skirts, Elspeth went to meet them.

Damn. They were a day early. Lucais battled down a wave of panic, then hurried after her. "Beth, I need to tell you..."

"Elspeth!" There was no mistaking that voice. Nor the face that appeared as the largest man tugged off his helmet.

"Da?" Alarmed, appalled, Elspeth staggered back a step, hands pressed to her thudding heart.

"Hardly a gracious greetin'," her sire grumbled. "And after I've come all this way to see ye." Lionel's eyes swept over her, narrowing as they came to rest on her face. "No matter. I'm here, as ye can see." He swung down from his horse, groaning loudly as his feet touched the ground. "We rode a far piece today, and my bad leg's gone stiff."

Lucais responded, but Elspeth couldn't make out his words over the rushing in her ears. *I willna faint.* She repeated the litany until she'd bested the worst of her dizziness.

" 'Tis a fine spot ye ha' here," her father was saying. "I'll enjoy watchin' yer clansmen compete...after I've had a word wi' my lass. Walk wi' me, Elspeth."

Face averted, her heart lower than her boots, Elspeth took her father's arm and matched her stride to his halting one. It hurt, sweet Mary, how it hurt to see him limp.

"There's something about the Games that always stirs the blood," her father observed after a few moments.

Elspeth started from her dark reverie, realized they'd climbed partway up the hill. From here the field of play was a panorama of bright colors and swirling motion set against the verdant green. But even the shrill of the pipes failed to move her blood. It was frozen in her veins.

"Are ye happy here?" He sounded so concerned.

"Happier than I deserve," she managed past a lump of misery.

"What's this?" He put his fingers under her chin and lifted it so their gazes met, locked. The deep, abiding love shining in the violet eyes he'd bequeathed to her was Elspeth's undoing. She no longer deserved her father's love.

"Oh, Da," Elspeth gasped, and the dam inside her burst. Hot, scalding tears poured down her cheeks. Deep sobs ripped through her chest. Dimly she was aware of her father catching her as her knees weakened. He hugged her close, murmuring words her mind couldn't grasp, yet they soothed her aching heart.

"That's it, lass, cry it out." Lionel awkwardly patted her heaving back, gazing down at her shiny hair through a blur of tears. "'Tis all right."

"Nay, 'tisna." Elspeth raised her tear-drenched face. "Y-you dinna kn-know what I've d-done," she choked out.

"If ye mean that damned business wi' the ambush, I know all about it. 'Twas Raebert's doin'," he spat.

Shock dried Elspeth's tears in a flash. "Y-you know? But how? When did you know? Why did you nae tell me?"

Lionel chuckled and blinked the moisture from his eyes. "'Tis glad I am ye've recovered. Jesu, I'd rather face an army without my sword than comfort a cryin' woman."

"Da." She gave him an exasperated shake. "Tell me."

"Well . . ." He soothed the hair from her temple as he used to when she was small. "Much as I wish I could claim I'd been clever enough to figure it all out, 'twas Lucais wrote and told me—"

"Lucais! That traitor!" Blood boiling, she turned to run down the hill and confront the man who'd betrayed her confidence, but her father held her fast.

"Damn, but ye're an impetuous imp. Listen a moment—"

"I've heard all I need to." Elspeth ground her teeth together to keep from crying again. "He had nae right to spill my secret. 'Twas . . . 'twas dishonorable."

Her sire nodded. "That an honorable man such as Lucais would stoop to such a thing must tell ye how worried he was."

"Well . . ." Elspeth looked away from his probing gaze.

"Damn, I wish Ross were here," Lionel growled. "I'm nae bloody good at this sort of thing. But he didna want to leave Megan and their wee lad, so I came alone to—"

"The babe's been born?"

"Two weeks ago. He's named Ewan after Megan's brother who died at the hands of the cursed MacDonnel who killed our Lion."

"Megan is well?" she asked anxiously, concerned for her sister by marriage and conscious that in seven months she'd face that same, age-old trial herself. Even healthy women ofttimes died in childbirth.

"She's fine, but Ross hovers over her like a mother hen wi' an ailin' chick." He chuckled, then sobered, cocking his head as he studied her. "Yer face has an odd glow about it. Are ye breedin', Elspeth?"

"Da!" Her cheeks heated. "What an indelicate question."

He shrugged. "Ross is the courtier in the family. He tried to tell *me* how to handle this." If he felt Elspeth flinch at the reminder of why he'd come to Kinduin, it didn't stay her father's tongue. "I told him I didna need his advice . . . nae when it comes to dealin' wi' my Elspeth." He gave her shoulder a rough, companionable squeeze. "Ye're like me. Plain talk, that's what we value. Nae need to mince words. 'Twasna yer fault. Raebert's to blame for what happened to me."

"But . . . but I should have given him the jewelry."

"Never. Gi' in to scum like that and they'll eat ye alive. Next he'd ha' wanted the keys to the castle and the food from our clansmen's mouths. A Carmichael never surrenders."

"B-but your leg," Elspeth stammered, aching to believe her father might forgive her, but not quite daring to.

He scowled, reaching down to rub his thigh. "It pains me and stiffens when I sit too long," he said simply. "But Megan's worked wonders wi' the herbal rubs her own mother used on her leg when 'twas broken. If she can walk wi' scarce a limp, so can I."

"Oh, Da." Elspeth's eyes filled with tears again.

"Humph. Must be the babe ye're carryin', for ye were never one to weep," he said gruffly.

"Aye. I suppose it is." Elspeth sniffed and wiped the moisture from her cheeks with the trailing sleeve of her gown.

"Well, now that's settled." *Settled? Did he really think so?* "Could ye dig up a cup of ale for yer thirsty da? And something to eat." His face lit with relish. "I swear I havena eaten well since learnin' ye wed Lucais."

"You dinna approve of him?" Elspeth asked anxiously, falling into step with her father as he started back down the hill.

He stopped abruptly. "I feared he wouldna do right by ye. Ross refused to rescue ye...said ye were fine. And I wasna in any condition, then, to come myself." His grimace told her how much that had chafed his pride. "After what happened wi' Raebert, I wasna sure about Lucais. Never did like Raebert. Canna trust a man who hangs around the court lookin' for scraps from the king's table instead of makin' his own way in the world."

You dinna know the half of it, Elspeth thought. But from the fierceness of his expression, she wondered if he did know.

"Ye should ha' come back to us when Raebert threatened ye," he growled. "I'd ha' fought the church and the Munros to free ye if I'd only known then what I do now."

The lump in Elspeth's throat thickened. "I—I couldna."

"Pride." Her father sighed and raised his eyes to the jagged peaks of the mountains. "We all ha' too much pride...or so yer mama says. 'Tis both boon and bane." He turned back to Elspeth, pinning her with a hard gaze. "Are ye truly happy wi' Lucais?"

"Happier than I deserve to be." She stood on tiptoe and kissed her father's stubbled cheek. "Lucais is nearly as forgiving a man as you are, Da. He loves me, though I scorned and rejected him. He loves me despite my imperfections."

"Imperfections," her sire bellowed. "Ye're the bonniest, bravest lass in the world. And dinna forget it. 'Tis lucky he is ye were willin' to overlook his humble beginnings and—"

"Lucais is the least humble man I know. His people call him the Lion of the North," she said softly. Better her father hear it from her than be shocked later on.

Pain briefly darkened her father's gaze as it drifted to the field below and the tall, chestnut-haired man in the center of a group of cheering Sutherlands. "Accordin' to Ross's tales and what I've seen thus far, he deserves to carry on the name."

Elspeth smiled through tears that ran perilously close to the surface today. "If this babe's a boy, we'll call him Lion."

"Lucais has agreed to this?"

"I'm nae sure Lucais deserves a say in the matter, not when he went behind my back and wrote to you."

"A man does what he must to protect his womenfolk."

As though that excused everything. But Elspeth didn't bother to voice the sentiment, for her father wouldn't have understood. Besides, her quarrel was with Lucais, not the father with whom she'd just been reunited. "Come, Da, let's get your food."

"Aye. 'Tis good to see ye smilin' again. *They* didna trust me to soothe yer fears," he confided as he charged down the hill, tugging her along in his wake. "Just because I dinna show my heart to all and sundry, *they* think I'm hard as stone inside. But our wee talk made ye feel better. Did it not?"

The edge in his voice made Elspeth's smile grow. He looked like a lad anxious for approval. A large lad. "Aye, it did, Da."

"Good. I ken young Lucais ha' been that worried ye'd hold it against him for sendin' me that message."

"Oh, I do," Elspeth said softly. So softly her father never heard her, intent as he was on joining the festivities. She hadn't forgiven Lucais for sharing her secret. She just hadn't decided what form his punishment would take.

Lucais's steps dragged as he climbed the stairs and approached the door to his chamber. 'Twas late and most people had long since sought their beds or curled up on the floor in the hall. All save Lionel. Despite the huge quantities of both food and ale he'd consumed—not to mention defying his daughter and competing in the caber toss—Lionel was still awake and alert, exchanging war stories by the fire with Cathal and Wee Wat.

'Twasn't his duties as host, or his interest in their tales, that had kept Lucais in the hall for hours after Elspeth had retired. 'Twas fear. The same cold, stark terror that knotted his belly as he reached for the chamber door.

Elspeth had not spoken to him since her father's arrival. True, the day had been hectic, with many demands on her time as hostess and lady of Kinduin, but surely she could have found a moment to smile at him, to let him know she didn't hate him for having gone behind her back and told her father the truth.

Lifting the latch as silently as he could, Lucais carefully pushed the door open, fulling expecting Elspeth would have extinguished the candles and gone to bed.

The sight that greeted him was worse. The room was ablaze with light and Elspeth was up, pacing before a crackling fire. The gleam in her eyes as she rounded on him was no trick of reflected flame. She was furious. "So, you finally worked up the courage to face me." Arms crossed over the front of her fur-lined bed robe, she tapped her foot on the carpet in silent challenge.

That did it. Lucais's frayed nerves snapped. Slamming the door shut, he threw the bolt, then advanced on her. "I was entertainin' your father. Who seems to think all is well."

Elspeth's lower lip trembled, a crack in her armor that made Lucais's heart leap with hope. "Damn you." She whirled away from him, her inner struggle mirrored in her trembling body.

"Oh, Beth." His own anger fading, Lucais went to her, wrapped his arms around her, absurdly pleased when she sighed and sagged against him. "I'm sorry, love. I did what I thought—"

"Was best." For the first time in two months, he couldn't gauge her mood or her mind. "So Da said. But—"

Now it was Lucais's turn to sigh. "But you're angry with me." He kissed the top of her head. "I just wanted you to be happy, and though I know you love me and take joy in what we're buildin' here together, I've sensed your sadness and wanted to ease it. I tried gettin' you to visit your parents. You refused so adamantly I knew of only one way to solve matters."

The direct way. Nothing could have shown his love more clearly or diffused her remaining anger as thoroughly. "You shouldna have gone behind my back. That's what made me furious with you, and I fear my rage grew out of proportion because I couldn't shout at you with so many people about."

"We're private now, if you've a mind to shout."

"Nay. I dinna like the way you did it, but..." Turning in his arms, Elspeth rested her head on his chest. "But I'm glad 'tis out in the open at last. Da doesna blame me in the slightest." She was still awed by that.

Lucais hugged her tight and thanked God for the new maturity in Elspeth. "He's a wise man. He knows you were both victims of Raebert's greed and cruelty."

"Aye. 'Tis a blessing Raebert's line died with him." She felt Lucais shudder and looked up in time to see anguish twist his handsome features into a mask of revulsion. "What is it?"

"Naught." He closed his eyes, but the gesture was as telling as words.

"Raebert left a bairn behind." Given his morals, she wasn't surprised. "And you know where it is." He denied it with a shake of his head, but she knew he lied. Knew, too, that Raebert's child must somehow be a threat to them or he'd not have been so upset. "We agreed to share everything," she reminded him.

Growling something savage under his breath, he set her from him and walked to the hearth. He jammed his hands into his hair and stood there, trembling like a winded stallion. His posture reminded her vividly of her first day here and the confrontation that had ended with the revelation that Gillie was his daughter.

Only Gillie wasn't his daughter, she was Alain's.

Nay, not Alain's. Oh God!

"She's Raebert's." Elspeth's agonized whisper had Lucais spinning in his tracks.

"Beth." Lucais went to her, scooped her up when her legs failed her, stumbled to the chair and sat with her on his lap. Her arms locked around his neck in a stranglehold and he held her tight, fearing her shivers would tear her apart. "I never wanted you to find out," he whispered.

"Me?" She leaned back and looked him square in the eye. "What of you? Forced to claim your enemy's bairn as your own. Why did you do it?"

"I did it for Gillie and for Jean. 'Twas my fault she came to Kinduin, my fault she fell into Raebert's hands. If I hadna gotten drunk that day in Edinburgh. If she hadna resembled you..." His voice trailed off, but Elspeth filled in the rest of the terrible story. "Jean told me who'd raped her. She wanted to die when she learned she was pregnant with Raebert's bairn." So he'd locked her up for her own protection. "She died birthin' Gillie, and I couldna turn the poor mite out."

"You did the right thing," Elspeth murmured.

He shook his head, eyes filled with regret. "I gave her a place to live and food to eat, never realizin' I was cheatin' her of the love she needed till you came along. Love I couldna find in my heart to give her. 'Tis why I couldna tell you the truth. Knowin' how you hated Raebert, I feared..."

"That I'd turn my back on her." Elspeth ran her forefinger over the hard line of his mouth, pleased when his lips softened for her. Truly he was the most wonderful of men, strong, yet tender. Never had his tenderness been more evident than it was now. To think she had feared he'd reject Gillie if he knew she was Alain's, never guessing the truth was far more horrible. "Once I might have shunned her for the hurts Raebert inflicted," she admitted with brutal honesty. "But you've taught me forgiveness, love, you've healed me in so many ways." She replaced her finger with her mouth, seeking to kiss away the pain.

When she let him up for air, Lucais exhaled and gathered her close, glorying in the feel of their two hearts pounding in unison. "I could send Gillie away if—"

"Nay." Elspeth smiled, gently kneading the tense muscles in his broad shoulders. They'd borne burdens that would have felled a lesser man. But now she was here to help carry the load. Nor did she find the duty onerous. "Gillie is a sweet lass. I see far more of Alain in her than Raebert. I think she'll make a good sister in a few months' time." She glanced up at him through her lashes to see if he'd caught her hint.

"Mmm." His eyes were closed, his head resting on the back of the chair as she massaged his neck.

Drat. "I fear I willna be able to wear that silk gown of mine for seven months or so."

"You'll need warm wool durin' the winter, but I doubt the cold will last seven months."

For a perceptive man, he could be dense at times. "Have you noticed I've put on weight?"

"Mmm." His hand moved up from her waist to slip inside the vee of her robe and cup one breast. "They do seem fuller. 'Tis nice." His thumb flicked over her nipple, making her groan. "Very nice." Eyes still closed, he lowered his mouth, covered the aching nub and drew down gently.

Desire spilling through her, Elspeth threaded her fingers into his hair and held him there. "Aye. 'Tis very nice, but enjoy it while you can, for come March you'll have to share me...."

His head flew up, eyes narrowed possessively. "Share you? Never." She knew the moment when realization dawned, because his eyes went round and his mouth dropped open. "You're breedin'."

Elspeth rolled her eyes. "Men are such rude—"

"Jesu...you are. Oh, Beth." Wonder, joy and concern chased across his rugged features, but the emotion that moved her was the love shining in his eyes as he gave her a quick kiss and a hug that stole her breath. "Oh, Beth."

Head nestled against his heart, Elspeth smiled. " 'Tis a lad and we're going to name him—"

"Lionel. Does the old devil know?" At her nod, he grinned. "I'm surprised he didna spill the news tonight."

"I threatened to tell Mama about the caber tossing if he said a word. Some people respect others' secrets."

"Beth," Lucais warned, not wanting to rehash that.

"Dinna fret." She smoothed a lock of hair from his forehead. "I mayna like your methods, but the results please me greatly."

"You're happy?"

"Very. I'd be happier still if you'd take me to bed."

"With pleasure," Lucais replied. As it turned out, they were both mightily pleased with the way the evening ended.

In the sweet aftermath of their loving, wrapped securely in Lucais's embrace, Elspeth listened to his even breathing, the crackle of the dying fire, the soft whisper of the wind against the shutters. Contentment seeped through her. Truly this was where she belonged. It had just taken her a while to realize that her destiny lay here in the wild Highlands with her proud Lion of the North.

* * * * *

Harlequin® Historical

From award-winning author Theresa Michaels

Harlequin brings you—The Kincaids

A series with all the Romance and Adventure of the Old West

July 1995

ONCE A MAVERICK HH #276
Former fast gun Ty Kincaid helps a beautiful young gambler track down the man who killed her father.

Winter 1995

ONCE AN OUTLAW
No one but the strong-willed widow could lure Logan Kincaid off the outlaw trail.

Spring 1996

ONCE A LAWMAN
Sheriff Conner Kincaid finds more that he bargained for when he helps a feisty woman look for her missing brother.

Follow the saga of the unforgettable Kincaid brothers in Theresa Michaels's dramatic new trilogy from Harlequin Historicals.

Harlequin® Historical

What do A.E. Maxwell, Miranda Jarrett, Merline Lovelace and Cassandra Austin have in common?

They are all part of Harlequin Historical's efforts to bring you longer books by some of your favorite authors. Pick up one of these upcoming titles today and see what a difference an historical from Harlequin can make!

REDWOOD EMPIRE—A.E. Maxwell Don't miss the reissue of this exciting saga from award-winning authors Ann and Evan Maxwell, coming in May 1995.

SPARHAWK'S LADY—Miranda Jarrett From this popular author comes another sweeping Sparhawk adventure full of passion and emotion in June 1995.

HIS LADY'S RANSOM—Merline Lovelace A gripping Medieval tale from the talented author of the **Destiny's Women** series that is sure to delight, coming in July 1995.

TRUSTING SARAH—Cassandra Austin And in August 1995, the long-awaited new Western by the author whose *Wait for the Sunrise* touched readers' hearts.

Watch for them this spring and summer wherever Harlequin Historicals are sold.

PRIZE SURPRISE
SWEEPSTAKES

OFFICIAL ENTRY COUPON

This entry must be received by: JUNE 30, 1995
This month's winner will be notified by: JULY 15, 1995

YES, I want to win the Panasonic 31" TV! Please enter me in the drawing and let me know if I've won!

Name_____

Address _____ Apt. _____

City _____ State/Prov. _____ Zip/Postal Code _____

Account #_____

Return entry with invoice in reply envelope.

© 1995 HARLEQUIN ENTERPRISES LTD.   CTV KAL

PRIZE SURPRISE
SWEEPSTAKES

OFFICIAL ENTRY COUPON

This entry must be received by: JUNE 30, 1995
This month's winner will be notified by: JULY 15, 1995

YES, I want to win the Panasonic 31" TV! Please enter me in the drawing and let me know if I've won!

Name_____

Address _____ Apt. _____

City _____ State/Prov. _____ Zip/Postal Code _____

Account #_____

Return entry with invoice in reply envelope.

© 1995 HARLEQUIN ENTERPRISES LTD.   CTV KAL